Celestial Plane

Patrick Menzel

Contents

1

OPERATION CHAOS

O n the night of October 7th, 1989, electric currents of frenetic energy crackled through the baseball stadium. A throng of fans swallowed the venue whole, their excitement rising by the second. San Francisco Giants and Oakland A's devotees clashed in a passionate display of allegiance.

Thin, verdant frames bordered the glasses of Celsey Hail, a staunch advocate for the City's ball club. At nineteen, she displayed the loyalty of a seasoned supporter, despite the team's recent struggles. Nestled sparrow-like between her parents on the upper bleachers amid the jubilant masses, she waved a giant foam finger with unbridled enthusiasm. Her father's gaze, a weathered atlas of life's hard-won battles, riveted upon the diamond's lush canvas while her mother, ever vigilant, scanned the surroundings for anything amiss.

Nearby, a concession stand released an enticing aroma—a blend of sizzling meat, toasted bread, and smoky char from the grill, mingled with savory notes of mustard and ketchup—as they awaited the first pitch. This sent hollow pangs gnawing through Celsey's insides. She held out her hand, eyes pleading, the universal sign for 'feed me' as clear as a neon sign.

Mrs. Hail chuckled, coins jingling as she rummaged through her purse. "Get three."

Celsey leapt to her feet, a grin spreading across her face. She began navigating the crowded assembly, her raven hair swaying in a loose ponytail. As she moved, she tucked unwieldy strands behind her ear, causing her jersey sleeve to shift, revealing a glimpse of a tattoo on her arm. It was a skull fossil, cradled in a fiery blossom of pink and red.

Not far from the stadium, a veiled group garbed in ceremonial attire ghosted through the serene residential neighborhood. Their leader grasped a timeworn grimoire in one hand and a torch in the other as they approached a subterranean entrance along the side of a home under construction. Two minions stepped forward and pulled the handle on the door, unaware a sinewy figure, known as a Roamer, watched their every move. "That's right, my pets," he hissed. "Tread forward and open the door."

His command reverberated inside the leader's mind, causing him to stop dead in his tracks. He searched through the distance, but saw no sign of life.

I knew you'd come. You just better keep your word.

Soon, the metal door creaked open, revealing a stone staircase that disappeared into darkness. The group stood frozen, their guts churning with dread. Then, as if puppets to some unseen master, their feet began to move slowly and dreamlike.

As they descended into the gloom, the air grew thick and musty. Each of them kept stealing glances over their shoulders, half-expecting to see whatever force controlled them. The walls seemed to close in, whispering secrets in a language too old for human ears. Every shadow might hide a threat, every sound a monster waiting to pounce, but still, they went deeper.

When the overseer's feet crunched on gravel at the bottom of the stairs, his outstretched hands brushed against something cold—a metal bracket embedded in the rocky wall.

Perfect, he thought, placing the torch into the slot.

As he turned to survey the room, his eyes fell on a weathered antique table. Without hesitation, he approached it and dropped the spell book onto its worn surface. The thud echoed in the stillness.

Behind them, the door slammed shut with a finality that made them all flinch. In an instant, the air felt thicker, heavier. They were sealed in, their fates now tied to this suffocating enclosure.

Taking a deep breath, he opened the ancient tome; its rough pages only stretching his nerves further. By the time he flipped through half the book, an eerie aura compelled him to rethink his actions. Chills raced down his spine as his eyes lingered on the title written in the margin: The Gateway Spell.

An immense burden weighed upon his shoulders as his finger traced the ancient text, uttering, "Aperi ianuam hanc, iubeo."

Their voices blended into a haunting chorus that reverberated through the sanctuary. Cracks snaked through the bunker's walls, driven by the ruptured ground. Tangible energy filled every crevice, ready to burst as the occupants focused on their task.

The ground beneath the field groaned, a deep rumble that started under the pitcher's mound and rippled outward like a stone dropped in still water. Cracks spider-webbed across the field, chasing fleeing players as the tremors reached the stands.

Debris rained down over their heads while the soil convulsed in a cataclysmic dance of destruction. Unbeknownst to them, nature itself had become a nefarious puppeteer, tearing the earth apart with merciless fury.

As athletes and spectators battled a surge of panic, Celsey lay pinned beneath a toppled concession stand. She gritted her teeth and heaved the structure off herself, her skin tearing against the rough pavement. Blood beaded along her forearms as she wobbled to her feet. After a few deep breaths, she turned to spot her parents still atop the bleachers. Without pause, she shoved through the stampede to reach them, wincing as the crowd jostled her raw limbs.

She halted about two feet from the bleachers and watched as her parents hurried over towards the beam. But before they could make another move, the lower half crumbled to the ground in a loud steel yelp. Not letting fear control her, Celsey rushed over with a message. "Hey! You have to jump!"

"Are you outta your mind?" Mrs. Hail exclaimed. "We could break something."

"Bones heal," Celsey remarked.

The congregation pressed forward, their voices resolute despite the trembling walls. Suddenly, an eerie crimson halo burst forth, filling the air with the acrid scent of sulfur. Before they knew it, a colossal creature tore through the chasm, showering them with debris as it touched down on the ravaged land.

The hole yawned wider, its edges crumbling like wet sand. Screams cut short as chunks of concrete and steel rained down, swallowing the congregation in an avalanche of debris. In seconds, where people had stood, there was only a mound of rubble, settling with final, ominous creaks.

The Roamer materialized under a battered streetlight before the creature, revealing pale pink skin stretched taut over muscles, straining to contain him. "Fifteen seconds," he said. "That's all it took to unleash havoc on this land."

Unfazed by the shuffled topography, the creature growled, its lofty presence radiating confidence. "Man-made creations are fragile," it declared. "I have never felt concern for the mortal realm."

A charged silence enveloped them as hollow eyes dug into the Roamer. With each step the creature took, the atmosphere thickened. At last, the demon broke the silence with a question that demanded answers. "Why exactly have you sprung me, Haines?"

"I need to find Lucifer's burial site, and who better to help than a demon?"

"What? Why would—"

"Doesn't matter. What matters is that I haven't been able to do so on my own and now I have a plan. You see, with mass destruction-"

"The angels would be sent to investigate," the creature interjected. "So, hold on, let me see if I got this right—" Incredulity steamed the air between them. "—you believe the forces of Heaven will guide us to our destination? A bold claim indeed."

"Precisely." The Roamer's sly smile showed approval. "But before we embark on this perilous endeavor, we must attend to your unmistakable countenance. Drawing unnecessary attention is the last thing we desire."

Repulsed by the idea of being confined within the fragile shell of a human form, the demon recoiled. "You expect me to bind myself within the constraints of a human?" it sneered. "Fine, but when we're finished, you had better free me from this gargoyle form."

"Yeah, sure." With an elegance that belied his nefarious nature, Haines recited an ancient incantation full of power and knowledge. The unclean spirit watched as he guided his hand in a fluid, graceful arc. In an instant, its lofty figure transformed into a more human-like shape. Now, the demon stood tall and slender, dressed in modern attire, its monstrous visage hidden beneath a veil of mankind.

With a nod of satisfaction, Haines assessed the creature's new appearance. "Now that I have bound a fraction of my essence to your being, you will have the fortitude to withstand the celestial hosts."

For a moment, he believed they were ready to unleash havoc upon the world. But his belief dwindled when he peered into the creature's abyssal eyes. They were an unmistakable reflection of its true nature, a darkness that threatened to expose their nefarious undertaking. "We must devise a means to conceal those orbs from prying eyes."

His words hung in the air, a portent of the chaos to come. As the pair plotted their next move, the world continued to turn, oblivious to the encroaching darkness.

***

One month later, deep within the vast expanse of the Australian outback, the fruits of their nefarious plan unfolded. Two vehicles, a Coach and the Trans City Express, were about to collide, tearing through the arid earth, their engines roaring like beasts eager to tear each other apart. Nature's relentless sun cast a merciless glow over the rust-colored terrain, which formed elongated shadows across jagged rocks and dried-up riverbeds.

From the desolate backdrop, Haines emerged, his presence sending a shiver down the spines of those who dared to look upon him. He turned his intense gaze on the Coach as it careened around a perilous turn. With a twirl of his finger, he commanded the bus to pick up speed.

Adrenaline surged through the driver's veins. He wrestled to regain control of the hurtling vehicle with anguish dripping from his furrowed brow. Despite his frantic efforts, the bus pressed forward, propelled by an invisible malevolence that defied logic. The operator's eyes jittered between the pedals and the looming horizon as he tightened his grip on the steering wheel.

Haines shifted his focus to the Trans City Express, repeating his previous gesture. Both engines roared in a fierce struggle for dominance. A discordant cacophony swallowed the breeze as the buses raced towards an inevitable crash.

The catastrophic impact tossed passengers and seats alike through shattered windshields, transforming once pristine vehicles into a bloody crime scene. The dark, omniscient orchestrator stood in silence with a fixed gaze on the devastation. A perverse satisfaction simmered within as he took twisted pleasure from the suffering.

As chaos unfolded, Haines's ally embarked on its own mission, halfway across the world, in a coastal Town of East Hampton, NY. The entity sidled up to Lighters Restaurant, a place that reeked of musty upholstery from the '70s. Above the door, golden letters clung to life under a sputtering caution lamp. It stopped and stared at an unfamiliar reflection through the door, letting out a deep sigh as it gripped the door handle.

Inside, its eagle eyes crept over the diners. A woman's bubbling laughter caught its attention. Her partner knelt in front of her, presenting a velvet box. The creature suppressed a growl of disgust as its glance fell upon friends bent over an ancient tome and a cluster of waiters singing "Happy Birthday" to a beaming boy.

At last, the hostess—a vision of sunshine in a floral dress—welcomed the diabolical entity with a radiant smile. Her golden name tag read Sara. "Hello! Welcome to Lighters! Just a party of one tonight, sir?"

A wicked grin spread across the demon's face, its eyes now slivers of ravenous veins, boring into Sara's essence. "Oh no, the revelry ends now."

Before the hostess could comprehend the gravity of the threat, malignant tendrils snaked up her arms and neck, marking the demon's dominion over her soul. Sadistic satisfaction gleamed in its eyes, while it watched the hostess, now a hollow vessel under its control, drift into the kitchen. Behind her, two busboys, witnesses to the unsettling encounter, trailed after her.

Concern glued their mouths shut as Sara, stripped of identity, shattered bottles and a few bags of sugar onto the floor. From the foot of the oven, commotion jerked the chief—a goliath of a man—to the extended counter. A tarnished silver cross graced his sweat-beaded chest as he mirrored that of a boxer's grace. With machine precision, he edged along the enclosure to the busboys. His calloused hand reached out to tap their shoulders.

He locked eyes with the busboys, pressing a finger to his lips before gesturing toward the dining area. His message was quite clear: keep quiet and protect the customers. With surprising agility for his size, he snuck up behind Sara. In one fluid motion, he wrapped his arms around her waist, pinning her arms to her sides.

Although he tried to steer her toward the double doors, she twisted free with cat-like reflexes and lunged for the sink, grasping a carving knife. Before the chef could react, she slashed at him, the blade biting deep into his forearm. He stumbled back, eyes wide with shock and pain, his breath catching in his throat.

Sara smirked and pulled a windproof lighter from her pocket. The erratic flame twirled in her hollow eyes as she turned her attention to the nearby gas line. With careful intent, she approached the volatile connection, the lighter held aloft like a sacred offering.

***

As the world held its breath, ten arduous months crawled by. The devastating inferno that ravaged Lighters Restaurant was but a single incident among many more. Yet, despite the widespread chaos, Haines found himself plagued by uncertainty. Then a chilling whisper slithered its way into his consciousness. "Your resolve better not waver."

Startled by the unexpected voice, he turned his head. "Oswald is that you?" he asked.

An eerie, melancholic voice enveloped the air, casting an unsettling aura. "Of course. You have ensnared the divine's attention."

"If that's true," Haines retorted, "why hasn't the Heavenly warriors descended?"

"The Supreme Arbiter sensed your potent display ever since your spectacle with the buses in Australia," Oswald explained. "He determined that Lucifer bore no responsibility—that there's a greater threat."

Haines sighed in frustration, the weight of their precarious situation settling over him. "So, what do you suggest I do next?"

The voice offered no further enlightenment, leaving him bewildered by the sudden silence. As he surveyed his surroundings, he noticed a crumpled flier discarded at his feet. Its once pristine surface, now marred by creases and folds, revealed details about a theatrical production called "Lucifer's Child," a one-woman play of considerable renown, scheduled for its twenty-eighth performance at the esteemed Music Box Theatre.

A sly grin curled on Haines's lips. "What do we have here?" he mused, feeling fate align with his dreary aspirations.

The next day, he and his ally lurked in the shadows of the crowded theatre, waiting for the perfect moment to strike. "I've decided what to call you," Haines said. "Victor, because together, that's what we shall be."

The creature glared at its prospective comrade with profound contempt for the mortal name. It refrained from a verbal assault, however, since it knew the Roamer's indifference. Moments later, its gaze shifted downward at Haines's hand. "I can't fathom how you stumbled upon this event," it said. "Perhaps there is a higher power interfering."

Amusement flickered in the Roamer's eyes as he convinced himself that fate had aligned with his aspirations. Once the theatre curtain rose, the smell of rotten eggs permeated the room. Those who caught a whiff looked around, covering their noses, but decided there was no cause for alarm. Seated in the front mezzanine row, Haines positioned his arms at his sides.

With a flourish of his index fingers, he unleashed sound waves which bounced off the walls. The actress's voice echoed through the hallowed halls, captivating the audience. Yet, it was the sudden apparition of the Devil that demanded attention. The projected figure, adorned with horns and wielded a pitchfork, dominated the stage. Whispers of fascination rippled among the captivated spectators.

Questions hung heavy, a mix of terror and excitement swirling in the hearts of those who witnessed the devil's appearance. The atmosphere tightened, sending a shudder down the actress's spine with a primal fear she couldn't shake. At a frantic pace, she spun around, her heart pounding in her chest, only to be met with a bone-chilling sight.

There, standing before her, was a figure that seemed to ooze malevolence. Its demonic features twisted into a haunting smile; the very essence of evil that made every hair on her body stand on end. Her eyes froze on the unholy presence invading her world. And then, with a sudden burst of inhuman speed, the apparition darted toward her.

The flickering image closed its hand around her delicate neck with a vise-like grip. Only when it eased its grip did she collapse onto the stage.

Fueled by panic and terror, the audience erupted into thunderous applause. Those in the front row—those who'd seen the struggle for breath—felt the weight of despair settle upon them. The actress's fight for life filled the room, desperate gasps and choked cries blending into a symphony of agony, a dissonant melody that clashed with the blissful ignorance of the crowd. And as screams pierced the air, everyone stampeded to escape the wrath of the malevolent force.

Amid the pandemonium, the wicked entities remained seated, their expressions twisted with sadistic delight. They reveled in the fear, basking in the darkness they had conjured. "Incredible," it said with glee.

Haines eyeballed the creature, his face set like concrete. "It is time to execute the next phase of our plan," he declared.

Dispensing with verbal niceties, Victor teleported to the heart of Times Square. Lost in thought, he strolled along the crowded street, his mind consumed by the malevolent game they were playing. Oblivious to his surroundings, a tall man, engrossed in his phone, collided with him. The impact pried his attention from the device.

While moving onward, the man stumbled and dropped his phone, diverting his attention at the most opportune time. At that moment, darkness slithered up his neck and face. Vein-like wicked tendrils seeped into his skin.

A nearby pedestrian rushed forward, but her act of kindness transformed into a nightmare as the possessed man seized her by the neck and tossed her to the ground. In a frenzy of violence, he mounted her prone form and tore at her face. Despite her valiant struggle, the woman stood no chance against her assailant, who ripped her head from her body, painting the street with the spectacle of his deranged bloodlust.

Victor continued his voyage and stumbled across a small group of bystanders, their faces etched in terror. Curious, he slowed his pace and observed the scene. The panicked cluster huddled together, some squeezing their phones in trembling hands, while others whispered frantically among themselves.

The possessed man, his body twisted and hunched, arms outstretched like a twisted imitation of an ape, turned toward the onlookers. He lunged towards them, driven by a hunger for violence that knew no bounds.

But then, a police officer tore through the chaotic streets of Times Square, his valiant spirit fighting against the sinister force permeating the square. Yet, as he drew closer, darkness crept across his body like an insidious infection. Within seconds, it settled into his skin. He jerked his gun up and pulled the trigger with reckless abandon, targeting anyone and everyone he could see. The once-lively square became an unexpected, grotesque battleground.

Inside the frenzied madness, Victor commanded attention from every corner. The vibrant pulse of the city unraveled, giving way to a macabre theater of violence. Innocent bystanders turned into frenzied predators, friends became enemies, and loved ones transformed into sworn adversaries, the insatiable bloodlust claiming them all.

Satisfied with the havoc unleashed, Victor melted into a wisp of smoke, his malevolent intent carrying him across the ocean. In a matter of seconds, he found himself standing before the enchanting elegance of the Eiffel Tower. He slithered past a young woman, her face aglow with the artificial light of her phone as she posed before the looming tower.

But her stomach churned over the sight she saw on her screen. Her youthful visage sagged and withered like rotting fruit. Wrinkles carved deep furrows into her skin, eyes sinking into blackened sockets. A banshee's wail erupted from her throat as the phone slipped from her spasming fingers, disintegrating on the cold, unforgiving pavement. The sound of breaking glass was lost in the cacophony of her scream.

In a frantic rush, she flitted about, the taste of bile rising in her throat. To her anguish, she found her friends clawing at each other with feral snarls, as if lifelong bonds had dissolved into primal hatred.

Back at the Music Box Theatre, chaos had also taken hold. An athletic man stumbled and fell onto a chair, gasping for precious oxygen as his gaze locked with the apparition that loomed over him. Desperation gripped his every breath as he fought for air, his struggle mirrored by the turmoil swirling within his eyes. And then, as he clung to the last flicker of hope, Victor took shape in the seat beside Haines. They both delighted in the unfolding nightmare.

"It is done," the demon said.

The Roamer grinned, pleased with how far they'd come. He believed it wouldn't be long now and sat back to relax.

***

A year had slipped by since the haunting events at the Music Box Theatre, but the burden of failure still clung to Haines like a shroud. Perched on a weathered bench, he found himself lost in a labyrinth of his own thoughts, the weight of the past pressing down upon him. His gaze skimmed the tribute article, a chilling account of the survivors' encounters with the devil himself. Despite the gravity of the situation, he couldn't shake the nagging question of why the Heavenly Cavalry had yet to descend.

Compelled by an irresponsible urge, he read the stark headline, 'Community Hospital Fatality.' In a moment of heavy silence, he pushed the newspaper aside and lifted his eyes, only to be blinded by a radiant halo that tore through the darkened sky.

Stoic in the face of its brilliance, he stared into the spectral light, driven by an unquenchable curiosity. He followed the invisible threads of power into the heart of the majestic Rocky Mountains. There, nestled among the towering peaks, stood an abandoned Anglican church, its former grandeur now marred by locked doors and boarded-up windows. A bitter dispute among the townsfolk had left this once-sacred place deserted, shrouding it in a desolate silence. Haines perched atop the mountain and stared, transfixed, at the dissipating radiance.

Three ethereal figures stood at the church's entrance, crackling with unparalleled power. They each assumed human-like forms: Gabriel, divine messenger, took on a slender figure adorned in pristine white garments; Raphael, known as the healer, appeared as a tall man clad in a verdant blazer and trousers; and Archangel Michael, renowned as a noble warrior, donned a tailored blue suit and somber black tie, proclaiming authority.

Without hesitation, the noble warrior swung open the door. His angelic retinue stood poised at the threshold, eager to receive revelations regarding the tumultuous upheaval gripping the world.

Despite harboring doubts about the likelihood of the devil's tomb being confined to holy grounds, Haines kept his vigilant gaze fixed on the celestial warriors. A tempest of questions churned deep within his mind.

Just then, an unseen voice pierced his consciousness. "The Supreme Arbiter has brought the divine mortal into existence." Oswald's voice echoed within the Roamer's soul.

A devious smirk brandished his features as he absorbed the gravity of the situation. He exulted in the knowledge that the cosmic equilibrium was shifting in his favor.

Michael soon reappeared alongside his angelic comrades, ready for the final judgment. "He is not only shielded within these old walls, but our protective incantation, woven as a barrier, holds strong." His words held clear conviction.

Raphael arched an eyebrow. "That means someone must be deceiving us."

Michael, his gaze fixed on the distant horizon, commanded his companions' attention. "Raphael, rid this mortal realm of the demonic affliction before it is further corrupted," he ordered. "Gabriel, guard the gate with unwavering vigilance. Allow no intruders to breach this sacred sanctuary."

Gabriel nodded in obedience while Raphael's disbelief threatened to erupt. "Do you intend to face this danger alone?"

"One archangel shall suffice to protect the fragile human child," Michael answered.

Raphael shot Michael a disapproving glare, his initial reluctance flickering across his face before yielding to Michael's authority. In a swift motion, two of the archangels vanished from view, leaving Haines concealed amidst the rugged terrain. A revelation dawned on him, shedding light on the reason for his previous failed attempts to locate Lucifer's hidden resting place.

"These uncivilized heathens must have interred him beneath a sacred edifice," he realized. "But fear not, for I possess the knowledge to bypass this obstacle." He murmured incantations under his breath, invoking the 'Veil of Shadows,' a spell that cloaked his vital force and energy to elude angelic detection.

With a flick of his wrist, he materialized inside the abandoned church. The chamber unveiled life-size statues of the archangels, each positioned prominently in the four corners of the frigid room. Due to an electrical shortage, only natural light could send him on his path. It wasn't until he ventured deeper into the heart of the chamber that his eyes flashed a menacing red. He had finally found it. His lips moved, releasing only a whisper. "This—this must be—" His eyes traced the intricate patterns on the floor that pulsed with immense energy.

He knelt down, laying his hand on the cold, hard surface of the tiled floor. A shiver coursed through his body as he closed his eyes, allowing the ethereal energy emanating from beneath his feet to envelop him. As the power flowed, his muscles rippled, growing stronger and more robust with each passing moment. Soon, a set of initials materialized on his left shoulder—M, R, and G. "That settles that," he muttered to himself.

Meanwhile, in the quaint town of Healdsburg, California, another small restaurant unwittingly became the stage for a nefarious plot. Within its walls, a group of hapless individuals found themselves trapped, their pleas for mercy dissolved into the callous walls of apathy. A brawny man battered the door, his face contorted in terror as sulfur's stench choked the tavern. Victor savored the devastation, bearing a wicked grin as his eyes morphed into an empty void that cast an ominous glow.

Just as he prepared to unleash further havoc, Haines materialized behind him and placed a hand on his shoulder. In a burst of unseen force, the door swung open, and the panic-stricken patrons fled for their lives.

"You party pooper," the creature sneered, rolling its eyes in exasperation. "Do you have any idea how much fun I was having?"

"You'll find others to afflict, I'm sure," Haines countered. "Alas, we have work to do now that I've located Lucifer's tomb. Too bad your feeble nature forbids you from treading upon sacred soil. I'm not about to risk being discovered; hence, you must seek a mortal to carry forth our mission."

The fiend stared at Haines, a derisive snort escaping its lips before watching him fade from sight.

"Well, I suppose we are done here," Victor muttered under his breath. Irritated by the Roamer's abrupt departure, he disappeared as well, leaving the chaotic scene behind.

Then, as if the cosmic tapestry itself recoiled from the depravity below, the firmament shuddered and rent asunder, birthing a shimmering portal of divine light. Through this ethereal breach, Raphael descended, his very essence a beacon of celestial righteousness. Mighty wings, iridescent with the emerald hues of creation, unfurled to pierce the shadows. In his grasp, a jewel-studded halberd pole thrummed with unrivaled power, its argent shaft adorning arcane sigils that entranced mortal eyes.

With a voice that resonated the force of his divine mission, Raphael's proclamation thundered through the air. "I have found you, nefarious fiend!"

His words rumbled off the ruins, penetrating the eardrums of both friend and foe alike. With a purposeful motion, he unsheathed his weapon. Its gleaming axe head caught the scarce moonlight, magnifying its divine potency.

The battlefield cracked under the weight of Raphael's presence, for his arrival signified the embodiment of justice and salvation. Amidst the chaos and despair, a glimmer of hope blossomed, a beacon of light piercing through the murk. The Archangel Raphael had come, bearing the celestial might and unyielding resolve necessary to vanquish the encroaching darkness.

However, Victor evaded Raphael's attack, leaping backward just in the nick of time. He fixed the angel with a glare, concealing his frustration and rage behind his foreboding facade. His fists clenched so hard his nails dug into his skin, drawing blood that disintegrated into ash upon hitting the ground. A wicked smile played on his lips as he mocked Raphael's perceived lack of skill and intelligence.

Undeterred, Raphael tightened his grip on the halberd pole, preparing for another confrontation, but Victor had his own plans. His eyes landed on two terrified waitresses who huddled at the side of the restaurant, and his grin grew with malevolence. "Fortune favors me today," he boasted, teleporting behind the unsuspecting women.

A shiver traversed the waitresses' hunched spines as the demon's icy hand muzzled their screams, plunging the area into a suffocating silence.

"Unshackle them at once!"

"By all means," Victor sneered. It seemed like he was going to comply until a strange transformation burrowed into their once-innocent features. Inky veins snaked across their skin, revealing the unmistakable signs of demonic possession.

Raphael lowered the pole, his eyes fixed on the women who had become mere pawns in the demon's wicked scheme.

How is this fiend able to go toe to toe with me? It is unfathomable.

Relishing in the game it had set into motion, Victor grinned. "Looks like your table is ready. How about some potstickers?"

Heaven's healer sought his opponent's presence as it already plotted an escape. Before he could make a move, the waitresses, their bodies fueled by a surge of adrenaline, hurtled toward the angel, desperate to bring down this celestial being. But the heavenly host refused to yield. Raw power flowed through his palms in a dazzling display of his formidable strength. With grace and agility, he dodged their strikes in a blur of motion.

Raphael lunged forward, his palms aglow with divine energy as they connected with the waitresses' foreheads. An infernal miasma lifted from their eyes, returning them to their true selves.

"Let us finish this!" Raphael's voice thundered. But when he turned around to confront the demon, it was already gone.

Within the aftermath of his declaration, the archangel faced the space where the nefarious fiend had stood moments before. This opened a doorway to unease in the recesses of his mind. What cunning machinations had the demon concocted, and where was he going?

Elsewhere, in the hushed corridors of the local community hospital, Michael found himself drawn to a room where a newborn infant had just entered the world. The room hummed with quiet intensity as the archangel's piercing gaze fixed on the infant, his keen senses attuned to the subtle energies that pulsed within her tiny form.

He leaned closer, his voice a mere whisper on the edge of perception and addressed the newborn with awe. "I did not expect your reservoirs to brim with such formidable power from the very onset." The weight of his words belied the innocence of the child before him.

A young nurse, her blonde hair a halo of light in the dim room, entered with a reverence that matched the solemnity of the moment. Cradling the infant in her arms, she turned her gaze to the radiant mother, her eyes alight with curiosity and wonder. "Have you thought of a name yet, Mrs. Puller?" she asked.

The mother, her expression suffused with a love that transcended words, met her baby's hazel eyes with a gaze filled with unspoken promises. A smile, tender and luminous, graced her lips as she spoke the name that would forever bind mother and child in an unbreakable bond. "Emily," she declared, her voice a melody of certainty and tenderness that resonated with the weight of a lifetime of love.

The nurse mirrored the mother's joy, her smile wide and warm. "Emily, it is then."

Peace and contentment radiated the room as the mother and child embraced the warmth of their new bond, unaware that they were under Michael's watchful eye.

2

THE MEETING

J ump forward to 2011, a time of hidden truths. Emily, a young woman with penetrating hazel eyes, stood in line at a bustling coffee shop. Her sable waves, kissed by midnight's caress, caught the soft illumination from the café's warm lighting. Gathered in a messy bun, stray threads draped down her back. In her hands, she held a book titled "Tar Heel Travels: Exploring North Carolina's Hidden Gems," its glossy cover adorned with bold letters that beckoned her to embark on a journey. She exuded a serene composure, familiarizing herself with the southern state.

However, when the line inched forward, a man ahead of her disrupted her peaceful introspection. His gruff voice pierced the air, carrying a sense of arrogance. Heavy bags weighed on his tired glare as he barked orders. Tension emanated from him, adding a jarring note to the otherwise harmonious ambiance. Emily's façade of serenity crumbled from his unpleasant presence, her fingers tightening their grip around the edges of her book.

The man's tirade made each passing minute last an eternity as he berated the barista with an unwarranted air of superiority. Emily couldn't help but feel an annoyance simmering within. She clenched her jaw and narrowed her eyes, attempting to will the man to leave. At last, the barista handed him his drink. His foul mood lingered like a dissonant chord. A wave of collective relief washed over the establishment as he stormed out, leaving behind an uncomfortable silence in his wake.

Emily took a deep breath, catching the rich, nutty fragrance of fresh coffee and warm pastries. She closed her book and approached the counter, ready to order and immerse herself in the simple joy of a well-deserved moment of respite. While awaiting her turn, a timid figure shuffled through the door. Neither tall nor imposing, he was an unremarkable presence, his uncertain gait betraying his lack of confidence. She observed the subtle signs of nervousness displayed in his darting glances.

Captivated, he examined the intricate floral design carved into the tiles beneath his feet, each petal and vine etching a sense of delicate beauty into his mind. He made his way towards the counter, each footstep a careful ballet of grace, as if unsure of his own existence inside this bustling café. But in an unfortunate moment of clumsiness, his body collided with Emily's, causing him to stumble backward as if the very ground had betrayed him.

"Oh, God! I'm so sorry!" he blurted; his face now flushed with a radiant shade of crimson that mirrored the roses on the cafe's wallpaper. His heart thumped within his chest cavity as he awaited her response. "I didn't get anything on you, did I?"

Emily, her words soft like the feathers of a dove, cast a quick glance at her pristine paper cup. "Not even a drop," she reassured, raising her eyes to meet his gaze.

Her lips parted as she took a deliberate sip of espresso, lifting her eyes to meet his. Above the enraptured pair, an ephemeral oceanic hue reminiscent of sunbeams filtering through crystalline depths tinged the overhead light before fading away. It seemed the universe itself conspired to connect their souls.

"I'm Caleb, by the way," he introduced himself, offering a hesitant hand.

She reciprocated with her name, accompanied by a tender smirk, intertwining her fingers with his.

Finding solace at a table in the quiet corner of the café, Emily gently placed her glossy-covered book beside her cup, its blue sleeve showcasing an intricate engraving of Burney Falls. As Caleb joined her, his leg shook as he took a sizable sip of his drink, almost finishing it. After setting the cup down, where it teetered on the edge, Emily couldn't help but tease, "I guess someone's thirsty."

"Just a bit," he retorted, staring at the table. Thanks to the ambient lighting, the dust jacket shimmered with an array of colors, capturing his attention. "So, do you travel a lot?" he asked, his deep tone washing over the table.

Emily's face lit up with joy, the glow of possibility dancing in her eyes. "I do," she replied, her voice carrying the softness of whispered dreams. "I'm working on becoming a travel photographer."

"That sounds exciting!" he said, expressing genuine interest. "Have you ever been to North Carolina?"

Her adventurous spirit beamed with delight as she pondered alongside a subtle smirk.

Why is this guy so jittery? She answered the posing question as Caleb finished the remnants of his drink. "I'm planning a trip there next month," she stated. "I've traveled a lot and captured thousands of scenic photographs."

Sharing a prolonged stare sprung a rare sense of genuine warmth, stirring emotions he never allowed himself to explore. Through her enchanting gaze, he found a haven, unable to contain a profound smile from overtaking his features. "Well, take it from someone who grew up there. You should visit Catawba Falls while you're visiting," he said.

"I'm sure I will. So, what brings you all the way to the Big Apple?" she questioned.

With a shy grin, Caleb spoke, his words filled with excitement. "I'm a writer. I just finished my first book signing down the street."

Intrigued, she leaned in with sparkling eyes. "That's really cool. I'd love to give it a read. What's it called?"

"Mystery and the Unknown. It's a collection that delves into unnatural phenomena and unsolved cases."

Before they could continue their conversation, Caleb's glare shifted onto a powerful, Herculean man with a cleanly shaven head and a hint of stubble, who settled just a couple yards away. With a newspaper in his hands, the man engrossed himself in its contents until a sudden surge of astonishment overcame him, spraying his beverage from his mouth. Caleb couldn't help but fixate on this unexpected display because it seemed a little over dramatic. Upon returning his sights back on Emily, he saw her glance at her watch.

"Oh no," she exclaimed, rising from her seat. "I have to go."

"Well, it was great getting to know you," he said. "Can we continue this conversation later?"

"Of course," she replied, flashing a smile.

Caleb, feeling overzealous, stood up and retrieved his BlackBerry Bold. Anxiety gripped him, a familiar sensation born of his lifelong struggle with attractive women. Yet, to his surprise, this interaction had unraveled without a hitch.

With measured discretion, the unknown man folded his newspaper, peering towards Emily as she entered her number into the author's phone. Once they tidied up their chairs and tossed the cups, the adventurer departed. At that moment, Caleb turned to confront the observer, determined to get answers. But on the cusp of approaching, a melodious tune emanated from his pocket. Glancing at his phone, he saw his agent calling and dismissed it. He needed to question the mystery man, and nothing was going to stop him.

In tandem, the man laid his newspaper down and stared towards the window. A veil of mystery cloaked him while casting a pervasive presence. Stepping before him, a sense of inner peace seeped into Caleb's essence, soft murmurs caressing his ears, easing his taut muscles. Struggling to shake off this sensation, he clenched his fists and glared ahead at the unknown figure standing with arms folded behind his back.

"Why were you watching us?" he asked, his tone assertive.

The man leaned back in his chair, his expression calm. Letting out a deep breath, he met Caleb's gaze with unwavering intensity. "You should step aside, mate," he retorted. With a penetrating stare, he positioned his left hand, ready to unleash something unimaginable.

Despite a pit forming in his stomach, Caleb claimed a seat on the opposite side. "No, I don't think so," he remarked.

Just outside the cozy coffee shop, however, Emily rushed across the bustling street toward the bus stop. Oblivious to her surroundings, she remained unaware of a green Mustang hurtling down the road, its body sporting two sleek black lines running parallel on both sides. As a nimbus cloud took shape in the sky, a few drops of rain fell onto the open sunroof.

With no time to react, she instinctively closed her eyes, while thrusting her hands outward to protect herself. And then, in a moment of awe, the mystery man snapped his fingers. To her amazement, the car screeched to a sudden halt, mere inches away from her trembling form.

The thunderous roar of the vehicle's engine pierced Caleb's ears, drawing his focus towards the window. His heart throttled his throat as he leaped out of his chair, the disbelief in his eyes undeniable.

How is it possible? He couldn't have just stopped that car with a finger snap...could he?

A whirlwind of thoughts swirled in his mind as he rushed to her side, his feet carrying him through the swarm of astonished bystanders. Concern overtook his face, mirroring the worry that gnawed at his heart.

"Emily! Are you okay?" he rang out, placing a hand on her shoulders, hoping to offer some solace.

His mere touch ignited a wildfire of perplexity in her mind. A mix of emotions—shock, fear, and profound disbelief—swallowed her as the world around her spun like a dream-turned-nightmare. How could she make sense of the car's inexplicable stoppage?

From inside the cafe, the mysterious savior observed their well-being through the window.

Caleb's voice boomed across the street, laced with a mixture of anger and relief as he admonished the bewildered driver. "You need to be more careful!" he yelled. Uninterested in a remark, he diverted his attention back to the adventurer. Her panic-stricken expression left him worried.

The driver hunched over with his left sleeve torn, revealing a bruise on his shoulder. "I'm sorry, I don't know what happened," he stated.

These words reached the mysterious savior's ears from within the small shop, drawing a disapproving shake of his head. Once more, he snapped his fingers, and the once-frozen car resumed its cautious journey, leaving behind a perplexed driver and a lingering sense of bewilderment. "I was afraid of that," he said, as if confirming a suspicion.

The sound of his voice faded, drowned out by Caleb's frantic questions as he gave her shoulders a gentle shake, desperate for reassurance.

"Emily, are you alright?" he implored.

After a moment of dazed disorientation, Emily pieced together her awareness. A shaky smile adorned her lips as she found her voice. "Yeah... I mean, I don't know how, but I'm okay," she whispered in disbelief.

Caleb enveloped her in a tight embrace. Holding her close, he noticed the mysterious savior's absence. Breaking the hug, he gazed deep into Emily's eyes.

"It's a miracle," he whispered. "If it's okay, I want to make sure you get home safely."

Grateful for his support, she replied, her tone tinged with vulnerability. "Thanks, but you don't have to do that; accompany me on the bus or anything."

But he was determined to reassure her of his intentions. "Nonsense," he began, intertwining his fingers with hers. "Besides, I don't have anything else to do today."

Uncertainty lingered in his mind, a remnant of surprise that hadn't yet faded. "Are you sure?" she asked, her voice trembling with gratitude.

"Absolutely," he said, while squeezing her hand with newfound resolve.

Guiding her to the bus stop, he pledged to stay by her side through the uncertainty. After a few moments of quiet, they boarded the bus and found an empty seat. Emily leaned against the cool window, while Caleb settled beside her. A calm silence enveloped them, offering a brief escape from the emotional whirlwind of moments ago.

"You said you were a photographer, right?" he asked, breaking the silence.

Emily reached into her pocket and retrieved her digital camera, her eyes lighting up with enthusiasm. "Aspiring to be," she corrected, passing the camera over to Caleb.

He examined the captured moments with a growing sense of awe. Soon, his gaze fell upon a breathtaking picture of Burney Falls. He couldn't help but exclaim in amazement. "Wow, this is good! You took this?"

Nodding in self-assurance, she confirmed her passion for photography with a confident, "Yup!"

He continued to explore the digital realm, captivated by each amazing snapshot. His laughter filled the air as he reached a photo of Emily diving into the cascading waters.

"You are fearless."

The corners of her mouth curved, shaking her head. "No, I just tried not to let fear hold me back."

As they moved on to the next image, a peculiar shot caught his attention—the mysterious savior, his face obscured by an outstretched hand.

"Who's this?" Caleb asked.

Emily tugged his hand, tilting the camera's screen for a better view. "Oh," she began. "He took the other picture for me, so I asked if I could take one of him, but he was hesitant." A puzzled expression crossed her features.

The next photo that appeared on the screen sent a chill down Caleb's spine. It captured the mysterious savior, but his azure orbs mirrored the emptiness of a cloudless sky. His gaze lingered on the image, his mind racing to comprehend the inexplicable. Slowly, he tore away from the haunting photograph and met Emily's concerned stare.

"Are you okay?" She asked.

"I'm fine," Caleb forced, masking the unease that gnawed at his core. Scanning the bus and passing scenery, he searched for any signs of their inexplicable follower. The weight of his realization bore down on him, but for now, he kept Emily blissfully unaware.

3

GUARDIAN ANGEL

After ensuring Emily's safe arrival in a nearby hotel, Caleb returned to the coffee shop to retrieve his car. About a half-hour later, he pulled into the parking lot of a bar on the outskirts of town, where a neon sign buzzed and sputtered, turning the vicinity into a stage for clandestine affairs. He turned off the engine, but stayed in the vehicle, fixated on the photo he'd snapped from Emily's camera. The image revealed a peculiar man with an inexplicable ability to freeze time, a mystery that Caleb was determined to unravel.

With a deep breath, he slid the photo off his screen and dialed David Bryer, a young scientist renowned for his intelligence. As the phone chirped, he tapped his fingers on the steering wheel. Soon, the scientist's faint vocals greeted him, leery of attracting attention from his colleagues.

"Caleb? What's up? I'm still at the lab," he murmured, staring through the glass on the door behind him.

"I know," the author acknowledged. "But it's important. If I send you a photo, can you show it to your cousin to see if he can identify someone?"

"I can ask. What's going on?" David replied in a subdued tone.

Caleb lowered the phone, his fingers navigating his gallery to find the photo he wanted to send. He cursed the sluggish internet at More Mellows Bar, each agonizing second increasing his impatience. His eyes remained glued on the intriguing image, while tapping his fingers on the dashboard.

At last, the 'sent' notification appeared, and he brought the device back to his ear, ready to share the details.

"I've just sent the picture," he informed, his gaze drifting out the window. "I'm certain this guy is stalking a girl I met at a coffee shop today."

"Well, it's good to hear you connected with someone. I'll do what I can," David replied before ending the call.

Later that day, inside a snug hotel, Emily savored the last drop of deep red wine while preparing a delectable dinner. An aged photograph hung on the refrigerator, capturing a tender moment shared between her and her younger sister, Kota Reels. In it, they both beamed with genuine happiness while clambering on a jungle gym.

Intoxicating flavors enraptured her senses when a knock sounded at the door, injecting a surge of excitement in the air. The door's smooth surface yielded effortlessly to the touch of the visitor's hand, bestowing a refreshing coolness upon the knuckles just beneath the displayed room number 1111.

This pushed Emily to her feet. "No way, is she here already?" She asked, looking at the time on the microwave.

Certain of the visitor's identity, she sat the wine bottle on the table and rushed over. In one swift motion, she swung the door open. "Welcome, Ko! I'm so glad you came." Wrapped in each other's arms, she couldn't miss the chestnut fur decorating Kota's jacket. "I guess you had Mugsy today?"

She brushed off a few strands, loosening the embrace. Soon after, her sister removed her coat. "A few days ago. I swear, that little guy has mad energy, and his fur just gets everywhere, ya know," she replied. The young visitor then kicked off her shoes at the door, exhaling a sigh of relief. After several advancements, she absorbed the opulent surroundings. A plush carpet sent a soft sensation beneath her polka-dotted ankle socks.

It was akin to walking on clouds, and Kota's attention wandered from the tasteful artwork hanging on the walls to the burgundy velvet couch decorated with vibrant throw pillows featuring various shapes, some accompanied by playful tassels on the corners. "Wow, this is a hella rad place!" she marveled.

Emily joined her in admiring their temporary abode, her focus drifting towards the large window. "Right, who knew New York could be this beautiful?"

Out of nowhere, Kota yelled, "HELLO!" In response, the adventurer lunged over in concern, but found her sister bearing an innocent expression, admitting, "I wanted to see if it echoed."

Amusement flooded her demeanor as she claimed Kota's travel bag. "Just wait till you see the bedroom." After stepping through the threshold, she dropped the luggage beside a king-sized bed.

Her visitor, however, stopped at the entrance, amazed by the high-quality linens on the elegant rural oak bedside table topped with a Dove Castle lamp. "Wow," she gushed. Just then, her stomach let out a loud growl in response to the alluring scents that seeped in from the kitchen.

"Good, I see you're hungry," Emily remarked.

A twinkle appeared in her kin's eyes as she exclaimed, her mouthwatering at the delicious smells, "Totally famished!"

She gave a comforting pat on Kota's shoulder before returning to the cooking area. Not long later, her sister emerged from the bedroom, holding her own painting, darting over to an open wall in the living room. Intrigued, the adventurer hurried over to witness the artwork being affixed beside another piece. The vintage one depicted mist-covered mountains under merciful rain, which was showcased as fine, diagonal streaks flowing throughout the canvas. She stood back, brimming with pride at the artwork she had contributed to the masterpiece. "There ya go. Now it'll be like a tiny bit of me is hanging with you while you're here," she said.

"I love it," Emily stated, staring at the unique painting. Then, as if remembering something important, she added, "Oh, I almost forgot; here's an extra keycard in case you need it for any reason."

Kota snatched it up and stashed it in her pocket before bolting to the food. Not long after, they settled at the table, encompassed in the glow of a fluorescent light, exchanging laughter and anecdotes. However, her excitement proved to be infectious as she fidgeted with her fork and tapped her foot to an imperceptible rhythm. "I still can't even believe how quick you got the peroxide!" she exclaimed.

The adventurer joined in, recounting a tale of splinters, providing vague details of the incident. "Luckily, we weren't too far from the cabin," she mentioned.

"Yeah, but like, did you have to pour half the bottle in my hand?" Kota questioned.

"Hey, you kept screaming to get it out, so I tore the lid open and did what I had to," she said, pouring blueberry juice into a glass while avoiding eye contact.

Midway through her meal, the young visitor offered her culinary critique with a touch of nonchalance. "This is dank, by the way." She pushed a strand of hair behind her ear, a faint scent of lavender shampoo permeating the space.

Emily's glare crinkled at the corners with a smile, absorbing the unexpected praise. She leaned in, taking on a more conspiratorial tone. "I'm glad you like it. I was worried it was going to be too spicy for you."

Kota snorted from the mere notion; her stare shot heavenward. "Oh, please, I can totally handle the heat," she said, her inflection reeking of mockery.

"Okay, challenge accepted." A momentary silence blanketed them while they both took a drink from their respective glasses. "I'm surprised you made it here already. I wasn't expecting you for a few days."

Mild exasperation took over her sister's movements as she zeroed in on the remnants of two emptied wine bottles resting on the counter. Taken aback, she dropped her fork. In a moment of reproach, she pointed out one subtle detail. "Is that why you haven't cleaned up?"

Surprised by the inspection, her words stumbled. "What? No, I -" Having forgotten all about her earlier indulgence, she turned in search of what the young visitor could have found. Upon discovering her carelessness, she met her sister's gaze, trying to plead with her. "I can exp–"

However, Kota wasn't having it. She got up from the table and relinquished her dish into the sink. "No, I get it," she murmured. "Seeing how much it helped my dad with his anger issues wasn't enough for you," she said in a sarcastic tone.

"That's not fair," Emily retorted.

"Isn't it?" the visitor inquired, Turning to face her sister. "He found me, by the way. He called a few times this past week and the other day he left a message saying that he was going to swing by. So, I left and came here."

"Kota, I didn't know."

"Of course not. How would you? It's not all bad though. I met a guy online, and he's a local. He's going to show me around the area."

Curiosity sparked within Emily as a sudden knock interrupted their conversation. Kota hurried towards the door, eager to discover who awaited on the other side. As she squinted through the small peephole, a young man with black hair wearing a khaki jacket came into focus.

"Yo, can I help you?" she asked, standing against the door.

"Uh, yeah. I'm Caleb," he began. "Is Emily here by chance?"

Kota eased the entrance ajar, ensuring the security chain remained intact so she could get a better look at him.

"Hey, who's out there?" Emily asked as she approached.

The young visitor turned to her sister and gave her the only information she had-a name. Much to Kota's surprise, a subtle flush colored Emily's cheeks. "Emmie, who is this dude?"

"A friend," she said, staring at the young man. "Sorry, this isn't a good time."

"Are you alright?" he inquired; his gaze locked on his coffee companion.

"She's fine," Kota asserted. "I'll just get out of the way." With that, she pivoted, aiming for the bedroom door, her steps purposeful.

However, a firm tug on her upper arm prevented her from taking another stride. Emily's grip was gentle, yet insistent. "This is my sis, Kota," she introduced with a touch of pride.

Feeling the pull of her sister's loyalty, the visitor spun back, facing their guest once more, who remained in the hallway.

Caleb held a hand up in a placating gesture. "Well, it's nice to meet —"

"Half-sister," she interjected, her gaze locked with the author's, defiance clear in her stance. "She kinda forgets to mention that part."

"Cause it's not important."

"Yeah, no biggie," Kota shrugged, retreating to the quiet alcove. Despite being stoked about her sister's blossoming relationship, she couldn't help but feel like she had to compete for her sister's attention.

"Kota!" It was at that exact moment her cheeks blazed with embarrassment, realizing the author was still standing in the hallway. She spun around, unlocking the chain, her words a hasty apology. "Oh, my gosh. I'm sorry!"

"It's fine. No worries," Caleb reassured, his voice carrying a soothing undertone.

"Would you like to come in?" she offered.

Stepping into the cozy abode, his eyes widened, sweeping over the inviting sanctuary. Enthralled by the brilliant décor, he advanced deeper into the room. "This is more spacious than my home," he said, looking at the chandelier above.

After closing the door behind them, Emily joined his side. She cast a glance at the interior design, then back at her guess, somewhat amused. "I think it's all the extra ambiance. Which looks nice, don't get me wrong, but, honestly, I can do without it."

Caleb's gaze lingered on her for a moment longer, his lips curling into a faint smile. There was a glint of recognition in his eyes, as if he comprehended the sentiment behind those words. Emily, too, held a stare, sensing an unspoken understanding.

Before long, he found himself immersed in a magnificent painting that adorned the wall, depicting the Eiffel Tower right after a refreshing rainstorm. Its vibrant colors and graceful lines brought an air of sophistication to the room. The painting seemed to capture a fleeting moment of tranquility, the raindrops glistening on the tower's iron structure as if frozen in time. Each brushstroke conveyed the artist's skill in capturing the essence of a Parisian evening, evoking wonder in his mind. "Wow," he whispered, his voice filled with awe. "This is remarkable."

The adventurer nodded with a radiant smirk. Her deep pools of hazel sparkled with gratitude as she stared at the painting before her. "I know. It's all Kota's creation," she disclosed. "But let's keep it between us."

"Why would she feel embarrassed about this?" Caleb wondered, stepping closer to the captivating artwork hanging in the living room. His eyes widened at the sight of tiny yellow dots strewn around the iconic structure. "Are those fireflies?" he asked.

Emily accompanied him on relishing the work of art with a sense of pride. "Yes," she confirmed. "She told me she was bored one weekend, and then this masterpiece came to life."

Caleb's admiration deepened as he marveled at the artist's talent. "To think she created such beauty in just a few days! I hope she's taking art classes to nurture her incredible skills."

Emily nodded. "I believe so. It's been quite some time since we last caught up."

Lost in their shared moment, the pair locked eyes, a sense of comfort passing between them. The room seemed to fade away as their connection intensified. Before too long, she broke the silence as she stepped back, sitting on the arm of the couch. "You know," she murmured, "I'm grateful that you're here."

Inspired by a sudden thought, she retrieved her iPhone 3GS from her pocket and navigated to a playlist titled 'Dance Songs.' Once the first melodic notes drifted through the evening air, she placed her phone down on the table, swaying to the rhythm.

Captivated over what was happening before him, Caleb watched in merriment as Emily showed off her moves. A playful grin tugged at the corners of his lips. "Wow, that thing's like an antique."

She turned around, donning a mischievous glimmer in her eyes. "Yeah," she replied. "I haven't had a chance to upgrade."

"That's okay."

Before he could speak another word, Emily leaned in close, pressing a finger to his lips with a soft 'shh'. Their proximity created an intimate bubble. "Let's just dance the night away."

With renewed vigor, her body continued to sway to the beat of the song. Lost in the infectious joy, he ducked under Emily's outstretched arms, dashing over to the couch. Their lightheartedness intertwined, creating an aura of pure bliss.

After pulling his phone from his pocket, a gentle vibration broke the rhythm of their dance. With laughter still echoing in the room, he rushed to check his messages, discovering a text from David. His eyebrows furrowed as he read the words on the screen.

I gave Jason a copy of the picture you sent me. He said he'll run it through the database; the message revealed.

Gratitude filled Caleb's heart as he prepared a response. His fingers moved across the keyboard with exact precision. Awesome, thank you, he typed.

Worry knitted Emily's brow when his phone entered her view, prompting her to ask, "What's going on?" She inclined her head towards the device, hoping it wasn't anything serious.

A reassuring grin played on his face as he replied, "Yep, just some work stuff."

Relieved by his response, her expression brightened, beckoning him closer to the couch. "Great! So come on, dance with me!" she exclaimed, her voice brimming with contagious enthusiasm.

He let out a self-conscious, aware of his lackluster dancing abilities. "I'm not the best dancer out there. In fact, 'worst' might be a more suitable adjective," he admitted, a hint of self-deprecation lacing his tone. Yet, his body waggled, attempting to find a rhythm.

Emily closed the distance between them, her gaze filled with warmth and understanding. "Come on, it's just us. Don't worry about looking stupid," she urged, her eyes brimming with excitement.

The words danced in the air, coaxing Caleb to shed his inhibitions. He gazed at her, his face breaking into a radiant smile, reassured by her infectious energy. The weight of self-consciousness lifted from his shoulders, for he knew he couldn't afford to appear foolish before her. "Come on, we can just jump around. It'll be fun," she continued, her voice brimming with enthusiasm that mirrored the mischievous glint in her eyes.

And in that very moment, as if the universe itself conspired to align with her desires, a familiar melody unfurled. The opening notes of "Jump" by Van Halen reverberated from her phone, filling the room with an electrifying energy that matched the spark in her enchanted beam.

A look of delight adorned her face, as if the song was a testament to some cosmic force at play. Grinning from ear to ear, her smile carried a flirtatious allure that was hard to resist. "Wow, this song couldn't have come on at a better time," she remarked, her voice laced with playful charm as she locked eyes with Caleb.

"Yeah, it would almost seem as if you planned this," he responded, his tone infused with a playful jest. His gaze met hers, and in that fleeting moment, a silent understanding passed between them. There was a shared sense of camaraderie, a tacit agreement to embrace the spontaneity of the present moment.

Giving in to the pulsating rhythm of the music, their bodies became vessels of unbridled joy. They leaped and twirled with carefree abandon. Soon, laughter spilled out, intermingling with the melody to create a symphony of pure bliss. In that whirlwind of motion, their worries and troubles dissolved, leaving only the exhilaration of the present.

In the serene haven of the bedroom, Kota sat cross-legged atop the bed, her back facing the luminous fixtures as her slender fingers glided across the smooth surface of her phone's screen. A pang of longing spread at her core. With a creased brow, she tapped away at the keyboard, each stroke a silent plea for guidance. She typed 'how not to be forgotten' in the search bar. As results popped up, she clung to any answer that would present itself. The harmonious sounds from the other room circulated through the air, punctuated only by the occasional click of a button.

Meanwhile, a nocturnal pulse throbbed beyond the hotel walls. Amidst a row of parked cars on the side of the building, one vehicle sat apart. Smoke from a cigarette rose through its window. But when the man went to take another drag, a dark presence walked up, sporting a lab coat, and pulled back the man's arm that was dangling along the side of the door. "I'm sorry, but–"

Quick to react, he opened and closed the door, loosening his assailant's grip. Unfortunately, this also knocked his arm from its socket, making it impossible to get free. Through the mirror, he saw the tip of a syringe peeked from his attacker's coat. Willing to deal with the pain, he clutched the door handle once more, but this time, the presence retaliated, slamming his body up against it.

The man stifled a cry by holding a hand over his mouth, while the other positioned to prick himself with the needle. "For the time being, you may continue to act as the shell of a man you are, until told otherwise."

Back inside the room, a notification flashed across the display, breaking the spell of concentration.

Just pulled up on the side of the house, it read.

Her heart quickened as she absorbed the contents of the message. A surge of adrenaline coursed through her veins, nudging her along to rise from the bed.

She pocketed her phone upon nearing the threshold, but before getting any further, a raucous symphony of laughter burst forth from the duo in the living room. Its infectious melody filtered through the air, weaving its way into her eager ears. The sound enveloped her, swirling and twirling as her hand dawdled above the cool brass doorknob.

On one side, the vibrant atmosphere beckoned Kota, tempting her to abandon all responsibilities and immerse herself in the carefree revelry happening just beyond the door. On the other, just beyond her sights, laughter erupted like champagne bubbles, filling the living room with a joyous crescendo.

Her phone emitted a persistent buzz, its call tugging at her desires. Each hum sounded, making her heart skip a beat.

The decision weighed heavily on her, a choice between the tangible comfort of familiar smiles and the intangible promises of a blinking screen. Should she succumb to the allure of laughter and carefree abandon or explore the unknown possibilities ahead?

In the end, Kota's resolve solidified. She turned the doorknob, feeling the smooth resistance yield to her touch, and stepped into the swirling chaos of the living room.

Upon re-emerging, she shielded her gaze from the questioning looks of her friends. Concern washed over Emily's face as she asked, "Where are you going?"

Kota met her sister's glare with intensity. "I have to go," she confessed, "but I'll be back soon." Rather than wait for a response, she left in haste.

Across the room, Caleb noticed Emily's shaken demeanor and asked, "Is everything okay?"

Emily, still reeling from the sudden departure of her sister, retorted, "Just sister stuff," her voice almost incoherent above the laughter and conversation.

A cool breeze brushed against Kota's face, carrying whispers of adventure. Sprinting across the dew-kissed lawn, she approached the familiar black jeep, its presence a beacon in the nocturnal landscape. Settling into the passenger seat, she fastened her seatbelt, a tangible reminder of her desire for safety and control.

"Better late than never, Simon," she whispered, irritation oozing throughout the vehicle.

Simon rolled his eyes and started the engine. "The night's full of surprises," he said. As soon as they pulled away from the curb, Kota's annoyance faded, replaced by a growing curiosity.

On the other side of town, the imposing edifice of Creation Labs loomed tall against the skyline, its grand silhouette dominating the surrounding landscape. Its pristine architectural lines became a driving force for innovation and progress. Huge reflective glass windows cascaded down the building's façade while at its pinnacle, towering spires reached towards the heavens. In the depths, however, David moved with shadow-like grace through the labyrinthine corridors.

Unable to stop himself, he walked up to a door embedded in the wall and punched in the password. After tapping the last key, the door lowered into the wall, revealing a freezer full of samples waiting to be studied.

Clenched tight behind his back, he hid a blood sample behind his colleague, Kyle, who inquired about their meeting. With a calculated move, the scientist plunged a syringe into his associate's shoulder, injecting him with a sedative.

As his colleague's face met the floor, David sprang into action. He hurried to the nearest table where a microscope awaited, its lens ready to unveil the secrets within the blood sample he drew.

He rested a glass slide on the base and held the syringe aloft like a conductor's baton, waiting for a single droplet of blood to bead at the brink. With precision, he allowed the ruby drop to coat the slide, watching the scarlet liquid spread, revealing microscopic mysteries.

David's breath caught in his throat as he watched the intricate dance of white and red blood cells in combat through the ocular lens. "I wasn't expecting this. The virus's effect is unprecedented," he whispered, astonished over his discovery.

4

DISCOVERED

February 1992

The creature pursued a sinister scheme that extended far beyond merely liberating Lucifer from hell. Prowling the lab's lit corridors, an assemblage of lanky silhouettes scattered on the walls under fluttering lights. Like a predator stalking its prey, it became fixed on the cluster of scientists engrossed in their groundbreaking experiment aimed at curbing plastic proliferation. Yet, an unsettling feeling gnawed the edges of its consciousness, whispering that not all was as it appeared.

Its conviction solidified as time elapsed, driving it to uncover the true nature of these individuals. When they dispersed in groups, it scoured for ulterior motives, beginning with Kyle Heem - a young, solitary scientist who seemed the perfect target for its machinations. From the Abyssal realm, a parallel dimension full of decaying particles, it trailed the scientist's every step.

It stopped when the scientist reached the sanctuary of a modest apartment building, surrounded by Callery Pear trees lining the street. From the parallel realm, those gnarled arboreal specimens appeared infested with fungi, their rotting fruit emitting a pungent odor.

Kyle ascended the wooden stairs, his footsteps shuffling through the empty hallway. Treads groaned underfoot, intensifying the night's stillness. Upon crossing the threshold, he barricaded the door. Only then did he discard his shoes, venturing deeper into the inner sanctum of his dwelling.

As he reached the bedroom, he held out a hand in search of the light switch. With a flick of his wrist, he illuminated the space until it shortened out, plunging the entire house into darkness. Frustration mingled on his features, bewildered over what just happened. "Not again."

Soon, his gaze shifted, drawn toward the stove's clock—a beacon of digits laden under a fiery sunset that proclaimed the hour: 6:06. Desperation crept into his actions, repeatedly flicking the switch, hoping for even a glimmer of light, but nothing changed.

He made his way toward the exit when a dash of movement demanded his attention, teasing the periphery of his vision. His tired mind, strained from the ceaseless demands of the day, played tricks on him. Doubt and unease crept into his thoughts, like tendrils of smoke slithering through his consciousness.

Okay, Kyle. He thought to himself, trying to quell the unease that settled in his bones. You need to get some sleep.

As those words lingered in his mind, an eerie phenomenon unfolded before him. A baleful glow skulked through the building, its wickedness flickering in a vile resurgence. Mesmerizing displays painted the walls, casting a haunting radiance across the room. An inexplicable chill crawled up his spine, causing his muscles to tense.

In an instant, the door slammed with a bone-rattling thud. Fear, a vice tightening around his chest, rendered him paralyzed. Panic awakened his adrenaline to a higher state as he searched for an alternate escape route.

Invisible on the mortal plane, the creature's intent pervaded like a heavy fog.

He's a nobody. I could end him, and not a single soul would bat an eye.

Yet, fate had a peculiar way of rearing its head at the most unexpected times. Just as his sinister thoughts took shape, something stole his attention—a tattoo of a slanted dagger, dripping blood at the tip, on Kyle's right shoulder. This compelled him to lower his power, ceasing the lights' erratic whirl, giving way to deceptive calmness.

A wave of realization washed over the dark entity, pleased by its discovery. "Well, doesn't that just change everything?" An ear-to-ear grin curled onto its features. "You'll be far more useful when you're working for me."

The following evening, it tracked a new target—Celsey Hail—a science prodigy about to enter the local bar. He stood in the middle of the parking lot, occupying the parallel dimension, scouring his memory. Images of the burning remnants from a restaurant, reduced to ashes, replayed in his consciousness. Then, a bench across the street, bearing distinct writing: 'Sara works here', stole his attention.

Alas, he snapped back to the building, its bold letters on the sign above the entrance riveted him: 'More Mellows Bar.' The invitation ignited an insatiable gnawing emptiness within him. "You're just tempting me."

Inside the bar, Celsey crossed the threshold into a spirited melody of excited banter and clinking glasses. Behind the sleek counter, the bartender's movements were well-practiced. Deft and fluid, his hands poured liquid merriment into vacant glasses, filling them to the brim.

Among the eclectic mix of patrons, her eyes locked with those of her cherished friends—Ashley, her vanilla blonde highlights framing her flushed face, and Rachel, whose wavy dark brown hair and gemstone earrings caught the light. Their expressions lit up with excitement upon seeing her.

They hurried over to greet her. "Well, look at you," Ashley said, genuine awe lacing her tone as she admired her. "You could have been a model with that gorgeous hair."

In a tender ballet, she traced the cascade of Celsey's hair, each strand a velvety weave of rich, mosaic locks.

"Thanks, Ash." Celsey tried to hold Ashley's arms to prevent her from pouring another drink. "But maybe you've had enough."

Rachel leaned over and caressed her shoulder. "I'm surprised we got you out of the lab," she slurred, the gemstone studs in her ears twinkling.

"Oh, you know, there's only so long one can stare at formulas and hypotheses."

"Well, I for one, am astonished that you managed to get into a prestigious lab like Creation at such a young age," Ashley said. With a delicate touch, she rubbed the golden cable chain gracing her neck. On it dangled a pendant—a grand cursive 'A'—a regal emblem of her identity.

"Almost dying really puts things into perspective," Celsey informed, settling onto a leather stool between her friends. "I wasn't going to just sit by hoping to one day reach my dream, so I studied—"

"We know. Couldn't even get you out of your house to meet boys," Rachel said, slurping the last remnants of her drink.

"Wait, she did meet that one guy. What's his name?"

"Oh, yeah. Kyle, right?" Rachel wiggled her brows and bumped shoulders with Celsey.

"Okay, maybe I should get you guys home."

"Come on, at least have one drink with us," Ashley insisted.

"Maybe another time. I think you two have had enough for all three of us already."

They executed perfect eye-rolls before fumbling to retrieve their purses as a sluggish man approached. Despite an air of confidence, his hesitant gait betrayed him. He sauntered over, interposed his arms between them, and inclined his head to greet Rachel with a soft, "Hey there."

"Whattup, boy?" Rachel blurted, halfway looking up at the newcomer.

Celsey cleared her throat to get his attention and lifted Rachel's hand, holding up her ring finger. "She's married, sorry."

Despite an apologetic smile, embarrassment overcame him, prompting him to lower his head and scuffle off. Upon reaching the table in the back from which he came, Ashley peeked over at him. "Wat 'bout me?"

"Come on," Celsey said, turning back to Rachel. "We should go."

"No, no," Rachel protested, her tone infused with nostalgia and longing. "You've gotta have at least one drink with us for old times' sake."

Her resolve faltered, giving in to the infectious spirit of camaraderie. She nodded, settling onto the leather barstool next to Ashley. "Just one. So, what are you guys drinking?"

"Oh, you know us. Anything sweet." Still swaying, Ashley's tone left a trace of indulgence that colored her cadence as she whispered to the bartender, "white gummy bear."

Concealed near the window, the demon stifled a yawn, bored by the festivities. In search of entertainment, he drew on his energy, his eyes shifting from their mortal appearance to the eerie blackness of his demonic form. Yet, before he could set his wicked plans in motion, the Roamer materialized behind him, his mere presence thwarting the hell-spawn's intentions.

"I know what you're planning," Haines declared, an ironclad resolve in his voice. "But Celsey Hail cannot be the one to open Lucifer's tomb."

Intrigued by this notion, the demon's eyes returned to their mortal state, its expression twisting into a scowl as it turned to face Haines. A low snarl escaped Victor's maw, betraying the primal fury simmering beneath the surface. "And why not?"

"Because she's already playing her part," Haines revealed cryptically.

"What does that mean?"

"It's not your concern," Haines replied, then disappeared from the demon's side.

On the subsequent night, the creature trailed Boris Linderman, the mastermind behind the current experiment at Creation Labs, from the Stygian void. His pursuit led him through the intricate pathways of the city streets. Curiosity buzzed within him as he contemplated the clandestine business awaiting them.

What shady affair are you getting into, eh, Boris?

Oblivious to the dangers that awaited, Boris turned the corner, making his way to the edge of a bustling beach path. A salty tang mingled with the earthy smell of decaying seaweed, saturating the air. On a bent knee, he delved into his pocket and pulled out a small, vibrant orange plastic bag, ready to gather bits of discarded wrappers, fragments of forgotten picnics, and glimmering shards of glass one by one.

This infuriated the creature, pushing it to crack its knuckle so hard that its fists oozed inky sludge. Beads of slime fizzled upon touching the sandy ground. Repulsed by the scientist's actions, it departed the dimension where the surface was riddled with deep fissures, thirsting for even a drop of moisture, and ventured into the mortal realm.

During his self-imposed mission, a growl ruptured Boris' fragile tranquility. Startled, he whirled around to find the demon disguised as Victor, standing only inches away.

"Holy heck. You scared the living daylights out of me."

Victor relished in the brief scare, knowing it was only the beginning. "You are as pathetic as you appear. Do you think that a mere mortal like you could single-handedly cleanse the vast depths of the ocean?"

"Well, I–"

"Save it." Closing the distance between them, their breaths mingled in the cool night air. "You are going to help me free Lucifer from his entombment."

Boris held his ground, feeling the weight of the world pressing upon his shoulders. "Yeah, I don't think so."

The fiend's eyes turned as dark as a starless night, resembling bottomless pits that bore into his soul. Its clenched fist trembled with an animalistic urge. Yet, amidst the tempest of its rage, a sinister grin grew, for he knew, with chilling certainty, that he had found the perfect pawn for his wicked intentions.

"Oh my God!" Boris spluttered, terror suffocating his quivering spirit. The small bag slipped from his grasp, its contents abandoned and forgotten, as he turned and fled from the beach. Driven by sheer survival instinct, panic compelled his legs forward.

His heart thumped as he dashed towards his front door, fighting to regain control of his racing mind. After fumbling for the keys several times, a surge of relief took over.

However, when he arrived at his destination, he encountered a nightmarish sight. His once peaceful home had transformed into an unfamiliar landscape. Murky vapor billowed from the kitchen, casting an eerie haze over everything, as if it had a life of its own, creeping into every corner and wrapping vines around his perception.

He stared in disbelief at what he saw before him. What was once a place of comfort now lay in ruins. His stove stood firm, poised to unleash its scalding contents. A pot, bloated and simmering, taunted him with defiant hisses and sizzles. The scorching heat radiated, fusing with the unmistakable odor of sulfur.

A sense of derision hung in the undulating mist, resembling ethereal creatures, mirroring his frantic footsteps. Whispers of forgotten, inaudible utterance plagued his ears, each a haunting remnant of his past. Images were next to come, clawing their way to the forefront, twisting reality into an intricate tapestry of memories.

Yet determination continued to burn within, urging him to conquer the madness and reclaim his sanctuary. Guided by instinct, he approached the treacherous pot, snatching a towel, prepared to confront the boiling contents threatening to overflow. He hurled the cookware into the sink, unleashing a torrent of water that extinguished the crackling flames, drowning out the fiery orchestra.

Quick breaths and shallow gasps consumed Boris as he struggled to make sense of the situation. After stumbling back from the once devouring flames, fear breached his mind. "Rylee?!" he cried out, his voice echoing through their besieged home.

The sound filled the air, absorbed by the unsettling silence that seemed to foretell the horrors awaiting him in the depths of their dwelling. Each panicked stride resonated with Boris's distress as he ventured into the dining room, where framed photos of smiling children lined the walls. Before he could reach the staircase, his foot struck an abandoned toy truck, sending it flying across the hazy space while he tumbled forward.

When standing back up, he blinked away the thick smoke that obscured his vision and called again for Rylee, her name a plea on his quivering lips. Amidst the deafening silence, he sprinted up the stairs. At the summit, two rooms loomed, once havens of solace now transformed into unforeseen nests of despair. Urgency drove him as he dashed to the nearest door, eager to uncover its secrets. Trepidation gripped him as he grasped the knob, but dissipated when he found everything undisturbed.

Dread pulled him to the next chamber, his hand trembling as it pushed the door ajar. But what awaited him sent a sharp shiver down his spine and stilled his beating heart. There, on the icy floor, Rylee knelt, a haunting portrait of anguish etched on her tear-streaked face. A menacing presence loomed behind her, casting a cloak of darkness over their lives.

"Took you long enough," it taunted. "So, now you're going to help me free Lucifer from his tomb."

Boris's throat constricted, his words stifled by the nightmare unfolding before him. Panic seized him to his core as the demon's talon closed around Rylee's neck. Entranced by each other's gaze, tears of sorrow trailed down their cheeks.

The creature savored the moment, its hollow pools shifting to black as it darted a disdainful glare toward its target. Still, thoughts of salvation flooded Boris's mind.

I will free you from this wretched place, my love. Together, we will find a sanctuary untouched by evil.

Unfortunately, the unclean spirit intercepted his thoughts, reveling in the anguish it had incited. A twisted smile contorted into an enraged scowl over this audacious aspiration.

"What's this? Did you think I wouldn't hear your mundane thoughts?" it said.

This realization silenced his feeble outcry. In a breathless moment, he bore witness to the unthinkable. The demon's merciless claw pierced Rylee's flesh, slashing her throat with savage brutality. Devastated, Boris crumbled to his knees, the weight of grief and despair bearing down on him like an insurmountable burden.

A stifling quietude settled over the room, broken only by the creature's twisted taunts. Its endless wells glimmered with malicious delight, reveling in the brutal erasure of the scientist's once-beloved 'honey-do' list. "Well, Boris," it jeered, the eerie proposal dripping like venom from its lips, "it seems you now have an abundance of free time on your hands. Why don't you lend me a hand in resurrecting dear old Lucifer, hmm?"

Seconds ticked by as the demon's pools returned to a human state. Its impatience grew, manifesting in a clenched fist that betrayed its escalating agitation. With steadfast strides, it distanced itself from Rylee's still form, discarding her like a forgotten doll.

As a torrent of emotions drowned Boris, he struck the floor with all his might. Paralyzed before the malevolent presence, his heart torn by the cruel fate that had befallen his beloved.

Frustrated by the scientist's lack of response, Victor erupted, slicing through the oppressive hush. "Snap out of it!"

Boris's glare seethed with anger as he confronted the sinister figure. He brushed away the anguish that stained his cheeks, summoning strength within his haunted countenance.

"Oh, that's right. I know you have three kids, and I know exactly where they are right now."

Under his tormentor's weight, despair reached its zenith, his heaving chest led a booming, building roar that shook the rafters - "ENOUGH!"

***

Dawn's canvas unfurled in the present, its golden rays spilled into the room, awakening Emily from her slumber. The sunlight painted the walls in vibrant hues, casting an enchanting glow that turned the room into a surreal dreamscape. Sparkling rainbow diamonds danced through her window, infusing the room with an ethereal magic.

She thought about what the day may offer as she perched on the opulent Italian leather couch, her limbs extending and acclimating to the dawn. From the plush velvet cushions to the suspended grand chandelier, the hotel room exuded elegance.

A sudden far-off growl of a beat-up pickup truck sent her back to the events at the coffee shop. However, her unease dissipated when her gaze fell to the floor, where she found her partner lying on the plush carpet, still lost in slumber. Charmed by the spectacle, she rested her feet on his back, a tender touch that conveyed their connection without words. The morning light enveloped their entwined forms, beaming a burning halo of contentment.

Well aware of the serendipitous moment that had befallen upon their shared space, a knowing grin curved her face. "Good morning. What a delightful surprise."

Caleb stirred, his peepers fluttering open with a slow, deliberate grace. "Hey, sorry, I didn't want you to feel alone."

Their eyes locked, presenting an opportunity for him to notice a mystical hue of purple swirling within her hazel irises. Thinking it was from the angle at which the sunlight hit her face, he rubbed his eyes. By the time his vision cleared, Emily had moved away from the couch, withdrawing her feet from Caleb's lap. Bending closer, she planted a gentle kiss on his cheek, a gesture teeming with gratitude. As her lips met his skin, he felt complete comfort in their shared moment. His pout etched closer, seeking to reciprocate, but fate had other plans. At the last moment, she shifted, causing their mouths to meet in an ephemeral touch of surprise.

In that split second, panic flooded Caleb's mind, fearing the consequences of his impulsive action. But as he pulled away, a gentle warmth enveloped him when she reacted to the occasion.

After parting, Emily's eyes reverted to their natural hue, exuding a hint of reassurance—a tacit confirmation that their impromptu kiss had not fractured their connection but strengthened it.

"So, that was okay?" Caleb asked, vulnerability in his voice.

Emily grinned. "Of course."

In the other bedroom, Kota stumbled inside and collapsed on the mattress, staring at the ceiling. Panic surged through her veins as nausea jolted her upright. Staggered footfalls guided her towards the locked bathroom. Driven by an insistent impulse, she stumbled towards the kitchen sink and convulsed into the drain.

Unaware of her sister's ordeal, Emily busied herself laying out an outfit until the retching shattered the peace. Alarm painted her brow as she hurried to investigate. On the other side of the cooking area, she saw her sister bent over, clutching her stomach.

"Kota? What's wrong?"

"I'm pretty sure I drank too much."

"Since when do you -"

No longer able to hold it back, Kota bent forward to vomit into the sink. Emily took a step closer, resting a hand on her sister's back. "What's going on with you?"

"How do you do it?" The only resonance was the gentle purr of the air conditioner as Kota looked up to catch her sister's glare. "Mom died in front of you, too. Do you not have nightmares?"

"Not a moment goes by that I don't think about it, but crawling in a hole somewhere isn't what she would have wanted."

"So, your solution was to run away?"

"What? I'm here to pursue my dream."

Regret consumed Emily following those words. "Sorry, I didn't mean..." She paused, taking in the surroundings once more. "I'm just trying to make a living."

Burdened by unspoken words, Kota's continued silence spoke volumes, revealing the complex emotions swirling within her.

"I've done my best to raise you, to protect you."

Kota's focus shifted downward, her voice carrying a raw vulnerability. "Protect me from what? Why did you have to come all the way out here?"

A wave of nausea overwhelmed her as she stood up, forcing her to stumble towards the sink once again, where she succumbed to uncontrollable retching. Emily moved closer to pat Kota's back. "I've never been more than a phone call away, you know that."

Charged energy hung heavy between the sisters, their unresolved hurt forming a fractured wall. In the next room, Caleb remained oblivious to their fraught exchange as his gaze transfixed upon the glowing screen, its hopeful text a slow-burning beacon. He believed that, in time, the mystery surrounding the savior would unravel. Eager to explore the digital realm, his fingers hovered over the keys. But a sudden glint drew his gaze, freezing his actions—a silhouette of a man crouched atop the nearby bank, the barrel of a rifle gleaming in the sunlight.

Swifter than thought, he spun to find them teetering upward. "GET DOWN!" His sonorous breath ruptured in a stern decree.

His shout rendered their half-risen shapes frozen. Yet a skittish finger's tremor triggered staccato gunfire, shattering the pane above them.

Despite his fear, Caleb crawled towards the danger to get to Emily. In a subdued tone, he asked, "Are you guys alright?"

He noticed sweat glistening on both Emily and Kota's foreheads, their wide eyes and lips drawn tight in a grimace of fear, never leaving him, their expressions mirroring the prickling atmosphere.

They nodded in response, unable to find their voices. No sooner had Emily gripped his hand than another gunshot rang out, a bullet puncturing the floor mere inches from their knuckles. The duo recoiled with pounding hearts, realizing the sniper must have spotted their movement. Everyone stayed motionless, fearful of the next shot. But the ominous silence stretched on, broken only by the ringing in their ears.

Perched on the edge of the rooftop, the sniper stared into the high-powered scope of his rifle. His finger tightened around the trigger as thin rivulets of crimson blood trickled from his flared nostrils. A searing, white-hot pain lanced through his skull, causing his vision to blur. With a guttural cry, he released his grip, sending his weapon clattering to the rain-slicked surface as his hands clutched at his throbbing temples. In a wretched wisp of a voice, the words slipped out through gritted teeth, "I don't have to do this."

Warm blood streamed from both ears, staining the collar of his dark tactical gear a deep shade of red. His legs buckled beneath him, and he crumpled backward, his body hitting the hard concrete with a dull thud as he sprawled motionless, chest heaving with labored breaths.

Minutes later, a patrol car screeched to a halt behind an ambulance. Shrill wails of sirens pierced the air as two officers got out of the vehicle, their footfalls carrying them towards the grim sight. Lieutenant Cortez, his shirt collar askew and a cigarette dangling between his fingers, approached Caleb and Emily, who stood on the steps of the hotel. Captain Javier, a seasoned veteran, met with the paramedics.

"Got anything?" he asked.

"I'd say the time of death is within the last thirty minutes," the paramedic said.

A foul wind gusted forth, whipping the nearby leaves into a frenzied panic. The foliage curled, veins darkening to an angry purple as they took on a sick, mottled appearance of blight and decay. When the corrupted leaves touched down across the street, their substance seemed to shrivel, as if brushing against some malign psychic force.

Javier recoiled his face into his shirt, muffling his voice. "And the cause?"

The paramedic pointed at the marksman's scarlet-stained ears and nose. "Given the other recent cases, I'd wager he met his demise from exsanguination, but the autopsy will confirm it." He then eyed the captain. "Is the smell getting to you?"

"Oh, no way that's from this body."

In contrast, Cortez shook off the icy breeze, exhaling a plume of smoke as he stopped in front of the synergistic threesome. "Can you tell me what happened here?"

Caleb sought to shield his comrade from the nightmare, blanketing Emily in a comforting embrace. "We have no idea. Some lunatic up there just took a shot at us," he said, glaring at the sniper's vantage point.

"And you have no idea who'd want to target you?"

"No," Caleb said.

"Look, dude," Kota interjected. "The guy lying dead was whacko. My sister and I never met him. Now, I can't say the same for her guy friend here, because we just met, but it's a safe bet that none of us knows who he was or why we were targeted."

Cortez reached into the tailored inner pocket of his coat, fingers brushing against the silk lining as he retrieved a spiral-bound notepad. Frayed pages from countless reviews bore his tight scrawl. He combed through its dense contents, each section filled with scribbled notes and bullet points from his recent cases and gathered clues.

As he neared the end, where the pages became murky by repeated handwritten additions, his gaze settled on one entry. There, underlined emphatically in the margin with a heavy pen stroke, were the words "coffee shop" - two simple words that carried unanswered questions. "This isn't the first time someone may have been out to get you, though."

"what?" Emily asked, her full attention on the officer.

Kota also stared at the duo, searching for a tell on either of their faces. The only hint of something hidden came from Caleb's reaction - facing the ground while blinking more than usual. She spun back towards the lieutenant when he filled them in.

"You were afraid that some guy at a coffee shop was trailing you."

"Are you for real?" Kota asked.

"Did you find anything?" Caleb inquired, making eye contact with Cortez.

"Uhm, no, not at this time."

"Wait a minute. Who was after us at the coffee shop?" Emily asked, looking up at her partner.

"I'm sorry I didn't tell you. I just didn't want to make you worry, especially if it's all for nothing."

Tension peaked while the demon loomed across the street, its arms dangling at its side. A jarring glint in its eyes froze the air, harpooning the trio in a baleful stare. "Thanks for the assist, angel. Seems I have located my prized possession."

Later that afternoon, Haines stood in the ruins of the Bayshore Roundhouse, a dilapidated building with shattered windows and walls covered in vibrant graffiti. He crossed his arms and gazed out of a broken pane. Behind him, the creature tiptoed over cracks in the foundation. "I believe I have found the mortal," it said.

Haines unfurled his eyes, revealing a glint of skepticism as he turned to face his ally. "Do not toy with me, demon. My patience wears thin. The day of reckoning draws near, and I have awaited this crucial information for a long time."

"Toy with you? Remember who you're talking to!"

A surge of demonic energy pushed him to channel some of his own, transforming his eyes into an ethereal white, pure as untouched snow, with a vibrant red light outlining his pupils. Massive balls of crackling electricity soon materialized, snapping close to the dark presence. "It would be wise for you to calm down."

"I'm serious! The humans know her as Emily Puller."

Haines arched an eyebrow. "And?" he said, impatience seeping into his tone.

"Everyone we targeted with the virus has either perished or fallen ill. But twice now, this girl has escaped unscathed." The Roamer's eyes, sharp as frostbitten arrows, stirred a restless tremor in the demon's limbs, coaxing it to gnaw on its own tongue. An exasperated breath escaped as he continued to speak. "Earlier today, I sensed a presence just before the sniper fired."

"A presence you believe to be Michael," Haines concluded, his voice trailing off as he pondered. He turned his back to Victor, mind racing with possibilities and implications.

"I have dispatched that shifty scientist to keep a vigilant eye on the one she's grown fond of," revealed the creature, a cunning gleaming in its glare.

Haines nodded, acknowledging the strategic move. "Smart. Perhaps such a loss will serve as a catalyst, awakening her dormant power."

5

THE ATTACK

That night, a ferocious storm unleashed its fury upon the city, its menacing clouds churned overhead, pregnant with impending doom. A thunderous rattle breached the sky, as if an unseen force had besieged the earth.

Inside Creation Labs, Kyle jolted awake, his eyes snapping open to the somber truth that he was stuck in place. Paranoia set in, sharpening his senses to notice the rough texture of duct tape securing his wrists and ankles to a wooden chair. Bound by these restraints, he had limited leeway to maneuver.

On the other side of the room, David remained unfazed at his desk, engrossed in examining a blood slide under a microscope. A confident smile played on his lips as he observed the results of his groundbreaking cure.

"Please, you have to let me go."

The scientist's indifference hung heavy in the air as he continued to scrutinize the slide. He turned his glare towards Kyle, their eyes locking in a tense standoff. "Luckily for you, it seems like my cure is working," he said, his intense jade eyes focused on the microscope. "But I need you to play your role, like one of them."

"One of whom? What are you talking about?"

Well aware time is of the essence, the scientist averted his attention back to the microscope. "Memory loss, it seems," he mused. "Tell me, what's the last thing you remember?"

Anxiety crept into Kyle's voice as he scrutinized his captor's face for any signs of malevolence. "I'm not sure," he admitted.

"Come on, dig deeper!"

Kyle squeezed his eyes shut against the backdrop of a throbbing headache, but his determination didn't falter. He retrieved a fragment of memory from what felt like mere hours ago. "I remember Boris. I believe... he—"

"Yes, Boris, and..."

"He summoned us for some kind of important discovery. You said you weren't feeling well, though."

"Wait, that's your most recent recollection?" Doubt colored David's tone, staring at his captive as if there's something wrong with him.

"Yeah, it just happened. I'm sure he and Celsey will be here soon."

"No, Kyle. That was months ago. What Boris inflicted upon you, upon all of you that night... I will find out." David said, returning to his desk to slide a fresh slide beneath the microscope.

As the storm raged outside, a powerful gust propelled a pebble against the window. This startled David, which coaxed him out of his chair. Rainwater seeped through several cracks, staining the floor. With quicksilver pace, he headed to a cabinet in the corner of the lab. He pulled out two buckets and placed them in the middle of the desks to catch the drips.

"Let me go so I can assist with the cleanup," Kyle implored.

"I can't until you're cured of the virus."

In another part of town, Emily and Kota settled into a new hotel. Their movements set off motion sensors, bathing them in a warm glow. As they crossed the threshold, the duo shook off the serenade of nature's lullaby. Kota's exaggerated twirl sent droplets everywhere from her soaked clothes. She took in their newfound accommodations and said, "Talk about a microcosm shift from the previous vibe." They scanned their surroundings while wrinkling their noses at a subtle musty odor.

Punctuated by an ostentatious swish, Emily flung their bags between the two plush, king-sized beds. "We're safe here, Ko. That's what matters," she said, leaning her hip against the solid oak footboard.

With a tough grip on the polished wood, she delivered a series of defiant kicks, worming her way out of the squishy, waterlogged boots. The soggy footwear thudded to the carpet, puddles already forming.

Adrift in her reverie, Kota slid onto the plush comforter's edge, her clammy shoes leaving a faint mark. It took a flurry of snaps from her sister, almost grazing her face, to ground her to the present. However, before she knew it, her water-soaked clothes touched down on the bed and released droplets of moisture all around her. She jolted back to her feet as Emily's eyes landed on the watery halo trailing to the floor, eliciting an incredulous, "Seriously?"

Why is this even bothering me right now? She wondered.

"Hey, ease up. It was an honest mistake, okay? I can't think straight from all the craziness going on," Kota stated.

"I get that."

Emily lifted her suitcase on the pillows, her eyes drawn to a trio of vibrant state ribbons tied to the zipper. The sight triggered a rush of nostalgia, transporting her to simpler times. One of them boasted a deep azure hue, depicting lush landscapes and an elegant silhouette of an alligator, a nod to the Everglades' unique charm. Nestled between them was a ribbon bursting with the warm tones of red and yellow, accented by sparkling sapphire blues, showcasing whimsical illustrations of the beloved characters Mickey and Minnie Mouse, evoking the enchantment of a magical theme park. She rested a hand over the last ribbon, its soft pastel shades of mint green, blush pink, and golden hues captivating her, reminiscent of the ever-changing seasons in Central Park.

As she unzipped the suitcase, her sister took in their new surroundings. The bed dominated the room's layout, leaving only a narrow path to the window, where curtains obscured any view. Kota leaned closer to Emily, their shoulders almost brushing against each other in the confined quarters, and whispered, "This place reminds me of the box back home."

Intent on pushing forward, Emily turned and reassured her, "I swear I wasn't even thinking about that. We needed to get as far away from that hotel as possible, that's all."

"Well, hats off to you. I mean, the Statue of Liberty is right outside," Kota quipped, making her way into the bathroom.

After hearing the door shut, Emily glanced outside, catching sight of the iconic statue standing tall in the twilight, a symbol of freedom and hope shining in the distance.

Elsewhere, Caleb sat on the couch, his thoughts consumed by earlier events. Lost in a vacant gale, he drifted back to a few hours ago when he sped down the road. In a fit of rage, fearing for Emily's safety, he called the scientist.

"Did your cousin ever find out who this guy is?" he probed. Before he could get an answer, however, the streetlight up ahead turned red, forcing him to slam on the brakes. His car slid a few feet, but still came to a screeching halt.

Concern grew in David when the sound of protesting rubber fighting for traction flooded the airwaves. "Caleb, are you okay?" he asked.

"I'm fine, man. What can you tell me?"

"Not much," the scientist said. "It's not like he talks to me about this stuff."

Caleb's frustration boiled over, his agitation swirling into a Supercell tornado as he slammed his phone onto the worn leather of the passenger's seat. "Come on, this is important!" he yelled.

Vibrations from the device brought him back to the here and now, drawing his gaze downward to the screen, ablaze with a text from David.

'I don't know what's going on, but you need to understand there's a chance your mystery man won't be in the database.'

Taking a deliberate breath after reading the message, he regained composure. His muscles contorted, betraying the strain that stole his movement. He knew what he had to do and held his phone up to dial Emily's number. Each ring connected them during his inner struggle.

Several harmonious tones, mirroring a bell tower, played in Caleb's ears. It didn't take long for his palms to be coated in sweat. After lowering the device, primed to hang up, he heard her voice call out, "hello?" It was a gentle breeze that carried the soothing whispers of a summer's eve.

"Hey, Emily, are you okay? Did you find a new place to stay?" His profound distress stirred in the timbre of his voice, seeking solace in her response.

"Yeah, Kota and I actually just got here a little bit ago."

"Oh, I'm glad to hear it," he said. "You know, you guys are more than welcome to stay with me."

"That's kind of you, but I don't want to impose, besides you seemed to have something on your mind. I mean, you took off pretty quick."

"Yeah, sorry for that. Uhm, listen, I know it's kinda late, but I'd wager none of us has eaten yet and if you haven't either–"

"I can't tonight, sorry," Emily's voice, a gentle interruption, halted his train of thought. "It's been a long day and I don't want to leave Kota alone."

"I get it. That's why I'm inviting her to join us. What do you say? We can always explore that charming restaurant downtown that has garnered exceptional reviews."

"Oh, is it that Chinese place that just opened? I heard it's really nice there. But are you sure?" Her excitement grew at the mere prospect of dining out with him at the acclaimed venue.

"You bet," Caleb affirmed, his words tinged with assurance and a hint of eagerness.

"Okay." A carnival of sunshine burst forth, painting her features with the vibrant hues of wildflowers. "What time do you want to pick me up?"

"How about seven?" Butterflies swarmed in his stomach, causing his leg to tap a rhythmic dance of anxiety.

"It's perfect."

"Awesome. I'll see you then. Text me the hotel you're at and room number," Caleb said, his words brimming with an organized precision. "Will do."

Once the call ended, Emily hugged her phone in a bear-tight embrace. Excitement crackled from the depths of her soul. She pressed her phone to her chin, taken aback when Kota entered the alcove with damp, loose, wavy hair that flowed beyond her shoulders.

"So, good news, I take it?" she queried.

"It's Caleb," she began. "He wants to take us out to dinner."

"Us?" Kota asked.

"He knows we've had a long day and wants to help."

"I don't want to be a third wheel." Kota's words trailed off, her gaze shifting around the room. "I'll be fine here on my own."

"It's already settled, Ko, and you're not getting out of it," Emily asserted, her movements purposeful as she retrieved a fresh set of clothing from her bag.

Back at his house, Caleb stood in front of the mirror in the dining room, his apprehension reflected at him. With each laborious loop, the fabric of his tie became a complex dance partner, challenging his trembling hands to master its intricacies. A gentle scrape of the wind against the windowpane broke his focus.

He shook his head over this minor scare before returning his attention to the mirror in front of him. In this silent battle between man and fabric, every movement carried weight, as if he were striving to synchronize the universe itself with his meticulous actions. The subtle tremors of his fingers betrayed his nervousness, yet his determination was unwavering. Beads of perspiration dotted his forehead as he wrestled with the quest for perfection.

A sigh, laden with fatigue, escaped him, breaking the tangible tension that ensnared the room. At last, he emerged victorious. The silk tie now lay with immaculate precision against his crisp button-down shirt, its deep-blue hue polished his strong jawline.

Drawn by the bouquet adorning the table behind him, Caleb's azure eyes danced with anticipation. A profusion of vibrant petals stood tall like his euphonic emotions, intertwining to mimic the complexities of his own heart. But when he reached for them, the lights flickered. With lightning still flashing outside and the sound of the raging storm intensifying, the house fell into an ominous energy.

The very air smelt of fear, weaving through the shadows that danced along the walls. Caleb's heart pounded in his chest, his entire body poised and ready for the impending clash. Between thunderclaps, he slunk along the tenebrous hallway, his footsteps muffled by an old, worn carpet, wrapped in a stagnant lull. Would it be a dangerous criminal, armed and ruthless? Or perhaps a lost soul seeking refuge from the violent storm? He gripped the weathered baseball bat, its familiarity providing a fleeting comfort in the face of impending danger.

As if an omen, the sound of an explosion filled the air, a volatile surge of electricity breaking through the locked front door. Caleb's heart skipped a beat, his body propelled forward down the hall and into his bedroom by an impulse fueled by adrenaline and an instinctual desire to protect what was his. Pride surged within him; a ferocity sparked by the breach of his sanctuary.

A brief second of respite tore to pieces as Boris advanced in a calculated manner, checking each chamber along the way. He inched closer to Caleb's covert refuge while adrenaline pumped through his veins. The slightest sound could give away his position, demolishing the tenuous cloak of secrecy.

His only protection was a door that erupted in a blinding hail of wooden shrapnel, succumbing to the intruder's relentless assault. Shards scattered like deadly caltrops through the dim corridor, jagged splinters whipping through the air. One lashed his face, a crimson rivulet slashing down his cheekbone, beads of scarlet welling and dappling his pallor. Coiled for an inexorable resolution, he braced to unleash fury onto the encroaching threat.

He clutched onto the remnants of the door, his fingers grazing the cool plaster of the wall behind him. The world seemed to hold its breath alongside him, every heartbeat spreading through the darkness like a distant war drum. Boris stepped into the room with obvious intentions. "I don't have time to play cat and mouse, so make it easy on yourself and just come out," he demanded.

But a fierce resolve gripped Caleb. He edged from the entryway to position himself. His little league bat melded to his fist - an oaken extension of his iron will. The force behind a powerful swing produced a long, jagged crack along the side as soon as it struck. For a moment, victory seemed certain. "You broke into the wrong house," he declared, shaking where he stood.

Rebellion whipped into his soul as his words pierced the charged energy, daring fate to challenge him. But the intruder did not falter. Rising from the floor, holding the remains of a wooden sword.

"What, did you come here to give me a few splinters?" Caleb said.

Rather than heed a response, Boris lunged towards his target, weapon prepared to strike. Yet, despite a sudden drop to the floor, he delivered a powerful kick that propelled the intruder into the wall behind him. Quick on his feet, he seized the baseball bat and swung it with extreme force, disarming his attacker. Upon seeing this, he relinquished the bat, dropping it on the floor.

The intruder's face, a mask of sneering disdain, bore into his bloodied hand. "It's obvious you've never been in a fight," he scoffed. "Or you wouldn't have lowered your guard so soon."

With no sign of hesitation, he dealt a forceful blow to the author's head, followed by a ruthless onslaught to his stomach. Collapsing, Caleb coughed up blood, his voice strained as he looked up at his assailant. "Why are you doing this?" his plea carried a desperate confusion, his eyes searching Boris's face for any sliver of understanding.

"Unfortunately, a powerful man wants you removed from the equation," Boris answered, his voice a chilling whisper.

Caleb defied all odds as his attacker prepared to deliver the decisive blow, summoning the strength to rise and tackle the man to the ground. In a blind rage, he unleashed a maelstrom of fists, each blow bruising flesh. His gaze spied on salvation's beacon: the wiffle wand, a promise of deliverance hewn from the heart of a hardwood tree.

With no time to spare, he charged ahead, fingers outstretched like a drowning man's last grasp. But Boris, swift as Judas, plucked away this final ember of hope and smashed the tip against Caleb's forehead, sending him to the hard floor.

He hovered over the battered young writer, aiming blow after blow upon his already injured arm. Every hit ripped a guttural scream, a discordant note that cut through the sepulchral hush.

Recognizing the futility of resistance, Caleb's cries melded with the symphony of pain. Boris's shoulders slumped, his chest heaving with exertion and dread. The bloodied bat p from his scared palms, clattering at his feet.

Contemplation shadowed his face as he grappled with the unbearable weight of his next decision.

In a swift motion, he seized his victim's throat and hurled him backward into the dresser. Upon impact, Caleb thrashed to the ground as the weight of the furniture fell atop his legs.

Boris took a deep, judderous puff, confronting the gravity of his actions. "I'm sorry," he whispered, his voice laced with sorrow and resignation. "But I have to protect my family."

Encamped in a haven of refinement, an unsettling sense of unease permeated the air. She dialed her partner's number, waiting anxiously for confirmation of their plans. However, the call diverted to voicemail, leaving a pit in her stomach. Her heart leaped in her chest when an unexpected melodious chime fluttered from the clock on the wall. Startled, she dropped her phone on the couch and sat down beside it.

A thunderous whip cracked across the sky, its lengthy tendrils slicing through a rhythm of electric branches against the night's void.

"Oh, spooky," Kota quipped, her weak jest a doomed flare against the encroaching unease. Her fingers fretted at her nail beds as her gaze roved the dusky enclosure. Emily's face, a rictus of apprehension, snagged her concentration. Immersed in helplessness, she forged a more plausible tale. "He's probably just running late. Maybe his phone died, making it impossible for him to call. Any minute now, he'll be here."

For a brief interlude, hope alighted on Emily's face, ignited by a passing car outside. But as its taillights dwindled into the distance, her optimism waned, occluded by an oppressive pall of augury.

Like a wilting flower, she curled inward; her gaze intertwined with Kota's, a silent conviction left unspoken. "I knew there was something wrong," Emily confessed, her voice laced with vulnerability. "I could feel it deep in my gut."

Kota, ever the provocateur, maintained her playful tone. "Or maybe you dodged a bullet." In an ephemeral pause, a smirk glimmered, attempting to coax a smile from her sister, yet her jest withered beneath Emily's disapproving stare. "I'm serious."

6

DIMINISHING LIGHT

Back in the cradle of 1992, Boris laid shattered on the floor as the fiend clutched its wrist and dissolved their bodies into a blur and re-materialized inside the rugged terrain of the Rocky Mountains. The air, saturated with an earthy reek, filtered into their lungs as a distant howl permeated the valleys. Victor clenched his jaw and tightened his fists, quashing the urge to let his frustrations devour him.

Haines curled his lip, flicking his eyes between his two comrades. "This is the human you've chosen to aid us?"

The creature twisted its visage. A derisive sneer revealed yellowed fangs. "He's just a nobody, a speck."

"Careful, you're breaking through the guise." Haines whirled to face the Anglican Church.

Boris scrambled back, his eyes darting for an escape, but before he could bolt, his gaze locked onto an uneasy spectacle - the horrid sight of the creature's wide grin. He tried with all his might to flee, but his body refused to obey. The power radiating from those coal-black eyes had him in its grip.

Victor prowled to the scientist, hands clasped behind his back, each step deliberate. He leaned in close, his breath hot on Boris's face. "Did you forget the cost of defiance?" it asked. "Eternal torment might intrigue me, but it repels your kind, doesn't it?"

Without warning, it shot out a hand, grabbed Boris's collar, and shoved him towards Haines.

The creature continued to tower over the scientist as its shadow engulfed the trembling man. "Are you done with your foolishness?"

Boris flinched. His voice came out a mere rasp. "Y-yes, sir."

Haines's eyes flickered. A crimson hue rimmed his pupils as he intoned the invisibility incantation. The air shimmered, a veil of enchantment descending around them. At the Anglican Church's door, Gabriel's vigilant gaze swept the scene.

The Roamer, sensing the holy presence, jerked his chin towards his ally. "Wait here, demon, until we return."

Victor's lips twisted in a sarcastic grin. He spread his hands wide. "Of course. It's not like I can prance right in."

Haines seized Boris's wrist. The world blurred and solidified into the ethereal interior of the opulent church. Boris staggered, his eyes wide. He spun around, mouth agape, trying to comprehend how they'd crossed miles in an instant.

"It's called teleporting," he said, grabbing his capture's arm, fingers digging into flesh. "Now, move. Lucifer rests beneath our feet."

Boris's gaze drifted downward, his eyes widening in alarm as he gazed upon opulent floor tiles, unable to fathom the task awaiting him. "How am I supposed-"

"You're a scientist," the creature interjected. "You'll come up with a clever solution to our problem. We need to get under the floor, so figure it out."

Because of the imminent threat to his family, Boris stared ahead with nothing to say. His clammy hands then pulled a pocket knife from his jacket, redirecting his gaze towards the floor and striking it with all his might. Haines beheld the mortal from afar. After several hard strikes, confusion etched on his features. "Why do you need me for this?"

"Because this way, I can remain hidden from your creator."

"What?" He paused and turned to face Haines. "You're afraid of God?"

"Enough with your questions," the Roamer snapped. "Focus on breaking through the floor."

With the threat of the demon's wrath hanging over him, Boris continued to stab at the floor. Every command had to be obeyed, or else his loved ones would get dragged to hell and sentenced to eternal torment. Tears welled up in his eyes as he pondered those chilling words.

Soon, he carved a sizable hole into the floor and dropped the central piece onto the earth beneath the church. Boris looked up at Haines, who now stood hovered above him.

"Now it's time for you to get your hands dirty," Haines stated.

Before long, Boris found himself covered in dirt, having dug himself into a deep hole in the heart of the catacombs. Exhaustion weighed on his weary body as he caught his breath.

"Who said you could stop? We don't have all day."

Boris sprang back into action, dread coursing through him as he pierced one of the many tunnels. As he delved deeper, a sharp object grazed his hand, leaving a trail of blood. Curious about the source of his injury, he felt around the dirt until something pointed poked his fingers.

He excavated the area, causing dirt to cascade away in small bursts and revealing a hidden tunnel entrance. Next to it lay a small wooden dagger. Boris grasped the weapon and tucked it into his jacket's inner pocket. He switched on his flashlight and prepared to crawl into the exposed tunnel.

Above, Haines peered down, a smirk of contentment playing on his lips, unaware of the scientist's disappearance. "Foolish human," he said, shaking his head.

Boris navigated the tunnel, searching for another escape route. Unaware of the dangers lurking in the shadows, he rounded a corner and ventured deeper into the catacombs. As he approached the end of the next passage, unsettling sounds crept through the darkness.

He swept his flashlight across the area but found nothing. Just as he considered retreating, a small, skeletal creature sprang forth, its twisted limbs propelling it towards him. The creature emitted a shrill screech, calling to its hidden companions. Boris winced, clamping his hands over his ears.

The echoes of several creatures reverberated through the darkness. Boris stepped backward, edging towards the tunnel's exit. The creature darted out of sight on all fours.

In an instant, Haines materialized behind the scientist. "You really thought you could escape me?" his voice dripped with disdain.

As Boris turned, the Roamer shoved him to the ground. A creature lunged at them, but Haines intercepted it mid-air, grasping its head. An ephemeral apparition of his opponent took shape, its gaze directed at the rampaging monster.

Haines stared Boris down. "Lucky for you, my abilities remain detectable in these tunnels. Now, let's move."

They squeezed back through the hole Boris had made and navigated the catacombs. Upon their return, the scientist prostrated himself before Haines. "Please, don't disturb the tomb."

The Roamer seized the man by his neck, forcing eye contact. "You'll dig, or you'll share this tomb. Understand?" After clawing at the dirt several times, he struck something solid.

As he brushed away more soil, Boris leaned in to see what he'd found. "Holy hell. It's here." A shiver ran down his spine, but he continued to uncover more. An iron chain wrapped around the tomb came into view.

Haines's gaze fixed on the contents. "They spared no precaution."

"Well, we did our best," Boris said.

Without another word, Haines vanished, leaving the scientist all alone. He glanced over his shoulder, half-expecting to see a figure lurking in the shadows of the catacombs.

This can't be happening, he thought, looking down at the tomb. Forgive me, world, but I can't let him hurt my kids. Besides, if this is all real, then so are angels, and I believe they'll put an end to this.

He unearthed more of the chain, revealing mysterious Enochian scratches that covered its surface. "Did these markings stop them from doing this themselves?" He grasped the chain, praying for a solution to present itself.

In the rugged wilderness of the Rocky Mountains, the Roamer stood beside the demon, who grew agitated by the devil's emergence.

Victor bit his lip. "What the heck is taking so long?"

"I expected your impatience, which is why I wanted to keep you informed," Haines said. "Lucifer's tomb is being brought to the surface as we speak." His voice then grew icy and stern. "But let us be clear. Should you divulge any information about our arrangement to Lucifer, it is you who will lose everything."

He warped inside the church and hovered above the hole in the floor. Satisfaction radiated from him as he observed the unearthed tomb. He then noticed the chain was still intact and folded his arms. "Come on, exert yourself," he admonished.

Boris dropped his pocketknife and grabbed onto the chain. "This isn't going to—" he stopped as the rusty links snapped under his efforts.

A brilliant red light erupted from the tomb, growing fiercer with each heartbeat. The top convulsed until it burst open, slamming against the dirt wall. The scientist fell to his knees, his heart racing. A loud crack reverberated through the air as Lucifer's hands emerged from the tomb, followed by his ascent. Taking on a human form, the red light faded, revealing piercing crimson eyes staring down at Boris.

"Now, why would a mere mortal set me free from Hell?" Lucifer's voice was smooth as silk, but with an undercurrent of danger.

Boris, unable to respond, locked his gaze with the devil's fist looming over him, a promise of violence on every knuckle. In a flash, Haines shed his facade, morphing into Victor's true demonic form.

"He didn't have a choice," Haines revealed, disguised as Victor.

Lucifer froze mid-strike, his gaze locked on the entity. He rose, hovering above the ground. "And how is it possible that you stand on these sacred grounds?"

"I devoured countless demon souls to gain the power necessary to escape from the Infernal Realm," explained Haines in his disguised form. "I mean, underworld. And it appears this act has made me a stronger demon."

Lucifer's eyes narrowed. "Perhaps. Now, explain why you've buddied-up with a sinner."

"There are greater forces at work," the Roamer explained. "God has created a human with the powers of an archangel."

Lucifer's eyes flashed with intense fury. "Not only did God get to dictate the rules, but now he selected which rules to break?" His voice dripped with venom.

Outside the entrance, Gabriel felt a sudden surge of dark energy. He unsheathed his sword and spun to confront the door. Behind him, a vortex of crimson and obsidian feathers erupted, igniting in a burst of sulfuric flames. As they receded, Lucifer emerged, his hands poised above the angel's ears.

"You are powerful, brother, but I'm smarter," Lucifer's words echoed inside Gabriel's head. "Know that I could have ended you right here without a struggle. Lucky for you, I may require your assistance."

An intense burgundy illumination emitted from the devil's palms, striking Gabriel and causing him to collapse. Lucifer glanced around, realizing the demon had fled. "Coward," he whispered.

The Roamer reappeared beside the creature in his own form. "I think it's time for you to become reacquainted with your dark lord," he said, placing his hand on its shoulder to transmit some of his energy. "Just tell him what he needs to know, then get out of there."

Victor nodded, feeling Haines' power course through his veins. He teleported into the church. While staring down on Heaven's warrior, Lucifer's voice oozed sarcasm. "At least you had the nerve to come back, even if it's only because I immobilized the angel. Now, tell me more about this human who possesses angelic powers."

Emily arrived at Caleb's house in a cab the next day while the driver chatted about the recent discovery of Kepler-11 having six planets orbiting a single star. She clutched her bag as the vehicle stopped. Without a moment to spare, she stepped out, greeted by the crisp morning air, and shut the door in one fluid motion. The driver turned around and chuckled at her efficiency, noticing the payment placed on the seat.

He drove away while Emily's heart raced. She stood there by the curb, dialing Caleb's number for the third time that morning, but once again, it went straight to voicemail. She sighed and glanced at the car parked in the driveway, a sign that he should be home. Determined, she strode across the lawn, the soft grass tickling her bare feet, and approached the front door.

With each unanswered knock, her anxiety grew as she reached for the doorknob. To her dismay, it creaked open, yet she hesitated to cross the threshold.

Her voice quaked when she called out, "Caleb?" Summoning her courage, she entered the house, only to be greeted by the light spilling into the clean-living room, illuminating the space with a gentle warmth. The pristine white walls seemed to catch the sunlight, reflecting it back in defined rays that danced around the room.

Her eyes wandered across the room, taking in the details as she moved closer to a bookshelf. Rows upon rows of books lined the wooden shelves, their spines arranged like soldiers standing at attention. Amongst the collection, her gaze lingered on the mystery novels, their colorful covers beckoning her to dive into their pages.

The faint strains of 'Carry on my Wayward Son' by Kansas reached her ears, its second verse playing from a distant radio. She followed the melodic thread, each note guiding her down the hall towards Caleb's bedroom.

Her steps betrayed her as she noticed the door discarded on the floor, mingling with small wood particles that clung to the carpet. She stepped over the debris and found traces of a struggle on the walls and furniture, the telltale signs of a violent altercation. Worry etched into her features as she processed the grim reality. She had to find Caleb to ensure his safety.

As she neared the fallen dresser, her senses heightened, her ears attuned to the faint sound of the radio playing in the distance. A familiar tune echoed through the house, soothing yet haunting as it filled the silence. It was a soothing balm, reminding her that hope still lingered. Then she looked across the room to find Caleb lying underneath the furniture.

"Oh, my God!" Her gasp echoed through the room as her hand flew to her mouth and her face contorted into a mask of shattered dreams.

Upon reaching him, she mustered all her strength to push the weight off him. Afterwards, she knelt beside him, her touch gentle and trembling as if afraid to hurt him further. Tears welled up in her eyes, tracing a shimmering path down her anguished face. Pulling out her phone, she unplugged the radio from the wall outlet behind her and dialed for help.

"Yes, yes, hello?" Her words rushed out as the dispatcher answered her call, her voice strained with desperation. "I need help right away. Someone attacked my friend!" The words tumbled from her lips, each syllable laced with fear and urgency, her trembling hands clutching the phone as if it were a lifeline.

Within moments, the shrill wails of sirens pierced the air as the police arrived on the scene. Emily dashed down the hall, flinging the front door open just as the lieutenant raised his hand to knock. Hurrying, she gestured towards the hallway, almost taking his hand to follow suit. "Yeah, yeah, yeah, please come in," she urged, her eyes watering in fear. "He's in the last room down there."

As the lieutenant made his way down the hallway, followed by his captain and a paramedic, the worn detective assigned to the case stayed behind with Emily. She closed the door with a determined click and joined the officers in Caleb's room.

"Hang on a sec," the detective said, his voice gruff but filled with empathy. "Are you Emily?"

Taken aback, Emily nodded with a "Yeah" so soft it could have been mistaken for an exhale.

"I'm Detective Jason Silverton. Caleb told my cousin he was worried that someone you guys met at a coffeehouse may have been following you."

"Yes, I know. But I still don't have the foggiest on who he's afraid of," she said.

"Well, I ran the picture he sent through the database and there were no hits. Still, I don't think it's a coincidence that someone attacked him. It's likely that this guy is the culprit; we just need more time to track him down."

Meanwhile, David found himself bound to a wooden chair in the corner of his living room, the ropes prickling against his skin like a golden net. His captor had secured his wrists and ankles with duct tape, rendering him immobile. As he regained consciousness, his eyes widened in realization, memories of the previous night's attack flooding back.

He soon locked onto the intruder, who stood before him, a complex mixture of emotions flickering across his eyes. He couldn't help but feel conflicted, torn between seeing Boris as an evil man and detecting a hidden battle within him.

"Why are you doing this?" the scientist asked, his mind racing to make sense of the situation.

Boris glanced at the tear in his glove, a momentary vulnerability exposing itself, before he reached into his coat pocket, retrieving a syringe. Aware of the contents, David struggled against his restraints, desperation radiating from every fiber of his being. His efforts proved futile as the intruder jabbed the needle into his shoulder, injecting him with the virus.

"Don't fight it," he advised, slipping the syringe back into his coat pocket. "You'll only die faster. First, I need you to destroy the cure you've created."

7

THE NARROW GATE

As David valiantly struggled against the virus's insidious control over his body, he stumbled into the opulent lobby of Creation Labs. Every step was a battle, his muscles throbbing with resistance, but he refused to surrender. Breathing heavily, he approached the grand door, his trembling hands clenching it with desperate strength. With an outburst of force, he swung the door open, its hinges creaking in protest, and stepped into the hallowed halls of the building.

"Cease this madness," he whispered, knowing deep down that he possessed the strength to resist.

Despite his plea, he found himself irresistibly drawn to the laboratory, his feet carrying him towards the cabinet where he had concealed both the samples of tainted blood and the elusive cure. A moment of hesitation gripped him as he glanced at the vacant chair that had kept Kyle bound.

"How did he escape?" he questioned under his breath; the weight of bewilderment heavy upon him. As he turned away, his eyes landed on the fresh marking—a deep, narrow gouge, on the side of the chair.

Crimson beads cascaded from his nose, etching ruby stains upon the pristine floor. Resoluteness surged through his veins, propelling him towards the cabinet. He clenched his molars like an iron vice and, with a fierce grip, smashed the vials containing the cure against the wall. The shards glistened like falling stars. In his torment, a guttural symphony of despair fought to stave off the virus consuming his consciousness.

He stumbled towards the sink like a wounded warrior defying the agony that clung to every fiber of his being. The cure, the elixir of liberation, flowed from his trembling hands, seeping into the cracks beneath his feet. It became a requiem for the extinguished spark of hope. With shaky knees, he collapsed, gripping his head as if suffering from a migraine.

Meanwhile, Emily arrived at the hotel, her footsteps echoing through the stillness of the bedroom. Weary and burdened, she trudged towards the patient room. The weight of the day pressed down like an oppressive force. Her mind raced like a frantic sprinter, doing everything it could to solve the intricate puzzle that lay before her. Back and forth, she paced, creating a frantic orbit around her bed, each step sending shivers of uncertainty rippling through her entire being. It was as if she was traversing the perimeter of her own inner labyrinth, trying to piece together the fragments of information that held the key to unearthing the identity of the enigmatic figure that haunted the recesses of Caleb's mind.

Then, in a sudden burst of clarity, Emily's memory transported her to a moment that had previously gone unnoticed. She vividly recalled the subtle shift in Caleb's demeanor, an invisible tension gripping his body, his eyes betraying an unspoken fear. And in that moment, her eyes widened as realization flooded her senses. It was the picture. That innocuous snapshot she had casually captured, frozen in time, seemingly insignificant at the time but now bearing the weight of untold secrets. Like a dormant volcano about to erupt, hope surged through her, an electric current coursing through her veins as she reached into the depths of her bag, hands trembling in anticipation to retrieve her trusted camera.

Just as her fingers grazed the cool metal of her prized possession, a cacophony of sounds cut through the silence, jerking her out of her single-minded focus. The door creaked open as Kota tentatively entered the room. Concern danced in her eyes as she acknowledged the weight that hung heavy in the air.

Utterly absorbed in her curiosity, she acknowledged Kota's presence with a distracted glance, her voice betraying a tinge of exhaustion. "Everything's fine," she responded. "I'm just trying to figure something out."

Kota, sensing the impenetrable fortress that had descended upon her sister's mind, leaned against the doorframe, her gaze unyielding as it bore into Emily's troubled face. She interjected cautiously, her voice a gentle offering of support, "Anything I can help with?"

Emily's eyes flitted towards her sister's concerned expression, grateful for the unwavering loyalty of her sister. "No, but thank you."

Her attention snapped back to the camera as she flipped through the multitude of pictures, searching for the hidden answers that lay within their frames.

Kota, undeterred by Emily's solitary pursuit, remained rooted in the doorway, intently studying the space between them. A mischievous grin played at the corners of her lips as she ventured to lighten the heavy atmosphere.

"I'm just gonna come out and say it, men can be pigs. Remember Bradley Donovan in your sophomore year? That guy was..." Her voice trailed off, lost in searching for the precise words to convey their shared understanding.

"Kota, no," she interjected. "Why would you even say that?" Emily's interruption had a hint of annoyance as she rolled her eyes.

The young visitor shrugged, her smile holding a wry charm. "Well, you did mention that you were figuring things out. Isn't that the universal code for someone messing up in a relationship, and now you're on a mission to untangle the mess?"

A tired sigh escaped Emily's lips as her shoulders slumped slightly, feeling a bittersweet appreciation for Kota's attempt to infuse levity into the weighty circumstances. "Well, you're not entirely wrong," she admitted. "But you're wrong about Caleb. Look, Kota, I just need a little bit of time to make sense of things, that's all."

Kota's shoulders sagged, the disappointment and concern intermingling on her face as she reluctantly accepted the explanation. "Yeah, okay. Whatever," she muttered, before turning away, leaving her sister enveloped in the solitude of her room.

Emily watched her walk down the hall with a pang of guilt. She hated the thought of keeping her in the dark about the potential danger that lurked around them. When she looked back down at the camera, she found the pivotal image staring back at her.

"Eureka!" she exclaimed, holding the camera aloft like a triumphant conqueror.

As she lowered the camera back down to look upon the mystery man's picture, she felt an overwhelming sense of calmness brush over her like a tidal wave. She was taken aback by this. Why aren't I nervous? she wondered. This is the man who may have attacked Caleb.

Her brow furrowed, staring at the captured image, which was overburdened with a calming presence that belied the mystery and conflicted with her instincts.

Soon, she began recalling the sound of the soothing and constant roar of the rushing waterfall, which could be heard from a distance.

I stood on the cliff as the mist from the crashing water filled the air, creating a serene atmosphere. It was then that a yellow feather caught my attention because it seemed to be out of place. I picked it up, feeling a sense of wonder and excitement building within me.

A subtle breeze brushed against my cheek as if it were a gentle touch from another realm. That's when a feeling of caution washed over me, like a warning whispered in the wind. I turned around, half-expecting to see someone standing behind me. But there was no one there.

Shaking off the strange sensation, I called out to a stranger who was standing nearby. I asked him to take a picture for me, handing him my camera. As he approached, I couldn't help but feel warmth.

After a few moments, he said he was ready to capture the perfect shot. I counted down and leaped into the water, feeling a rush of exhilaration. Just as I disappeared beneath the surface, the camera clicked, freezing the moment forever.

When I got out of the water, I saw the stranger waiting for me, holding the camera. He returned it to me with tenderness in their voice. "Here is your device," he said.

I couldn't help but notice a faint steam rising from their hands, though I didn't really suspect anything. My mind was more focused on the photo he took. I gasped in awe. The image was beyond anything I could have imagined. The surrounding trees appeared to sprout vibrant purple wings as if touched by magic, while a halo of light hovered above my head, casting an ethereal glow.

Excitedly, I went to share my amazement with the stranger, but they had already started walking away. Determined to capture their image, I called out to them. I wanted to remember the person who had taken such an incredible photo.

He turned, a hint of wariness in his eyes, but I didn't let it deter me. I snapped another picture, capturing his gaze. While reviewing the photo, I noticed something peculiar. The lighting was normal, except for their eyes, which seemed to emit a radiant glow.

Curiosity consumed me, and I raised the camera to take another photo, but to my surprise, the stranger had vanished without a trace. I searched the surroundings, hoping to catch a glimpse of their presence, but they were nowhere to be found.

Perplexed, I tried to make sense of what had just happened. It was as if they were there one moment and then gone the next. I couldn't shake off the feeling that there was more to this encounter than met the eye.

Lost in her thoughts, Emily's phone suddenly rang, jolting her back to reality. An unfamiliar number appeared on the screen, piquing her interest. With apprehension, she answered the call, ready to embark on a new chapter of this mysterious journey.

***

Emily dashed through the doors of the hospital, her heart pounding in her chest. She rushed to the information desk, eager to find out why she was summoned. However, the nurse requested that she wait patiently. Frustrated and anxious, she made her way to the waiting area.

As she sat down, a peculiar sensation washed over her. A lingering scent, reminiscent of morning dew on fresh grass, filled her nostrils. She glanced towards the window and found it firmly shut. The crisp, clean inexplicable aroma transported her from the sterile hospital environment to a serene meadow at dawn. She shook her head, trying to focus on why she was here.

Time seemed to slow to a torturous crawl when she caught the sound of gossamer-thin whispers.

They're coming for you. You have to run.

She whipped her head around in search of the source of the warning. But the waiting room remained as it was - quiet. Finally, a scruffy man draped in the white coat emerged from the sea of uncertainty. His steps were purposeful as he approached Emily in the waiting room. His voice, tinged with sympathy, reached out to her in the midst of her confusion.

"Excuse me, are you Emily Puller?" he asked, his presence comforting yet ominous.

Her lips trembled as she took a deep breath, her voice barely above a whisper. "I am... Can you please tell me what's going on? I got a call to come in, and I did, but now nobody's talking."

With delicate care, the doctor settled beside her, his steady gaze trying to soften the blow of the impending truth. "My apologies, Ms. Puller," he began. "Caleb woke up earlier. He called out your name and then..."

Desperation filled the space as Emily interrupted. "Then what? What is it?"

Silence stretched between them, a heavy weight hanging in the atmosphere. Time seemed to stand still as the truth was finally revealed. "I'm sorry. He's in a coma."

The room spun, and Emily's world crumbled around her. Shock, disbelief, and anguish intertwined within her. The doctor's comforting pat on her shoulder was but a fleeting touch as he rose from the chair and left the waiting room. Tears brimmed in her eyes, blurring her vision as she leaned back, her gaze fixed on the cold, unforgiving floor. Her heart broke, shattered by the devastating news she never saw coming.

Grief consumed her like a powerful tide. The weight of betrayal hit her as she felt the sting of knowing that Caleb had kept this secret from her. Her broken heart morphed into anger, a fire that burned within her. Rising from her seat, she placed her face in her trembling palm, desperately trying to make sense of this painful reality.

Across the room, the demon watched Emily's emotions unfold. Dissatisfaction etched across his face. Frustration boiled within him as he clenched his fist, his body tense. He abruptly stood from his seat, exiting the building in a whirlwind of raw emotions. The moment the door closed behind him, he disappeared, teleporting back to the Bayshore Roundhouse, where Haines and Boris awaited his return.

In the depths of fury over Caleb's condition, Victor marched towards Boris with an unstoppable force. Unleashing his rage, his fist connected with Boris' stomach, striking the newly acquired scar tissue. Boris crumpled to his knees, a mix of agony and satisfaction playing upon his face. To Victor, this pain was a sign, a confirmation that his target was still alive.

Seeking answers, Haines observed the scene, his voice laced with curiosity. "I gather from your actions that the mortal still breathes," he stated.

A growl escaped Victor's lips, his anger barely contained. "The sinner knocks on purgatory's door. He's sinking into an endless slumber, though it is not yet definitive," he spat out. "It seems that Boris has failed to deliver the final blow."

"What? No, I did my part," Boris defended himself, pain shimmering in his eyes. "If Caleb's still alive, then it's pure luck."

Victor's teeth grit together, his tone venomous. "Luck? No, I suspected your failure." He paused, a sinister grin spreading across his face. "No worries. I'm giving you one and only one chance to rectify the situation, or it'll be your family who suffers."

Boris's departure left the room shrouded in cold silence. Haines turned, his gaze fixed upon Victor, searching for the reasons behind his unwavering loyalty to the mortal despite the chaos that followed.

"I don't know why you're still working with the mortal," Haines mused. "You already got him to release Lucifer and create your virus."

Victor's eyes gleamed with dark amusement as he revealed his twisted plan. "There's nothing as fulfilling as corrupting a pure soul. I told him it's the only way he can save his family. What he doesn't know is that the more he listens to a demon, the darker his soul becomes, and then I'll drag them all to hell in eternal flame."

As he exited the room, the liming sound of Oswald's voice echoed in the Roamer's mind, commanding his attention.

"I need you to sow the seed and orchestrate a chain reaction, starting with Detective Jason Silverton."

"What for?" Haines remarked, seeking clarification.

"Lay down the right cards, and we shall ensure that the angels don't stop Lucifer before he steals the mortal's angelic powers."

Amid the sinister orchestration of hospital sounds, Emily languished in a seat, enveloped by her despair. Time slipped away unnoticed as a constant stream of patients ebbed and flowed around her, their lives intersecting with hers, their untold stories swallowed by the somber atmosphere. Lost in her own realm of anguish, her phone pierced through the haze, its shrill intrusion initially slipping past her consciousness. Ignoring the urgent calls clamoring for attention, she allowed them to tumble into voicemail, relinquishing herself to the burden of grief until the ceaseless ringing became a persistent reminder of her solitude.

"What?" she said in haste, her voice overshadowed by a heavy cloak of sorrow.

"It's Kota," the voice on the other end crackled with concern. "Simon told me he heard about Caleb on the news. Did you honestly believe you could shield me from this in a small town like ours?"

"I didn't want to burden you," Emily whispered.

"Burden?" Kota's tone held a hint of frustration. "You need to see me as an equal, not someone who needs protecting. I assumed you would be at the hospital, so I'm having Simon bring me there."

"No, I mean, I appreciate the gesture, but I don't want you to miss your classes because of me."

"Well, sometimes being there for you is more important."

"Kota," she began before realizing she had hung up. "Damn it."

8

THE JOURNEY

I nside the relentless fury of a tempestuous storm in downtown New York City, nature's wrath unfolded with hailstones the size of golf balls and lightning bolts crackling through the sky. The once-familiar streets were veiled in an ethereal mist, tinged with a haunting burgundy hue. Inside the fog stood a prominent law firm known for its excellence. Unbeknownst to its inhabitants, a malefic presence was about to change their lives forever. Alas, Lucifer appeared with an ominous light. His intense gaze swept across the building, seeking out those who work for the Roamer. With unwavering purpose, he breached the thirty-third floor, casting an impenetrable shroud. Without hesitation, the Prince of Darkness extended his arm with a terrifying glow.

"I don't know who has released you from your crypt, but I have no qualms about sending you right back after you tell me where I might find Haines, that is."

However, what he perceived as a faceless demon was just an ordinary man, terrified by the sight of his glowing figure. Picking up on his bewilderment, another worker sauntered over, oblivious to the impending doom in their midst. Soon he recognized the fear in his friend's eyes and hastened to intervene.

"What's going on here?"

But, in the serpent's menacing gaze, he saw the worker transform into yet another faceless demon who dared to challenge him.

"It appears that you weren't the only one to have escaped," he sneered.

A blaze erupted from Lucifer's palm as he closed in on the distorted image. Petrified, the worker found himself immobilized, unable to flee as his attacker extended a hand inches away from his face, forcing him to burst into flames.

Fear-stricken wails brought the devil's attention towards the other man, who flew into the nearest office. With a mere stare, the fortified door crumbled to dust, dispersing in the air. The work caught his burning pools and began inching closer toward the desk.

"I fail to comprehend why you are fleeing from me. Cowardice is such a human quality," Lucifer taunted as he stepped into the office. His eyes returned to their normal state after taking notice of the presence of a woman. "Ah, I see you sought reinforcements. Clever."

He continued to battle every creature he thought he encountered inside the building. Although lacking his full strength, he utilized the jagged lightning bolts from the storm to strike down all forces that dared to move on the other floors.

Faceless demons loomed in the epicenter of Lucifer's mind, provoking him to attack. When the opportunity presented itself, he teleported in front of the male worker, driving his fist mercilessly into the man's chest. Meanwhile, the woman attempted to escape, rising from her desk to reach the exit. Yet, as she reached out for the handle, the locked door mysteriously lifted from the ground and clicked seamlessly back into place on its hinges.

Panicking, she tugged at the unyielding door, only to find Lucifer turning his attention back to her, holding the worker's heart within his grasp. After callously dropping the organ, he spun around to face his envisioned enemy, who now wielded a sword adorned with cryptic Enochian scripture. With lightning reflexes, the entity lunged at him, swinging the sword with deadly intent. But Lucifer eluded the strike by a hair's breadth. This brought forth a wicked brilliance boiling inside his being, compelling the fiend to erupt into blazing flames. In reality, it was the woman succumbing to the searing inferno. Only then did he survey the remnants of his own delusions, his handiwork entwined with his troubled mind.

"You cannot hide from me," he declared, his voice resounding through the room. His eyes pierced the ceiling as if it held the secrets he sought. "I am going to find you, Haines!" The walls carried his vow, a promise drifting into the ether.

Several towns over, in the sanctum of the Community Hospital, Emily stood by Caleb's bedside, watching the monitor display the reassuring rhythm of his heartbeat. The soft beep of the machine filled the room, a steady reminder of life, as she held his hand, her fingers intertwining with his. She lowered her gaze to his face, longing to see the warmth of his eyes once more. Her grip tightened as if willing him to awaken.

"Why didn't you tell me?" she whispered.

A sudden knock resonated against the door, interrupting the solemn atmosphere. Startled, she turned her attention to the entrance, finding Kota and Simon standing in the doorway. Their presence brought a glimmer of comfort.

"What are you doing here?" she inquired, quickly adding, "Not that I mind the company or anything."

"Did you really think I'd leave you alone right now? You've taken care of me practically my whole life; the least I can do is be there when you need a shoulder to lean on."

A grateful smile graced Emily's face, a flicker of warmth softening the lines of worry. "Thanks, Kota," she expressed, feeling the weight of their unspoken bond.

"No problem, sis," she said, a mirrored smirk adorning her face. "You don't think I'd be there for you? Do you really think so little of me?"

Emily's hand found its place on her sister's shoulder, seeking solace. A single tear escaped her eyes, tracing a path down her cheek, its evidence of her vulnerability. Without hesitation, she wrapped her arms around Kota. Her trembling lips curved into a genuine smile as she embraced her sister.

"No. My head's just not right, right now," Emily confessed, her tone subdued but laced with gratitude.

She wiped away the tears that threatened to overwhelm her, refusing to let her mask of serenity crumble. Kota had always been her pillar of strength, even during their teenage years when Emily was plagued by bullies. She'd urge her sister to turn the other cheek, to rise above their hurtful words. Yet, deep within, she cradled thoughts of confronting those who tormented her sister, offering them a taste of their own medicine. However, the stakes were higher now. The image of Caleb lying motionless, his very presence a testament to the danger that lurked, shattered her resolve.

"So, anything I can do?" Kota's voice broke the silence, her words laden with concern that pierced through the darkness.

"Can you take me to the hotel? Please."

"Sure. But there's somewhere we need to go first. It's the only stipulation, and you have to trust me. No questions asked."

Emily regarded her sister with a dubious stare. "Why don't I like the sound of this?"

"Don't stress. It won't be the worst thing you've ever done," Kota assured her, a playful chuckle escaping her lips. "Nah, that title goes to Bradley Donovan, your sophomore year—"

"Oh my God, Kota! Ew! Brad was such a sketchball!"

"You were the one who went out with him."

"Well, this is the second time today you've brought him up. Methinks someone's got some repressed feelings," she pushed, relishing the lightness that overshadowed their worries.

"Gross, man! He's, like, almost old enough to be my pops!"

"Hey! What are you trying to say?"

"Nothing. Nothing." After a brief pause, she continued, "But seriously, how am I supposed to forget a dude who made you a mixtape with 18 songs, all with Emily in the title? And on top of that, he spray-painted your name on the hood of his van."

"Yeah, like I said, total creepster," Emily shuddered, memories of her younger self weaving through the tangled web of teenage relationships resurfaced.

"How did he even have a van, being a high school sophomore, anyway?" Kota questioned.

"He wasn't a high school sophomore, that's how. Anyway, you said we had somewhere to go?" Emily rose from her place by Caleb's side and headed for the door.

"Wait. What?" Kota asked, her confusion unraveling those words. She sped up to Emily to catch her at the threshold. "You told me that he was a sophomore."

"Yeah, I did. And he was. Just not a high school sophomore," Emily clarified.

"Huh? I don't—"

"College."

"What?! Ew! Emily Marie Puller!" Kota exclaimed, the pieces of the puzzle falling into place.

"Hey, you even said it yourself," Emily reminded her.

With a mischievous twinkle in her eye, she opened the door, her gaze enticing Kota. "That he was nearly old enough to be your dad."

After a short drive, Simon and the sisters found themselves in front of a bustling ice cream parlor called Big Scoops. As they entered, Kota's eyes widened in excitement, scanning the array of delectable flavors behind the glass display. Her excitement was unmistakable as she ordered a cone so large it required the support of both her hands. Carefully, she started licking the sides of the vanilla ice cream coated with rainbow sprinkles, savoring every lick to prevent the creamy treat from dripping onto her hands.

Beside her, Simon enjoyed a double chocolate sundae, the rich layers of chocolate sauce, whipped cream, and crushed nuts creating a dessert masterpiece. On the opposite side, Emily enjoyed her vanilla and chocolate swirl cone, adorned with the same colorful sprinkles.

Concern overtook Kota's face when she turned to her sister. "So, are you feeling any better?"

Emily responded with a warm smile. "I am," she said, her gratitude evident. "Thank you, Kota."

Their mother used to take them to Big Scoops whenever they felt upset or troubled, a tradition that somehow made their sorrows melt away like ice cream on a hot day. Emily recognized Kota's attempt to bring comfort, but this particular problem felt too weighty for even their favorite ice cream parlor to solve.

Interrupting the serious moment, Simon interjected, "Alright, who wants seconds?"

A spark of excitement lit up Kota's eyes, transforming her usually composed demeanor into one of eager anticipation. "Me!"

However, her enthusiasm faded when she noticed Simon's distant expression. She nudged him with her elbow. "Something on your mind?"

But he just blinked and said, "Oh, it's nothing. Just thinking about a project I have to get done."

When Emily finished her cone, she looked over at a quaint bookstore across the street. An idea flickered in her mind. She opened her bag and retrieved a weathered notebook adorned with dog-eared pages. Flipping it open, she revealed a meticulously curated list of books she yearned to read. On the margin was written Mystery and the Unknown, capturing her attention. Emily glanced at Kota, her face smudged with remnants of ice cream, and made a decision.

"I'll be right back," Emily declared, gathering her belongings, heading for the inviting bookstore, her steps propelled by both curiosity and a longing for answers.

Kota watched her sister's retreating form, nodding in acknowledgment. "Okay, I'll be here," she affirmed, a sense of support evident in her voice.

Meanwhile, the hospital buzzed as Boris and Victor navigated their way through the sterile hallways. The flickering lights overhead danced like ethereal fireflies, casting a haunting glow onto their resolute expressions as if the very walls were whispering secrets. Shadows stretched and swirled like dark specters, amplifying the air of tension that enveloped them.

"Inconspicuous, huh?" Boris quipped sarcastically, his voice tinged with annoyance. Victor was quick to silence him with a stern gaze, positioning himself in front of the door. "He's in here," he announced firmly, his voice carrying the weight of the situation.

Boris took a deep breath, preparing himself for what lay ahead. But Victor's words cut through the tension like a cold blade, stripping away any sense of camaraderie. "Not we, just you. It's your mess. You clean it up. I'm only here to make sure that you finish it this time. And that's more than I should have to do," Victor stated, his arms folded across his chest as he leaned against the wall. Determination mingled with frustration marked his expression.

Victor pushed the door ajar, gesturing for Boris to enter. As soon as the scientist stepped inside, however, the creature shut the door, trapping them both in a closed-off world. Boris proceeded to approach Caleb with hesitant steps, his eyes clouded with remorse for the damage he had inflicted. He studied the still figure before him, frozen in time, bearing the weight of their choices.

"I truly am sorry," Boris whispered, his tone full of regret. "It's not really clear to me as to why, but these guys want you off the board pretty bad."

In the distance, the sound of footsteps echoed down the hallway. A concerned nurse noticed Victor standing outside the room and hurried over to him; her worry etched across her face.

"Can I help you?" she inquired, her voice laced with compassion. The fiend met her gaze, piercing her with his intense eyes.

"My friend heard what happened and wanted to come and visit his brother," he explained.

"Brother?" The nurse's curiosity prompted her to peer through the glass on the door, only to be met with a shocking sight. Boris stood inside, clutching Caleb's pillow in his hand.

A rush of panic surged through her as she attempted to open the door, but Victor pushed her aside, protecting their secret. "They're brothers," he insisted, holding her gaze.

Faced with the unexpected revelation, the nurse stood silent, her eyes betraying disbelief. Victor, adept at reading minds, filled in the gaps. "You don't say. So that means Emily has been his only visitor," he mused aloud, gaining valuable insights. Realizing their error, he swiftly opened the door just as Boris was about to smother Caleb with the pillow. "Plans have changed. We have to go right now."

Just outside the hotel, the car carrying Simon and the girls pulled up in the parking lot. Emily grasped her bag tightly, gratitude evident in her voice. "Thank you, this was fun."

Kota questioned, hesitant to leave her alone. "Are you sure you don't want me to stay?"

"Yeah, I'll be fine. I promise."

She stepped out of the car and made her way to the front door. The creaking hinges welcomed her into the silent house. Seeking solace, she headed to the kitchen, pouring herself a glass of rich red wine. She savored the taste as it danced upon her palate, the velvety liquid soothing her nerves. Glass in hand, she retreated to her bedroom, relishing the comforting embrace of solitude. Closing the door gently behind her, she placed the glass on her nightstand, a shimmering ruby in the soft glow of lamplight.

Emily settled onto her bed, eager to lose herself in the pages of a book. Opening her bag, she retrieved the book that had captured her attention. It began by recounting the chilling events of the Hill Town Massacre in New York, vividly describing the brutal murders of six families over three consecutive winter nights in 1988. The words painted a haunting picture of fear and despair.

The next chapter transported her to a place she knew all too well—Burney Falls, California. As she continued reading, a cold shiver ran down her spine, raising goosebumps on her skin. More than twenty-six people had mysteriously vanished in the area over the past few years. Memories flashed through her mind, recalling the bulletin with pictures of the missing, further fueling her curiosity.

Eager to uncover Caleb's thoughts, she closed the book, a sense of unease settling within her. Her mind drifted back to the moment she had leapt into the tranquil waterfall. Just before her feet left solid ground, a glimmer had caught her eye, tantalizing her with its mysterious allure. As she floated weightlessly in the water, her gaze was drawn toward a distant cave nestled against the expansive ocean.

Out of nowhere, her phone rang, breaking her concentration. Without bothering to check the caller, she answered.

"Hello?"

"Hey, Emily, I'm with Creative Minds," a voice on the other end greeted.

Searching for a response, she replied, "Okay," only half-engaged in the conversation.

"I'm calling to let you know the position that you were supposed to interview for earlier today is closed, but I can put you back on the waiting list if you'd like."

Half-truths and possibilities swirled in Emily's mind, wrestling for attention. "Um, yeah, that sounds great, thanks. I'm sorry, but I can't talk right now," she murmured distractedly, ending the call.

Her eyes darted to the final sentence on the page, where Caleb had penned his speculations about what lay within the enigmatic cave. Excitement mixed with trepidation coursed through her veins, igniting a fire within her soul.

9

THE BOOK

F ar away from the city's fast-paced energy, an unkempt man maneuvered his vintage '96 Buick LeSabre into the weather-beaten parking lot of a dilapidated Cowboys gas station. The faint hum of the city's ceaseless activities faded into the distance, leaving only the quietly rustling leaves and a hushed stillness that enveloped the location. With measured steps, the man emerged from his vehicle, leaving his wife and young daughter cocooned inside its protective confines. He gravitated upward, entranced by the flashing lights suspended overhead.

Out of nowhere, the creature emerged from the distance and presented itself as a street preacher of sorts. "Excuse me, sir. How do you feel about the impending doom to your planet?" It asked.

"What?!" The man retorted, bewildered by the threat as he removed the nozzle from his car. "Get away from me."

"No problem."

An eerie smirk overtook the preacher's face, staring deep into the man's eyes before departing, leaving behind an air of amusement as he headed inside the small convenience store.

Unbeknownst to the man's wife, who was happily engaging with their daughter inside the car, an unsettling force clouded his mind. In the midst of playing peek-a-boo, she looked up just in time to witness a disturbing sight. She saw her husband drenched in gasoline, holding the customized Zippo lighter with their daughter's handprint and name she got him for their tenth anniversary. She screamed at the top of her lungs and opened the door.

"What on earth are you doing?!"

The sound of her voice jolted the man out of the trance as the dark veins that had consumed his face dissipated, leaving him shocked by the abhorrent act he was about to commit.

Within the confines of the store, the creature whispered under its breath after realizing the absence of any distinct scent in the air.

"Haines, this is undoubtedly your doing," it declared.

"I see nothing escapes your keen perception," the Roamer said, his voice carried by the wind.

"I have delivered your message, so now I'd like you to keep your word and free me from this gargoyle entrapment. Then, if possible, never cross each other again. If Lucifer discovers our collaboration, my fate will be sealed."

"Tell me, what is it about demons? You all consider yourselves to be the darkest threats to the world, yet you are terrified of a single being." Haines began, materializing beside his reluctant ally with crossed arms. "By the way, what's with the new getup? Are you trying to hide from me?"

"No, I'm not that foolish," it said. "I'm just trying out a few tricks."

"Well, for now, you are free to do as you please, but soon, I will require your assistance in another attack on the human, merely to ensure that the previous incident was not a mere fluke," Haines affirmed.

"Are you serious?"

"I am. Which means your true form will have to wait."

Miles away at a quaint cottage nestled amidst the lively backdrop of downtown New York, Boris bolted into his bedroom and pushed the bed away from the wall. In doing so, he revealed a concealed safe embedded within the structure, further fueling his mounting anxiety. With palpable apprehension, he retrieved a weathered wooden weapon reminiscent of the fabled Sword of Freyr, albeit with a damaged handle and worn edges.

"With this, I shall vanquish you, demon," Boris proclaimed.

All of a sudden, a creaking sound emanated from the door, immediately catching his attention. However, his apprehension grew as a familiar voice seeped through the doorway.

"What're you gonna do with that, pop?" Leigh asked, her voice filled with concern.

Not wanting to scare her, Boris spun around, locking eyes with his daughter, who stood in the entrance. Yet, the glimmer in her eyes revealed not anticipation but rather a fear rooted in what her father might be capable of. Rising to his feet, he concealed the broken sword in the inner pocket of his denim jacket, eager to reach her. In response, however, Leigh backed away, the lines of trust and safety blurred in her uncertain gaze.

"You have no reason to be afraid of me, Leigh. You don't know what happened that night, but I assure you, I am innocent," he pleaded.

"We got back home from the sleepover and found Mom... she wasn't moving in the bathroom. I kept calling you again and again, thinking there's gotta be some reason, but you never picked up," Leigh retorted.

"Please, listen to me," he pressed, stepping closer. "There are real monsters out there."

Suddenly, Noah entered the room, positioning himself just behind his sister's protective stance. "We are well aware, Dad," Noah interjected, his voice carrying a sense of accusation. "One of those monsters is standing right in front of us."

"One day, I will prove my innocence to you, but right now, there is something that I have to do."

As he attempted to make a swift exit, both Leigh and Noah converged upon the doorway, adamant about preventing their father from slipping away. Frustrated by their intervention, Boris locked eyes with Leigh, his heart aching at the fractured trust resonating within her gaze. Cursing his circumstances, he adjusted the broken sword concealed inside his denim jacket pocket, contemplating his next move. But before he could execute his plan, both Leigh and Noah resolutely refused to yield, their presence acting as an impregnable barrier.

"You have got to let me go!"

Leigh glanced upward at her older brother, seeking support and validation amidst the uncertainty that befell them. Meeting her gaze, Noah responded, his voice firm and resolute. "The authorities will soon descend upon us. We are ensuring that you do not attempt to evade their pursuit."

His daughter locked eyes with him as she uttered, "I'm sorry, pop. You didn't leave us any choice."

Resolute yet cornered, Boris muttered to himself, despair weighing heavily upon his shoulders, "No, I have to get out of here." Turning his back on his children, he headed towards the window.

As he opened the window, the sound of approaching patrol cars reverberated through the house. His heart sank as he whirled around, sprinting away from his children's sight. He raced down the hallway and dashed into the kitchen, intent on reaching the back door. At the same time, multiple footsteps echoed throughout the house, escalating the tension that filled every crevice of his being.

Desperate to make his escape, Boris flung open the back door and rushed into the yard. However, his fleeting hopes were shattered as he overheard Noah's voice shouting, "He went down the hall!" Determined to evade capture, Boris hastily closed the back door behind him, his movements calculated and quiet as he also turned off his phone.

Peering through the narrow openings of the wired fence, he surveyed his surroundings, his heart pounding in his chest. Two officers, sensing his presence, decided to give chase on foot, their rapid footsteps echoing behind him. Simultaneously, the officers within the house scrambled to their patrol cars, their aim to intercept him down the road. Back within the house, Leigh and Noah fervently watched as the officers sprang into action.

As the adrenaline coursing through their veins subsided, Leigh turned to her older brother and pleaded, her voice betraying an undercurrent of doubt, "Tell me we did the right thing, Noah."

"Of course we did," he said.

Not too far, in Woodley Park, a golden draft rustled nature's quilt, humming with the jubilant tunes of singing birds. Effervescent daffodils, flaunting bright trumpets, and delicate daisies carpeted the lush greenery beneath a canopy of mature trees. A rainbow of butterflies danced around Michael as he bestowed his guidance upon Emily.

"This appeared to be a calm enough place for you to commence your training," he said. "Sit down and close your eyes, allow the breeze to whisper its secrets."

Emily settled herself on tuffs of wild grass, her eyelids fluttering shut. Yet, even in her closed state, her gaze remained fixed on Michael, seeking his wisdom amidst the darkness. As she immersed herself in the calmness surrounding her, Michael's voice floated to her ears like a distant melody.

"Release your fears and doubts," he urged. "Embrace the harmony of nature, for it shall be your guide."

When his guidance began to intertwine with the winds, an intrusive sound cut the tranquility—a vibrating tone from Emily's phone. An expression of both annoyance and disappointment crossed Michael's face.

"Seriously? The time for distractions has long passed," he remarked, admonishment clear in his voice.

Against his criticism, she peeked through her eyelashes, extracting her phone from her pocket and answering the call.

"Hey, what's happening?"

Concern underscored Caleb's every word, rushing to inquire about her well-being. "Oh, good, you're okay. When Jason left, he... he said the hallway was... empty."

"You're worried about me even after waking from a coma." A tender smile graced Emily's face. "Michael brought me to a secluded spot in response to some strange occurrences with the lights. He's teaching me how to harness these powers."

The extent of her unawareness dawned on Caleb. He teetered on the edge of interruption, compelled to disclose information of utmost importance, but waited til she finished speaking.

"Em, there's something... you need to see."

The importance in his tone led her to agree to meet him. Once the call ended, she rose from her seated position. "I've got to get back to Caleb. He needs me to see something that cannot wait," she announced, conviction lacing her words.

Unamused, Michael rolled his eyes but conceded to her request. "Very well, I shall take you to him. However, when this task is done, our training shall commence with no interruptions."

In the blink of an eye, Michael transported her back to the hospital. Overhead, a lacework of faults sprawled across the scarred plaster, bathed in the stuttering glow of temperamental illumination.

"Did I do this?" she asked.

"Do what?" Caleb retorted, looking up at the damaged ceiling.

"Her heightened emotions are overpowering her rationality, and if left unchecked, they will lay waste to the world. Therefore, it is imperative for her to commence her training."

"Not 'til she sees it," he demanded, turning toward the archangel. "She needs... to know what... she'll be signing up for." He started at the archangel as he got off the bed and placed the gown on top of the blanket.

"Perhaps it will provide some clarity," Michael said, recognizing the validity of this request. "The both of you should go to the cave. I will return to Heaven to regain my strength."

"You do that. I'm sure we... will see you... again." His focus, noble yet straining, left him breathless.

After watching the archangel fade out of the room, Emily turned to face Caleb as he sat back on the bed. "The cave? Are you referring to the one from your book?"

Her inference sparked a smirk over his features. "You read it?" he inquired, holding a hand to his head.

"Well, only a part of it. What made you decide to write about the Hilltown Massacre?"

"I was contracted... to write about... something real," he paused, taking in a lung full of air. "Stories involving cold cases... they're quite popular... these days. I stumbled on it online... and it really stood out... as one of the most... perplexing cases."

"It's just that it hits a little too close to home," Emily revealed, her voice tinged with unease.

"What do you mean?"

"My uncle used to live in a cabin near that area, and it dredged up some memories."

"I'm sorry for making you feel uncomfortable." With a firm stance, he approached his partner, resting his head against hers. Then, he planted a tender kiss on her forehead. "Come on, we should... get going." he said, grimacing as he stood.

Emily moved to support him, concern etched on her face. "Are you sure you're up for this?"

"We don't have... a choice." Caleb's determination overrode his physical discomfort. "Let's move before anyone tries to stop us."

Just then, the doctor entered the room with his clipboard in hand. "Mr. Lansworth, I'm glad to see you're up and about," he said, moving in to check his patient's vitals.

Emily stepped aside, giving the doctor room to conduct a thorough check-up. Her heart pounded as she watched Caleb's chest rise and fall with each breath.

"Listen, doctor."

"Your breathing is still a bit labored," he informed, turning to Emily. "I'm going to have to ask you to keep your visits brief. Caleb has to take it easy."

"Yeah," his patient began. "I need to... be discharged."

"Is this a joke? You just woke up from a coma."

"Okay. How... about this? If I can take... a stroll outside and... be fine. Then, I can leave."

Against his better judgment, the doctor agreed. "Alright, but we're going to do this the right way. Nurse," he called out the door, "bring a wheelchair, please."

Caleb opened his mouth to object, but a gentle squeeze from Emily's hand silenced him.

Moments later, a nurse wheeled in a chair. "This is non-negotiable," the physician stated. "You'll use the wheelchair, and we'll take a short trip to the garden area. If you can manage that without issues, we can discuss your discharge."

Caleb settled into the wheelchair, his jaw clenched shut. Emily moved to push him, but the nurse took control. "I'll handle this," the nurse said kindly. "You can walk alongside us."

Once they reached the garden, a small oasis of greenery where flowers bloomed in tended beds, he braced himself to stand back on his feet. Emily wanted to help, but the doctor wanted to see him manage on his own.

"Alright, if you can walk a lap around the path here, I'll sign off on your release. Emily, you can walk beside him, but please don't offer physical support unless he's in danger of falling."

As they began their slow journey, Emily held her head down, watching her worn sneakers scuff against the gravel. But her mind was a million miles away. Caleb acknowledged her despondency and took her hand, hoping to lift her spirits. She raised her gaze to him, her eyes squinting against the bright sunlight.

"It's strange to think how much has happened while you were... asleep," she began. "Did you know there was a massive earthquake in New Zealand last month? And all that unrest in the Middle East - they're calling it the Arab Spring."

"Em—Emily," he pressed, coming to a halt in front of her. "We will get justice... for what they did. I promise." Their eyes locked in a shared struggle, understanding where the other was coming from. "I promise."

The rest of their walk passed in a contemplative silence, each lost in their own thoughts.

Hours later, they exited the hospital. A massive cumulonimbus cloud loomed overhead, its towering form a churning mix of deep blues and rich purples. The cloud's anvil-shaped top spread across the sky like a cosmic bruise. As if on cue, rain began to pour from the darkened heavens.

Relentless droplets slammed against the pavement with audible force. Each raindrop exploded on impact, creating a misty haze. The parking lot soon became a sparkling mirror.

Lightning flickered within the cloud, illuminating its majestic structure. The low rumble of thunder followed, a sound so deep it penetrated the earth.

Caleb, strengthened by the powerful display, picked Emily up in his arms. With a burst of vitality, he sped across the slick pavement, each step sending up a small spray of water.

"Let's stop at the burger place ahead," he said, his voice rising above the storm's cacophony. "We can get out... of the... storm and, I don't know... about you, but... I'm starving."

His endurance waned as his words became more labored, each phrase punctuated by gasping breaths. The effort of carrying Emily, combined with his recovering body, took its toll. This caused his steps to become unsteady.

Emily felt the muscle spasms in his arms fighting to keep them both upright. "Caleb," she started, concern evident in her voice.

But before she could finish, his knees buckled, controlling their descent rather than falling outright. Suddenly, Emily found herself half in his lap and half on the wet pavement.

Caleb's chest heaved as he struggled to catch his breath, his face pale from exertion. Water streamed down his face, mingling with beads of sweat on his brow. Despite his exhaustion, his arms remained protectively around Emily.

"I'm... sorry," he panted. "I thought... I could..."

Emily shifted, moving to support him rather than be supported. "It's okay," she assured him.

They sat there for a moment, rain pouring down around them, the pavement cold beneath them. Her hair hung heavy around her shoulders while looking around for viable options. That's when she noticed they were more than halfway to their destination.

"Look!" she said about the thunderous roar. "Fast burger is right there. I'll go and get you food. Hopefully that'll fix you right up."

As she advanced closer to the restaurant, she noticed fumbling lights shining through the word "Fast" on the large, neon burger sign. Instead of heeding a warning from the oddity, she continued forward. However, reaching for the door gave her goosebumps. Her muscles coiled as if preparing for fight or flight. She peered through the windows and caught a glimpse inside.

At first glance, everything seemed normal - Customers sat motionless at their tables, burgers half-raised to mouths that no longer chewed. The cashier stood frozen behind the counter; eyes fixed on the door. But as her perception adjusted, she noticed a family near the window shift in her direction, their gazes unnervingly fixed.

She blinked, and for a split second, could've sworn she saw sharp teeth flash across their eyes. This caused her body to tense and take an involuntary step back.

Seeing this, Caleb clung to his feet once more. "What's wrong?!" he asked.

"I'm not sure. I think we should maybe stop at the place down the street," Emily confessed.

Inside, the establishment's occupants sat in an eerie silence. An employee queued at the counter stared at the customers filling their stomachs. At the same time, they all paused and stared at one another. It was as if they were awaiting Emily to enter their domain.

"Okay, let's do that," Caleb agreed.

She walked back up to him and placed his arm around her to keep him vertical.

Still sensing her unease, he squeezed her hand, silently communicating that he understands as they resumed their walk down the rain-soaked road.

10

DIVINE PROVIDENCE

Bathed in the golden embrace of the midday sun, Boris crept along the perimeter of the majestic hotel. The imposing structure stood tall before him, its grand facade adorned with elegant carvings and opulent decorations that spoke of a bygone era of wealth and prosperity.

As he neared the rear of the hotel, a vigilant security camera affixed to the side of the building went unnoticed. Its unblinking lens scanned the path he traversed. Yet, by some surreal trick of fate or cunning, the camera seemed oblivious to his presence. It focused instead on the barren land, transmitting an image of an empty world devoid of any trespassers.

Boris approached the partially opened window. His stomach churned with each step. The panes creaked in the calm breeze, amplifying his racing heartbeat. Beads of sweat trickled down his temple, his breath becoming shallow as he mumbled a curse word under his breath.

His fingers swayed the closer he got to breaching the sanctity of the room. With measured deliberation, he clasped the window ledge, its cold metallic touch sending a jolt up his arm. He hesitated, the realization of the precariousness of his situation sinking in, before mustering the determination to hoist himself up and over the threshold of forbidden territory.

Boris squeezed through the narrow window, his body contorting to fit into the room beyond. As he stood upright, he surveyed his surroundings with a careful eye, muttering, "People really need to be more cautious about their security."

He looked around, taking in its pristine cleanliness. Not a single dish cluttered the sink, nor a crumb marred the spotless table. He couldn't help but be impressed by the meticulousness of the occupant. His attention was drawn to the refrigerator, adorned with a few small pieces of artwork. Among them was the picture Emily hung up when she settled in.

"Dang it," he whispered, as he approached the refrigerator. His finger traced the edge of the photo before unclipping it from the magnet that held it in place. His eyes darted around the room once more, his mind racing with the need to eliminate any evidence. With a final glance, he tore the picture into pieces and dropped them into the sink. When the last shred diminished, he produced a lighter and set fire to the torn remnants, reducing them to mere ashes.

From out of nowhere, a pungent and foul smell filled the air, like a mixture of burning sulfur and decaying flesh. It clung to his nostrils, inducing a nauseating sensation that threatened to overpower him. The stench carried with it an essence of pure evil that seemed to seep into every crevice of his being.

A wintery sigh curled through the air, wrapping Boris in an icy cocoon. Goosebumps erupted across his skin. His breath misted in front of him, shivering against the unexpected cold. It was like the very presence of the demon sucked away the warmth, leaving a suffocating aura.

Visions of darkness and torment flashed through his mind, like his very thoughts were being invaded. He turned around in sheer fear to discover the creature standing before him.

"This doesn't surprise me one bit," it began. "I know full well sinners aren't to be trusted. Now, tell me what you burned in that fire."

"Maybe it was already burning when I arrived," Boris suggested.

"No, I don't think so," it retorted. "The fear in your eyes tells me that you found something vital."

A casual wave of the creature's hand extinguished the flames and restored the picture to its original state. It observed with satisfaction before shifting his gaze to the scientist's shoulder, causing it to pop out of its socket. Boris howled in pain, his body paralyzed by the demon's power.

"I think I've been more than fair with you, considering I left your children alone all this time as promised," it taunted. "Maybe you need another reminder, something to prove that you don't get to call the shots."

"N-no, wait. Please," Boris begged, desperation seeping through his voice. "Just take me. I can tell that's what you really want to do."

"You're not going to get off that easily."

His gaze shifted from the picture on the wall to Boris, who stood trembling before him. "Now, you must make a choice - between your children, Leigh, Ava, and Noah."

Tears streamed down Boris's face, fully grasping the gravity of the situation. "Please, don't do this," he pleaded, his voice breaking with desperation.

"If you don't choose, then I will. Either way, the blood will stain your hands. And let's not forget, you haven't seen them since that fateful night you murdered their mother," it sneered, delighting in the anguish. Boris's injured arm quivered as if contemplating a futile escape from the clutches of this demonic tormentor.

"But I did not do this!" Boris erupted, denying the accusation. He mustered a brief moment of defiance, his uninjured arm wrenching away from the oppressive wall.

"Perhaps you forgot that the last time they saw you was the evening before I took your wife's life. When they returned home, finding her corpse, you were nowhere to be found. What other conclusion could they draw?"

"You son of a—"

"If you don't decide, I will," the demon said.

Boris continued to plead for mercy, but his cries fell on deaf ears. It seemed there was no escape from the misery thrust upon him. Then, without warning, the creature vanished from sight, but a flicker of movement on the television concurrently caught his attention. The screen became a tormenting window, urging him to witness Ava's demise.

He watched in paralyzed terror as his youngest daughter, hand-in-hand with an unfamiliar companion, ventured along the Appalachian Trail. The trees seemed to close in, their twisted branches slithering along the gravel. Cold dread consumed him, forcing him to come to terms with the enormity of lost moments. His focus locked onto Ava's finger, noticing an engagement ring. But before he could lose himself in that fragile moment, the creature appeared before them as just another man walking the trail.

"No!" his anguished scream pierced the air, reverberating through the hotel.

Meanwhile, Emily descended into the hidden room. As her foot touched the last step, a brilliant blue light engulfed the space, dissipating into darkness as the lights burst around her. Undeterred, she reached into her bag, her trembling hands seeking the reassuring warmth of the Dorcy Lantern. With a soft click, the room bloomed with light, revealing unsettling sights. Bookshelves lined the room, filled with stacks of paper, but it was the pentagram paintings adorning the walls that sent shivers down her spine.

"What is this place?" her voice faltered.

Despite being immersed in the unknown, she ventured through the room until her foot got caught on a folded chair. The unexpected mishap sent her crashing onto the furniture. As she struggled to regain her composure, she uncovered a hidden tape recorder beneath the seat. She sat against the wall, her heart pounding as she pressed play.

"This is Donovin Puller, and I never imagined finding myself doing something like this, but the bizarre events of the past few weeks leave me no choice. It all started before the Hilltown Massacre just outside this cabin," his voice crackled through the tape. Emily hovered over the pause button. Her breath caught in her throat. The hairs on the back of her neck stood on end, her uncle's words echoing in the silent room. She found solace in the comfort of the folded chair as she continued to listen to her uncle's unsettling audio diary.

"I needed some time alone to clear my head, so I spent the day by the pool. But no sooner had I settled, with my feet dangling in the water, when a peculiar man dressed in a perfectly tailored blue suit appeared before me. It's odd, though; not only did he know my name, but he also knew about my niece, who was only going to be two in a few weeks. He requested that I free up my time for the coming weekend and spend time with her. I asked him how he knew me and little Em. He, in turn, told me there wasn't time to answer any questions and that I just had to trust him. I finally stared into his eyes, which is when I noticed the marble blue glow that radiated from his eyes. Yet, somehow, I felt completely at ease even after he seemed to disappear the moment I blinked."

Emily stopped the tape, her mind engrossed in the words of her uncle. She couldn't shake the belief that the unknown man from the coffee shop was the one responsible for the brutal attack on her friend, Caleb.

Near the staircase, Michael watched her intently, a sense of unease settling over him. He had hoped that she'd remain oblivious to the dangers until she's ready, but he now realized her instincts were leading her closer to the truth. "I needed to check things out at the church after Gabriel's failed mission."

Unwilling to delve further into her uncle's shadowed past, Emily set the tape recorder down and rose from her seat. Determined, she grabbed the flashlight and proceeded upstairs to uncover more pieces of the puzzle. Michael stayed rooted to the spot for a moment, his mind filled with doubts. "Mr. Donovin always appeared so astute, a respected police officer. How could he have possibly thought his men would listen to him about us?" he whispered to himself.

With the floorboard back in place, Emily took a deep breath and stepped out of the cabin. The crisp night air embraced her as she made her way towards the dirt road, clutching the book tightly in her hands. With each step, she opened its pages and continued reading the aftermath of the chilling events. She furrowed her brows, intrigued yet skeptical of the story. "This tale is captivating enough without embellishments," she mused, closing the book.

Her mind whirled with the implications of her discoveries. Each step was automatic, her thoughts replaying the information she'd uncovered. Suddenly, the ground disappeared beneath her feet. She flailed, a startled gasp escaping her lips. Darkness engulfed her as she plummeted into the unseen ditch. She winced from the sharp pain in her back, taking a moment to catch her breath. Slowly pushing herself up, she rummaged through her bag until her fingers closed around the familiar shape of her flashlight.

Composing herself, she aimed the beam of light in different directions, trying to discern her surroundings and figure out her next move.

"What on earth?" she asked, realizing she had fallen into the heart of an underground tunnel. The hole loomed above her, leaving no other choice but to forge ahead. With each uncertain step, the tunnel stretched out before her, its walls covered in layers of damp moss, giving off a musty odor that hung in the air.

After reaching a crossroads, Emily hesitated briefly before choosing the only available path, her curiosity guiding her through the eerie passageways. Minutes turned into eternity as she weaved deeper into the labyrinth, the silence broken only by the sound of her own footsteps echoing off the cold, stone walls.

At last, ahead in the distance, she spotted what appeared to be an exit. A glimmer of hope ignited within her, urging her forward. Stride by stride, she began to notice several weathered wooden floorboards jutting out, seemingly pointing at an opening. Not thinking twice about it, she mustered her strength and leaped, using the boards as makeshift handles to pull herself up toward the surface.

Her body trembling from the effort, she clung to the floorboards, taking in her surroundings. The fading sunlight revealed an image of an old abandoned house in front of her. The dilapidated structure stood as a haunting witness to the passage of time, its walls marred by years of neglect and decay.

"Holy." Her heart soared with relief the moment one of the floorboards gave way, prompting her to loosen her grip and tumble to the ground. Pain seared through the arm she landed on, leaving a trail of scratches in its wake. She locked her eyes skyward, irises dilating like twin moons as the gravity of her plight dawned upon her - she had found herself beneath one of the six houses where the infamous massacre had taken place.

Summoning her courage, Emily lifted herself up, wincing at the throbbing pain in her injured arm. She reached for the flashlight she had brought along, its comforting glow illuminating her surroundings. As she took a shaky step forward, images of past horrors haunted her thoughts, intensifying her nervousness.

"Who would have dug these tunnels under these homes?" she wondered aloud, lost in the dark recesses of the subterranean world.

Ready to march on, Emily continued her journey, the dim light revealing a wider space within the tunnel. It was here that she noticed peculiar markings etched into the walls - intricate Enochian wardings telling tales of forgotten secrets. To an untrained eye, they might appear as mere random scratches, but to Emily, the significance was palpable.

"How many people have come down here?"

Back on the surface, Michael stood in front of one of the desolate houses, searching for her presence as an unsettling absence set in. "Where are you, Emily?"

That's when a peculiar sight stole his attention. The ground before him, disturbed and displaced, formed a puzzling path connecting one house to another. His gaze swept over the deserted ruins; realization dawned on him that all the houses were somehow connected.

A soft whoosh of air blanketed him as his feet lifted off the ground. His eyes blazed a piercing marble blue light, dispelling the shadows across the landscape. He soared upward, watching the houses below shrink to miniature models, eager to unravel the mystery.

"What in the world is going on here?" he mused in a bewildered tone, his voice hushed.

Without any inkling, Victor materialized in front of him. "There is no need for you to concern yourself with that, Lightbringer."

Michael's azure eyes widened. "Why am I unable to sense your power?" he asked.

"A little gift from my partner in crime, you could say."

A name escaped Michael's lips like a hushed prayer, barely audible in the wistful gale. "Lucifer..."

The creature, however, stared at him and proclaimed, "It's time to remove you from the board."

"You are a fool if you believe that you even have a chance," Michael retorted, his eyes blazing with a fervent blue light. He extended a hand toward the demon, his palm radiating a blinding brilliance. Before long, holy energy burst forth, engulfing Victor.

Yet, to Michael's astonishment, the demon remained unscathed, protected by some unseen force. "That's not possible."

Elsewhere, deep within the labyrinthine tunnels, Emily pressed on, her steps echoing softly against the worn stone walls. A chilling silence enveloped her, punctuated only by the faint sound of something slithering and crawling, lurking just beyond her vision.

As she strained to discern the source of the approaching footsteps, fear crept through her veins, causing her breath to hitch erratically. Suddenly, she spun around, her heart pounding within her chest, only to find herself face-to-face with a gaunt and twisted creature, once human but now reduced to a contorted figure crawling on hands and knees. The flashlight's beam pierced the creature's cloudy eyes, causing it to recoil and flee into the shadows whence it came.

In that moment of respite, Emily glimpsed another aberration, its arms flailing in a grotesque display of deranged limbs. It lunged at her, viciously knocking the flashlight out of her grasp. Without wasting a second, she scanned the area and stumbled upon a sliver of light beckoning her further down the tunnel.

She sprinted toward the distant glow, her eyes catching sight of a glimmering object reaching out from the darkness. It was the handle of a gun, a small glimmer of hope amidst the encroaching nightmare. But before she could seize it, a third creature pounced upon her, slashing its claw-like fingers across her ankle, eliciting a searing pain that dropped her to the ground, clutching her leg in agony.

In a desperate bid to escape, Emily kicked and screamed, summoning every ounce of strength concealed within her. With an adrenaline-fueled burst, she managed to dislocate the creature's shoulder, wrenching herself free from its grip. Gasping for breath, she pushed herself onto unsteady feet, but the pain radiating from her injured leg forced her knee to crash heavily against the unforgiving dirt below. Realizing escape on foot was no longer an option, she resolved herself to crawl, her hands instinctively propelling her away from the encroaching terrors.

The creature, with its menacing gaze locked on her, snapped its dislocated shoulder back into place with a sickening crack. As she crawled, Emily could sense more of them slinking along the walls, their presence sending shivers down her spine. Determined not to let any distractions hinder her, she kept her focus solely on reaching the gun.

Unable to stand, she fumbled back, collapsing onto the floor. Desperate, she rolled until she found herself under the flickering light. With the creatures closing in, she spotted the gun lying by her waist. Without hesitation, she snatched it up, swiftly turning around and firing several shots at their feet. But instead of deterring them, the gunshots only seemed to enrage them further, their frenzied movements propelling them toward her with reckless abandon.

One of the creatures extended a hand into the pool of light, only to recoil in agony as its skin sizzled and burned. Their raucous cries pierced the air, causing the rest to halt in their tracks and fade back into the shadows, retreating from the searing brightness.

Meanwhile, on the surface, the battle raged on. Michael lunged towards Victor, aiming a punch at his face, only to be halted by a powerful gust of wind. Confusion etched his face as he questioned the source of this unexpected force.

Victor, his face calm and collected, smirked. "My wings can do more than just help me fly," he revealed, his voice carrying an air of superiority. The sound of rushing air filled the area as Michael's eyes began to radiate a piercing blue light, thrusting the demon several feet backward.

"If that's all you've got, then maybe you should bring your sword into this fight," the demon taunted, a wicked grin spreading across his face.

Thoughts raced through Victor's mind as he contemplated his next move. "I've been on Earth for too long. I may not have the power to wield it now," he pondered silently. Nevertheless, he stood his ground, unwilling to be defeated so easily.

"Pity, if this is all I'm going to get, there's no reason to drag this out," Victor responded, his eyes turning obsidian black as he tapped into additional powers. In a fluid motion, he leaped into the air, his arms raised, revealing his clawed hands.

As he grazed Michael's chest, the porch lights of the nearby homes began to flash an enchanting emerald green. Well aware of the significance of this sudden change, the fiend froze.

"Release him or face my wrath, demon!" The words thundered through the air as Raphael made his presence known.

Victor removed his claws from Michael's chest, teleporting effortlessly behind Raphael. "Show me what you've got," he taunted, his voice dripping with arrogance and defiance.

Raphael's emerald eyes blazed with determination as he turned around, only to find his opponent hovering above him. With a grin dawning his face, Victor unleashed a devastating punch that would have surely brought the archangel to his knees. However, Raphael managed to evade the blow, leaving the demon stunned by his failure.

"How are you this fast?" Victor asked, his voice laced with frustration.

"It pays to know the right entities," Raphael replied, his eyes continuing to emit a vibrant green light. Then, he whirled around, attempting a counterattack. But before he could make contact, Victor, seizing the moment, used his borrowed powers to send Raphael crashing down to the earth, his impact causing the ground to tremble.

"Raphael!" Michael's weakened voice echoed through the chaos.

Back inside the damp, dark tunnels below, Emily lay on the ground, her body trembling with exhaustion and fear. Tenacious in her quest to escape, she reached out towards a loose floorboard, gritting her teeth against the pain coursing through her. Realizing that going back into the unknown darkness was not an option, she mustered the strength to pull herself up.

As she struggled to bridge the gap, Emily fell over a small stone, causing her to lose her balance and fall against the wall. Her hands grazed the cracks in the decaying foundation, fueling her determination. Ignoring the pain, she decided to use the rugged surface as leverage, pushing against it to gain some height. However, this choice plunged her once again into the encompassing darkness, the creatures inching closer with each passing second.

Aware of the encroaching danger, Emily summoned every ounce of strength, using her feet to push away from the wall. Suspended in the air, she desperately reached for the floorboard, her fingertips just shy of grasping it. The creatures closed in, their presence suffocating.

Refusing to succumb to fear, she continued to fight. Slowly but surely, using both her trembling hands, she managed to pull herself up onto the kitchen floor of the derelict house. Feeling a surge of relief, she rolled over into the adjacent room, putting as much distance as possible between herself and the gaping hole in the ground. Moments later, the weight of the building above caused a portion of the floor to collapse into the tunnel, crushing the creatures beneath.

Gasping for breath, while her body trembled from exhaustion, her phone began to ring. Still processing the events that had just transpired, she answered the call with a mixture of weariness and apprehension.

"Yes?" she answered.

"Emily!" Kota's voice rang out from the other end. "I'm so glad to hear your voice."

"Kota? Is everything okay?"

"Yeah, I mean, I didn't know if something happened to you. You left without saying a word."

Relief flooded Emily as she reassured her sister. "Oh, no. I'll be back. I just had to check on something."

"Okay, good. Cause I could really use my big sister's help right now."

Worry etched on her face; Emily sat up on the cold dining room floor. "Kota?" she pressed.

"Emily, get the cops here," came Kota's urgent plea.

The call cut out, sending shockwaves of panic rippling through Emily's body. "Kota! Kota!" she desperately redialed the number, only to be met with the cold comfort of voicemail. Her tears mingled with the mascara streaks on her face as she rose to her feet, her limp forgotten in the urgency of the moment.

The battle continued to rage on the surface as Raphael knelt beside Michael, his hand pressed against his brother's stomach.

"Do not fear," he began. "I sensed something amiss when I felt your strength waning yet found no trace of the demon. That's why I put Gabriel on high alert."

"But I fear even Gabriel may not stand a chance against him," Michael replied. "There is something profoundly wrong here."

Raphael nodded, staring onward at the battlefield. "Yes, that is why we need him here. Perhaps the three of us can send this stain back to where it came from."

A malicious grin spread across the demon's face as he taunted his opponents. "Looks like I'll have the pleasure of taking down two archangels today."

Alas, as if already aware of the unnatural circumstances, Gabriel appeared before Victor in an ethereal display of mystical aura. The atmosphere around his arrival transformed into a dazzling white light that enwrapped him completely. As he emerged, the radiance shimmered, casting an enchanting glow upon his figure. In his grasp, he held the majestic golden pike; its unique design, accentuated by intricate carvings and ornate patterns, possessed a divine energy that emanated from its very core.

Gabriel stared into the unwavering eyes of the demon. With a hint of curiosity, he inquired, "Mind if I join in?"

"I almost forgot you were sent down with them. No matter, perhaps now things will finally become interesting."

"Why does this abomination feel no fear in our presence? There is something deeply unsettling about all of this," Michael exclaimed, his eyes fixed upon Victor.

"Both you and I have been harnessing our powers since our arrival here, while Gabriel has had no reason to. He should still possess his full strength," Raphael shared, his attention never wavering from the ferocious battle before him.

Gabriel's eyes blazed white, the spiked pike becoming a blur as he swung it toward the demon's face with lightning speed. Just as Victor attempted to evade the blow, his moment of escape was abruptly halted by a carbon copy of the archangel he was fighting. The spikes on the angel's weapon tore through the demon's flesh, eliciting a piercing shriek that reverberated through both the air and the very ground beneath them. Gabriel withdrew the pike from Victor's mangled face, watching as he fell to his knees, writhing in sheer agony.

"It is time for you to return to the realm whence you came," the archangel declared, his voice resolute.

"Ah, Gabriel, the angel of trickery. I am far from being defeated," Victor retorted, his wounds beginning to heal before their very eyes.

"This should have been his end. Is he somehow immune?" Raphael pondered, his brow furrowed with a mix of confusion and concern.

11

ENTRAPMENT

In the frigid, damp alley, brimming with a cacophony of overflowing dumpsters and debris of human wastefulness, Lucifer's piercing gaze swept across the desolation, contorted in an expression of utter disdain. With each step he took, his foot sunk into a soaked garbage bag, sending forth a torrent of water that added to the putrid environment. With much disappointment fueling his very being, he clenched his fists so fiercely that all the rocks in the alley burst into flames.

In a low, muted hush, he said, "And God deemed these mortal creatures worthy of bowing before them."

Releasing his pent-up fury, Lucifer set ablaze the very bag he had crushed beneath his feet, the flames leaping and dancing at the edges of the mangled plastic. The inferno served as an unwavering testimony to the destructive capabilities that humans possessed, fueling his unyielding resolve to bring retribution and justice to this chaotic world.

Suddenly, a disheveled, destitute figure emerged from the shadows, his tattered rags clinging to his emaciated frame. In a desperate display of survival, he brandished a blunderbuss at the devil's countenance, his voice reeking of fear.

"Alright, give me your money!"

Lucifer's eyes, gleaming with contemptuous enlightenment, locked with the disheveled man's gaze. An incredulous smirk danced upon his lips as he surveyed the pathetic sight before him, a mosaic of poverty outlined by tattered fabric and an overpowering stench.

With an air of audacity, he retorted, "Excuse me? Look at you, my good man. Your threadbare trousers are marred by gaping holes and the pungency that radiates from your demeanor is simply unbearable. However, I have a proposition that surpasses any pecuniary transaction." As he took a purposeful step toward the robber, he halted. "On second thought, let's add some thrill to this encounter."

The thief's knees wobbled under the weight of the adversary's hostile stare, a mere mortal cowering before the embodiment of malevolence.

Crimson fires seethed in Lucifer's irises, igniting a storm of panic within the man's heart. His body quivered, unable to withstand the overwhelming terror that coursed through his veins. In a desperate attempt to distance himself from the demonic presence, he stumbled backward, his own clumsy feet betraying him on the slick pavement. As he hit the ground with a resounding thud, the metallic clatter of his gun crashing against the concrete reverberated in the eerie stillness of the night.

Through the dim and murky glow of the alley, Lucifer towered over the fallen man, an ominous figure wreathed in darkness. Sinister anticipation emanated from every fiber of his being, accentuated by the malevolent glint that danced in his devilish eyes. His deep, menacing voice slithered menacingly through the air.

"Do you honestly believe you can pilfer from me and escape unscathed?" A twisted semblance of mercy flickered in his gaze, humoring the thought of compassion for the wretched soul before him.

However, he succumbed to a primal impulse and descended upon the cowering man with his fingers curling around the fabric of his collar. The distance between them diminished as he pulled the thief closer, their faces mere inches apart. The rancid breath of peril brushed against the man's panicked features. "Consider yourself fortunate that I deign to show leniency today," Lucifer hissed, a dangerous undertone lacing each calculated syllable.

The man's wide, fright-filled eyes wavered with an urgency to convey the magnitude of his understanding. A desperate nod punctuated his silent plea for mercy.

In a gesture of finality, Lucifer released his grip on the quivering man, watching intently as he scrambled to his feet, his limbs betraying him in his haste to escape. The ethereal glow of Lucifer's presence followed the fleeing figure as he merged with the world beyond the somber alley. Standing there, the devil relished in the intoxicating rush of power that accompanied his ability to instill terror in mere mortals.

As the man made his way onto the main road, a symphony of screeching tires pierced the stillness of the night. This cacophony wrenched Lucifer's attention away from his momentary amusement. A Ford Explorer hurtled towards the hapless robber, a force of unyielding steel on a collision course. The air thickened with tension as the SUV connected with flesh in a macabre dance of inevitability. Silence gave way to the sound of impact, followed by the thud of a body crashing against the brick wall of a nearby building.

Lucifer's fixed upon the lifeless heap that now rested on the unforgiving ground, remnants of a vessel that once housed a soul. A twisted smirk tugged at the corners of his mouth as he murmured to himself, savoring the taste of power that lingered on his tongue.

Far away, in a nearby parking lot, Kota made her way towards Simon's car, carrying two bags brimming with the treasures of her recent shopping spree at the Arts and Crafts store. As she settled into the passenger seat, she placed the bags delicately on the floor, their weight serving as a palpable reminder of the relief she had sought through retail therapy.

Her annoyance seeped through her words as she addressed Simon, "You were supposed to come inside after you finished your cigarette," her voice dripping with exasperation at his careless actions.

Ignoring her frustration, Simon fired up the engine, momentarily drowning out the mounting tension within their cramped space with the growl of the car. His detached response hung in the air, a clear indication of the unease plaguing his mind.

"I can't help but think there are more important things we could be doing right now rather than picking up new art supplies, like being there for your sister while she wallows over her crumbling relationship." His words bore down heavily, lacking any moral substance.

Kota's initial urge to react waned when she noticed a small puncture mark on Simon's neck. Images of news reports flashed through her mind, detailing victims with similar wounds. Nervously, she bit back her words and sank back into her seat.

"I think I should call Emily," she suggested.

"Good idea."

After a few rings, the phone call was redirected to voicemail. Kota made a second attempt, only to receive the same outcome.

"We need to go back home," she insisted.

"We're already on our way."

Once they had passed the grocery store, situated just a brief stroll from the hotel, she allowed the panorama outside to engross her for the remainder of the ride. Worried thoughts of Emily consumed her mind. As soon as Simon eased the car into a parking spot, Kota sprang out to the door. Her restless hands reached for her pockets in search of the keycard. To her dismay, she discovered that it was missing. and a wave of panic washed over her.

Realizing that the keycard had slipped out in the car, Kota turned on her heel, only to collide with Simon, who was standing a few steps behind her. He extended his arm towards her, clutching the precious keycard in his hand.

Relief flooded Kota's senses as she retrieved the key from Simon's outstretched arm. With swift movements, she swiped the keycard against the sensor, granting them access to the hotel. The moment the door swung open, Kota dashed inside, her heart pounding against her ribcage.

Frantically, she called out her sister's name, her voice echoing through the empty hallways. Silence greeted her plea, intensifying her worry. Steadfast to find any trace of Emily, Kota conducted a search in her sister's bedroom. In a feverish bid to make contact, she whipped out her phone and speed dialed the first number on her recent call list. The persistent ringtone filled the air, but there was no response on the other end.

Dread gripped her as she murmured, "Damn it, where are you?"

Every passing second felt like an eternity in her fretful sweep of the empty room. She almost jumped at the sound of Simon's voice behind her.

He stood at the entrance and gave a tongue-in-cheek reassurance: "Don't worry." Then, drawing closer, he stopped almost nose-to-nose. "I'm sure she's alright. Probably just went out to get some fresh air."

Seeing a glimmer of fear in her eyes, Simon turned around and navigated his way to the living room where he sank into the embrace of the couch. Before he could get too cozy, a trickle of blood escaped his nose, staining his sleeve, a reminder of his condition. Still, he proceeded to lose himself in a trance, fixated on the blank wall before him.

Kota, on the other hand, remained in the other room, standing near Emily's bed. Although fear gnawed at her, she resigned herself to exit and headed to the main door. But, as the hallway opened into the living room, her pace slowed, uncertainty prickling at her thoughts—where is Simon?

Upon reaching the room, she caught sight of him, eyes fixed on the plain wall. Unease grew to new heights, but left with no other options, she pressed on.

Outside, the enclosed space crackled with erratic electricity, signaling the creature's presence. "I don't think so," it hissed, its steaming hand claiming the metal door handle.

The mechanism turned dull red, then brightened to a searing orange. Kota's hand mirrored the creature's action inside, only to recoil from the burning heat. She fixated on her hand as angry blisters formed and raw, red skin surfaced, the pain like needles of fire piercing her flesh. Her eyes watered, smearing her eyeshadow as she swallowed a gasp, glancing back at Simon, who remained eerily still.

A piercing ringtone disrupted the tense silence from the bedroom, catching her off guard. She recognized the tune and sprinted back to pick up in time. The sudden noise also stole Simon's attention as he grinned while keeping his gaze on the wall.

Kota ran up to the bed and shook her bag upside down until her phone tumbled out. Before it could touch the pillow below, she caught it and answered the call.

Immediately, Emily's voice sliced through the air. "Kota, are you alright?"

The two embarked on a serious conversation about Kota's situation. Not one to admit defeat, she stared at her scared hands and thought.

Of course there still might be something I can try.

She burrowed through the contents that lay atop the bed. "Come on, where is it?"

"What do you mean you're trapped? Is he holding you somewhere?" Emily continued.

Tears blurred Kota's vision as the faint sound of creaking floorboards inched closer. Her breath hitched, her phone almost slipping from her sweaty palm as she turned around, coming face to face with Simon's looming figure.

"Listen to me. I'm on my way, but right now you need to hang up and call the police," Emily's voice rang out.

Faster than a flash, he swiped the phone from her hands and threw it against the wall. Fragments of glass that scattered across the floor. Not one to be taken down easily, Kota searched her pockets for a hidden weapon.

"You're so feeble, unable to put up a fight. Pathetic," Simon scoffed, towering over Kota, his eyes filled with malice, feeding off her terror.

Seizing an opportunity, Kota delivered a swift knee to Simon's stomach, causing him to bend forward in pain. In a split second, she followed up with a powerful kick to his face, sending him crashing to the ground with a thud.

"I knew you weren't Simon anymore," she said, pulling out a can of potent pepper spray from her pocket.

Simon, his nose bleeding profusely, pleaded with her, his voice filled with desperation. "No, please don't do—"

Before he could finish, she unleashed a spray of incapacitating mist into his face.

A shrill cry of agony echoed through the room as Kota leapt over him, her singular focus on reaching the exit. But as she slid the keycard into the slot, Boris was right there to thrust the door open with commanding vigor, blocking her escape.

"Looks like someone can use a helping hand," he said, stepping into the house with a chilling air of superiority.

Once again, at the Hilltown massacre site, Emily limped as quickly as her injured body allowed, retracing her steps to the nearest bus stop. Michael felt her presence once again as concern clouded his thoughts.

"She is wounded."

Raphael turned his attention to his brethren, clearly sharing his concern. "The mortal?" he inquired, searching for confirmation.

"Yes. I lost track of her when the stain emerged," Michael confirmed, responsibility weighing heavily upon him.

"Well, that could pose a problem," Raphael mused thoughtfully, his focus reverting to the relentless battle unfolding before them. As his hand extended, the emerald light erupted, conjuring the majestic Halberd pole. "Be cautious, Gabriel. This could very well be a trap."

Gabriel, his angelic countenance etched with wisdom, considered Raphael's words. "You may be right. Perhaps it is wise for Michael to return to his post."

Unexpectedly, Victor appeared behind the archangel and placed a hand on his shoulder. In an instant, as if obeying an invisible force, Michael found himself kneeling on the ground, burdened by an unseen weight.

"What sorcery is this?" Michael questioned, incredulous and bewildered by the overwhelming power exerted upon him.

The Halberd pole gleamed like an emerald gem as Raphael swung it towards the hell spawn. Just as the blade on the side of the weapon was poised to strike, Victor vanished before Raphael's eyes, only to reappear silently behind him. The attack was abruptly halted by Gabriel's swift action as he thrust the golden pike into the demon's unprotected back. A surge of energy seeped from Victor's eyes, a momentary display of the pain he felt.

The sensation caught the creature by surprise. Haines' energy was clearly fading, leaving him vulnerable. Pulling the weapon from his seared flesh, he winced, feeling the burn scorching his palms.

Raphael confessed with a heavy sigh, "Our weapons seem futile against him."

"We have one remaining gambit," Gabriel proclaimed, his eyes shimmering with an ethereal radiance.

He raised the Halberd pole high above his head and summoned a beckoning glow in the darkening sky. Raphael mirrored his companion's actions, hoisting the golden pike aloft. Together, their weapons created an enigmatic vortex, a gateway to an otherworldly power. The sky howled with the fury of a storm, accompanying several lightning strikes which electrified the angelic arsenal, charging them for one final assault.

Victor grinned, his focus set on Michael, his voice brimming with sinister resolve. "Cease this resistance or watch as I pulverize your precious warrior."

"We cannot afford to let you triumph," Raphael maintained.

"Michael understands that," Gabriel interjected.

As anticipation intensified, their weapons ignited with an incandescent torrent of electricity. Suddenly, within the heart of the swirling vortex, vivid white and green sparks began to dance in harmonious fusion. They coiled around one another, building up an immense reservoir of power, until finally, they unleashed a cataclysmic blast, aiming directly at Victor.

When the smoke and ashes finally settled, the angels surveyed the battlefield, searching for any trace of the demon. Amidst the swirling darkness, not even a whisper remained of Victor's presence. A renewed sense of hope emerged as Michael rose to his feet.

"We have prevailed," he announced with a triumphant edge. "The battle is won."

Their familiar shades reverted to their natural hues, yet Raphael's iris emitted a delicate wisp of smoke, a testament to the energy he had expended. With a weary expression, he acknowledged the grave reality. "That exertion depleted us greatly. If we are to stand a chance against Lucifer, we must return to Heaven to replenish our power."

Michael looked up at the heavens, his voice laced with both longing and determination. "Yes, my brother, we are acutely aware of that fact. Yet, we cannot access the solace of Heaven until our mission is fulfilled."

Miles away, in the safety of Bayshore Roundhouse, Victor stood before Haines, enclosed within a protective shield of pulsating energy. He felt a mix of surprise and satisfaction at his own survival.

"I'm still alive," he said, relieved by Haines's presence.

"You see, I told you the temporary boost would be just enough for our plan to come to fruition," Haines explained knowingly. "Boris and the others have already made our rendezvous, and the arrival of the one called Emily is imminent."

"Excellent," Victor remarked, relishing the moment. "It is time for me to bring Lucifer up to speed."

Haines interjected, a shrewdness gleaming in his eyes, "But not until she awakens her dormant powers."

Later, in the illuminated kitchen of David's house, he stood by the sturdy wooden table adorned with an array of napkins and paper plates. His gaze fixated on these mundane objects, his imagination yearning for them to come alive under his telekinetic control. But alas, his efforts yielded only frustration as a throbbing headache reverberated through his skull, accompanied by a crimson trickle of blood escaping his nose. Defeated, he collapsed into the nearby chair, cradling his pounding head.

"I made a branch sway with my mind. Surely, I can unleash this power upon these inanimate objects," David muttered, his voice fueled with determination.

Minutes slipped away as he continued to fixate on the stationary items before him. His vision blurred, yielding to exhaustion that began to envelop him. Fighting to remain conscious, he battled against the ravages of the virus coursing through his veins. Yet, his strength waned, and he surrendered to the insidious grip of fatigue.

Suddenly, a voice intruded upon his waking world, piercing through the fog of his fatigue. It was the voice of Victor, mocking his futile attempts at control. Startled, David jolted upright as if shaken awake from a terrifying nightmare. It was at that point where the napkins and paper plates on the table stirred, defying gravity's pull. They danced through the air for a second before cascading onto the floor. An overwhelmed David gasped for breath, his heart racing at the sight before him. "I did it," he whispered, awe-struck by his newfound power.

While the storm raged outside, its thunderous roar swallowing the surrounding city, a sudden darkness eclipsed David's triumph. The power succumbed to the fury of nature, plunging him into an abyss of shadows. With arms still splayed across the table's surface, he battled against the oppressive darkness that cloaked the room, searching for solace in familiar shapes and contours. But what he found was far from ordinary—instead of his hand's silhouette, a monstrous claw loomed before him. Panic surged through his veins as he questioned the limits of his imagination. Was this a sinister trick played upon him? Fear took hold, compelling him to flee from the chair in fear of the impending horrors that threatened to befall him.

Back at the hotel, the flickering lights revealed a horrific scene. In the living room, Kota, her vibrant spirit dimmed by the cruel twist of fate, was bound to a weathered wooden chair. Duct tape bound her ankles, wrists, and stomach, ensnaring her in a web of captivity. Vulnerable and desperate, she strained against her restraints, her body yearning for release. Standing ominously behind her were Kyle and Simon, their presence a haunting reminder of the torment she endured.

In the midst of this sinister tableau, doubt riddled Kyle's mind. The burden of his actions pressed upon his conscience, shattering the veil of villainy that once cloaked him. Unease knit his brow as he remained transfixed, immobile in the face as blood began to seep from his nostrils, a visible sign of internal conflict. But the torment didn't cease there, for his left eye mirrored the bleeding, staining his cheek with a disturbing conjunction of scarlet hues.

"Come on, man, clean yourself off," Simon urged, his voice filled with excitement.

Through a slender crack in the blinds that covered the windows, Boris caught a glimpse of a vibrant yellow taxi pulling up in front of the house. He took a deep, steadying breath, preparing himself for the impending event about to unfold.

On shaky feet, Emily entered the house. She scanned the room and discovered Boris and the others, standing like statues in the pall of a faint light. However, before she had a chance to take in her surroundings fully, Victor materialized behind her, his grip firm and unyielding.

"Hey, I have this under control!" Boris yelled. He wanted to reassure Emily that there was no cause for concern. But his plea fell on deaf ears as Victor guided Emily forward, her body pressed against Kota's, who sat bound in a chair.

On her knees, Emily peered up at her restrained sister, her pleading eyes tainted with a mixture of fear and confusion. Despair dripped from her voice as she implored her captors for mercy, "Please, why are you doing this?"

Victor's visage hardened, his expression devoid of empathy. With a chilling calmness, he declared, "You're going to help us by unlocking the hidden powers within you."

"What are you talking about?" Emily's voice quivered as she struggled to make sense of the unfolding nightmare.

Boris shifted uneasily, struggling to find the right words. "Unfortunately, there seems to be only one known way to awaken those powers."

Emily's glare darted back to the distressed scientist. She could tell he didn't want to be there. He didn't want to be involved in what would happen next. She could see his muscles shake. As she tried to understand him, Simon produced a pocketknife, its silver blade glinting in the dim light. With a cruel resolve, he yanked Kota's head back by her hair, the knife's cold touch grazing her delicate skin.

As her sister's pained howls echoed through the room, Emily's heart twisted with a painful mixture of fear and determination. She made a desperate attempt to intervene to protect her sister from the impending harm. But Victor's strength proved insurmountable as he forcefully pushed her back down to the ground, a silent warning to stay put.

"It's simple," the creature retorted. "You know what we want. Show us that you can harness these powers on your own, or we'll be forced to do things our way."

A fierce defiance appeared in Emily's eyes as she mustered the strength to challenge their assertions. "I am not special in any way. I do not possess any kind of extraordinary power."

At that moment, Emily's gaze locked with Kota's, tearful eyes meeting in a melancholic exchange. However, as Emily's tears fell from her eyes, a mesmerizing purplish hue shimmered within each drop, an inexplicable phenomenon that left Kota bewildered.

Caught in the intensity of the situation, Victor exchanged a knowing glance with Simon, issuing a silent command. A malevolent grin spread across Simon's face as he brandished the pocket knife, his hands trembling with a twisted sort of excitement. "It's been fun, babe," he taunted before slicing Kota's throat.

The world shuttered, shaking violently as Emily's grief and rage manifested into an unstoppable force. A surge of power coursed through her veins, bursting forth explosively. Simon, caught in the maelstrom, was launched backward, his body crashing into the adjacent wall. The impact inadvertently caused his own pocketknife to pierce through his neck, sealing his fate.

While the house groaned under the strain of Emily's unleashed power, shards of glass erupted from the windows, cascading to the ground below. Violent hues of purple lightning danced around the room, illuminating the chaos that unfolded. Emily's eyes darted around her surroundings, her newfound power pulsating within her. And yet, amidst the destruction, her gaze inevitably fell back upon Kota's lifeless body.

12

REVELATION

"We may have vanquished the demon, yet the lingering presence of darkness persists," Michael asserted, his eyes glued on his brother of trickery with unyielding intensity.

Gabriel's features knotted as his knuckles turned white. "I have explained countless times that he snuck up on me. Stole enough of my power to render me unconscious."

"I do not care for your excuses, Gabriel. What concerns me now is the eerie calm that has befallen upon us," Michael declared, his voice tinged with an ominous tone.

Refusing to stand by and watch, Raphael interjected, "Enough! The vile creature has returned to which it came, and we must unite in our quest to track down Lucifer."

In an instant, a formidable force surged through the land, threatening to overwhelm the angels. They recognized this energy and exchanged knowing glances. Michael gazed skyward.

"Something is amiss," he said. "This power - it belongs to Emily."

"That means we have fulfilled our orders, right?"

Michael's expression soured, his voice heavy with unease. "This energy is veiled in sorrow and despair."

Straightaway, a set of shimmering wings took shape on his back. They emitted a searing light until he blurred out of sight.

Meanwhile, a powerful storm whipped through the county hospital, demolishing windows like fragile glass ornaments. Its forceful gusts even knocked out the electricity, plunging the entire building into darkness. Luckily, the hospital's backup generator rumbled to life, sending a current of electricity through the veins of the institution.

As the lights flickered back on, the once-silent hallways came alive. The sounds of beeping monitors, humming ventilators, and rhythmic puffs of breathing machines filled the air. Doctors and nurses, their faces etched with determination and urgency, scurried through the corridors to attend to their patients with a newfound sense of relief.

In one room, the machine monitoring Caleb's vital signs indicated a gradual slowdown in his rapid heart rate. His eyes fluttered open, blinking away the remnants of sleep, only to meet the gaze of a startled nurse who had rushed into his room. Recognizing the urgency, she wasted no time and called for the doctor, her voice tinged with a mix of surprise and hope.

Back at the once serene hotel, Emily crawled with resolution towards Kota's body. However, her focus was abruptly diverted by a crackling sound emanating from the now desolate front lawn. The presence of the demon eclipsed her attention, its malicious aura seeping into every crevice of her shattered reality. In a moment of eerie calm, she rose to her feet, moving with purpose down the sparking hallway.

Outside, a wounded Victor loomed over Boris, whose body was littered with deep lacerations. A wicked grin adorned his face as he spoke. "I'm pleased to say I no longer have any use for you."

With his back pinned against the earthy gravel beneath a vibrant tree, Boris couldn't believe his ears as he cautiously asked, "What? You mean, I'm free to go?"

Victor's smirk widened, an air of superiority radiating from him like a sinister aura. "Absolutely," he retorted, his words laced with disdain, "Enjoy life as a wanted man."

An ember of anger burst into a flame on Boris's face; his features contorted with fury. "Oh, this ain't over, you son of a—"

Suddenly, the air echoed with the sharp report of a gunshot, a bullet finding its mark in the upper back of the diabolical creature. Its eyes widened in shock, its glare diving to the wound where tendrils of black smoke rose.

"You finally see what you're capable of. Yet you shoot me with a gun?" it questioned, turning around, expecting to confront Emily standing nearby.

To its astonishment, however, its inky pools found no one at first. Only after casting a glance toward the darkened corner of the hallway, did its gaze meet the still-aimed gun. A mix of surprise and realization washed over him like a chilling wave.

"I see; you're in denial." The creature's words carried a note of bitter resignation as it disappeared right before Emily's very eyes.

Fearful that the authorities would soon converge on the crime scene, Boris fought to push himself to his feet, his wounded body protesting every movement. Emily, however, had other plans. Stepping through the remnants of her once-secure window, she emerged into the raging storm. She held a firm grip on the gun, leveled against Boris's head.

Her heart raced within her chest, each beat more erratic than the last, drowning out the world around her. "Give me one good reason why I shouldn't put a bullet in your skull," she uttered.

Distraught, the scientist sought redemption. "Please, I didn't have a choice," he pleaded, his voice laced with remorse. "That thing you shot, it's a demon, and it threatened my whole family."

A bitter scoff escaped Emily's lips, her eyes narrowing in disbelief. "Okay, first off, demons aren't real," she said. "They're just things people make up to excuse their actions. Secondly, just because your family is in danger doesn't give you the right to destroy mine."

She stood in silence for a moment, contemplating what she would do. Her finger teetered on the precipice of the trigger with trembling hands. She squeezed her eyes shut, blocking out the reality unfolding before her as she braced for an irreversible choice.

But the very second her finger began to exert pressure on the trigger, salvation arrived in the form of a timely intervention. Michael appeared beside her, his hand reaching out to grab the pistol. A deafening sound crackled as a bullet found its place in the vast expanse of the sky above. His steady gaze met Emily's searching eyes, an unspoken understanding passing between them,

"Trust me, no good will come from this," his voice resonated with calm authority.

Memories flooded to the forefront of her mind like a streaming waterfall, yet, calmness overtook her. "You're the guy who took that picture for me at Burney Falls. A friend of mine ran into you at the coffee shop, and I know I saw you the other day when I almost got hit by that crazy driver. Why are you following me?"

"My powers have waned substantially during my sojourn on Earth. Were it not for this decline, I would have abided in the celestial realm," Michael explained.

"And now you're going to talk to me about powers? This isn't some kind of superhero film."

"No, this is your life. Whether you choose to believe me or not, I am the archangel Michael," he declared. "I have been tasked with the sole purpose of protecting you until such time you awaken these hidden abilities."

Doubt lingered in Emily's gaze, her mind grappling with the inexplicable nature of it all. But then, in a moment of illumination, she recalled her uncle's journal, the words etched upon its pages by his trembling hand. She remembered his accounts of the man with the glowing eyes and how he felt in his presence.

"It's you," she whispered, her voice a mixture of awe and wonder. "You're the one who told my uncle to watch over me."

The archangel's gaze softened, remorse etched across his features. "Something big happened, and I had to check it out. I thought I was doing the right thing," he admitted with a touch of regret.

Rage and resentment coursed through Emily's veins as the weight of her uncle's perceived madness settled heavily upon her soul. Her voice wavered as she confronted him, her tone a mix of sorrow and accusation. "You're the reason why people thought he was crazy."

Out of the blue, a patrol car jerked to a stop at the curb, its flashing lights painting the street in pulses of red and blue. Both Captain Javier and Officer Cortez emerged from the vehicle, already surveying the scene.

"This looks serious," Cortez remarked, his hand resting on his holster.

"Stay alert," Javier ordered.

As they approached, Javier directed his focus toward Emily, who stood almost like an empty shell of her former self.

"Hello there, remember us?" Javier asked, trying to offer solace amidst the disarray.

Emily nodded, her eyes still filled with defeat and unshed tears. She couldn't understand why her sister had been targeted. She didn't quite understand what happened to herself back there either, despite Michael's explanation.

"Wait, I called about two hours ago. Why did it take you so long to get here?"

Baffled, Javier and Cortez looked back at each other. "Ma'am, we got the call not ten minutes ago," Javier explained.

"W...what?"

"Please calm down," Cortez interjected.

"I called from Hilltown, you do the math!"

"Look, we're sorry we're late, if that's the case, but right now I need you to recount what transpired here?" Cortez said.

"They came for her," she began, her voice wavering. "These men... they came after Kota and... and they killed her."

"Who's Kota?"

"My sister. She was my sister," Emily responded, her voice low, racked with guilt as she limped toward the steps near the hotel.

Javier, beginning to grasp the situation, affirmed, "You understand we need to conduct an investigation, right?"

Fatigued and battered, Emily gave them the go ahead, taking a seat in front of the door.

The policemen commenced their examination, cautiously peering through the shattered window. Javier contemplated entering through the narrow opening, but Cortez intervened, approaching Emily instead.

"Hey," Javier whispered, "let's go."

Once inside the disorienting spectacle of a room on a count of the lights blinking on and off in rapid succession, the lieutenant discovered Simon's body pinned to the wall with a savage gash across his throat. Shocked and disturbed, he took a step back, uttering words of sorrow and regret.

"Oh no. I knew this kid. He had plans to join the academy after he finished school," he said in earshot of the captain.

Meanwhile, Javier stood over Kyle's body, noting the motionless figure before him. "We have another victim who appears to have bled out," he announced, kneeling beside the teenager. "You must be Kota."

Officer Cortez walked up behind him, catching sight of the body. "You know, it's always unsettling to find a victim with their eyes still wide open," he remarked, unable to tear his gaze away from the haunting stare of the deceased.

Captain Javier rose to his feet, closely observing his officer. "So, what are we thinking?"

He mulled over his response before crafting an official reply. "I don't know," he said. "It looks like an explosion went off, doesn't it?"

The two took a look at the extensive damage around them. The walls were marred with deep, jagged cracks, pieces of plaster and brick littering the floor. The windows had been obliterated, shards of glass scattered everywhere, leaving gaping holes where the panes once stood. destruction to the walls and obliterated windows.

"It does and my money is on Emily since she's the only one who walked away."

"Hold up. Now, you mentioned that one of them fits our case. Well, I'm still struggling to understand how traces of oak leaves were found in their bloodstream."

"I've heard rumors about a certain substance derived from the oak tree that can affect the frontal cortex," Captain Javier explained, his voice laced with an air of mystery. "I believe we are dealing with a puppet master pulling the strings behind these events. For now, we need to summon the crime scene unit and secure this area," he concluded.

Emily continued to sit beside the exterior when her phone rang out. Primed to silence it, she noticed the caller ID displayed the hospital's name. This sparked a hopeful glimmer as she eagerly picked up.

"Hello?"

"Hi, is this Emily?" a voice on the other end asked.

"Yes, what's going on?"

"I'm a nurse at the community hospital. I wanted to inform you that Caleb regained consciousness a little while ago."

"Seriously? That's incredible!" she said, brimming with gratitude.

As soon as the call ended, Emily stood, wiping away more tears from her eyes. Elated, she looked to the heavens, holding her hands close to her heart. "This news makes me very happy, but if you are real, can you please bring Kota back?" she said underneath her breath.

Before long, the officers exited the building with an update of their assessment. "This is now officially a crime scene," Javier stated. "It's clear there's more to the story. So, are you going to tell us what happened in there?"

"I told you."

"No, not all attacks end in such destruction. If you tell us, or even who you might have crossed paths with since this isn't the first time you were targeted, it would go a long way to bringing an end to all of this," Cortez added.

"I haven't done anything to anyone," she replied, a hint of disbelief mingling with her exhaustion. "I only got to town a few days ago."

"In any case, it would be wise for you to find another place to stay for a while," Javier advised. "I suggest remaining in the vicinity in case further questions arise."

"No problem. I don't think I want to stay here anymore. There's just one thing I need to grab."

The captain gestured at the door, giving her the okay to enter the hotel. Cortez followed a few feet behind. After entering, Emily went right to the bedroom, where her dresser, adorned with a mirror, revealed traces of smudged eyeshadow on her face.

With trembling hands, she wiped it away and took a seat on the stool in front of the dresser. She heard the officers' footsteps as they neared the room, prompting her to reach forward and slowly open the top drawer. Amidst a collection of clothes lay a polished black rock with a ring in the center, connected to a slender gold chain. Emily stared at the pendant, recalling the night she had lent it to her sister—a cherished memory now tarnished by tragedy.

It was right after Kota had a nightmare about the hit and run, which had claimed our mother's life, that she woke up with a broken heart. She sat at the edge of her bed when a flash of lightning illuminated the room through the window next to the dresser. She jumped over the subsequent thunder, but it was the screeching sound muffled within the loud bang that had truly frightened her. In a panic, Kota had gotten out of bed and ran for the door, making a beeline for my room.

"What's wrong, Kota?" I asked, waking up after she had turned on the light.

She told me she thought someone was inside the house. That it might be the man who got mom. I promised her that there was no one out to get us. And I know hearing it must have comforted her because she leaned down and gave me a hug.

"I still get them too," I told her, giving her a one-armed hug in return. It was at that moment that she removed her necklace. "You should have the whole pendant for extra good luck when you go take pictures around the world. Plus, maybe it'll help keep you from forgetting me."

As she went to hand it over to me, I told her to keep it. While apart, it held much more good luck than having it as one because the space in between wouldn't be as great.

She accepted my offer and held the necklace in her palm. I guess I couldn't sell it though because she called me out on it.

"What matters is that you do. You're the one who goes to church every Sunday," I said.

"Yeah," Kota began, putting the necklace back on. "It's where Simon and I first met."

"I remember," I replied, yawning as I was ready to go back to sleep. "Okay, goodnight, Ko. I'll see you in the morning."

A single palm to the door snapped Emily back into the here and now. "Hey," Cortez began. "Did you get what you wanted?"

Emily grabbed the pendant and stood up. "Yeah, I'm all set." But as she turned around, she noticed a half-crumpled sheet of paper laying by her pillow.

"Good, cause time is of the essence, and we don't have all day," Cortez interjected.

However, she had become more focused on the recent discovery. Aware that it must have been left by Kota, each approaching step took massive strength. Still, she persisted and unwrinkled the note. On it, were just four words: Simon. Bloody nose. Virus?

"You coming or what?" Cortez asked, cracking the door open.

Without any more delays, Emily exited the room and made a beeline to Captain Javier. "There's a virus going around, and you don't seem to be doing anything about it," she proclaimed.

"Excuse me? Ma'am, I assure you—"

"A lot of good that's done."

"Look, there are steps we have to take. Things we have to figure out, such as its origin or strain."

"Well, I'm pretty sure it isn't airborne. You should probably hunt down that Boris guy I heard about on the news."

"Boris? Who, Linderman? You think he's—"

"No, I don't think; I know it. That man was here, and he coerced Simon into killing..." Emily paused for a moment. "Just find him, please."

She then proceeded to exit the main lobby and walked up the hill to the nearest bus stop.

Meanwhile, at his house, David remained seated in the chair. Weakened from the vast amount of energy he had expended; he could hardly keep his head up. To his surprise, a knock at the door sounded through the abode.

"Come on, Dave, open up," demanded his cousin.

Although he didn't receive a response, Jason proceeded to open the door, unaware that the handle had already started to twist before his grasp.

"Dave are you here?" he asked, closing the door behind him.

"In here," the scientist said.

"Hey, my unit's on the way to investigate a crime scene," he informed, entering the kitchen. "I tried to call you since it's not too far from here, but you didn't pick up. Then, I got a call from the hospital. Evidently, Caleb woke up a little while ago. I'm heading there now to see if he can shed some light on the identity of the culprit."

"You do that. I'm gonna take a nap," he urged, resting his head on the table.

Satisfied to see his cousin unharmed, Jason made his way out the door. After wrapping his hand around the knob, he felt a sharp pinch in his palm and retracted. What he saw left him uneasy. There were deep jagged marks around both the edges and the keyhole. With David too exhausted to move, Jason proceeded to lock the door before shutting it behind him.

At the same time, Emily ventured up to the reception desk at the hospital. "Hello, I'm here to see Caleb," she said.

"Oh, you must be Emily. Come on, I'll take you to him."

"No need. I've been coming here a lot." As she took a step forward, a question dawned on her. One that hadn't crossed her mind until now. One that made her a little wary of the circumstances. This prompted her to journey back to the desk. "Uhm, sorry, I was wondering how you knew to call me?"

"Well, your name being the last thing he spoke before going into a coma, the doctor felt it would be a good idea to contact you. Especially since he doesn't seem to have any family listed."

"But how did you find me?"

"Dear, the digital evolution has exploded. All I had to do was type his name in social media and after a few scrolls, I found this lovely post about you. It was really sweet."

Emily, not knowing how to react, remained still.

He made a post. What did it say?

"Is there anything else?" the nurse asked.

Lost for words, she just turned and ventured down the hall. Eager to learn what he said, she took out her phone and logged into "Chatterbox." Immediately, she noticed a flurry of activity on her news feed. Friends had posted status updates, shared photos, and invited her to virtual events. She even had several new friend requests. It had been some time since she last went online, but still wasn't expecting so much news.

Ignoring the new posts coming in, she navigated toward the search bar and typed in Caleb. From there, it was only a matter of time before she found it. The post in question.

So there I was, nervous just walking into a coffee shop, barely holding myself together. You know, completely outta my element. But then came this remarkable moment. I mean, it took bumping into her, nearly making her spill her coffee. But there you were with your brazen smile, so warm and full of life, making me feel safe and at ease. Your kindness was like a beacon of light cutting through the fog of my nervousness. Thank you, Emily.

She sniffled a bit before putting her phone away and entering the patient's room. As soon as she saw him lying in bed, his face pale and drawn, she lost her composure and ran over to him. She brushed her finger along a thin layer of stubble on his face.

When he opened his eyes, the dark circles beneath them accentuated his weariness. The world around them seemed to fade, leaving just the two of them in that singular, profound moment.

"I'm so happy you're okay." She leaned over and wrapped her arms around him.

He returned her gesture with a mere ghost of an embrace, his arms resting on her back without any real pressure.

After lying back down, Caleb's gaze settled upon the doorway. In his peripheral vision, he saw the nurse exiting the room. But something about her movement seemed... off. Through the haze of his fatigue, he could have sworn her feet weren't quite touching the ground. It was like she glided out. He blinked hard in an attempt to clear his vision. When he looked again, the nurse was nowhere to be found, filling him with a vague sense of unease. Had he imagined it?

He returned his attention back to Emily. "Are you... alright?" he asked, pushing the strange image to the back of his mind. "I-I saw that... limp."

"Yeah, it's nothing," she said, brushing away tears from her face.

While staring into each other's eyes, she felt a lump in her throat. Without looking away, Caleb gently wiped a tear from her eye.

"That guy you were worried about," she began, holding his hand. He gave her a concerned look but remained silent. "He's claiming to be an angel. He showed up when these psychos came after me. I think they're musicians, though, cause they just vanished into thin air."

"Oh, Em," he leaned forward and kissed her forehead. "I admit I... was concerned. But now... I know it was... for nothing. Michael, he appeared... before me, too."

Emily pulled away from him, shaking her head in disbelief. "No. I don't care what that man says. If angels are real, then that means God is too. And if He's real, why is Kota dead?"

13

STRIFE

Lucifer, confined to a wooden bench outside a modest restaurant, contemplated his next move. Unable to conceal his anger, his fist rained down upon the furniture, shattering off a corner that scattered onto the ground. His eyes, laden with the burdens of past deeds, fixated on the bursting lights throughout the restaurant. Then, as if guided by an unseen force, he looked ahead and closed his eyes, sensing a presence before him.

"So, you haven't been caught by the angels yet, after all," he murmured.

In response, the creature stepped forward to reveal news of great importance. "I've come to inform you that the sinner has awakened her powers."

A perceptible smile tugged at the corner of Lucifer's face as he opened his eyes, reveling in the triumph of this revelation. "I know," he admitted. "I felt the marvelous burst of power a little while ago. But it also felt like she didn't achieve it on her own." He turned his glare upward to meet the creature's eyes. "Care to enlighten me?"

Well aware of the delicate balance between deception and loyalty, the fiend treaded on thin ice, carefully orchestrating his response.

"I wouldn't know. This is the first I've been able to track her," he deceived. "We must act now if you wish to seize her power."

A hint of intrigue danced across Lucifer's features, his mind pondering the potential of this newfound power. "Or perhaps this sinner may prove to be an ally on our path to taking down that treacherous Roamer," he mused, his voice low and husky.

Perplexed, Victor sought clarification. "Roamer?" he questioned, trying to hide the tremor in his voice.

The devil's eyes narrowed, his ire resurfacing as he contemplated the source of his current predicament. "Yes. Surely you remember the vile insect that encompassed you in that gargoyle shell?" he questioned. "That monstrous being was also the architect of the war in heaven."

"And do you truly believe this sinner will aid you in bringing down such a formidable adversary? It seems preposterous," it suggested.

Lucifer, ever the enigma, smirked, his confidence unshaken. "Perhaps," he responded, his voice carrying a hint of mystery. "Only time will tell."

Meanwhile, amidst the vibrant atmosphere of More Mellows bar, a haven for those seeking solace and connection, Celsey found herself perched on a solitary barstool. Her eyes fixated upon the dynamic glow of the news channel playing on one of the smaller televisions. A myriad of messages popped up across her phone's screen, a testament to the thriving love lives of her cherished companions, Ashley and Rachael.

Startled from her reverie by the bartender's inquiry, she placed her phone back into her pocket, a brief respite from the digital hum of relationships on display.

"Alright, what'll it be?" the bartender asked.

"Oh, uhm, I'll try a floating gummy bear."

As the barman placed a glass of rum on the counter, the pub fell into an all-pervading quiet as a news reporter's voice resonated through the airwaves. The name Kyle Heem echoed in her head like a thunderclap. Celsey brought her hand to her quivering lips and formed a fragile barricade against the shock that reflected in her wide, searching eyes.

Compelled to act, she dug into her purse, clutched her Galaxy S, and zipped out. After reaching her vehicle, she got in and dialed a friend's number. As she prepared to back out of the parking spot, a young woman's voice echoed through the device.

"Celsey? What's wrong? I thought we were done for the day," the voice said.

"Kyle's dead," she retorted, her voice strained with sorrow. "And I am willing to bet Dave is behind it. I need you to be the Seeker once more and dig up any dirt you can find on him. Something doesn't feel right."

"Whatever you need." The Seeker's response exuded unconditional loyalty. But for Celsey, resolving this tragedy became her sole purpose. Harshly brushing away a tear, she steeled herself for the journey ahead.

I'll get justice for you, Kyle. I promise, Celsey declared to herself with steadfast determination.

Elsewhere, within the sterile walls of the hospital, Emily leaned up against the cold brick wall. "I didn't expect you to be the religious type."

Caleb, still recovering, but breathing easier, replied, "Trust me... I never believed... in supernatural beings. That changed when I... I woke up. He appeared. No one else saw him," he paused, taking a deep breath. "My fear... vanished. Instead, I felt peace, like nothing... nothing was unconquerable."

Emily raised an eyebrow with bitterness tainting her words. "He's also pretty good at ruining people's lives."

In an abrupt ballet of luminescence and obscurity, the wellness enclave's lighting wavered, projecting transient brilliance across the space. Caleb's gaze anchored on his partner, yet from the periphery of his vision, he beheld the resplendent archangel Michael materialize behind her. A profound, ethereal warmth enveloped Emily in a serene embrace. She whipped around to behold the formidable celestial warrior.

His gaze bore down upon her with a message of absolutes. "Your uncle made his choice."

"You could have left him out of it," she shot back.

"You do not understand. We had received word that Lucifer had been set free. My priorities shifted momentarily, but still I ensured your safety."

As a means to halt the bickering, Caleb raised a hand, forming a silent "T" to signal a pause. "Hold up," he interjected. "Are you saying... the devil is... walking amongst us?"

Emily, her stare unwavering, replied in disbelief, "According to the stories I heard from Kota, the devil would bring about the end."

Before they could continue, a knock at the door disrupted the course of the conversation. It was none other than the detective entering the room. A single fluorescent light's erratic sputter stole his focus as he shut the door. It wasn't long until it settled back into harmony with the other lights in the room. A wave of apprehension tugged at him, leaving an unsettling sensation of being under scrutiny. He swallowed hard, reminding himself to push past the creeping paranoia and maintain his focus.

"I'm Detective Jason Silverton," he said, his keen eyes darting around the room, absorbing the details with the precision of a seasoned detective. "Are you Mr. Lansworth?"

"Yes."

Jason's glare soon settled on Michael, standing stoically in the corner. Beneath the mundane surface, he couldn't shake off a lingering doubt.

"Hold on," he said. With a quivering finger, he pointed toward the angel. "Isn't he the guy?"

"Oh, no," Caleb said, shaking his head.

Unable to keep his focus, Jason's attention drifted to the dark recesses of the room. A fleeting and elusive specter seemed to haunt the edges of his vision, a figment of his own imagination rather than a corporeal presence. It danced about, taunting his senses with its intangible existence.

The wraith-like shape eluded him, looming just out of reach like a puzzle waiting to be solved. It teased and toyed with his mind, its form adapting and shifting on a whim. It was a manifestation of his own paranoia, an intangible reminder that not everything could be easily explained. Though his intuition of scrutiny intensified with every passing second, he fought against the urge to surrender to his growing unease.

Plagued by an imagined watcher, he remained steadfast in his ability to untangle the web of mysteries embedded within the chamber's dimensions. It took Caleb's voice, asking if he was alright, to bring him out of his paranoid state. He took a deep breath and calmed himself as he turned back toward his possible witness, who was waving his arms to get his attention.

"Sorry, yes," he began, answering the posed question. "I thought I was going to sneeze. So, where were we?"

"I was trying to tell you that this man just resembles the guy from the picture."

"He sure does. Anyway, I came here to gather a description of the assailant who attacked you."

Seizing an opportunity to converse with Emily, Michael positioned himself before her, securing her focus. Aware of the detective's presence, he suggested they continue their discussion in the hall. She rolled her eyes and looked over to her partner, expecting support. However, he returned her gaze and assured her, "It's okay. I'll be fine."

Out of excuses, she stood up from the chair. But her legs gave way, forcing her to collapse. Michael caught her in the nick of time, his eyes glowing a faint, translucent sapphire light. As she lay in his arms, he noticed the blood-soaked cloth wrapped around her ankle. "This could be serious."

These words clung to Caleb's ears, beckoning his concern. "Is she okay?"

"Yes," Emily retorted. "I'm fine."

"We need to get this taken care of right away." Michael continued to hold her in his arms as he opened the door. Upon entering the hallway, to the human eye, he appeared to be a young doctor, his features sharp and reassuring, pushing a woman who sat slumped in a wheelchair, her hair streaked with silver weaving through once jet-black curls. Her leg, encased in a cumbersome cast, jutted out with a bright blue crutch propped alongside it.

As he approached an unoccupied room, a woman, her face masked in worry, stepped into his path just outside the waiting area. Her eyes, red-rimmed from lack of sleep or tears, looked up at him imploringly.

"Doctor, please," she began. "My brother's undergoing cardiac surgery right now. Can you tell me anything? How's he doing?"

Michael paused and looked upon her with a gentle, reaffirming demeanor. "Your brother, Joseph, is in good hands," he said. "The best surgeon we have is with him right now."

The woman clung to his words, though weariness still etched her features. "Thank you. It's been so hard waiting..."

"Yip, yip," his patient blurted, glaring upward with sharp hawk-like eyes behind a pair of reading glasses perched on her nose. She clutched the armrests with tense-fisted intensity, her fingertips showing slight hints of arthritis with each taut grip, tapping a staccato rhythm of irritation.

"Apologies, but I really must be going."

At last, he entered the empty room and laid Emily on the bed. Not wasting a moment, he spread the blinds across the window and readied himself to call upon Raphael. He took a step back when he saw Emily's puzzled expression.

"Yip, yip, what am I—a feisty elderly woman?"

"In the eyes of Ms. Sargeant, yes."

"I could not risk mortal healers seeing me carry you or they may have wanted to do an examination and there is just no time."

"I don't understand. What do you mean, no time?"

Instead of providing more answers, Michael cut off the conversation and called out for his brethren. In a heartbeat, the hands and numerals of the clock on the wall bathed in a leafy tint. Soon, Raphael stood at Michael's side.

"I am here."

"Good," Michael remarked. "I need you to heal Emily so she can begin her training."

His palms shimmered an emerald green hue as he walked up to her. With a mere touch to her shoulder, her wound shone green until it evaporated. Once more, Emily could walk again, but her disbelief only grew.

How is any of this possible?

"It is done," Raphael stated. A brilliant flash of emerald light flooded the room, his majestic wings blurring into motion. They moved so fast that he phased out of sight.

As Emily's strength returned, she slid off the bed.

"If a higher power truly watches over us, then why are psychos lurking at every turn? Why is the world in such bad shape?"

"We are not here to correct human error," Michael asserted, his tone firm yet compassionate.

Emily's voice trembled with emotion as she countered, "Human error? That's all it means to you? The people of Hilltown were slaughtered, and the innocent kids who were blamed took their own lives. Recently, I saw my fair share of monsters, but no evidence of angels."

"One cannot exist without the other," Michael remarked matter-of-factly, his eyes piercing into her soul.

The mention of her past losses filled her with raw, vulnerable pain. "After my mom died in a hit-and-run right in front of Kota, I... I raised her. She was just a kid. If you're an angel, then bring her back to me," she pleaded.

Her hands crackled with small bursts of purple electricity as they came together with interwoven fingers and thumbs planted against one another. Tiny arcs of energy danced between the narrow gaps.

Michael's glare shifted upward, sensing the cracking ceiling before a blinding burst of light engulfed them. Time was of the essence if he wanted to prevent a disaster. He placed a steady hand on Emily's shoulder, and in an instant, vanished from the hospital, leaving only emptiness and unanswered questions.

In a moment, they reemerged in Woodley Park, a verdant oasis embracing the surrounding cityscape. Tall, proud trees reached for the heavens, creating a canopy of. The grass beneath their feet tickled their senses as it swayed in unison, vibrant and full of life. It was a place of solace and serenity, a respite for weary souls.

Emily's world reeled as she materialized in this picturesque haven. Vertigo seized her, causing her legs to waver unsteadily beneath her. She took a cautious step backward, seeking support from the earth beneath her as her mind struggled to grapple with the reality of the situation.

"What did you do?"

Michael stood before her, his countenance serene and full of enigmatic wisdom. "Your emotions were spiraling out of control," he began, his words firm yet calm. "Had I not intervened, the hospital would have become a cataclysmic battleground, consumed by the tempest that raged within you."

Emily sank onto the leaves that danced in the gentle breeze. An overwhelming sense of peace washed over her as the touch of the angel's hand left traces of tranquility. She sobbed, releasing the pent-up anguish that had consumed her.

"There is great evil in this world; I do not deny it," Michael said, his eyes fixed on the horizon where the sun painted the sky in vibrant hues. "Lucifer, the serpent, is the embodiment of this darkness. You have been chosen to vanquish him, armed with the powers I can feel resonating deep within you."

She lifted her tear-stained face to meet the angel while wiping away remnants of her grief. When she spoke, her voice cut through the equanimity of the park. "What do I have to do?"

14

TEMPTATION

Far away from the city's fast-paced energy, an unkempt man maneuvered his vintage '96 Buick LeSabre into the weather-beaten parking lot of a dilapidated Cowboys gas station. The faint hum of the city's ceaseless activities faded into the distance, leaving only the quietly rustling leaves and a hushed stillness that enveloped the location. With measured steps, the man emerged from his vehicle, leaving his wife and young daughter cocooned inside its protective confines. He gravitated upward, entranced by the flashing lights suspended overhead.

Out of nowhere, the creature emerged from the distance and presented itself as a street preacher of sorts. "Excuse me, sir. How do you feel about the impending doom to your planet?" It asked.

"What?!" The man retorted, bewildered by the threat as he removed the nozzle from his car. "Get away from me."

"No problem."

An eerie smirk overtook the preacher's face, staring deep into the man's eyes before departing, leaving behind an air of amusement as he headed inside the small convenience store.

Unbeknownst to the man's wife, who was happily engaging with their daughter inside the car, an unsettling force clouded his mind. In the midst of playing peek-a-boo, she looked up just in time to witness a disturbing sight. She saw her husband drenched in gasoline, holding the customized Zippo lighter with their daughter's handprint and name she got him for their tenth anniversary. She screamed at the top of her lungs and opened the door.

"What on earth are you doing?!"

The sound of her voice jolted the man out of the trance as the dark veins that had consumed his face dissipated, leaving him shocked by the abhorrent act he was about to commit.

Within the confines of the store, the creature whispered under its breath after realizing the absence of any distinct scent in the air.

"Haines, this is undoubtedly your doing," it declared.

"I see nothing escapes your keen perception," the Roamer said, his voice carried by the wind.

"I have delivered your message, so now I'd like you to keep your word and free me from this gargoyle entrapment. Then, if possible, never cross each other again. If Lucifer discovers our collaboration, my fate will be sealed."

"Tell me, what is it about demons? You all consider yourselves to be the darkest threats to the world, yet you are terrified of a single being." Haines began, materializing beside his reluctant ally with crossed arms. "By the way, what's with the new getup? Are you trying to hide from me?"

"No, I'm not that foolish," it said. "I'm just trying out a few tricks."

"Well, for now, you are free to do as you please, but soon, I will require your assistance in another attack on the human, merely to ensure that the previous incident was not a mere fluke," Haines affirmed.

"Are you serious?"

"I am. Which means your true form will have to wait."

Miles away at a quaint cottage nestled amidst the lively backdrop of downtown New York, Boris bolted into his bedroom and pushed the bed away from the wall. In doing so, he revealed a concealed safe embedded within the structure, further fueling his mounting anxiety. With palpable apprehension, he retrieved a weathered wooden weapon reminiscent of the fabled Sword of Freyr, albeit with a damaged handle and worn edges.

"With this, I shall vanquish you, demon," Boris proclaimed.

All of a sudden, a creaking sound emanated from the door, immediately catching his attention. However, his apprehension grew as a familiar voice seeped through the doorway.

"What're you gonna do with that, pop?" Leigh asked, her voice filled with concern.

Not wanting to scare her, Boris spun around, locking eyes with his daughter, who stood in the entrance. Yet, the glimmer in her eyes revealed not anticipation but rather a fear rooted in what her father might be capable of. Rising to his feet, he concealed the broken sword in the inner pocket of his denim jacket, eager to reach her. In response, however, Leigh backed away, the lines of trust and safety blurred in her uncertain gaze.

"You have no reason to be afraid of me, Leigh. You don't know what happened that night, but I assure you, I am innocent," he pleaded.

"We got back home from the sleepover and found Mom... she wasn't moving in the bathroom. I kept calling you again and again, thinking there's gotta be some reason, but you never picked up," Leigh retorted.

"Please, listen to me," he pressed, stepping closer. "There are real monsters out there."

Suddenly, Noah entered the room, positioning himself just behind his sister's protective stance. "We are well aware, Dad," Noah interjected, his voice carrying a sense of accusation. "One of those monsters is standing right in front of us."

"One day, I will prove my innocence to you, but right now, there is something that I have to do."

As he attempted to make a swift exit, both Leigh and Noah converged upon the doorway, adamant about preventing their father from slipping away. Frustrated by their intervention, Boris locked eyes with Leigh, his heart aching at the fractured trust resonating within her gaze. Cursing his circumstances, he adjusted the broken sword concealed inside his denim jacket pocket, contemplating his next move. But before he could execute his plan, both Leigh and Noah resolutely refused to yield, their presence acting as an impregnable barrier.

"You have got to let me go!"

Leigh glanced upward at her older brother, seeking support and validation amidst the uncertainty that befell them. Meeting her gaze, Noah responded, his voice firm and resolute. "The authorities will soon descend upon us. We are ensuring that you do not attempt to evade their pursuit."

His daughter locked eyes with him as she uttered, "I'm sorry, pop. You didn't leave us any choice."

Resolute yet cornered, Boris muttered to himself, despair weighing heavily upon his shoulders, "No, I have to get out of here." Turning his back on his children, he headed towards the window.

As he opened the window, the sound of approaching patrol cars reverberated through the house. His heart sank as he whirled around, sprinting away from his children's sight. He raced down the hallway and dashed into the kitchen, intent on reaching the back door. At the same time, multiple footsteps echoed throughout the house, escalating the tension that filled every crevice of his being.

Desperate to make his escape, Boris flung open the back door and rushed into the yard. However, his fleeting hopes were shattered as he overheard Noah's voice shouting, "He went down the hall!" Determined to evade capture, Boris hastily closed the back door behind him, his movements calculated and quiet as he also turned off his phone.

Peering through the narrow openings of the wired fence, he surveyed his surroundings, his heart pounding in his chest. Two officers, sensing his presence, decided to give chase on foot, their rapid footsteps echoing behind him. Simultaneously, the officers within the house scrambled to their patrol cars, their aim to intercept him down the road. Back within the house, Leigh and Noah fervently watched as the officers sprang into action.

As the adrenaline coursing through their veins subsided, Leigh turned to her older brother and pleaded, her voice betraying an undercurrent of doubt, "Tell me we did the right thing, Noah."

"Of course we did," he said.

Not too far, in Woodley Park, a golden draft rustled nature's quilt, humming with the jubilant tunes of singing birds. Effervescent daffodils, flaunting bright trumpets, and delicate daisies carpeted the lush greenery beneath a canopy of mature trees. A rainbow of butterflies danced around Michael as he bestowed his guidance upon Emily.

"This appeared to be a calm enough place for you to commence your training," he said. "Sit down and close your eyes, allow the breeze to whisper its secrets."

Emily settled herself on tuffs of wild grass, her eyelids fluttering shut. Yet, even in her closed state, her gaze remained fixed on Michael, seeking his wisdom amidst the darkness. As she immersed herself in the calmness surrounding her, Michael's voice floated to her ears like a distant melody.

"Release your fears and doubts," he urged. "Embrace the harmony of nature, for it shall be your guide."

When his guidance began to intertwine with the winds, an intrusive sound cut the tranquility—a vibrating tone from Emily's phone. An expression of both annoyance and disappointment crossed Michael's face.

"Seriously? The time for distractions has long passed," he remarked, admonishment clear in his voice.

Against his criticism, she peeked through her eyelashes, extracting her phone from her pocket and answering the call.

"Hey, what's happening?"

Concern underscored Caleb's every word, rushing to inquire about her well-being. "Oh, good, you're okay. When Jason left, he... he said the hallway was... empty."

"You're worried about me even after waking from a coma." A tender smile graced Emily's face. "Michael brought me to a secluded spot in response to some strange occurrences with the lights. He's teaching me how to harness these powers."

The extent of her unawareness dawned on Caleb. He teetered on the edge of interruption, compelled to disclose information of utmost importance, but waited til she finished speaking.

"Em, there's something... you need to see."

The importance in his tone led her to agree to meet him. Once the call ended, she rose from her seated position. "I've got to get back to Caleb. He needs me to see something that cannot wait," she announced, conviction lacing her words.

Unamused, Michael rolled his eyes but conceded to her request. "Very well, I shall take you to him. However, when this task is done, our training shall commence with no interruptions."

In the blink of an eye, Michael transported her back to the hospital. Overhead, a lacework of faults sprawled across the scarred plaster, bathed in the stuttering glow of temperamental illumination.

"Did I do this?" she asked.

"Do what?" Caleb retorted, looking up at the damaged ceiling.

"Her heightened emotions are overpowering her rationality, and if left unchecked, they will lay waste to the world. Therefore, it is imperative for her to commence her training."

"Not 'til she sees it," he demanded, turning toward the archangel. "She needs... to know what... she'll be signing up for." He started at the archangel as he got off the bed and placed the gown on top of the blanket.

"Perhaps it will provide some clarity," Michael said, recognizing the validity of this request. "The both of you should go to the cave. I will return to Heaven to regain my strength."

"You do that. I'm sure we... will see you... again." His focus, noble yet straining, left him breathless.

After watching the archangel fade out of the room, Emily turned to face Caleb as he sat back on the bed. "The cave? Are you referring to the one from your book?"

Her inference sparked a smirk over his features. "You read it?" he inquired, holding a hand to his head.

"Well, only a part of it. What made you decide to write about the Hilltown Massacre?"

"I was contracted... to write about... something real," he paused, taking in a lung full of air. "Stories involving cold cases... they're quite popular... these days. I stumbled on it online... and it really stood out... as one of the most... perplexing cases."

"It's just that it hits a little too close to home," Emily revealed, her voice tinged with unease.

"What do you mean?"

"My uncle used to live in a cabin near that area, and it dredged up some memories."

"I'm sorry for making you feel uncomfortable." With a firm stance, he approached his partner, resting his head against hers. Then, he planted a tender kiss on her forehead. "Come on, we should... get going." he said, grimacing as he stood.

Emily moved to support him, concern etched on her face. "Are you sure you're up for this?"

"We don't have... a choice." Caleb's determination overrode his physical discomfort. "Let's move before anyone tries to stop us."

Just then, the doctor entered the room with his clipboard in hand. "Mr. Lansworth, I'm glad to see you're up and about," he said, moving in to check his patient's vitals.

Emily stepped aside, giving the doctor room to conduct a thorough check-up. Her heart pounded as she watched Caleb's chest rise and fall with each breath.

"Listen, doctor."

"Your breathing is still a bit labored," he informed, turning to Emily. "I'm going to have to ask you to keep your visits brief. Caleb has to take it easy."

"Yeah," his patient began. "I need to... be discharged."

"Is this a joke? You just woke up from a coma."

"Okay. How... about this? If I can take... a stroll outside and... be fine. Then, I can leave."

Against his better judgment, the doctor agreed. "Alright, but we're going to do this the right way. Nurse," he called out the door, "bring a wheelchair, please."

Caleb opened his mouth to object, but a gentle squeeze from Emily's hand silenced him.

Moments later, a nurse wheeled in a chair. "This is non-negotiable," the physician stated. "You'll use the wheelchair, and we'll take a short trip to the garden area. If you can manage that without issues, we can discuss your discharge."

Caleb settled into the wheelchair, his jaw clenched shut. Emily moved to push him, but the nurse took control. "I'll handle this," the nurse said kindly. "You can walk alongside us."

Once they reached the garden, a small oasis of greenery where flowers bloomed in tended beds, he braced himself to stand back on his feet. Emily wanted to help, but the doctor wanted to see him manage on his own.

"Alright, if you can walk a lap around the path here, I'll sign off on your release. Emily, you can walk beside him, but please don't offer physical support unless he's in danger of falling."

As they began their slow journey, Emily held her head down, watching her worn sneakers scuff against the gravel. But her mind was a million miles away. Caleb acknowledged her despondency and took her hand, hoping to lift her spirits. She raised her gaze to him, her eyes squinting against the bright sunlight.

"It's strange to think how much has happened while you were... asleep," she began. "Did you know there was a massive earthquake in New Zealand last month? And all that unrest in the Middle East - they're calling it the Arab Spring."

"Em—Emily," he pressed, coming to a halt in front of her. "We will get justice... for what they did. I promise." Their eyes locked in a shared struggle, understanding where the other was coming from. "I promise."

The rest of their walk passed in a contemplative silence, each lost in their own thoughts.

Hours later, they exited the hospital. A massive cumulonimbus cloud loomed overhead, its towering form a churning mix of deep blues and rich purples. The cloud's anvil-shaped top spread across the sky like a cosmic bruise. As if on cue, rain began to pour from the darkened heavens.

Relentless droplets slammed against the pavement with audible force. Each raindrop exploded on impact, creating a misty haze. The parking lot soon became a sparkling mirror.

Lightning flickered within the cloud, illuminating its majestic structure. The low rumble of thunder followed, a sound so deep it penetrated the earth.

Caleb, strengthened by the powerful display, picked Emily up in his arms. With a burst of vitality, he sped across the slick pavement, each step sending up a small spray of water.

"Let's stop at the burger place ahead," he said, his voice rising above the storm's cacophony. "We can get out... of the... storm and, I don't know... about you, but... I'm starving."

His endurance waned as his words became more labored, each phrase punctuated by gasping breaths. The effort of carrying Emily, combined with his recovering body, took its toll. This caused his steps to become unsteady.

Emily felt the muscle spasms in his arms fighting to keep them both upright. "Caleb," she started, concern evident in her voice.

But before she could finish, his knees buckled, controlling their descent rather than falling outright. Suddenly, Emily found herself half in his lap and half on the wet pavement.

Caleb's chest heaved as he struggled to catch his breath, his face pale from exertion. Water streamed down his face, mingling with beads of sweat on his brow. Despite his exhaustion, his arms remained protectively around Emily.

"I'm... sorry," he panted. "I thought... I could..."

Emily shifted, moving to support him rather than be supported. "It's okay," she assured him.

They sat there for a moment, rain pouring down around them, the pavement cold beneath them. Her hair hung heavy around her shoulders while looking around for viable options. That's when she noticed they were more than halfway to their destination.

"Look!" she said about the thunderous roar. "Fast burger is right there. I'll go and get you food. Hopefully that'll fix you right up."

As she advanced closer to the restaurant, she noticed fumbling lights shining through the word "Fast" on the large, neon burger sign. Instead of heeding a warning from the oddity, she continued forward. However, reaching for the door gave her goosebumps. Her muscles coiled as if preparing for fight or flight. She peered through the windows and caught a glimpse inside.

At first glance, everything seemed normal - Customers sat motionless at their tables, burgers half-raised to mouths that no longer chewed. The cashier stood frozen behind the counter; eyes fixed on the door. But as her perception adjusted, she noticed a family near the window shift in her direction, their gazes unnervingly fixed.

She blinked, and for a split second, could've sworn she saw sharp teeth flash across their eyes. This caused her body to tense and take an involuntary step back.

Seeing this, Caleb clung to his feet once more. "What's wrong?!" he asked.

"I'm not sure. I think we should maybe stop at the place down the street," Emily confessed.

Inside, the establishment's occupants sat in an eerie silence. An employee queued at the counter stared at the customers filling their stomachs. At the same time, they all paused and stared at one another. It was as if they were awaiting Emily to enter their domain.

"Okay, let's do that," Caleb agreed.

She walked back up to him and placed his arm around her to keep him vertical.

Still sensing her unease, he squeezed her hand, silently communicating that he understands as they resumed their walk down the rain-soaked road.

15

THE CAVE

Dressed in a sleek, all-black polyester bodysuit adorned with a gray utility belt cinched around her waist, Celsey ignited the engine of her car and zoomed down the highway toward David's house. The darkness outside seemed to match the intensity of her mission. A sense of urgency filled the air as she reached into her pocket and dialed the seeker's number.

"I need you to tell me if he's still at his bungalow," Celsey demanded.

"Yes," the seeker said. "Thermal imaging shows he hasn't moved."

"Excellent."

The car slowed down as Celsey navigated a turn into a quiet residential area. Not long later, she pulled into the driveway, her car creeping behind David's parked truck. Before stepping out, she slipped on a pair of black patrol gloves, prepared for any eventuality.

"You're not going to live to hurt anyone else."

She opened the armrest and retrieved a small metal box housing a face mask shaped like an infinity sign. As she slipped it on, she pulled her hood over her head, a cloak of mystery engulfed her very being.

Inside the house, David sat at the kitchen table, unperturbed, devouring a box of crackers. With a wave of his hand, he used his newfound powers to open the pantry, and float a can of spray cheese toward him. However, his attempt at a carefree moment was interrupted by the insistent doorbell.

"Hello?" David called out. A hint of unease crawled over him when no one answered. "You might as well leave if you're not going to say anything because I'm not opening the door."

The sound of a lock being picked filled the air, making his heart race. He stood up, bracing himself for the inevitable. Just as the door began to open, he swung his arm out, using his powers to slam the door shut.

Caught off guard by his resistance, Celsey clenched her fists and struck the rectangular window on the upper part of the door. To David's surprise, the glass cascaded onto the floor. With only the cabinet divider separating him from the intruder's view, he focused his powers. His brow furrowed when he locked onto the drawer near the sink. After mere seconds, he forced it open, and with a deliberate effort, willed a knife to float over to him.

Celsey thrusted her arm through the shattered window, turning the knob from the inside and flinging the door wide open. Upon entering, glass crunched under her heel while glaring round the room for any signs of movement. She treaded along the dining room wall, inching closer to the kitchen. But before she could enter, an invisible force pushed her back, throwing her off balance.

"What the heck was that?" she exclaimed, regaining her footing.

David, shielding himself between the cabinet divider and the assailant, couldn't help but wonder about the identity of this masked intruder.

"Who are you?" he asked.

"You can call me Huntress," Celsey announced, her eyes wandering to the pocket on her utility belt.

In the same beat, she hurled a ninja star toward her former collaborator. Without thinking twice, he raised his hands to protect himself, unintentionally making the weapon ricochet into the ceiling.

"Seriously, how are you doing that?" she asked, fueled with annoyance.

"Tell me who you are, and maybe I'll answer the question."

Growing impatient, Celsey retrieved three more ninja stars and launched them at David. One aimed for his head, another targeted his torso and the last was directed at his legs. Full of purpose, David swung his arm, deftly changing the trajectory of two of the stars. However, the third one found its mark, piercing his hand.

Pain seared throughout his body as he let out a pained cry. Yet amidst the agony, he maintained his focus on his attacker. His eyes locked onto hers as he summoned his powers, sending Celsey hurtling across the room, crashing against the wall.

"It's called telekinesis," he declared, walking over to her. "Now, let's see who you are."

He removed the mask, expecting to discover a stranger underneath, but, to his surprise, his attacker was someone he knew quite well. A whirlwind of questions flooded his mind.

"Celsey? What are you doing here? Did Boris send you?"

She paused, locking eyes with David. "Why would..." her voice trailed off in his gaze. "I've come to get justice for Kyle."

"You know, Boris is the one who infected him," David revealed.

"He may not be the kind-hearted man I thought him to be, but neither are you. You bound him to a chair in the lab."

"So, you're the one who freed him."

"Yeah, and a few days later, he's dead. I doubt that's a coincidence," Celsey retorted, her voice tinged with sorrow.

Like an unwanted serpent, a trickle of blood snaked its way down David's nose. He looked down the moment a drop hit his hand and unclenched his fists. As he wiped it away, a sudden headache diverted his attention. The distraction freed Celsey from the wall. After landing on her feet, she withdrew another ninja star, primed to launch it at David's leg. The projectile pierced his flesh just above the knee, forcing him to scream out in agony as he collapsed onto the floor.

"I know you two were close, but you have to listen to me. I was trying to cure Kyle," he pleaded, his voice filled with urgency despite the searing pain.

"Cure him of what?"

"Seriously?" David asked incredulously. "Boris created a virus and used him as his guinea pig."

"Why should I believe you?"

"Go to the lab. You'll find all the proof you need.".

"Fine," Celsey acquiesced, meandering toward David. "But you're coming with me." She bent down, pulled out the ninja star embedded in his leg, and grabbed disinfecting wipes from another component of her utility belt.

While she cleaned the blade, its metallic squeaks faded into the sound of rushing water...

The flowing cataracts of Burney Falls sparkled under the afternoon golden rays, each drop catching the light and creating a mesmerizing display. Proud and serene, the surrounding forest's foliage rustled in the crisp, invigorating air. On this picturesque day, the traveling duo strolled through the majestic landscape as the wind whipped around them, keeping foot traffic to a minimum. Caleb walked beside Emily, his voice cutting through the breeze when he informed, "It's not too far now."

"Good, cause I'm getting tired."

"You could be experiencing jet lag."

Emily smiled and replied, "I think it has more to do with the two-mile walk we did."

"Thank you by the way, for giving me the courage to get on a plane."

"What? You've never flown before?"

"Uhm, no I don't do heights," Caleb confessed.

As they continued on their way, a torn piece of paper danced at her feet. Intrigued, she picked it up and realized it was one of the many missing person's pages from the bulletin at the main entrance. Sadness flashed in her eyes when she recognized the scruffy man in his thirties from the photo. The flyer stated he had been missing since March 8, 2008, and noted a distinctive vine tattoo around his shoulder.

At the bottom, in bold letters, was a plea: "If you have any information about Charles Haskell, please contact the Shasta County Sheriff's Office."

As she held it in her hand, she found others blowing across the ground, each bearing different faces and dates. The wind seemed to be carrying fragments of countless lost lives.

"How many people do you think went missing here?" she wondered out loud.

"Too many, as far as I'm concerned." Caleb stood at the edge of the falls, peering around the delicate beauty around him, searching for the entrance to the cave. Then, a gust of wind passed by, catching his attention as several shining particles on the ground sparkled. "There it is."

Emily let her gaze drift upward into Caleb's gaze, her eyes filled with curiosity. "You know, I've seen him. Possibly everyone."

"What?"

"These missing people," she said, holding out the paper for him to see. "This guy, among others, was down there in the tunnels under those houses. They were definitely sun-deprived and possibly not even human anymore, but it was them."

He took the paper from Emily, his doubt about their survival fading away. "You're certain it was them?"

"Trust me, I remember the faces of anyone who tries to kill me."

"You said this was back in Hilltown?" he asked, his curiosity piqued. "I initially chose these specific crimes because I hoped to come across something the officials missed and find them."

Emily stayed by Caleb as they stared over the edge of the waterfall. "So, where exactly is this cave?"

"Down there. We just have to follow the trail," he informed, proceeding along the ledge.

"You know, we could just jump," Emily suggested, mischief glinting in her eyes.

"No way."

"Come on," she teased, a playful smile tugging at her lips. "It's so warm out; we'll probably dry off in a matter of seconds."

"Yeah, because that's the problem," he retorted, turning to see the mischievous grin on her face. "You really want to jump?"

"It's okay, I won't make you."

Caleb looked down at the water below, taking a deep breath before grabbing Emily's hand. "Let's do it."

"Really?!" her eyes widened with excitement.

Despite his reservations, he embraced his partner, holding her tightly. "I'm sorry we never got our first date," he whispered.

"No worries," she responded, her voice filled with reassurance. "We'll get another shot soon enough." Emily looked up into Caleb's eyes, her anticipation growing. "The water here is usually really cold, so we could either jump in fully clothed or—"

"Probably best we don't," he interrupted, removing his shirt. "We have a long walk back, and I don't want you getting sick."

Emily followed his lead, dropping their clothes on the rocky ground as she approached the waterfall. A chuckle escaped her when she saw Caleb squeezing his eyes shut and held his hand to help ease his fear.

"It'll probably be less scary if you keep your eyes open."

Taking her words to heart, Caleb opened his eyes as they both jumped off the edge, descending into the exhilarating rush of the waterfall. As they resurfaced, he swam towards the rocks to exit the water.

"It's not that bad," she stated, a playful energy in her voice as she swam behind him.

"No, it's pretty cold," he retorted.

After getting back on solid ground, Caleb looked along the side of the waterfall where the sparkling stones adorned a large burnt rock on the wall. With a triumphant point, he exclaimed, "That's it. The Burning Devil."

"The burning what?" Emily raised an eyebrow.

"It's what the locals call it. Look, at the top, it sort of looks like horns, and the bottom could be a rising pitchfork."

"Why is it burned?" Her curiosity burned bright.

"No idea, but the entrance to the cave is right above it."

Uncertain of what awaited them, Emily walked forward, carefully placing her hand in the middle of the burning devil. She looked up, attempting to visualize the imagery Caleb described. Instead, violent flames burst forth as the devil's voice echoed in her head, "Prepare yourself, child."

He stood there, his teeth tugging at his lower lip. His regard for his partner left him monitoring her well-being. Encompassed by his hold, Emily smirked at him. "Thanks," she said. "I just lost my footing."

Indomitable, she walked up the steps lining the wall of the cave entrance. Caleb joined her, his lighter illuminating the darkness that lurked within. As the flames flickered, Emily's eyes caught the scratches on the cave walls. "This is like hieroglyphics."

"The writing style used to predict prophecy."

She stopped at the center of the wall, her gaze fixed on an engraved image of two people holding hands. However, she beheld the deep crack in the wall where the hands met. An ember of intrigue stirred, nudging her to place a hand over it.

"If these hieroglyphics are about my life, then this must be Kota," she said as tears rolled down her cheek. The deep crack in the wall extended several feet, followed by what appeared to be an explosive event. "Is that supposed to be my power awakening, like what happened at my house?"

"I think that's a safe bet," Caleb inferred, moving nearer at an unsteady pace. Together, they beheld the outline of a woman seated cross-legged, her hands resting on her knees with palms facing upwards, encompassed by two circles—one around her head and another around her body.

"I've seen this picture before," Emily said. "It's meditating, a technique used to connect the body and mind."

"Check out what's next to it."

Both of them stared in wonder at the image: an eyeball, dotted by six markings—three on each side. Their eyes widened at the sight of a human figure, orbited by countless stars etched onto the adjacent wall.

"I don't understand. What does any of this mean?"

"Perhaps it's part of the training Michael spoke of," Caleb offered.

"Who drew all this?" Emily met Caleb's wonder, hoping for an answer.

"That's an excellent question."

She redirected her head to the furthest wall near the entrance. In the center, a person engulfed in energy fiercely battled a shadowy figure.

"What is all that stuff surrounding me, and who the heck am I supposed to be fighting?"

"Looks like you're destined to become very powerful." Caleb leaned a hand on the rock, tapping the image in question. "I know the shadow symbol usually means an unknown variable. In this case, I think it's safe to say you're battling the devil."

He circled his finger atop the figure's head. "These look like horns." Then, he moved his hand to the face. "And those rubies are definitely eyes." Finally, he pointed to its back. "And it's obvious these are wings."

When he faced his partner again, dread had manifested itself deep into her features. She stared ahead as color drained from her face. Her breath came in shallow, rapid gasps, while her lips parted, caught in a silent expression as if the sinister image had reached out from the cold stone and gripped her very soul.

You can deny all you want, but you know it's true. For if angels exist, then so do I. Lucifer's voice rang in her mind, warning her of the treacherous path that awaited.

Despite his weary form, Caleb hurried to her and shook her from the daze. Her eyes, glazed with terror, gradually focused on his fretful face. "Are you alright?"

She blinked, as if trying to wash away the haunting words that plagued her thoughts. A shiver ran down her spine, while bringing a hand to her forehead. Her breathing steadied when the world around her came back into focus. Comprehension, mingled with the remnants of fear taunted her as she locked eyes with Caleb and nodded.

"You sure?"

"Yeah," she said, realigning her gaze at the hieroglyphics. "So, you believe all this?"

"Right now, I think it's the only thing offering answers. To be clear, I am in no way suggesting you should do this. I mean, this looks like something they should deal with."

"What if they can't?" she asked, facing Caleb once more. "What if there's something we're not privy to?"

With this thought and the recent invasion to her mind, Emily's cool façade weakened. She hustled to the exit, unwilling to accept the weight of the literal writing on the wall. She leaped down the root-laden steps, her feet almost catching on the twisted vines that snaked through the rocky terrain.

Still inside the cave, Caleb gave one last look around. While trying to grasp the bigger picture, he glanced upwards at the stalactites, each one glistening with mineral-rich water. Speaking his wonder aloud, he murmured, "If all this is true, and she has to... well, then I think it's safe to say you have a funny sense of humor."

Moments later, as he stepped out, his ears perked at the sound of scuffling ahead. Anxiety twisted in his chest as he quickened his pace, navigating around rocky protrusions. Not too far, he found her, wrestling with the terrain, struggling to nudge her foot from between two stubborn rocks.

Her breath came in strained gasps, her face a mask of frustration. She wiggled about until she got free. After which, she tripped over the vines on the ground and stumbled backward, landing on her butt with a soft thud. That's when she saw Caleb rush over to her, offering a steady hand.

"What happened?"

"Stupid vines," she said, standing back up and wiping the dirt from her jeans.

He maneuvered to get close enough to hold her by the hand. "Don't worry," he said, standing in front of her. "Everything's going to be okay," he said, enveloping her in a warm embrace. "I will never let anything happen to you."

16

LIGHT MEETS THE DARK

As the sun began its descent, spreading a warm, honeyed glow across the vast expanse of the horizon, Boris found himself ensnared within a labyrinthine thicket of whispering trees deep in the heart of the dense woods. Each step he gingerly took, aware of each rustle of leaves beneath his worn-out shoes, was shrouded in a thick, impenetrable mist of uncertainty. His heart, an unwelcome drummer, thrummed a feverish rhythm against the fragile rib cage that housed it. Far from the safety of his sanctuary, he now sought refuge from the relentless pursuit of the law.

Miles stretched out behind him, each stride devouring precious moments of respite. Yet, even here, surrounded by the austere yet tranquil silence of his solitude, Boris found no solace. The haunting visages of his cherished children, their innocent countenances twisted with anguish and betrayal, etched themselves mercilessly within the deepest recesses of his memory. Their glimmering eyes were tainted with the heaviness of shattered trust, as though the darkness they held within mirrored the path he trod.

"I'll unearth damning proof of this demon," he whispered, willing this oath to seep into the very core of his being.

Within the labyrinth of his troubled mind, Boris sought solace, desperately seeking the shroud of darkness to cloak his transgressions. In this tenebrous sanctuary, he allowed himself to meld with the ephemeral whispers of the ancient trees, their gnarled branches outstretching like skeletal fingers, beckoning him deeper into their woody grasp. His heartbeat, a wild bird desperately flapping against the constraints of its ribbed cage, surged within him.

"In this hour of desperation, I need you, Rylee. Please guide me through this darkness," he beseeched.

The musty scent of damp moss and decomposing leaves tainted the air, bathing his senses in nature's potent alchemy. His footsteps became a dance infused with a sense of impending doom, painting a delicate tapestry upon the forest—a mosaic of choices between salvation and irreversible ruin.

Although ready to give up, something propelled him forward, coaxing him ever deeper into its primal embrace, its voice whispering a chilling reminder that if he stopped, all would be lost.

With the ethereal image of his beloved wife deeply etched within the fragile vaults of his memory, Boris collapsed, his trembling body engulfed within the soft embrace of the earth beneath him. Tears stained his dirt-streaked face, a testament to the immense burden he carried, borne not only by his broad shoulders but also by the void left behind by her untimely departure. His voice faltered, laden with raw emotion, as he questioned the cruel hands of fate that had mercilessly plucked her from the world.

"Why did you have to go?"

And then, like a fragile spark flickering within the encroaching darkness, a glimmer of hope began to bloom once more within his anguished heart. A memory, long buried beneath the debris of despair, resurfaced, its vibrancy illuminating the darkest corners of his mind's eye. He recalled the day his beloved wife's curiosity had been piqued by the discovery of a solitary gray feather delicately tucked at the base of her favorite tree. It had marked the beginning of a captivating odyssey, as it lured her deep into the enigmatic realm of Spirit photography—a mystical technique that captured the ethereal dance of supernatural forces on the surface of film.

Engulfed in his thoughts, Boris clutched his cell phone with an unwavering grip, his determination driving his actions forward. Memories flooded his mind, vividly replaying a conversation he had had with his wife. With a playful curiosity, he had questioned the existence of dark, menacing forces like demons, lurking in the shadows.

The unexpected response from his wife had caught him off guard: scoffing at the notion, she confidently dismissed the idea of a mere token such as a feather being the work of a demon. According to her, demons were far more vulnerable than people realized. She believed that merely knowing their name was enough to strip them of their power.

As he delved deeper into the mysterious realm of the spirit world, he found himself standing amidst a dense thicket of towering trees. With a deep breath, Boris took in the crisp forest air, his heart both exhilarated and filled with trepidation for the obstacles that awaited him.

Out of nowhere, the sound of approaching footsteps broke through the silence, jolting Boris from his thoughts. Refusing to retreat, he propelled himself forward, sprinting out of the woods, darting across the peaceful street, and hurtling down a steep incline. Ideas swirled in his head as he raced to outsmart the malevolent force that threatened his very existence. All the while, his mind remained focused on devising strategies to ensnare the enigmatic entity that eluded his grasp.

At last, at the bottom of the hill, the screeching sound of tires on asphalt reached Boris's ears, piercing his concentration. He recognized the distinct engine rumble of a Honda Accord speeding by, and a flicker of recognition ignited within him.

"Celsey? So, you're still alive," he whispered.

Aboard the car, David sat in the passenger seat, bound with unforgiving duct tape, his hands restrained behind him. Drops of sweat trickled down his face, each one landing on a wound on his leg, sending a sharp, stinging sensation through his body. Despite the discomfort, his focus never broke. He formulated a plan just before they reached their destination. His muscles strained, but the harder he tried, the more the tape clung around his wrists, refusing to give even a millimeter.

In search of understanding, David turned his sights on Celsey. "I didn't harm Kyle. I was trying to save him."

His colleague, however, remained set on vengeance. She looked at her engagement ring, adorned by a Sapphire gemstone which captured the light. "You left him alone, locked in the lab for hours. He was terrified when I found him. He claimed you had gone berserk."

David opened his mouth to speak, only for his glare to lock onto the ring on Celsey's finger. "I knew you two were close, but I had no idea it had evolved into something more."

"That's because we managed to keep our personal and professional lives separate."

A realization struck David like a bolt of lightning as he observed the scenery through the window. "The security tapes. I almost forgot," he whispered.

Celsey leaned closer; her voice tinged with curiosity. "What did you say?"

"There is undeniable evidence on those tapes, but it won't be what you want to hear."

She sped past the next green light and maneuvered the car a few blocks down until they arrived at an empty parking lot. Bringing the vehicle to a halt at the curb in front of the foreboding building, she stepped out, leaving David waiting for her to come around and free him from his confinement.

"Let's go," she demanded, swinging open the passenger door.

David complied, stepping out of the car and standing beside her while she shut the door. He spoke up, reminding her of his predicament. "You'll need to untie me."

To this, she raised an eyebrow. "And why would I do that?"

"Because you reminded me about the security tapes, which contain irrefutable evidence. But they're in the archives."

"Forget it. We're not going into the basement. You claimed there was evidence of this virus in the lab, so that's where we're going."

David let out a heavy sigh, realizing he had no choice but to show her the truth. He stopped in front of the entrance, gesturing for his hands to be freed. "If you release me, I give you my word I won't try to escape. We need to go down there, and I'll present the evidence to you. Otherwise, neither of us are going to leave this place."

Intrigued, she leaned forward, obliging her captive's request as she opened the door. Pushing him inside, she followed closely behind. "You better not be plotting something."

"Right, because the basement, away from the exits, is the best place to plan an escape."

"First, you claimed the proof was in the lab. Now, it's in the basement. Keep quiet and walk or I'll decide now if you're lying," Celsey retorted.

They continued down the corridor in silence, soon arriving at the staircase leading four flights down. Halfway down, Celsey's quick, shallow gasps created a fragile rhythm against the cold stone walls.

David glanced at her out of the corner of his eye, noting the anxiety in her every breath. "I see you're still not a fan of elevators."

"Just shut up and walk, okay?"

Not long after, they reached the archive room, its sterile atmosphere swallowing them whole. Soft hums of fluorescent lights buzzed overhead, bringing rows of metal shelves that held countless files and documents out of the darkness. Resolved to do his part, David approached the main computer, its screen a clunky CRT monitor. Its beige plastic casing, though only a year old, already seemed dated.

Multiple wires sprawled out from the back, connecting to a tangle of security feeds and peripherals. The buttons on the keyboard were noticeably worn, with some letters almost invisible from frequent use over the past year, and a joystick for manual camera control sat beside it.

At the same time, Celsey found solace in the plush rolling chair, situated next to the desk, her eyes fixed on his every move. "How far back are you going?"

"Four years ago, on March third."

Unsure what to make of that, she paused, her gaze glued to the screen. "Are you absolutely certain about the date?" she asked, as if peering into a different dimension of time.

"Yes, March third was the day I woke up paralyzed because I knew we had started something wrong," he affirmed, his words carrying unresolved trauma.

Celsey stared in shock, then repositioned her focus to the screen. She searched, with a keen eye, for that pivotal moment frozen in time. And then, with a slither of hope, she clicked on the selected date. In an instant, the surveillance footage unveiled the key to their shared past.

"Fast forward to around two-forty," he said.

With a steady hand, Celsey adjusted the timeline, navigating the labyrinthine threads of memories. She stopped a couple of minutes before the designated time. Soon, their eyes glued to the screen as they witnessed a scene that felt both familiar and deeply unsettling. It revealed Kyle pacing in front of a bathroom door, his mind riddled with doubts as Boris hustled towards him.

Despite the image fading in and out, it was clear that he had presented an engagement ring—the very one on Celsey's finger. "What the heck?" she muttered. She twisted the ring on her finger, anxious to learn the truth.

On the monitor, Kyle hesitated to accept it, his apprehension teetering on the precipice of revelation. Something troubled him, a burden that etched upon his weary face. "And you're certain this is necessary?"

"It is if you want her to stay alive," Boris proclaimed.

As they watched Kyle reluctantly take the ring, time stood still for Celsey. Her breath hitched, and the air felt thick and suffocating. Her eyes locked onto the scene, her thoughts swirling in a storm of disbelief and sorrow. The ring on her finger, once a symbol of their love, now felt like a cold, heavy shackle. Their relationship, once so full of promise, now felt contaminated by a sinister undercurrent. Was their love truly just a pawn in a cruel game of manipulation and survival?

"If it's any consolation, he really did care about you," David interjected.

"Really?" Her gaze shifted from the screen to her captive in search of reassurance.

"Annoyingly so. He constantly asked me if he had a chance with you."

Celsey's lips curved in a faint smile, a semblance of warmth blossoming amidst the chaos that surrounded them. However, her eyes darted back to the screen, drawn back into the enigmatic unraveling of their shared past.

"Look at Kyle's face after Boris walks away," David urged, joining her beside the computer.

Using her fingers, she zoomed in on her fiancé's tormented expression. "He's staring blankly at the ring," she observed.

"Take a closer look. Notice the conflict written all over his face. He's torn between doing what's right and keeping you safe."

The weight of the revelation settled upon her shoulders. Frustration simmered beneath the surface as she struck the desk with a clenched fist, the sound resonating in the hallowed room. "How do you know all this?"

"Because I was there. In fact, I was coming out of the bathroom, which was in the camera's blind spot, as Boris walked away. I asked Kyle about it, but he turned a blind eye." David revealed this as if it haunted his every step.

"And you claim he was protecting me. Protecting me from what?"

"Three months after that incident, we made a breakthrough in an experimental project—one that Boris promised would cleanse the air."

She took a deep breath, her fingers closing the file that held their shared history. Reluctant to accept the information, she entered a new date. The new feed brought up footage from inside the lab.

Though the image had a grainy tint, it was evident that Boris reclined in a chair, cradling a clear vial that encased unknown contents. The room itself seemed to wait for the inevitable clash of truth and deceit. And then, like a figure emerging from nowhere, Kyle stormed in, demanding he explain himself.

"Does the name Holly mean anything to you?" Boris asked.

Celsey's face tightened in confusion while inching closer. "Holly?" The name fell from her lips, unsure of the significance.

The conversation continued on the grainy screen, the audio scratchy but audible. Kyle's eyes fixated not only on the vial that stood between them but also on an envelope that held considerable evidence.

"What is that?" he asked.

"I don't think I owe any answers to a man who orchestrated a heist resulting in the deaths of two security guards and—oh yes, Holly."

Kyle's anger radiated through the room, each word punctuated with a fierce defense. "Those guards were about to shoot me. And as for the reporter, I have no idea how her car blew up."

"No, you simply drove away. Let me enlighten you—Holly survived the explosion because she wasn't inside when it went off. Paramedics arrived fifteen minutes later and rushed her to the hospital where she was pronounced dead on arrival."

"I'm aware, but that was not my fault?"

"Depends on how you look at it, I suppose. You may not have set the bomb, but if you had called for help, assistance could have arrived sooner, and Holly might have survived. I'm willing to bet maybe she saw something, and you didn't want to risk her writing about it in the paper like she'd done before."

"I've already done my time, man. What's this about?"

"You were locked up for the bank robbery, not the bombing. Had I known about this detail, I never would have welcomed you into my team."

"Because I had nothing to do with it.

"It doesn't really matter," Boris said, standing up from the chair. "What I need you to do now is collect ten kilograms of oak leaves and prepare the extraction and purification process."

Celsey's mind remained on the revelation of Kyle's past and shut off the computer. A moment of silence had fallen onto the room. She drew in a long breath, her mind working to unravel the unexpected revelations.

David, sensing her turmoil, ventured to reveal more details about the project. "From then on, Kyle and Boris, along with you and I, worked to perfect this virus."

"No, Boris said the experiment would improve the immune system so it could better fight off diseases."

"Do you think he'd be upfront about creating a virus that could manipulate the mind?"

"Besides, I got sick and missed the rest once everything was ready to go," Celsey began, looking towards her colleague. "If you knew about all this, why didn't you do anything to stop it?"

"I didn't know until Kyle had been infected and ordered to perfect the virus. At that point, there wasn't time to go to the police. Who knows how long an investigation would have taken. No, I knew each ingredient, so I buckled down and started working on a cure."

Overwhelmed, she removed the ring from her finger, and placed it beside the computer. "It's been four years."

"Yeah, well, it hasn't been as easy as I originally thought. Only recently, I started thinking outside the box and realized there was something Boris hid from us."

Celsey exhaled, a slow, deliberate breath, before pushing back from the desk. The chair's wheels grated against the floor. She began walking over to the exit, every step leading her into an uncertain future. Her hand paused on the doorknob.

David, still needing her to unbind him, stood up and asked, "Hey, what about untying me?"

She fidgeted with the knob before pivoting to face her captive. She retrieved a ninja star, its sharp edges glinting under the harsh glow. Confusion now guiding her actions, she commanded, "Turn around."

He complied with her order without resistance. In a swift, precise motion, she cut through the ropes that held him captive, freeing his wrists. Relief washed over him as he rubbed his liberated wrists.

The hinges on the door emitted a prolonged, metallic rasp as Celsey left the basement. When it clicked shut behind her, the sharp, resolute sound reverberated through the emptiness, leaving David alone with his thoughts.

17

GABRIEL'S WARNING

On the precipice of their destination, the intrepid pair neared Caleb's abode. While crossing the road, Emily lagged and came to an abrupt halt. Rooted to the spot, a flood of emotions besieged her. On the other hand, her partner continued onward, oblivious of her immobile distress. It wasn't until his foot touched the curb that he turned and rushed over to her.

"Everything's going to be okay."

"I hope you're right," she said. "Nothing seems real anymore."

"I'm real," he declared, placing a hand on her arm. "And I'm not going anywhere."

Emily clung to him, her embrace transforming into a bear hug. Her voice quivered as she asked, "How did you manage to come back from all this?"

"From what?"

With brine-streaked cheeks, her gaze lifted, meeting his weary eyes. As she went to wipe away the evidence of her sorrow, Caleb's touch intervened. His tender fingers swept the water from her face, each stroke a soothing balm to her aching heart. Her hand paused mid-air before lowering onto his arm, finding solace in the steadiness of his presence.

"When you were in the hospital, the nurse said you didn't have any family."

"That's concerning. My parents are both alive and well back home in North Carolina."

A somber chuckle escaped his lips, carrying a hint of incredulity. The absurdity of the situation filled his mind like a strange mist intertwining with the scent of antiseptic. In that moment, their mutual bewilderment lingered like a bittersweet melody. It reverberated through the air, an unspoken symphony that spoke volumes of the human condition. Boundaries of hierarchy and procedure proved fallible, the reality of human error seeped through the cracks.

"No brothers or sisters?" she inquired.

"Only child."

"I guess even hospitals can screw things up."

They released their grip on one another and readied themselves to cross the street. However, upon setting foot on the moist lawn in front of the residence, an unexpected chill seeped through Emily's shoe, sending an unpleasant shiver up her leg. She glanced down and discovered filthy mud water cascading over her foot, prompting her to retreat to the safety of the sidewalk. Caleb's face tightened with concern as he stepped beside her.

"Come, my lady," he said, sweeping her up off her feet.

Nestled in his arms, she held her head close, hearing the rapid, rhythmic thrum of a heartbeat brushing incessantly against his ribcage. Each beat mirrored her own despite his outward façade. She raised a gaze upward, offering unspoken comfort.

As they reached the porch, he sat her down so he could fish in his pocket for his keys. A metallic jingle pierced the silence as she watched him unlock and push the door open. He then gestured for her to enter first.

The moment her shoes made contact with the welcome mat, the sound of duck feet echoed through the house. She stood before Caleb, looking up at him with a mixture of gratitude and amusement.

"Feel free to take off your shoes. I'll dry them for you," he offered.

"It's all good."

"You sure? It's no trouble at all. I want you to be comfortable."

"If you want to," she said, leaning down to remove her shoes.

After handing them over, Emily took note of the home's distinct features. Its walls were adorned with periwinkle paint, giving the space a calm, welcoming atmosphere. Meanwhile, Caleb threaded his way through the modest sized kitchen to get to the laundry room. Lustrous stainless steel appliances opposed the honey-toned cabinets above a small island with a granite countertop that extended into the center.

Positioned right at the entrance to the laundry room was a refrigerator, marking a clear divide between the two spaces. Caleb placed the shoes on top of the dryer as he bent down to grab a bin from the side, where he kept an old newspaper.

When he re-entered the room, proud to be able to provide her with dry footwear, he noticed that her ankle socks were also soaked. "I can dry those too."

Emily obliged, knowing that it was something he wanted to do. She removed her socks and placed them in his hands with flushed cheeks and sparkling eyes full of gratitude. A chuckle escaped when she ambled over to the inviting couch, grateful for the much-needed levity that Caleb had brought into her life.

"Thank you," she began, her voice filled with heartfelt gratitude. "I really needed something to laugh about right now."

Immersed in his task, he failed to hear Emily's appreciation. His mind riveted by an unexpected mystery within her shoes. As he removed the insoles, a smattering of minuscule crystals descended onto the wet floor, their fragility shattered upon the merest brush of his fingertips.

Back in the living room, Michael materialized before Emily, his sudden presence jolting her to the very depths of her being. Captivated by an electrifying blend of shock and astonishment, a surge of adrenaline coursed through her veins, causing her body to leap in a balletic display of surprise.

"Holy hell!" she exclaimed.

"I do not understand that context, but we must get started right away," Michael said.

"Whatever, fine," she retorted, somewhat dismissive. "You need me to meditate, right?"

"Yes, close your eyes and breathe. Let everything else fade into the distance."

As she sank deeper into the process of meditation, Caleb crossed the threshold, clutching one of the shoes. "Hey, I don't know what to make of this, but..." he trailed off, after realizing Michael had returned. "I'm guessing this is you."

"There's the mortal who keeps imposing," the archangel retorted with a hint of annoyance. "So, what exactly are you accusing me of?"

In response, Caleb presented the crystal fragments that clung to his hand. "She stepped in a puddle outside, so I wanted to dry them for her. But, I found these crystals stuck on the insole."

"Perhaps it was Gabriel with an important message."

"You mean this is supposed to carry meaning?"

"How did you feel when you first encountered it?" Michael probed, his eyes scrutinizing Caleb's face.

"I... I'm not entirely certain. It just felt... off, somehow," he confessed, a faint tremor of unease infiltrating his voice.

"I feared as much. I suspect it was a forewarning of sorts. Guard over her while I seek out Gabriel." The archangel departed, plunging Caleb even deeper into the unknown than before.

Meanwhile, inside the Silverton residence, Jason sought solace in the bathroom, his face drenched as he vigorously scrubbed away the haunting voices echoing in his mind. The sound of water droplets hitting the sink filled the silence, interrupted by his wife Tori knocking on the door.

Concern laced her voice as she asked, "What's happening in there? Are you alright?"

"I'm fine," he said, his words failing to mask his inner turmoil. "I'll be out soon."

Tori's worry spilled into her eyes, and she gently suggested, "Maybe you should consider taking some time off. Remember what happened to your father when he witnessed those horrific crime scenes? I don't want you to suffer the same fate."

Jason swung the door open, clutching his head yet determinedly replying, "I am not going to have a mental breakdown, alright?"

With a flicker of hope, Tori pleaded, "You better not. Ally needs her father in her life."

"Don't worry, I'm not going anywhere."

In the midst of their conversation, Jason's phone pierced the air with the peculiar melody of a song. Tori let out a small smile as she remarked, "I still can't believe that's your ringtone."

Planting a quick kiss on his wife's cheek, Jason moved away to answer the call, his voice brimming with anticipation. "Hey, did you find something that could help us crack the case?"

"Yes!" The voice on the other end exclaimed, a palpable joy seeping through the phone.

"That's amazing. Stay calm; I'll be there in a moment."

Once the call ended, Jason turned around to face Tori, his excitement evident. "We finally have a lead."

Tori raised her hand, gesturing for him to leave. Hesitant to leave her alone, Jason locked eyes with his wife, detecting a subtle hint of concern in her gaze. Respecting her wishes, he nodded in acknowledgement before exiting the room. The moment he was out of view, Tori found herself lost in her thoughts, a single tear slipping down her cheek.

Far away, in the heart of the Botanic Garden in Claremont, California, a strange stillness encompassed the vibrant array of flora and fauna. Time itself hung in suspension, composing an eerie tranquility over the lush landscape. Suddenly, a cascade of enchanting blue sparks began to shimmer through the humid air, their glow mesmerizing in the deepening twilight.

Each petal of the delicate blooms seemed to hold its breath; their vibrant hues intensified by the whimsical dance of light. Tall trees, sentinels of the garden, stood motionless, whispering secrets to the shimmering air.

Sparks wove together in a harmonious ballet, creating a breathtaking spectacle. With each movement, they melded into a translucent portal, suspended like a window into another realm. Coils of smoky mist, reminiscent of spectral serpents, curled around its edge.

Through the haze, a figure emerged, clad in the robes of a nurse. Her presence existed on the edge of perception, a blend of earthly grounding and mystical agility. She moved like an astral apparition, as if conjured from the deepest wells of imagination.

"You have failed," a voice emanated from the shadows, its words etched with scorn. "The human is unlocking her potential."

"I truly believed that the creature would have prevented this," the nurse responded, a tinge of defiance coloring her words. "I am astounded that it refrained from taking its frustrations out on her. But I did my best to convince Mr. Landsworth, why he—"

A wave of energy shot out into the air, which held her in place. Her skin began to shimmer a soft, iridescent sheen, as if kissed by the light of a hidden moon.

"You should never have gotten in the creature's way."

"You said it was one life in exchange for the whole world, so I made a choice, but I will not kill anyone, do you hear me?"

"I should have realized the folly of aligning with a flawed organism."

"This is not my doing. It was you who attempted to sway the archangel's convictions and failed."

"You know what your kind excels at?" the voice sneered as the figure stepped out from the shadows, looming behind the nurse. "Power."

With a deep inhalation, the energy took on a ribboned shape, wrapping around her. In mere moments, she phased in and out of sight before completely disappearing.

"Perhaps a conversation with the Entitles is in order," the figure murmured, its words laced with a chilling determination.

As swiftly as it had appeared, the portal vanished, leaving behind only a handful of withered vines, mere remnants of the octopus-like plant's former splendor.

18

PREPARATIONS

In the depths of New Hampshire's White Mountain Forest, Lucifer loomed with an unsettling stature, imposing amidst the vast darkness that surrounded him. With a deft motion, he opened a gate, unleashing a torrent of flames from the eternal pit. As the fiery portal closed, a formidable entity emerged from its depths—the mighty Cerberus, a creature shrouded in savagery. The three-headed dog floated about; its nefarious stare focused on the King of Darkness. Closing the distance between them, Cerberus positioned itself beside the devil, a symbol of both loyalty and destructiveness.

"Hello, Cerberus. Perhaps you can aid me in gaining an advantage over that despicable Haines," he said, brushing a hand across the beast's heads. "I require you to familiarize yourself with my power, then scour this earthly realm until you find something akin to it. Once you have, come find me."

The three-headed animal traveled down the mountain, its energy radiating through the surrounding landscape as it embarked on its quest. At the same time, Lucifer lowered himself to the earth and inspected a deep gash on his hand. The pain fueled a lingering anger within him, a wrath that promised no mercy for Haines.

"When I find you, rest assured that inexorable vengeance shall befall you," he vowed. His oath rippled over to the quaint town of Portsmouth, where an old church bell inexplicably tolled.

Meanwhile, in the City that Never Sleeps, Boris departed a supermarket not far from his home. A worn, wrinkled blue face mask clung to his visage, appearing as though it had been mercilessly torn from an old, tattered shirt.

Securely clutching a brand-new HTC ThunderBolt in his hand, he hastened to the side of the building before embarking on a sprint across the street and into the dense embrace of the woods. Finally, upon reaching the bottom of the desolate hill, he halted his breathless journey and promptly discarded the pungent mask.

"Okay," he began, activating the camera on his newly acquired device. "Alright, for those of you who don't know, I'm Boris Linderman. A freaking scientist, someone who only believes in the cold hard facts. Well, at least, that's how I used to feel. I've been accused of a heinous crime–" he paused, tears welling in his eyes. "The murder of my beloved wife. But I swear on my soul that I am innocent. No, it was a vicious demon. And by the Gods, I am going to hunt it down and make it pay for the agony of ripping Rylee from my life."

He stopped, slipping his phone back into his pocket, his hand delving into the warm recesses of his jacket. His fingers wrapped firmly around what remained of the legendary Sword of Freyr. He stepped forward, aligning himself with a mighty tree several feet away. Taking a deep breath, his heart pounding, he steadied himself and raised the weapon, its gnarled and worn hilt reflecting the dim light.

In an instant, tranquility enveloped him, his breathing easing into a steady rhythm as he honed his concentration, fixating his glare on the target ahead. With a sudden surge of vigor, he propelled the sword through the air, its path flawless, aimed with lethal precision at the heart of the ancient trunk.

"Oh, yeah," he proclaimed, advancing confidently towards the tree. "That demon's fate is sealed."

Despite its fractured state, the blade retained an edge sharp enough to slice through the layers of weathered bark and strike the designated spot. The impact caused a piece of the handle to shatter against the trunk, breaking off and drifting gracefully to rest among a kaleidoscope of autumn leaves below. Undeterred by these minor hindrances, he remained steadfast on retrieving the weapon crucial for his impending battle. Yet, try as he might, the sword refused to release its hold on the resilient tree.

"Please, don't make this difficult."

Boris's hands, now marked by redness from relentless efforts, almost succumbed to exhaustion. With no viable alternative, he seized the handle with both hands, his feet braced against the sturdy, twisted contours of the trunk. In one last desperate display of strength, the universe seemed to align with his will. The blade let out a groan of resistance before cleaving into the trunk like a scythe through ripe crops.

As the massive tree crashed backward, Boris tumbled onto the cushion of leaves, narrowly avoiding the destruction. A sigh of relief escaped him as he glanced at the sky, thankful for its benevolence. Just as if the heavens wept in solidarity, raindrops began to fall, pattering softly on the ground beside him.

Later, at Caleb's abode, he found himself by Emily's side, keeping a vigilant watch over the room. His fervent hope rested on Michael's swift return with favorable tidings. His gaze drifted to the rain outside, only to be interrupted by the gradual dimming of the living room light, drawing his attention upward to the ceiling. Considering a mere bulb malfunction, he rose promptly from his seat, striding to the wall switch near the door. To his dismay, the switch remained unresponsive to his toggling.

Not wanting to show weakness, Caleb resisted the grip of panic and methodically scoured the room for potential makeshift shields. He struggled to reposition both the television and its stand closer to Emily's back, yet persevered until he achieved his goal. Driven by a newfound resolve, he maneuvered the couch in front of her, flanking her with a recliner on each side.

"It's a start," he remarked, surveying his handiwork.

Without delay, he reached for his phone, his fingers dancing across the screen as he delved into research on the vulnerabilities of demonic entities. However, his discoveries were confined to conventional wisdom, emphasizing the efficacy of materials like iron, salt, and holy water in repelling malevolent spirits.

"Salt should suffice, and---" His train of thought was interrupted by an intrusive ringtone. Opting to ignore the call, he continued unfazed.

He fumbled through the cabinet where he discovered a container of kosher salt, its pristine crystals fueling him with hope. He felt its smooth surface beneath his touch as he seized it. After heading back to the living room, he clutched the salt, its grains cascading through his fingers like fine sand. As the ringing persisted, he extracted his phone from his pocket and discerned that the caller was David. "Now's not a good time."

"Oh, really? Then make time."

Perplexed by his outburst, Caleb perched on the arm of the couch, a flicker of uncertainty crossing his features. "What's the matter?" he inquired, his concern escalating to new heights.

Within the jumbled whispers that tormented David's mind, pushing him to clutch his head in anguish, a clear directive emerged: Find Emily.

"Hey, are you there?" Caleb probed, breaking the oppressive silence.

"My colleague fell victim to the virus driving people to madness. It seemed he was fixated on locating your girlfriend. I just needed to be sure she was safe," David elucidated.

"She is," Caleb affirmed.

Unable to utter another word, David's phone slipped from his quivering hand and thudded against the cold floor, his body collapsing in the arched entrance of the archive room. His anguished screams reverberated through the space, causing the very foundations to tremble, cracks fissuring across the once sturdy desk and crimson rivulets trickling from his tear-streaked eyes.

Time was of the essence; David knew he had to eradicate this virus before it consumed him, too.

Caleb, however, lingered in the oppressive silence which overtook the call, misinterpreting this as a sign that the conversation ended. This prompted him to redirect his attention to the task at hand. Soon enough, he had constructed a protective circle of salt around Emily. Once the final arc of the circle was completed, he couldn't help but marvel at the peculiarity of this ritual.

And then, like a rampaging wildfire, realization struck him. There was one person he could always rely on, one person who held an unwavering belief in the mystical realm that he was now tangled up in—his mother. Grabbing the phone once more and speed dialing a number he knew all too well. It wasn't too long before he heard the sound of the other line picking up. "Mom?"

"Caleb? How's the book tour going, sweetheart? You've been away for so long," his mother's soothing voice flowed through the speaker.

"It ended weeks ago. I've been in the hospital. Didn't they inform you?" Caleb's concern was evident.

"What? No, no one reached out to me. Are you okay?"

"I am now."

"So, what's troubling you?"

"You never had a problem believing in God," he began, unsure how else to broach the topic. "Does that mean you also believe in demons too?"

His mother's voice turned pensive; the sound of her thoughtful pause carried through the phone line. "Of course. For one to exist, the other must as well. Do you remember the prayer we learned in church for protection?"

A wave of nostalgia swept over Caleb as he delved deep into memory, recalling the sacred words that were etched in his mind.

"I do, Mom. I used it once we got home, and that's when Dad revealed his disdain for religion and his resentment towards you for subjecting me to it."

"I have to get going; I'm sorry."

"Wait, I need to know. What was the prayer to bless water?"

Then, the realization that her son might be in trouble hit her. Ms. Lansworth froze as she started her car. She leaned over and pulled a Bible from the glove compartment and flipped through the pages in search of the verse in question.

"God our Lord, you caused water to flow over the sacraments, imparting life and abundant blessings. Today, I come before you, beseeching you to hear my prayer and manifest your glory and power by blessing this water. May this water, sanctified by your divine favor, be used to banish malevolent spirits and cleanse us of our sins. By your benevolent touch upon this water, we shall be delivered from all evil."

"Thank you," Caleb expressed.

After exchanging their final words, he proceeded to gather water in a large jug from the kitchen, feeling a renewed sense of hope.

19

CONTEMPLATION

In the oppressive gloom enveloping her, every corner had been devoured by a haunting emptiness. Emily's presence yielded to this void, where only whispers of her innermost thoughts drifted through the space. The shadowed landscape rendered this realm impenetrable.

What are you doing? You don't believe in a higher power. Why are you listening to this man? Her thoughts wrestled within her mind. If there was a God, why would He let Kota die?

These incessant Cognitions swarmed through Emily's consciousness, relentless and unforgiving. As she grappled for clarity, the air in her lungs grew thin, making it increasingly difficult for her to breathe. In this strange realm, she sought answers as her thoughts echoed repetitively, like a skipping record. And then, in a moment of revelation, she finally understood her surroundings—she was inside her own mind.

"So much for a peaceful meditation. This feels more like an out-of-body experience somehow," she mused. Her thoughts continued to assail her mind, their relentless barrage wearing her down.

Why didn't you stay with her? You should have protected her. Why didn't you warn her, for Christ's sake?

"ENOUGH!" she erupted.

Her breath became heavy, beads of sweat forming on her chin. It was then that a rift in the air materialized before her eyes. A powerful gust of wind surged forth from the opening, knocking her off her feet. Confusion clouded her mind, and she remained on the ground, fixated on the rift that loomed above her.

Kota, I have to go. Call me if you need anything. She heard herself say, the image of the hotel room emerging inside the rift, bearing an uncanny familiarity.

"Hey," Kota began, addressing her sister. "I think you should stay here for a little while. You know, be around family."

Emily turned to face Kota, contemplating her words.

"Besides, we always do game nights on Fridays when you visit, so how about it? Maybe it'll help get your mind off your boyfriend for a little while."

A conflicting surge of emotions nudged Emily along, driven by the need to unravel the mysteries surrounding Caleb's coma and the possibility of uncovering what might have been right in front of her. However, as she gazed into Kota's pleading eyes, she couldn't bring herself to refuse and posed a question.

"What game did you have in mind?"

Outside the unfolding scenes, Emily sank to her knees, tears streaming down her face, unable to contain her guilt.

"Why are my thoughts being thrust into the spotlight? I know I have failed!" she lamented.

Meanwhile, she heard a knock at the door, drawing her attention once more.

"See? I told you he'd be down for playing Monopoly," Kota remarked, shutting the door behind her as Simon entered.

A smug expression on his face sent a shiver down Emily's spine, chilling her to the core.

Fibers of reality began to extend beyond the scope of her subconscious. Plum sparks wrapped its spectral clasp around Emily's corporeal being. The light waned, swallowed by the encroaching darkness that bore witness to the extraordinary unfoldment.

In a swift display, Caleb arranged an assortment of vials lying on the table. Each container held precious holy water, shimmering with a celestial glow. Against the backdrop of foreboding shadows, the table became a haven of mystical power laden with potential salvation.

He moved in earnest, determined to get back to Emily. His knuckles clenched white, eyes reflecting a mixture of trepidation and resilience. "Oh no, no, please!"

The gravity of the imminent danger weighed on him. With steadfast resolve, he took control, hands gripping a vessel of salt as if wielding a tangible shield against the encroaching darkness. The grains, like precious tears of protection, cascaded forth, tracing a serpentine path along thresholds and windowpanes.

Again traversing the void of Emily's cognitive space, the trio gathered around the table, their faces adorned with smiles that beamed with the infectious joy of camaraderie. In the center of the board, a bowl of chips beckoned, its savory allure tempting their taste buds. Amidst the lighthearted banter, Simon reached out to grab a handful, his attention momentarily diverted. Yet, Kota's perceptive gaze fell onto a minuscule piercing adorning his wrist, a glint of enigmatic significance. Before she could voice her observation, the unexpected transpired—their lips met in a bittersweet kiss, a poignant farewell cloaked in passion.

"I'm sorry." His words were a bare murmur that brushed against Kota's ear, laced in a fragile apology that hung in the charged air. And then, for no rhyme or reason, he abruptly snapped her neck, a macabre act that disrupted the tranquility of their surroundings.

Emily recoiled in horror, her vocal cords unleashing a primal scream that rumbled through the vast emptiness. Desperately, she extended an arm to the searing image of the fading rift, clutching at her shattered reality, a futile attempt to reclaim what had been so brutally torn away from them. The weight of guilt descended upon her like an implacable storm, each droplet thundering through the corridors of her mind.

Haunting echoes of self-blame continued their assault, a dissonant chorus that threatened to consume her sanity. However, as if summoned by the indomitable will of her heart, a brilliant light materialized before her very eyes. She traced the contours of her chest as if seeking solace amidst the onslaught of remorse.

"Kota," she whispered, her voice a gentle caress that dissolved into the emptiness.

Her sister's voice resonated from the spectacle.

Emily, it's time to let go of the guilt. My life, brightened by your presence, was never stained by your actions. Don't bear this burden; it isn't yours to carry.

The ephemeral light dispersed, receding into the infinite darkness. Emily, overcome by a mix of awe and relief, closed her eyes, her breathing deep and deliberate. Seconds danced into eternity while the encompassing landscape underwent a metamorphosis. Whispers of the ocean's rhythmic cadence mingled with the melodious symphony of birdsong. And in this resurgence of vitality, her aura reached new heights, spiraling upward into the tense round void.

In the heart of this swirling vortex, a pinprick of light emerged. Its warm glow quickly expanded outward, pushing back the obscurity. As it brightened, intricate patterns began to form within its radiance, reminiscent of synapses firing in a vast neural network.

David discerned the unmistakable contours of a human brain before him. The right hemisphere pulsed with vibrant energy; each spark of activity visible in dazzling detail. However, the left side told a different story. Dark patches cloaked significant portions of the left cortex. But what unsettled him more than anything was the realization that these spots were not static—they writhed and shifted with a slow rhythm.

"I've never seen anything like this," he said, his voice laden with wonder as he held the cerebral imaging over a lamp at his workstation. The moment he placed the scan down, he made his way to the cabinet, where he retrieved a syringe. Now wasting a moment, he sought out a vein in his arm, the cool metal meeting his skin as he plunged the needle, securing a precious blood sample.

Confidence flowed through him, reassuring that his cure held promise. Perhaps a stronger dose was required, an adjustment to combat the insidious encroachment. However, just as hope tinged his thoughts, the lights flickered, and a familiar, chilling voice slithered in the wind.

"And then there was one." The creature's words oozed of malevolence, halting his action. Panic spread on his face, helplessly listening as it continued its taunting proclamation. "You're the last sinner carrying my virus."

The fiend grinned, its proximity to the scientist evaporating at an alarming rate. Soon, they were standing neck and neck. David couldn't help but lock eyes with his tormentor, refusing to succumb to the evil that sought to possess him.

"I know what you desire, and you will not find it within me," he declared.

His glare darted around the room when he caught sight of a forgotten water pebble. He called on his telekinetic prowess, hurtling the device toward the demon's head. Impact ensued, unleashing a surge of energy from David's eyes that shattered the water pebble, its contents erupting like an unleashed tempest. Amidst the chaos, a computer crashed into the creature's face. The impact ruptured the back panel and unleashed a torrent of inky black goo.

No sooner than David could bolt to the exit, did the fiend become vertical once more. "I have come for two things. Your soul and the location of the archangel, and I shall not leave until I possess them."

The scientist summoned every ounce of his power to unleash a fierce windstorm that would serve as a barrier between himself and the malevolent presence. With a powerful scream, the wind intensified, thrusting the creature against the door, stopping its advance.

The demon bellowed in frustration, flapping its unseen wings. This proved to be strong enough to reverse David's energy, hurling him across the room. In a resounding crash, he tumbled to the floor, his descent accompanied by the toppling of a desk.

As the creature approached with relentless determination, the sudden flutter of lights caused it to pause. It remained oblivious to the ceiling screws, which held the lamps in place, were loosening at a moderate pace.

"A mere light show meant to intimidate; I assume?" It scoffed, fixated on its target's fallen figure.

"Intimidation, no. Inflict pain, though, hopefully."

In an exhilarating demonstration of his power, David harnessed the shards of glass strewn across the floor, directing them at the fiend. As if choreographed by a vengeful orchestra, another desk levitated over its head. Just before he could execute his next move, an unseen force threw him backward, bursting through the wall and landing on the grass several feet away. The impact left his head and arms bloodied, rendering him unconscious.

In a dramatic twist, Haines emerged on the scene, coursing with inverted electricity that crackled around his being. "You assume mortals are impotent against you, allowing battles to prolong. But there exist forces in this world that can harm you, don't they?" He said, staring at the fallen demon.

A profound glare exchanged between the formidable adversaries. With focused intensity, the Roamer directed his power at the iron hook embedded in the creature's stomach, obliterating the weapon with only a thought.

In a moment that seemed to suspend time itself, the demon drew a breath as if resurrected from the brink of annihilation. "I suppose I should say thanks," it muttered, reclaiming his footing.

"Do not mistake my leniency for weakness," Haines retorted. "You are fortunate that I still require your assistance. Now, speak, have you discovered what we seek?"

"No, but I believe the sinner possesses the answers we need," the demon conceded.

"Thus far, he has proven resilient against your virus," Haines mused, shifting to the gaping hole in the wall. "With Lucifer pursuing me and the mortal that possesses archangelic abilities eluding our grasp, perhaps it is time to adopt a less aggressive approach."

20

LYING IN WAIT

Gabriel stood before Lucifer's vacant tomb inside the catacombs. A constellation of dust motes danced as he fixated on the iron chains lying in disarray on the cold stone floor. His fingers twitched at his sides, itching to examine the metal links. Slowly, he knelt beside it, his movement betraying a blend of fascination and perplexity. He lifted a section of the chain with a knitted brow. The Enochian symbols that once glowed with celestial power were now dull.

His eyes widened in realization—the spell had been erased, leaving no trace of its former potency. "It makes no sense," he began. "One moment, there was nothing, and the next—" His words trailed off, interrupted by the arrival of Michael, who stood at the entrance. "I do not know what you wish to accomplish here, but the mortal called Caleb received your message. However, it seemed to be incomplete."

Gabriel clenched his jaw, curling his hands into tight fists. He turned to face Michael with a glint of indecision in his eyes. "I was trying to warn you that the Entitles are gunning for the angelic mortal."

Michael's features contorted with disbelief. "What?! I thought we wiped them all out after they devoured many of our soldiers."

An oppressive repose settled onto the duo as their failure bore down on them. In no time, the angelic messenger divulged his knowledge. "Yes, I remember. I fear they may attack the very moment she realizes her full potential."

A brooding fog of suspicion enveloped them, while intertwining destinies drew near. Their watchful eyes stood as the final bulwark against the impending onslaught.

"Not if we remain vigilant this time," Michael asserted. "This time we shall be ready to act should they make a move."

Gabriel nodded in agreement, his eyes gleaming with a blend of determination and a hint of foreboding. "I believe they already have. I sensed terror and checked things out myself."

"Show me."

The catacombs dissolved around them, replaced by the harsh glare of streetlights. In an instant, the two celestial beings materialized several strides away from the familiar facade of the Fast Burger restaurant. Its once-vibrant signage flared in fits and starts, a testament to the faltering semblance of normalcy. Michael approached the blood-stained glass with calculated cadence. He leaned in close, his face mere inches from the crimson smear. His eyes narrowed as they observed every detail of the spatter—its shape, its consistency, the way it had dried on the smooth surface. He reached out, his fingertips hovering just above the stain, like he could read its history. The air thickened around them, heavy with the residue of fear and confrontation.

"We must be at the right place."

"Did you doubt me?" Gabriel questioned.

"Let us confirm what we are dealing with." Michael strode toward the door, poised to confront the lurking menace.

"I faltered but once," Gabriel lamented. "In the span of a heartbeat, Lucifer was freed."

The warrior angel's features hardened, his voice flowing in the purity of sacred rivers. "Your carelessness in letting him escape was a colossal mistake." He paused, noting the anguish in Gabriel's eyes. "You seek forgiveness? Then come up with a trick that will ensure victory in the coming battle."

He gripped the handle and swung the door open. His brethren followed only to find signs of unimaginable terror. All over the floor, a forlorn pool of blood colored the cracks in between each tile. The lifeless bodies of two crew members lay sprawled on the ground, their faces bearing the grotesque scars of scorching water used for frying fries. Beside them, the shift manager's body appeared unharmed, except for a ghastly wound on his neck. Even the custodian, once a humble keeper of cleanliness, now occupied the sullied mop water.

"What on earth? Rarely do Entitles unveil such brutality," Gabriel exclaimed, his voice tinged with incredulity.

"If they have sensed Emily's power, they will stop at nothing to possess it. This gruesome spectacle is but a means of augmenting their own strength," Michael said.

The messenger's voice quivered in anger. "If they dare to steal the life essence of others, then none are safe. We must—"

"No," Michael interjected. "We shall not act unless we receive the order."

Outraged, Gabriel succumbed to his boiling emotions and took his wrath out on the door. He was torn between his conviction to do what he believed in, regardless of the opinions of his fellow angels, and the consequences of disobedience, which could lead to exile or far worse.

Suddenly, a torrent of ethereal purple lightning pierced the heavens in an astonishing spectacle usually reserved for celestial planes. Michael and Gabriel, both attuned to this kind of raw power, raised their heads to the dilapidated ceiling.

"This is a dire omen, Michael."

"Despair. Anguish. Emily teeters on the precipice of surrender," Michael said.

"Can you blame her? Remember, she recently bore the unfathomable loss of her sister," Gabriel reminded.

"I implored her to let go of everything." In a radiant tableau of cerulean light, Michael clenched his fists, while still focused on the heavens.

"Do not overlook the fact that we are talking about a mortal."

In a wordless accord, Michael teleported to her. Gabriel, however, did not budge, pondering their conversation.

Your word is not always sound, Michael. The last time I heeded your words, several lives were lost in Hilltown, New York. Gabriel thought to himself.

The lights shimmered in Caleb's house, casting a marble glow as the Archangel materialized in the same spot he had occupied earlier. He looked on in bewilderment, beholding a fort made of cushions, encapsulating Emily. Surprised, he angled his head in a quest for comprehension. Then, the sharp click of a firearm being cocked reverberated from the depths of the kitchen. Still, he remained steadfast, refusing to divert his gaze.

"What is all this?"

After hearing his voice, Caleb swept into the room, adorning a necklace crafted from intertwining sticks, which created a makeshift cross. In his grasp, he clutched a pistol. A surge of relief washed over him at the sight of Michael's presence, allowing him to exhale a long-held breath of ease.

"I just about lost it," he confessed. "You've got to give some kind of warning when you show up so I don't freak out every time."

"Understand your emotions, and that will let you know I am near," Michael replied, taken aback upon seeing Caleb's disheveled hair and the water dripping from the pistol's barrel. "What did you do?"

"I infused holy water into a handful of bullets. Now, tell me—"

"It seems that you made an error somewhere along the way."

"Dang it," he whispered, his gaze falling upon the barrel with frustration.

He pivoted back to the kitchen, where he had left two buckets of holy water and a pack of ammunition. Upon opening the cylinder, he carefully removed the leaking bullets.

"I'm still curious, though; what did you mean about understanding my emotions?" he asked, deconstructing the bullets.

"You may have thought you were nervous, even scared, but your inner self should feel at ease," Michael stated, as he observed the fort.

"You're right," Caleb exclaimed, realization dawning on him like a bolt of lightning.

Michael walked up to the cushion citadel in wonder. "What is this?"

"You're an angel, you tell me," he retorted.

Unamused by his insolence, Michael teleported beside him. He exhaled heavily to ensure he'd get Caleb's attention.

"Okay, okay. I made a fort to try and hide her in case any unwelcome d guests decide to drop in," he stated, sluggishly whirling to lock with the Archangel's unwavering stare.

"And what about what you have here?"

"Oh, uhm, it's a cross imbued in holy water, and also filled these bullets with it."

"You do realize that the heat expelled from the gun after being fired will most likely dry it off. The most it might do is give the vile creature a bruise," Michael countered.

"Then what am I supposed to do, huh? She's in there right now, trying to tap into her powers to fight the devil. She shouldn't have to face it alone."

"She is not going to be alone."

"Well, I'm going to be there too," Caleb affirmed, a flicker of defiance in his eyes.

"If you insist on being stubborn, perhaps this may help prevent a casualty." He hovered a hand over the ammunition, etching pentagrams on the casings. "There, holy water is one with your weaponry."

"That was really cool," Caleb said, awe and wonder lacing his words.

"Now, tell me, you do not expect your fort to slow down demonic forces."

21

SIGNS OF EVIL

In the heart of the mountains, Lucifer stood tall, his left arm ablaze with flickering flames that alternated between an ominous black and a scorching yellow. With a commanding sweep of his hand, he conjured a luminous fireball in the palm of his right hand, its intensity captivating in its raw power. Drawing close his other arm, he allowed the fiery orb to absorb the surrounding flames, replenishing his own energy. Satisfied, he closed his hand, extinguishing the ball of untamed fire, a brief display of his restored might.

All of a sudden, a streak of pearly light pierced through the night sky, accompanied by a gale-force gust of wind, signaling the imminent arrival of his pet. Lucifer's eyes fixated on the distant horizon, a wicked grin spreading across his face as he sensed the approaching surge of energy.

"Well, that was astonishingly quick."

In a flurry of movement, Cerberus, the fierce and loyal hound, appeared before him, panting heavily in excitement, his eyes reflecting the satisfaction of having fulfilled his master's bidding.

"Let's see what you have discovered." He placed his hands delicately over Cerberus's eyes, a conduit to witness events unfolding in the laboratory. In an instant, he was transported, observing each unfolding moment as if he were physically present.

A shimmering fog materialized, and informed Lucifer that it was his target - Haines. Every fiber of his being resonated with recognition, confirming the identity of the elusive figure. His vengeful glare then fell upon the Roamer, extending a helping hand to an injured Victor.

"Well, well, well, a traitor lurking in the shadows," Lucifer whispered.

After seeing what he needed, the devil peered deeply into Cerberus's eyes, a gesture of gratitude and approval. Extending his hand, he generated a vibrant crimson energy beam, casting an emanation reminiscent of a delectable dog treat.

"You have done well, my faithful companion," Lucifer commended, tossing the animate treat high over the towering peaks.

Swift like lightning, Cerberus charged after his prize, a fleeting vision of loyalty and purpose. Believing he had the information necessary to track down Haines, Lucifer teleported within the confines of the lab itself, his presence commanding, amidst the remnants of the encounter between the scientist and the creature. In the flickering glow of malfunctioning lights, vibrant red electricity crackled impulsively, spasms of raw power cascading through the laboratory. Every pore in David's body quivered in terror. The chilling proximity to the devil sent shivers down his spine.

With immeasurable dread lurking deep within, David propelled himself forward, his heart racing at an accelerated tempo, reaching for his cellphone in a desperate attempt to make a call. Yet, to his unnerving dismay, the screen relentlessly flashed the unnerving digits of six hundred and sixty-six, searing through his already terrifying suspicions. Though gripped by a paralyzing fear, he sprinted forth like his very life depended on it.

Elsewhere, in a vacant spot outside the police station, Jason parked his car, but remained inside. He glanced at his reflection in the rearview mirror and adjusted it to get a clear view of what's behind him. He took a deep breath and emerged from the vehicle, forgetting to turn off the engine. As he made his way to the entrance, he jumped at every noise.

Once he stepped into the forensics lab, he heard country music blaring in the informational sanctuary. The walls were full of colorful posters of legendary country singers. In the corner, a worn-out dartboard hung precariously, evidence of the occasional respite from tireless work. A small CD player on the desk played these twangy tunes, adding an undeniable charm to the otherwise serious environment.

The analyst, a woman with a contagious enthusiasm evident in her every movement, donned a pair of glasses that accentuated her intellectual prowess. While sharing her latest discoveries about the virus, she cradled a minute container. Encased were remnants of a leaf.

"This peculiar specimen was discovered near the limbic lobe of the brain."

Javier lifted a brow in confusion as he examined the minuscule treasure. "And what exactly are we looking at here?"

A knowing smile formed on the analyst's lips as she leaned forward, focusing their attention. "Gentlemen, this leaf hails from a rare species of oak tree, exclusively found in the untamed lands of California. Locals call it the Death Oak."

A hint of somber realization crossed Cortez's face, his voice hushed with a mix of awe and horror. "No wonder how it got its name."

Inquisitive flames rippled through the detective, prompting him to come forth and join the conversation. "But how did this leaf end up there in the first place?" he asked. "What could be the significance behind it?"

"It was held inside the substance these people were injected with," she said, pivoting toward the computer screen.

In a calculated motion, she revealed a series of pictures which captured the essence of the pandemonium. They served as a chilling visual testament to the victims' wounds—punctures found on various body parts, be it arms, necks, or shoulders. Gender lines also blurred as these marks seared the canvas of both men and women, defying any predictable pattern.

A shroud of ambiguity swept across Javier's face. "None of them share any semblance of commonality, not even the puncture site," he shared, his voice faltering amidst the bewildering observations.

"None that we can see, anyway," Jason countered. He took a step closer and continued his train of thought. "Tell me, where was the last known crime scene?"

After several clicks, the analyst pulled the images of Kota, Simon, and Kyle, unveiling before them a clandestine visual narrative captured within the sacred confines of the hotel where Emily chose to reside—a cocoon teeming with secrets, patiently awaiting their discovery.

Jason, his pulse racing, turned toward the analyst, only to discover a shadow, dark and elusive, perched in the corner, commanding his attention.

"At last, I have found you," he blurted, propelled by unwavering purpose. His feet carried him to the shadows, his mind already weaving intricate narratives of revelation and triumph.

But alas, the moment his hand grazed the cold, barren wall, he came face to face with emptiness, with solitude. Confusion etched itself upon his features, his mind a labyrinth of unanswered questions, the mystery deepening with each passing moment.

What is going on? he mused, each syllable laced with a cocktail of bewilderment and fascination, his thirst for truth unyielding.

"Is everything alright?" the analyst queried.

"Yeah, I'm fine," Jason retorted with a hint of irritation. He headed back to the clustered group only to find the captain staring at him.

"Why don't you go home and get some sleep," he proposed. "I'll call you if we find any next leads, deal?"

"Yeah, okay."

Moments later, Jason settled into his vehicle. He held his head when a subtle shimmer enveloped the passenger seat. This drew him to start the engine. Haines, invisible to the naked eye, turned the radio on the very second the key turned in the ignition, awakening not only the mechanical mechanism but also the Roamer's plan.

A sharp jolt raced down Jason's spine as the radio sprang to life, seizing his attention with an iron grip. A foul voice slithered through the speakers and transcended the ordinary airwaves. Like an open book, it read his subconscious. The mention of the address, 696 Cold Stone Avenue, made his heart pound. Its thudding rhythm threatened to drown out all other sounds.

The voice on the radio reveled in its grotesque desires, passionately proclaiming a fervent wish to dismantle and ravage an unsuspecting family. Each word slithered through the airwaves, coiling around Jason's mind, tightening its grip on his fragile thoughts. A sense of impending doom seeped into every corner of his being, suffusing even the tiniest crevices of his consciousness.

Haines lingered close by, striving to comprehend the swirling depths of Jason's distress as if peeled back layers of a tormented soul. The physical radio appeared dormant, but the Roamer couldn't help but be ensnared by the enigma before him. Confusion clouded his thoughts as he grappled with the enigmatic nature of Jason's turmoil.

"What is he hearing?" he pondered, his curiosity igniting an ember on the edge of a consuming blaze.

"Precisely what I need him to," Oswald's voice reverberated within Haines's mind, mingling with shadows and secrets. "His unbridled fear will stimulate him to relocate his beloved wife and daughter and deliver them to those nefarious Entitles."

"Why tread such convoluted paths? If it is the family you seek, why not strike forthrightly?" He questioned, baffled by the labyrinthine plot unraveling before him.

A clandestine mirth entwined itself in Onward's tone, a dark symphony of sadistic amusement. "It's all too entertaining, don't you think? Besides, all the pieces have yet to fall if we're going to keep the angels at bay."

In a sudden frenzy, the car screeched to a stop, narrowly averting a collision from going past a red light. Jason's jittery hand jerked for the radio with his sights glued to the commanding stoplight. Undeniable fear colored his soul as he waited for it to change.

The velvet night, thick and impenetrable, draped itself all the way to Boris. The battlements of an aged church wept ebon tears for humanity's forgotten hopes. An eerie serenade from realms unseen pulled him into the quiet reverie of the forsaken churchyard. Driven by the ever-ticking clock, he directed all his pent-up rage into a fierce kick aimed at the side of the door.

The handle bore the brunt of his force, which dented the framework. Encouraged, he delivered another powerful blow, causing the stubborn door to yield just enough for him to slip inside. He then strolled to the font of holy water, situated near the entrance.

Uttering a fervent prayer, Boris bowed his head, seeking forgiveness from a higher power. "Forgive me, Father, for I have sinned," he began. "But you know my truth." His attention drifted upward, locking onto the magnificent ceiling above.

With wary hands, the broken man presented the sword to the light and lowered it into the awaiting font. Shards of the weapon splintered away, surrendering themselves to the holy water. As they floated, an unnerving drop in temperature froze the water, transforming it into an ice sculpture. Chills snaked their way down his spine.

"How dare you?" a menacing, disembodied voice growled from the shadows.

"W-who said that?" Boris stammered.

"We're the ones asking the questions," the voice replied.

A young man and woman, garbed in sixteenth-century attire, materialized before him. Their expressions twisted in disgust as they bore their reproachful gazes upon Boris.

"Of course there're more demons," Boris muttered under his breath.

"Did you hear thunder clapping or an ear-piercing screech? No? That's because we didn't come from Hades," the young man taunted with a hint of derision.

"Then what—" Boris began, only to be interrupted by the young woman's whisper in his ear.

"We are spirits of those who dwell beyond death."

Startled, Boris jumped, struggling to grapple with the incomprehensible circumstances that enveloped him.

"Your soul is marked for aiding that fiend in summoning Diablo from Hades," the young man asserted.

"Diablo, Hades...what? No, I never intended to unleash the devil. That demon slaughtered my wife and threatened to do the same to my children."

"So, you condemned the entire planet," the young man sneered, his anger seeping through his words.

"We don't have time for this," Boris pleaded.

An ember of anger ignited within the young man's eyes while his companion's gaze fixated on the weapon gleaming with holy water.

"Look, brother, isn't that—" the young woman began, her finger pointing towards the sword's hilt.

"It's Jack. What are you doing with him?" the young man asked, his voice laced with curiosity.

"With who? What do you mean? Where did I get the sword? It was buried deep within the catacombs."

"He has certainly seen better days," the young woman murmured, her eyes appraising the sword's worn form.

Boris couldn't help but voice his disbelief. "Why do you keep referring to this as if it were a person?"

"Because it is alive. It possesses the power to shape-shift. So why does it appear so forlorn?" the young woman replied, her words dripping with a sense of somber truth.

"Yeah, sure, why not. Demons are real, and apparently, spirits too. So, a living sword? I suppose that's not too far-fetched."

Intently examining the sword, the young woman unraveled Boris's plan for vengeance. "You mean to slay the fiend with this sword," she uttered, her hand hovering just inches away from the dull blade.

"It won't work, not unless you unlock its power," the young man added.

The scientist couldn't contain his wonder any longer. "How do you know all this?" he asked.

"We were part of Freyr's bloodline—the man who created this weapon," they both disclosed simultaneously, their voices harboring reverence and sorrow.

"Okay, then where is he? Maybe I can speak to him about utilizing his sword?"

"He's dead," the young man declared with unwavering conviction. "Although he may have been a God, he relinquished his powers to be with our mother."

"Of course he did," Boris sighed, a sense of resignation tingling his words. "One last question because I really must be going. Why are you sharing all of this with me? When you first appeared, you looked like you wanted to kill me."

"You are embarking on a mission to banish a great evil from your domain," the young woman stated.

"And we seek to purge as much malevolence as possible," the young man concluded, his gaze locking with his, full of resolve and an unyielding commitment to their cause.

A sudden loud bang reverberated through the stormy, rain-soaked sky. Boris turned his attention to the frost-laden window, just in time to witness a tempest raging outside. When he pivoted back, he discovered that the two spirits had vanished.

Filled with trepidation, he moved to exit the church, but the plaintive cries of a child echoed through the building, drawing him toward their source.

In a panic, he hurried to the altar where he took cover. Anxiety overtook him the second the door swung open. It was a boy in search of a place to hide.

He darted around, his breath coming in quick, panicked gasps. In a fumbling motion, he ducked down and scurried between the rows of wooden pews. The high backs easily concealed his small frame. His fingers trembled as he gripped the edge of a hymnal book, using it to shield his face.

An eerie silence descended over the sacred space, broken by the boy's muffled whimpers. As heavy footsteps began to echo through the nave, the boy's eyes widened in terror. It became clear that his hiding spot would not suffice.

In a burst of desperate energy, he scrambled from his hiding place, his shoes squeaking against the polished floor. His gaze locked onto the imposing statue of Archangel Michael that stood near the altar, its marble form radiating an aura of protection. He made a break for it in spite of his growing fear.

As soon as he reached the figure, he slid behind it and dropped to his knees, ending the time for indecisiveness. Without warning, the door creaked open once more.

A man shuffled in, his posture stooped and movements slow. His gray-tinged goatee framed a face lined with wrinkles, marred by fresh bruises. Still crutched behind the altar, Boris's breath caught in his throat when the glint of a butcher knife clutched in the man's hand caught his eye.

This wicked man crept forward, his free hand running along the tops of the pews. At each row, he bent down, peering into the shadows between the seats. The knife swayed with every movement, drawing him ever closer to the statue.

Boris clutched the sword, hoping that he could strike at the right moment. To his surprise, however, the weapon underwent a transformative metamorphosis. Its once dull blade and worn hilt breathed new life, revealing a supple leather grip accompanied by a thirty-inch double-sided steel blade.

Nevertheless, it wasn't until the man laid eyes on the boy that his composure dissolved. Despite the need to remain inconspicuous, he knew he had to save the boy from a grim fate. Fueled by this determination, he rose to his feet with the sword held high, and charged towards the wicked man.

Caught off guard by the unexpected presence, the man attempted to react, but Jack effortlessly plunged into his stomach. Blood spilt from his mouth as he collapsed, face-down, onto the floor. The child, rescued from imminent peril, fled from the church in a frenzy.

Boris beheld the gleaming sword. For the first time, his eyes took on the majestic form of Jack in all its original glory.

"So, you can shape-shift, huh? I don't suppose you can turn into a cloak of invisibility."

22

THE NEXT TRIAL

Michael stood at the doorway, his piercing gaze fixed on Caleb, who paced back and forth across the room. With each turn, he swiped across his phone screen, searching for more information that might offer protection against demonic forces.

He muttered under his breath a few times, pausing to jot down notes.

After what seemed like an eternity of this relentless search, Michael's lips curled into a satisfied smile. "Very few mortals handle the revelation so well," he said, his voice cutting through the tension. "You are doing remarkably."

A sharp rap at the door drowned their exchange. Caleb's brow furrowed as he took a few steps forward. He stopped and whirled around to grab the bag of salt lying on the table behind the Archangel. Preparing himself for the worst, he poured some in his hand while proceeding to the entrance.

"Who is it?" he asked.

"It's Dave," came the familiar voice from the other side.

Relieved but still wary, Caleb returned the salt to the bag and unlatched the door. As he opened it, he caught sight of a yellow cab pulling away from the curb. His eyes roved over the street, noting the absence of his truck.

"Dave?" he asked, glancing at the vacant curb. "You didn't drive here?"

The scientist remained on the doorstep, unkempt and haggard. "It's a long story. May I come in?"

"Of course." Caleb stepped aside to let David cross the threshold.

From the other room, Michael repositioned his gaze from Emily to the newcomer. In an instant, he materialized before them, his eyes fixed on the visitor. "You are not clean," he declared.

David's posture constricted, his shoulders curling in a reflexive guard. "Excuse me?" he retorted; his voice sharp with indignation. He turned to Caleb, confusion and wariness evident in his expression. "Who is this guy?"

Done with the pretense, Michael interjected, his tone grave, "The virus, you have it."

Caleb's pupils dilated, his forehead crumpling with confusion. He looked from his friend to Michael. "Can't you heal him?"

The Archangel's expression remained impassive, his eyes never leaving David. "No," he replied, his voice steady and matter of fact. "But I know who can."

The scientist shot his arms outward, suggesting they put a pin in their solution. "Wait, wait, let me show you something first. I think it can help."

He narrowed his concentration on the bag of salt lying on the table. At first, nothing happened, but a quiet twitch. Then, it became a violent tremble. Suddenly, the table groaned, inching backward across the floor. The next thing they knew, the bag tore open. A cascade of white crystals spilled out, scattering across the floor in a grainy waterfall.

Caleb's jaw dropped; his eyes wide with disbelief. He stared at the salt-strewn floor for a moment. "I don't believe it," he breathed.

With the shake of his head, he aimed for the kitchen. His voice drifted back, filling with a new sense of possibility. "You can help Emily fight the devil."

"Excuse me?"

"You said you wanted to help," he said, returning to the room with a broom in hand.

"Yeah, I meant to stop Boris from doing this to anyone else."

"Unlike you, I don't have powers," he informed, sweeping up the salt.

"Yeah, but—"

A soft gasp from the living room pivoted his concentration. Emily awoke from her meditative state.

She blinked in surprise at the wonders that encased her. Cushions stacked all around her like castle walls and a large, thick blanket draped overhead.

What in the world? she pondered.

"Uhm, what's going on?"

Caleb dropped the broom as her voice cut through the air. "You're okay!" he breathed, a profound sense of relief overwhelming him. With his heart pounding like a drum, he rushed to the other room, eager to meet her in the fort. His smile blossomed the instant his eyes met hers.

"Was this you?" she asked, reaching for the couch to help her up.

"It was a precaution," he informed, extending a hand to better assist her to her feet. "So, do you feel any different?"

"I'm not sure. I—"

"That was only the beginning. You have opened the door inside your mind. Now, it's time to harness your abilities," Michael asserted, towering over them.

"And how am I supposed to do that?"

"It's simple. You need to go through the door."

"Seriously, more med—"

"It's more than just meditation. Focus and delve into your darkest memories, only then will you find the door," he explained.

David, observing from the threshold, couldn't get past the devil remark, and voiced his concerns. "What makes you think Satan is out there? I mean, sure, there's been a spike in terrible events lately, but the world is full of nut jobs."

"There is no time to brief you on the situation," Michael said.

"My point is, angels are responsible for putting him back in his place, not ours."

"I forgot that you go to church," Caleb said.

"Yeah, but even so, it's clear they're all around. Just the other day, I was leaving the lab and saw Jeff—you remember him?"

"Isn't he the guy who always tried to get you to look over his physics homework during lunch?"

"Yes. He walked right up to Kim at the dessert bar. The moment he spoke to her, I felt a breeze pass by, only there was no wind."

"May we dispense with the idle chit chat?" Michael asked, urgency lacing his tone. "Emily must proceed with her training."

Swift like lightning, Caleb turned to face his partner, his touch gentle and firm, as he took her hands in his at her sides. The slight tremor in his grip revealed his anxiety about the situation. "You don't have to do this."

"I think it's a bit too late for that, don't you?" she asked, tapping his thumbs.

"Demons may exist, but they also have weaknesses," Caleb stated. "I'm willing to bet the devil does too."

Michael nodded. "He does, and she is standing right here."

Her partner shot a disapproving glare at him. "No, you can't make her relive past trauma."

"It is the only way for her to tap into her power."

Emily stepped between them, her eyes darting from her partner to Michael and back again. With a hint of exasperation in her voice, she said, "Will you please stop arguing with an angel?"

Once these words left her mouth, a wave of dizziness washed over her. She flung a hand to her temple, pressing against her skin in an effort to quell the throbbing pain behind her eyes. Her vision swam, the room tilting at odd angles.

"Whoa," she blurted, her free hand extending for support.

"As she swayed, Caleb jumped forward to steady her, wrapping an arm around her waist. "Emily, are you okay?"

"Yeah, I just feel exhausted," Emily confessed.

"It is the door inside your subconscious," Michael informed, deducing the cause. "Now that it has taken form in your mind, it must be maintained, or it will drain you."

"What?!" Caleb snapped his head up at the Archangel. "Funny how you left that part out."

"I assure you, there is no cause for alarm. Once the trials are complete, she will be fine."

The author glanced back at Emily, only to find her unconscious. Panic washed over him as he shook her, but his efforts yielded no response.

"Em," he whispered, dropping his head onto her shoulders.

"Is she okay?" David asked, concern coloring his words.

Michael stood his position, locked onto Emily's weary form. "She is going to be fine," he assured. "I sense a strong heartbeat."

Caleb scooped her into his arms, her limp body feeling light against his chest. He carried her to the couch and laid her down on the soft cushions. Kneeling beside her, he brushed a stray lock of hair from her face.

"Isn't there anything you can do for her?" he asked.

"This is something she must do on her own," Michael affirmed.

"Emily," Caleb called out.

23

MEMORY LANE

Caleb's words echoed in the vast expanse of Emily's subconscious. Her anxious heart thumped, each beat rippling through the empty void. Panicked breaths were the only sound in the realm. A faint glimmer of light seeped through a cracked door, casting long shadows that danced on the edge of perception. Whispers intertwined with the air, guiding her hesitant steps.

As she crossed the threshold, a new world unfurled before her. The door led her back to the memory of her uncle, his voice strained with urgency while trying to convey his theory about the Hilltown massacre. Emily, a young girl at the time, adorned a delicate blue ribbon in her hair. She stood beside her mother. Inside Don's office, a palpable air of orderliness prevailed. Papers were stacked on the desk, their edges sharp and unblemished. At the top of the pile, front and center, rested the case file in question.

In the pristine office, Don's jaw clenched, his fingers drumming an agitated rhythm on the polished desk. He slammed his fist onto the desk. He couldn't understand why no one wanted to go over the facts when he provided reasonable doubt.

His superior's words sharpened. "You need to calm down. All I'm saying is you need to take another look at the documents you submitted."

"Why?" he asked, nursing a bruised knuckle. "Because the truth contradicts your belief system?"

The captain's eyes narrowed, his voice dropping to a low, steely tone that brooked no argument. "You are an officer of the law, for God's sake. Do you want to be a laughingstock? It won't matter how many successful cases you've solved. Your credibility will crumble."

Don edged forward, his eyes fused with his superior's, a perilous spark of defiance flickering within. "Tell me, what exactly do you want me to change? Are you asking me to say that I believed those teenagers broke into those homes and ruthlessly slaughtered their victims?"

"For starters, yes. "We had DNA evidence, and their fingerprints were found at the crime scenes."

"Why do you think those suspects took their lives?" Don asked. "Do you think it was out of guilt or fear? Fear that whatever merciless force claimed the lives of those innocent people would come for them next?"

Apprehension marred the captain's face as he surveyed Don, now a shadow of the exceptional officer he once was. "What happened to you? Not two months ago, you were hailed as one of the finest officers this department had ever seen. You solve cases with unwavering reliance on facts. Now, you refuse to acknowledge the imminent closure of the Hill Town massacre case, instead clinging to a belief in the unnatural."

"Because there is something sinister at play."

Having heard enough, his superior came to a decision. "I am placing you on mandatory leave, effective immediately. I'll take your badge and gun."

Outside the office, Ms. Puller and her child glued their sights upon the closed door. Unaware to all, a subtle surge of purple electricity coursed through young Emily's eyes. In the doorway, present-day Emily stood, silently observing, her presence a reminder of forgotten memories.

"I don't remember this," she whispered, her voice carrying a hint of confusion. "Mom and I had come to surprise Uncle Don, but instead, he was being reprimanded. So, we went back to the car."

As she delved deeper into the recesses of her memory, she took notice of her surroundings. Although she hadn't left the office in the traditional sense, she sat in the confines of the vehicle beside her younger self. "How did I end up here?" she asked, realizing she was alone. "Where's mom?"

In the waking world, a loud thud reverberated through the room as Emily's hand struck the floor. Velvet hues sparked at her fingertips, sending electric tingles dancing through the cracks. Caleb's breath seized in his throat, spellbound by the spectacle. He reached out to her with a shuddering hand.

David backed out of the room, getting out of dodge from the smoke left by the electricity in the floor. When he looked over and saw Caleb about to touch Emily's hand, he just about freaked.

"I wouldn't do that!"

In an instant, Michael materialized beside him, already clutching his hand. "Trust me, you do not want to do that."

Mesmerized by the light in the Archangel's eyes, he froze, but in a calm manner. When Michael turned to face Emily, a radiant glow emanated from his outstretched hand, enveloping her fragile form.

Back inside her consciousness, Emily heard his voice calling out to her. Then, as if by magic, he appeared in the passenger seat.

"What is going on?"

"Due to your incredible power, it occasionally emerged without restraint."

Confused, Emily pressed for further clarification. "What does that mean? Why don't I remember?"

"You were a mere child, tapping into a vast well of untold powers. I had no choice but to shield you from those memories until you were ready."

The next thing she knew, they were standing back inside the office. Her younger self sat in a chair against the wall. Not a moment too soon did Mrs. Puller walk up, her face dawning worried lines. "There you are," she said with a sigh of relief "Where'd you run off to? The bathroom?"

Present-day Emily turned to face the Archangel, still pondering his words. Her frustration boiled to the surface. "You manipulated me. My mother was run down, and my sister brutally murdered. You haven't kept me safe at all. If anything, I would have been better prepared to face these things if it weren't for you."

Michael glared at her as their surroundings morphed into Emily's childhood home in California. She scanned the room and saw her seventeen-year-old-self writing: happy birthday Kota on a vanilla cake. "No, I don't want to be here," her present self said.

Meanwhile, in the house, a purple mystic light devoured the wall facing her open palm. The violet incandescence sparkled, bathing ethereal hues around the room. It was like amethyst glimmers had descended, instilling a warm calmness over Caleb. His clenched hand softened as he watched in awe.

Soon, the wall began to vibrate along the upper corners, causing tiny specks of paint to rain down. The honey-toned cabinets and island below pulsed with energy. Seeing this, David turned his gaze back to Caleb.

"I think we should get out of here," he said.

"You can go, but I'm staying."

A low hum littered Emily's ears as she redirected her focus to the window, joining her excited younger self.

I can't sit back and watch this. She thought, hearing her inner voice ricochet across the vast space.

"You cannot change a memory," Michael retorted.

Then, the sound of a neighboring door slamming shut stole her attention. As her younger self ran to put the candles on the cake, present-day Emily turned her gaze toward the source. She saw a disheveled man staggering down the steps outside his door. A fresh bruise marred the skin over his right cheekbone, partially hidden by the tangled mess of his beard. He moved with a limp, his palms—showcasing bloodied knuckles—pressed against his forehead. Once inside, he wasted no time in starting the vehicle and darting out of the driveway.

A smooth and steady purr dragged her focus forward where she found her mom and sister sitting in the car for a moment. She could see her mom talking to Kota in a stern manner.

Come on. Drive away. You forgot something.

Her wishes weren't met, however, as the doors swung open. The moment her mother got out and Kota's foot touched the grass, the wailing cries of a foreign vehicle veered toward the curb at an alarming rate. With no time to react, Mrs. Puller dashed to the curb and pushed Kota back inside the car. This action placed her in harm's way, hurtling her into the tree with its exposed roots.

Hearing the loud thud sent shivers down young Emily's spine as she darted towards the window and found her mom pinned against the trunk.

"Mom!!" she bellowed, releasing violet waves around the window, which also cracked along the exterior and the door. Thick smoke twirled in the wind, devouring all of her surroundings. Present-day Emily looked down as a violet tear slid down her cheek.

Michael fixed his gaze on her, bearing witness to her fading form. In a heartbeat, she resurfaced in her physical form, springing upright on the couch.

Caleb sprinted over and dropped to his knees to make himself eye level. He rubbed her back and met her stare.

"I'm so glad you're back."

"Me too," she said, engulfing him in a bear hug.

All of a sudden, the drywall gave way, disrupting the moment. Dust and debris showered upon the floor. The trio jumped, though only Emily appeared shocked.

"I saw that coming," David said, inching his way into the room. He greeted her with a stationary wave. "I didn't get a chance to introduce myself. I'm Dave."

"Uhm, hi?"

Caleb followed her stare on the fractured wall. "Don't worry. It's nothing that can't be fixed."

"Did I—"

"Indeed you did," Michael interjected, materializing before the trio. "Your powers are awakening, but you lack control."

Emily's eyes glittered with cold fury as she looked up at him. "Why didn't you warn me?"

"That would have only exacerbated your emotional state."

Still glaring at him, she inquired, "what exactly happened back there?"

"It's called Astral Projection," Michael clarified.

"Astral," Caleb began, his gaze fixed on the angel. "Isn't that when the soul leaves your body?"

Confusion clouded Emily's mind as she recalled appearing inside her mom's car after thinking where she wanted to go. And at the same time, how she watched herself disappear from the vehicle.

"Can you explain exactly what happened?" she asked.

"Unable to deal with the negative energy around your uncle's office, your mind sought an escape. Just like the last memory, you wanted to run so the moment you saw what you needed to, you fled back here."

Caleb's voice lifted, tinged with the shimmer of hope dancing in his eyes. "So, does that mean the trial is over?"

Michael's eyes burned with a fervent glow, reflecting the heavy burden of unfulfilled duties. "No, there are still five more abilities she must unlock, and we must proceed right now."

24

ALLIANCE

I n the pulsating heart of the office building, called Enerwave Tracks, where cubicles and workstations stretched as far as the eye could see, a symphony of clattering keyboards and ringing phones painted the air with a tangible sense of urgency. The clerical work had accumulated like an insurmountable mountain, forming towering stacks of paperwork that threatened to engulf the employees.

Amidst this ocean of chaos, a young man sat at his desk, a lone soldier in the battle against the endless tide of information. With determined focus, he wiped his glasses, his gaze unwavering from the glow of his computer screen. The desk displayed his name plaque, a symbol of his identity and place within the corporate hierarchy - Scott Cunningham.

Scott's fingers tapped away at the keyboard, entering data regarding the recent surge of energy that had plunged several towns into a dark abyss. Upon nearing the final sentence of the first paragraph, a chill in the air seized the room. Tendrils of inky black smoke materialized, like whispering phantoms breaking free from the confines of their dimension.

Unbeknownst to the office denizens, the aging mail clerk shuffled through the room, his weary eyes fixed on the day's task. Ignoring the eerie spectacle dancing before him, he steered in its direction. Time slowed to a crawl as the misty tendrils extended their reach, a sinister appendage fueled by malevolence. In an instant, the oblivious mail clerk had been propelled across the room, colliding with the rigid walls that resonated with the force of impact.

Scott shot up from the chair, his body tensing with a surge of fear. The sense of impending danger permeated the air, his heart threatening to burst from his chest.

A voice emerged from the ominous shroud of smoke, slicing through the silence like a sharp knife.

"You can drop the charade. You are not fooling me," it declared. "I know what you really are."

Devoid of any emotion, a man and woman rose from their adjacent cubicles. Their movements seemed almost mechanical, guided by an unseen force. With calculated detachment, they glided towards Scott and the swirling darkness. While the entity's words hung in the air, they fixed their gazes upon the billowing mass of dark vapor. No flicker of surprise or fear marred their stoic expressions, only wonder.

"Calm yourselves, I am not here to fight," the voice continued as a presence engulfed in shadows stepped forward.

Scott furrowed his brow, attempting to comprehend the situation at hand. "So, what is it that you want?"

"I know you are in pursuit of the unawakened archangel. I share your desire to stop her. However, she is protected by the Archangels."

"You are a phantom, an entity that strikes without warning. How can an angel thwart you?"

"He had assistance."

"But how are we expected to succeed where you have failed?"

The woman joined the conversation. "We appear as ordinary mortals. Our powers remain concealed until the moment of attack, making it too late for anyone to intervene, even an Archangel."

Scott couldn't help but express his skepticism. "If you possess all the answers and insights, why don't you just strike—"

"My kind will be lurking within the shadows, observing your every move. We await the opportune moment when you manage to catch her off guard."

A tinge of doubt seeped into the woman's voice as she dismissed the proposed plan. "That approach will never work."

Without warning, the phantom took shape behind the two unsuspecting Entitles who approached from their cubicles. In a swift motion, its hand rose up, hovering above them. It drained the very essence of life until their corporeal forms disintegrated into ethereal wisps.

As the dust floated in the air, the phantom bore its eyes into Scott, emanating an intensity that sent a shiver down his spine.

"We have no time for this. Either take my offer or perish where you stand."

Fear gnawed at the last Entitle's gut, intertwining with a fierce survival instinct.

Worlds apart, in the ethereal expanse of Heaven—a place where the very fabric of existence shimmered with celestial splendor—Gabriel made his way into Raphael's sacred quarters. The closer he got, his presence announced itself with a transcendent glow. As soon as he entered the quarters, his eyes were drawn to a panorama of wonder and divine artistry.

The chamber itself adorned walls woven from threads of luminescent gold and silver, glistening in eternal twilight. Suspended in the air were emerald orbs. In the center stood Raphael, his form a vision of pure reverence. He bowed and unfurled his wings.

"Apologies for interrupting your solace, Raphael, but we must converse."

"What troubles you?"

"You sense it too, right? I presume that is why you are here."

"What is happening below?"

"The Entities have returned and are in pursuit of the mortal."

"Then we must eradicate them, once and for all," Raphael declared.

"Yes, but are you prepared to disobey orders? Michael contends that they pose no threat."

The emerald radiance gradually faded from the healer, as he pondered the opposing question. "Michael has yet to understand that waiting for orders sometimes results in devastating consequences."

"He is attempting to expedite her training so that she will be able to take matters into her own hands," Gabriel explained.

"But if she completes the final trial, she shall possess a power that our enemies can hone in on," Raphael stated.

"The Entitles have already managed to eliminate a significant number of our men; there's no guarantee that she will be strong enough to withstand their onslaught."

"Well, Gabriel, I presume you have a well-thought-out plan."

Concealed beneath a veil of white flames, Haines and Victor positioned themselves across the street from Caleb's suburban home. An eerie stillness devoured them as they observed their target, remaining invisible to anyone who might have chanced a glance in their direction.

Their glare fixated on the house; Haines broke the silence with a hushed voice.

"Just look at them in there," he whispered, his words infused with disdain. "They actually thought they'd be safe here."

Victor, unwavering in his focus on the house, contemplated the situation, the weight of uncertainty etched on his furrowed brow.

"How far along do you suppose she is in the trials?" he questioned.

Hesitant, Haines offered a measured response. "I'm not sure," he mused, his words muffled by the crackling of unseen flames. "But if they continue on uninterrupted, it won't be much longer."

25

INNER THOUGHTS

Dark clouds draped themselves heavily across the horizon, their weight pressing down on Jason as he hunched over the steering wheel in his car. A bleak shadow fell over him, the sky's pallor reflecting on the windshield. The engine hummed, its sound merging with the unsettling comments from the radio. Voices grew more sinister, intertwining with the rhythm of his racing heart, filling the confined space with an eerie tension. Each word became a sharp sting aimed directly at him. His fingers clenched the leather steering wheel, the pressure building with each passing second.

How could someone allow these creeps to spew their horrible desires over the airwaves?

Suddenly, Tori arrived with their daughter in the backseat. His urgency catapulted him out of the car, his anxious footsteps echoing on the concrete. As Tori opened her car door, he hurriedly beckoned her, desperation consuming his voice. "Come on," he implored, swinging the door open. "We need to find a safe haven for you and Ally."

Perplexed, Tori stepped aside, momentarily blocking the path to her car door. The weight of their daughter's recent struggles hung heavy in the air, overshadowing any other concerns.

"Today was supposed to be a day full of joy for Ally. We were finally about to be next in line at the teddy bear factory. You can't disrupt it like this. Your job is taking a toll on your sanity."

Frustrated, Jason tried to explain the gravity of the situation, but Tori began to hear the sound of static noise. As she approached his car, she discovered that he had the radio turned nearly all the way up.

"It's nothing but white noise," she observed, staring at the radio.

She inched towards the receiver, determined to shut it off, but he grabbed her by the wrist and spilt out the details about the horrifying messages that had streamed from the radio. The voice promised the uncertainty of their fate, in an unknown timeframe which they would be subjected to its malevolence.

Fear coursed through his veins like icy tendrils, jolting him into action. He urged Tori to get back in her car and leave with Ally.

"You have to go now," he insisted, his voice dripping with desperation. "It's the only way I can keep you safe."

Tori's shoulders slumped as she sank into the driver's seat. Her eyes dimmed, reaching for the window crank. With a trembling hand, she rolled it down and stared up at him. Her voice crackled with a mix of emotion, longing for a resolution to her husband's inner demons.

"You need to rest," she asserted. "I'll continue with our plans for the day without you. We'll be back later tonight."

Realization set in that his pleas had fallen on deaf ears. His lips pressed into a thin line, a twitch forming at the corner of his mouth. He let out a subtle huff, flaring his arms around. The window absorbed the force of his punch, a testament to his mounting anguish as his wife vanished from his sight.

Jason sauntered and inserted the key into the lock when an idea hit him like a ton of bricks. "That's it," he said. "If I change the lock, she'll have no choice but to stay at a hotel or something."

This idea prompted him to retract the key, get back in his vehicle and head for the nearest hardware store. A streetlight that lingered on red, halted his tracks. During which point stationed him near Caleb's home.

In the messy living room, Michael approached Emily with a sense of authority. "Close your eyes and release the grip of your nerves. Leave behind all distractions that pull at your attention. Quiet your mind, and hone in on Caleb's thoughts."

Unsure of what was about to happen, Emily raised an eyebrow and questioned, "What?"

"The next phase of your training is to tap into the minds of others. And surely unraveling your thoughts will not pose much of a challenge."

Her partner expressed his excitement. "Wow, so she's going to be able to read minds?"

"Among other abilities, yes."

Emily listened, immersing herself in the moment. With every breath, she prepared herself for the next stage of her training. Sensing her readiness, Michael shifted his attention towards him, his gaze now fixed upon the other crucial player in this intricate interplay.

"Alright," he began. "Clear your mind of any lingering negativity. Embrace a state of serenity."

In the neighboring houses, the Entitles barged inside, unleashing fear on the unsuspecting residents. Frantic screams pierced the air as the occupants fled. Not willing to relinquish his prey, Cunningham gave chase, only to be stopped by his colleague.

"Let go of me, Morgana," he strained.

"No. This isn't why we've come." Conceding to her reasoning, he sighed, his fear of the phantoms getting the better of him.

Out on the front lawn, Haines closed his eyes and tuned into the currents of dark energy swirling in the atmosphere. "We are not alone," he declared.

Victor tilted his head and raised his hand, fingers grazing his chin. His pools darted at the Roamer. "What do you mean?"

"It seems those resilient little Entitles have at last caught up with us."

"But how? I thought they had been eradicated long ago."

Haines shrugged, a smug confidence creeping into his response. "Well, it appears that a few managed to slip through the cracks. Nevertheless, they shall not impede my plans."

Weary from the interminable wait, Victor curled his hands into fists. In the same beat, his eyes transformed into unfathomable pools of darkness. But just as his impulsive urges threatened to take control, the Roamer cast a glance in his direction, compelling his body into a state of unnerving stillness.

"This is precisely why demons consistently falter. They are too consumed by their impatience, unwilling to bide their time until all the intricate threads align."

Haines felt the creature's immense agitation give way and loosened his vice-like grip, granting his comrade the freedom to turn and face him.

"This prolonged game has reached its limits. Sinners will eternally remain slaves to their filthy emotions," Victor declared.

Haines attempted to reason with his ally's perception. "While your observation of their triviality is correct, rest assured that our grand design unfolded precisely as planned. However, if the thirst for bloodshed consumed you to such an extent, why not focus your wrath upon those who were on the brink of launching an attack? I must caution you, though, exceeding the thresholds of power safeguarded by the protection spell I wove around you would expose your presence to the Archangel."

In a jarring encounter, an Entitle sprang forth from the shadows, its gnashing teeth poised and ready to devour the demon, seeking to drain him of his potent energies. Reacting swiftly, Victor lunged forward, seizing the sinister entity in his powerful grip, his hand mercilessly crushing its fragile throat. Smoke billowed forth from the entity's blood, scorching the creature's fingertips with an acrid burn.

Enclosed once again in the living room, Emily shifted her concentration, tapping into the fragments of the angel's memories. She wanted to use this time to unveil any secrets her mentor may have kept. At first, Caleb's thoughts hit her with a resounding force. His worry and love for her became apparent. But after a little focus, she tapped into Michael's aura. Once there, a series of shockwaves reverberated through her very being, pulling her out of the serene sphere of meditation. Her eyes fluttered open with the weight of her newfound knowledge.

"That was fast," the Archangel began. "So, tell me, what occupies this mortal's mind?"

"I haven't the faintest idea," Emily retorted, her voice tinged with a subtle edge. "But you, on the other hand, orchestrated this whole thing."

"Excuse me?"

"I believe I witnessed events from the past. You were outside the coffee shop nestled on the corner of First and Second street long before my arrival. You set the stage where I'd meet someone, hoping to tether me to a specific location."

Michael, choosing to dismiss these claims, interjected, "You disobeyed my instructions."

"Wait, so our encounter wasn't a chance occurrence?" Caleb queried.

"No, it was nothing more than a precise and calculated deception orchestrated by this purported angel."

"It is true that you were always going to visit that coffee shop at some point. I simply expedited the process by arranging for your book signing event to conclude ahead of schedule."

"You were the, quote unquote, person my agent mentioned, the one who purchased all the remaining copies of my book."

"And what about my feelings? Are they products of manipulation, or are they genuine?" Emily asked.

A knot tightened in her chest, her breathing becoming shallow and rapid as the realization of Michael's betrayal settled in. Her mind raced, questioning every interaction, every moment she'd shared with Caleb. Was any of it real? Had she been nothing more than a pawn in some celestial game? The memory of their first meeting flashed before her eyes, once warm and serendipitous, now cold and calculated. She saw Caleb stumbling into her, spilling her coffee - had that been orchestrated too? The thought made her head spin.

"How dare you?" she voiced in a contained fury. "You had no right to manipulate our lives like this. Who gave you the authority to play God with our emotions?"

Anger and betrayal warred with confusion and a stubborn hope that somehow, despite it all, her connection with Caleb was genuine. She turned to him, her eyes searching his face for any sign of complicity or deceit.

"Did you know about this?" she breathed, her words a fragile whisper.

Caleb shook his head, looking as shocked as she felt. "No, I... how could I have known."

Her gaze darted between the two, unsure of who she could truly trust in this web of divine manipulation. The room seemed to spin around her, the foundations of her reality crumbling beneath her feet.

"I need some air," she muttered, pushing past both of them and heading for the door. As she reached for the handle, she paused, turning back to Michael with eyes that blazed with hurt. "This changes everything. How can I trust anything you say now?"

Without waiting for an answer, she wrenched open the door and stepped outside, leaving a stunned silence in her wake.

Soon after her exit, David entered, his brow furrowed in confusion. He glanced from Michael to Caleb, then to the door. His lips parted, as if struggling to process the scene before him. "She does understand the stakes, right?" he mustered. "Because it seems like, she lets every emotion distract her from what's important."

The author's gaze snapped to David, a flicker of defensiveness crossing his features, while Michael remained impassive, his eyes still fixed on the doorway where Emily had disappeared.

While tensions rose, the ripple effect of celestial machinations spread further. In the heart of the city, Gabriel and Raphael materialized in Scott's office at Enerwave Tracks. The faint scent of ozone lingered, a residual whisper from their emergence. Their eyes traced the contours of the space, but it was the tingling resonance blanketing the four walls that captured their attention, assuring them they had arrived at the right place.

"They were here," Gabriel announced, his decisive movements bringing him to the computer atop Cunningham's desk.

Raphael, fixated on the wisps of smoke spiraling upward from several tiles on the floor, responded with a resolute nod.

"I concur. The lingering presence of malevolence is still palpable within these confines."

"Then let us purify this space and continue on our quest." Gabriel's ethereal form radiated an intensified luminosity that engulfed the entire edifice in its divine essence.

Brilliant beams of pure, radiant light emitted from their core and shot out in every direction. A searing wave of benevolent heat, then rippled outwards, purging every taint of darkness and malevolence. Whispers of a fading hymn disintegrated into motes of sparkling dust.

The explosive purification spread far and wide, touching the burnished disk of the sun's rays. It cast sharp beams that played against a timber maze in walking distance of the abandoned church. Hidden within the labyrinth of trees, Boris wedged himself into a hollowed-out tree. His body pressed against the rough, moss-covered walls, camouflaging him within nature's hideaway.

All around him, officers combed the area, their voices low but urgent. Dogs barked sporadically, their keen noses scanning for his scent. Flashes of sunlight glistened in Boris's eyes, reflecting off the badges. Still, he remained stone-still, his heart pounding in sync with the footsteps that occasionally drew too close.

As they advanced beyond the tree, he let out a quiet sigh. His mind soon drifted to better times. A time where Rylee brought him to the woods and talked him into climbing the tallest tree with her.

"Alight," Rylee began, looking up at a lively tree. "This one should do."

"For what?"

She glanced back at Boris with a smile. "We're going to climb it." Shifting her focus upward, she continued, "The higher you go, the more calming it gets."

"Are you sure about that?"

"It's what I do whenever I feel like I'm drowning," she'd explained, already reaching for the first branch.

Well aware of the need to stay focused, he shook his head, drowning in a sea of consequences. He'd climbed even higher than ever before, not in altitude but in the stakes of his predicament. Voices of the search party became distant, granting himself a silent sigh of relief. He drifted his stare to the bark near his face and noted twisted symbols accompanied by jagged lines engraved in the wood.

"What was that fiend doing near hallowed ground?" He wondered.

Once the coast cleared, he descended the tree with cautious steps. After reaching the base, a glint of light caught his eye, drawing his focus to a small, inconspicuous object half-buried in the soft moss. Curiosity piqued, he walked over and knelt down to brush away layers of leaves. Upon removing several handfuls, a weathered key graced his sights. Would this chance discovery prove helpful or ineffective in his quest?

Of all the things I could find out here. I've got to find out what this might open.

A thoughtful expression overtook his face as he held the mundane object in the palm of his hand. Its intricate black and red pattern etched with a golden border drew him in even further. He flipped it over and found three letters—T.A.S—carved into the middle.

Back to the battle, which thanks to Haines's magic, remained concealed just beyond the confines of the house. An amber tint moved around Emily while she stood just outside the door. She folded her arms and stared at the sky where flashes of light illuminated the early evening clouds. The sun, not yet set, cast long shadows across the yard as it dipped towards the horizon. Her mind raced, still reeling from the revelation of Michael's manipulation.

Caleb joined her in the fading daylight. "Em?" he said. "Are you okay?"

She turned to him, her eyes glistening with unshed tears. "I don't know, Caleb. How can any of this be okay? Our entire relationship...was it all just part of some divine plan?"

When he opened his mouth to respond, Morgana set her sights on the unawakened archangel. But before she could close in, Victor sprang into action. A billowing mass of black substance erupted from his eyes, splitting into nine distinct parts as it hurtled towards her and her army. Upon impact, the air crackled, creating a strong gust of wind that swept across the yard.

Emily's hair whipped around her face as Caleb pulled her close, shielding her from the sudden chill. "Whatever brought us together," he murmured, his voice barely audible above the wind, "my feelings for you are real. I know that in my heart."

She looked up at him, conflict evident in her eyes. After a moment's hesitation, she nodded, allowing herself to lean into his embrace. "Let's go back inside and figure this out."

As they turned to reenter the house, Haines observed as an arm launched out from the murky depths of the inky substance and constructed a vice-like grip around Morgana's hand.

"It's been a while since I've witnessed this particular ability," he retorted.

His eyes fixed upon the black morphing substance that began to replicate the very likeness of Victor. A semblance of curiosity mingled with a trace of caution colored his words, heightening the suspense thickening the already tense air.

Scott's lips curled into a subtle yet defiant smile as he surveyed the emerging copies, a calculated plan surging within his mind.

"These entities find sustenance in the energy they siphon," he elucidated. "Yet, they shall find none from my duplicates, for it is my essence alone that fuels their ephemeral power."

Thus commenced a relentless clash as the replicas surged forward, a collective force determined to vanquish Scott and his army. A maelstrom of fury and determination ensued, their bodies moving in harmony with practiced agility, blades shimmering like silver in the midst of the tumultuous fray. Each strike reverberated through the air, a symphony of clashing steel, mingling with the thunderous cadence of footsteps upon the blood-soaked ground.

In the crucible of battle, anguish coalesced with unyielding resilience. Blood and sweat mingled as each warrior confronted their relentless adversaries, the earth thirstily absorbing the vibrant hues of their struggle. Yet, despite the searing pain etched upon their weary forms, Scott and his comrades defied despair, rising from the ground with triumphant grins spreading from ear to ear.

A renewed fire ignited within their eyes, unwavering in the face of adversity. They pursued their targets, refusing to succumb to defeat.

Amidst the exhilarating chaos, Haines's voice carried a tinge of frustration blended with a trace of longing. "This would be considerably easier if we didn't have to worry about the nebulous presence of the angel."

In the blink of an eye, the battle took a treacherous turn. The air crackled with tension as sharp, circular blades tore through the Entitle's hands, stomach, and shoulders, leaving behind rivulets of crimson. Victor's replicated forms, brimming with intent, poised themselves for a vengeful assault, their movements synchronized and lethal.

But their anticipation was met with bewildering surprise. Their enemy, shrouded in an enigmatic prowess, seemed to disappear before their very eyes, as if blending into the fabric of time itself. The rapidity of this ethereal vanishing cast a perplexing haze upon their senses, leaving them disoriented and vulnerable.

"Where did he go?" one copy questioned, searching desperately for any residue of their elusive adversary.

In that desperate moment, confusion became their undoing as one of the Entitles thrust its sinewy arm into each of the replica's bodies. The malign force coursing through their fragmented forms receded, leaving them to revert back to their original, mindless state.

Amidst the mournful remnants of their defeated replicas, Haines's voice cut through the lingering silence, marked by equal measures of frustration and determination. His eyes found Victor, imploring him for guidance within the chaos.

"Got any more bright ideas?" he inquired, searching for a glimmer of strategic ingenuity amidst the tumultuous battlefield.

26

DISOBEDIENCE

Emily and Caleb stepped back into the house, the wind pushing the door shut with a firm thud. A peculiar sight rested in front of them. Both David and Michael stood rigid by the battered window. The defiant piano chords of "Gives You Hell" by The All-American Rejects broke the silence.

She'd forgotten all about Kota's chosen ringtone for her father - once a shared joke between sisters - now felt like a punch to the gut. Caleb shut the door as Emily dug into her pocket. Once the intro began to replay, she took a deep breath, brushed her hair out of her face, and accepted the call.

"Hello?"

"Well, it's about time you pick up," the agitated voice crackled over the speaker.

"Frank, I—"

"Shut up. You had the audacity to tell me she would be safer with you. And on top of it, I had to hear about her death from your cousin Caroline? Are you kidding me!?"

Emily flinched, tightening her grip on the phone. "I'm—"

"I don't want to hear it," he interrupted again. "Oh, and just so you know, no one wants to see you at the funeral either."

The line went dead, leaving Emily broken. She leaned back onto the wall, hunched over. Seeing this, Caleb went to consult her, but she steadied herself and walked away.

"I'm fine," she said, passing her partner and further entering the adjacent room.

David stepped closer to the window, beholding the ground, where tiny particles of dirt defied gravity, hovering inches above the earth. In the same breath, these specks broke apart into microscopic pieces.

"Are you seeing this?" he asked, his voice a mix of awe and confusion. He turned to the others, seeking confirmation that he wasn't imagining things.

The duo exchanged puzzled glances and moved closer to the window. Meanwhile, Michael studied the peculiar pink haze outlining several clouds.

"I need you to meditate again to clear your mind," he said, facing Emily. "I will return as soon as I can." He then phased out into the void.

She nodded and pivoted to the living room where she sank her knees into the thick, slate-colored rug. Caleb followed; his footsteps muffled by the dense pile. Compassion carved valleys in her partner's features. His eyes, pools of empathy, fixed on his partner and in response, softened his posture.

"Are you sure you're up for this right now?"

The floorboards groaned under David's steps as he twirled to face them. "She doesn't have a choice."

That remark pinched Emily's eardrums, snapping her head up. The intensity of her glare made him take a step back, "Excuse me, I do have a choice," she said with a firm voice. "And this is it."

She then looked ahead and closed her eyes, her lashes fluttering against her cheeks. After taking a deep breath, a sense of calm washed over her. She acclimated to a new awareness, the Celestial Plane.

A cacophony of frequencies vibrated within her consciousness, each one distinct, yet part of a greater harmony. From the ether, a discordant note struck her senses, leaving a void where there should have been balance.

"Something's wrong," she whispered.

Caleb knelt in front of her and leaned in. "What do you mean?"

"I'm not sure. It's like a pool of unnatural energies trying to converge." Emily's eyes flew open as if pushed out of her meditation.

David tensed as he noticed her pupils dilate with shock. "Oh, I have a bad feeling about this."

Water cascaded down the tiers of a marble fountain, its gentle gurgle a counterpoint to the bustling New York street. Coins glinted at the bottom, wishes cast by hopeful passersby. Just beyond, the Sweet Tooth Dessert Bar hummed with activity. A winding line of customers stretched down the sidewalk, the air thick with the scent of sugar and freshly baked pastries.

At the end of the queue stood the messenger and healer, invisible to mortal perception. Gabriel's sapphire eyes glistened. "Do you feel that? The sourness draped in human covetous desires."

Raphael kept shifting his head in search of anyone who may detect their presence. "I do. There is a curtain of deception that obscures this gathering."

The once lengthy line dwindled to a trickle after fifteen minutes. Sable and Lyra, two female associates, exchanged a high-five, their excitement palpable. They'd almost sold out their entire array of desserts.

Their celebration waned when Enzo, their robust and muscular boss, strode into the room. At first, a motionless expression dawned his features. A prompt grin followed, stretching far and wide. "You did well today," he said, pride evident in his voice. "Ready for a grand feast to celebrate your triumph?"

Both women smiled, sharing their excitement. Lyra untied her apron, feeling liberated, while Sable flipped the light switch. Eager for the evening's festivities, they both exited the establishment and slumped onto a bench. The moment they sat down, Lyra lifted her feet and peeled off her flip flops. She winced, kneading the tender soles.

A light puff of wind stirred the grass, carrying an inexplicable sweetness. The blades straightened, aiming skyward as if in reverence. In the periphery of the worker's vision, the air sparkled like a heat mirage. Two figures stepped forth from the distortion: Raphael and Gabriel, their presence infusing the area with an otherworldly radiance.

From the entryway, Enzo glued his sights upon the celestial hosts. "Angels," his voice rumbled with fury.

Gabriel clenched his jaw in righteous anger while Raphael's serene demeanor vanished, replaced by a stern glower that could intimidate even the bravest of souls. They beheld the laid back Entitles with such vigor.

"Be gone, vermin!" the healer's voice boomed. His emerald gaze, reminiscent of ancient forests, shone bright.

The messenger's eyes gave way to an alabaster shine. It wasn't long before the combination of their energies consumed the property. As quickly as the brilliant light came and went, it left a tableau of destruction in its wake. But among the remnants, Michael stood tall, his fists tightened at his sides. His eyes, narrowed and cold, swept over the devastation before settling on his brethren.

Surprised to see him, Raphael broke the silence. "What are you doing here?"

"I could ask the same of you," Michael retorted.

"You know these filthy things pose a threat to the mortal," Gabriel interjected, his words laced with a touch of righteous indignation.

"We are ending the battle before it ever starts," Raphael concluded.

The warrior's words cut through the tension like a sharpened blade, aimed solely at Gabriel. "I told you we had not been given the order to proceed in this manner."

A thunderous crack disengaged the angels' heated discussion. They turned, transfixed by the bar's overseer. Enzo's presence commanded reverence, his left arm pulsing with exposed energy. Blue blood seeped from his right shoulder, carrying fragments of a deep sea nebula. Each droplet held specks of emerald green, fiery red, and golden yellow orbs dancing like tiny galaxies.

But he paid no mind to his wound and surveyed the destruction. To his horror, he found Lyra and Sable lying still under the rubble.

"When will you angels realize that not all of us want to fight?!"

Raphael seized the opportunity to taunt the Entitle, dismissing its desire for peace. "No, of course not. You just want to feed in peace."

Fueled by a surge of defiance, Enzo refused to let such accusations go unanswered. Its response cut through the heavy atmosphere, each word a blade honed with resolute defiance.

"On the energy from buildings!" he said.

Michael stepped forward to confront the formidable energy-absorbing being. "Prove your words and we shall leave," he assured.

However, Enzo's hope for a peaceful resolution faded. His eyes locked onto the angels, the intensity of his gaze betraying his ruthless intent.

"Oh, no, negotiations are over."

The entitle lifted its hand, fingers grazing the wound on his head, tracing the contours of the deep gash. His facial expression darkened, a flicker of anguish replacing his usual unbridled confidence.

A collective dread settled upon the group as Gabriel voiced the growing worry that swelled in the air. "This does not look good."

Enzo's arms lunged forward, fingers splayed and ready to explode into motion. His stance shifted, one foot sliding back as he bent his knees, grounding himself like a coiled spring. A deranged look in his eye took hold as he prepared to attack.

Michael raised his hand towards the heavens, his authoritative gesture summoning the celestial power within his sword. The blade responded, glowing with a radiant light that pierced the very fabric of the sky. Beside him, Raphael extended his hand, the air shimmering around it as the majestic Halberd pole solidified from a golden mist. Gabriel closed his eyes in deep concentration, and from the core of his being, a surge of pure electricity crackled to life. It arced and twisted, taking shape into the formidable Golden Pike, glowing with an intense brilliance. With their divine weapons in hand, the Archangels stood poised, their senses heightened as they prepared for the coming battle.

Michael took the lead and charged forward. With a deceptive glint in his eye, Enzo leaped ahead, his body language telegraphing an imminent attack. But before long, he teleported, reappearing behind his foe. His decisive blow sent Michael off-balance.

His brethren rushed to help, however, found their attacks thwarted as well. Enzo twirled, seizing the Halberd pole mid-strike.

"Impossible," Raphael said, pushing harder.

The Entitle turned his focus on Gabriel, realizing he gripped only air. "Where's your weapon, angel?" he asked.

"Here!" Gabriel shouted, hurling the Golden Pike at him.

The captured version of Gabriel dissolved into white light. Enzo wrenched the Halberd pole from Raphael, striking him with brutal force. The impact sent Raphael crashing through the glass partition, far from the dessert bar.

An eerie grin grew on Enzo's face as he stared upon Gabriel's incoming energy attack. The blast slowed down when a vortex opened in his chest, ringed with razor teeth. It consumed the energy and the Golden Pike's radiance. Drained of power, the mighty weapon crumbled to pieces.

Power flowed through Enzo, his muscles swelling to new proportions. Michael leaned on his sword, struggling to remain vertical. "You might as well surrender now, you fiend. I saw what just transpired."

"Oh, sure, I'll surrender. Right after I annihilate you."

"Michael, what are you doing?" Raphael inquired.

"Engaging in this meaningless squabble."

With an intense blaze, the archangel's eyes emitted a piercing blue hue as he executed a powerful swing of his sword, driven by the fervent desire to sever the Entitle in twain. Alas, his efforts were thwarted as the entity intercepted the blade, catching it in his hand. Blood trickled down the Entitle's arm, a testament to the sword's relentless incision, gradually slicing through the supple flesh.

"You really think you can beat me like this?" Enzo taunted.

"Not a chance," Michael said.

Abandoning his weapon, his feet propelled him up the colossal arm of the Entitle. With a burst of momentum, he launched himself from the entity's broad shoulder, his intent fixed on striking the vulnerable expanse of its neck. Yet, in a display of lightning-like reflexes, Enzo intercepted the angel's audacious assault, ruthlessly slamming him down at his feet.

As the impact reverberated through his body, Michael's eyes reverted to their normal state. However, determination ignited within him, as a radiant blue light enveloped his left hand, which stayed clenched at his side.

"Do not dare claim victory, you wretched fiend!" The Archangel's voice thundered, his arm outstretched towards the Entitle, unleashing a formidable wave of energy.

Yet, to his dismay, another vortex, bristling with razor-sharp teeth, materialized within the depths of Enzo's stomach. Unfazed, the Archangel continued to unleash his blast, simultaneously employing his right hand to reach out towards his sword. With an almost supernatural force, the weapon responded, hurtling into his grasp with a resounding impact. In an instant, the blade pierced his foe's shoulder, eliciting a guttural cry of anguish that reverberated through the heavens.

"You have lost," Michael declared, pulling the weapon down, removing his arm completely.

As the limb fell onto the ground, it disintegrated into a viscous void. The warrior stood tall once more while his brethren watched in astonishment.

"They are vulnerable while eating, that is why he pushed Raphael aside," he informed, his keen perception earning him praise.

"Nice observation, Michael," Gabriel commended, his tone full of admiration.

Rather than accept the win, the warrior lamented in regret. "This battle should never have been waged in the first place."

Enzo gathered his bearings, rising to his feet with boiling fury. He lunged after the Archangel, unaware of his own weakness. "This is far from over, angel. I will return for you," he blurted.

With a spiraling motion, he vanished, leaving Gabriel and Raphael poised to give chase. However, Michael stepped in front, effectively blocking their path.

"It is not up to us to bring about the demise of the Entitles," he asserted with unwavering conviction.

"Understood, but what if he manages to reach Emily? What course of action should we take then?" Raphael inquired.

"In such a dire circumstance, I envision that we would receive the imperative to smite the entity, but only when absolutely necessary."

"What convoluted reasoning is this?" Gabriel asked.

Michael looked at his brethren. "In light of your disobedience, I shall banish you from earth."

As he spoke, his eyes blazed with intense energy, consuming the very essence of the surrounding area. A profound stillness descended upon the aftermath of the chaotic battle, enveloping the scene in an eerie silence. Inside this hushed space, a single leaf, transformed into a crystalline structure, descended from above, alighting upon the grass at the base of a majestic tree trunk.

27

BROKEN SPELL

B ack at the battle site cloaked by magic, Victor extended his arms to unleash a swarm of vibrant red and black beams towards an imposing Entitle. Powerful winds enveloped him in a captivating display of force. Although it kept his foe at bay, three swirling vortexes formed inside the energy-eater's body, drawing in and absorbing its malevolent power.

Haines monitored the surroundings and approached his ally. "If you persist in this manner, you'll soon deplete your reserves," he asserted, his gaze fixed upon the formidable entity.

"I ought to have an ample amount of power to vanquish this creature," Victor declared.

With a roll of his eyes, the Roamer employed teleportation, resurfacing behind his ravenous foe and applying pressure to its vulnerable neck. At the same time, the power emitted by the demon propelled the incapacitated Entitle off the lawn, giving way to a brief respite. But, the reprieve was short-lived as two additional energy-eaters threw themselves at the Roamer.

In a blur of motion, Haines glided to the side, avoiding his foe's desperate lunge. With a swift twist, he spun around, his fist cutting through the air like a speeding bullet, aiming for the pressure points near the Entitle's shoulder.

The impact reverberated through the entity's essence, disrupting its advancement. Haines's strike unleashed unfathomable power, drawing in the very air itself.

Unshaken by its companion's setback, the remaining Entitle pressed on, its gnarled knuckles closing in on the Roamer like a vice. However, he summoned a spectral apparition of himself. The ghostly image materialized, leaving an ethereal trace in its wake, as Haines phased behind the entity, his movements fluid and precise.

With a forceful blow, he struck the pressure point along the creature's neck, the impact resonating with bone-crushing intensity. The Entitle, once a formidable force, now laid neutralized.

In a seamless motion, the Roamer landed back on solid ground. He set his gaze upon his ally, whose brow glistened from beads of sweat. "Not everything needs to be a battle."

Victor, his eyes wide with curiosity, couldn't help but ask "Why didn't you do that in the first place? Why go through the struggle?"

A smile curled at the corner of Haines's lips, a glimmer of amusement dancing in his eyes. "I was hoping you would have come up with a logical way of fighting these guys."

Victor's face flushed with shame. He believed that fists were the only way to settle a fight. The Roamer, well aware of this fatal flaw, decided to coax him through.

"Now, show me what you've learned," he said.

The creature nodded, his gaze shifting to the remaining army of Entitles, their dark figures dotting the landscape like an ominous storm approaching. He took a step forward, ready to face the onslaught, his every movement brimming with a fierce determination that matched the intensity of the battle.

In the confines of the house, Emily continued to sit cross-legged, reentering a meditative state. She focused on steadying her breath, each inhale and exhale deliberate. Through the pandemonium of recent events, she found peace by delving deeper into her inner world.

Caleb, on the other hand, spread a line of salt on each windowsill, creating a protective force field. He paused at each one, muttering a quiet prayer under his breath, hoping that this simple act would be enough to keep the encroaching darkness at bay. He shook the last remnants of the bag onto the final windowsill, watching the grains scatter like tiny, crystalline sentinels. With a sigh, he glanced over at David, who paced along the rug.

The scientist had transformed the edge of the fabric into his own private labyrinth, his feet tracing and retracing an intricate pattern. Each turn punctuated by a soft mutter or a quick gesture, as if he were conducting an abundance of ideas.

Intrigued, Caleb crumpled the bag and threw it into the garbage bucket in the corner. From there, he continued on, exiting the kitchen, and shifting between Emily and David.

"Is everything alright in here?"

David stopped mid-step and spun around, his eyes gleaming with an unsettling theory. "I think we should use Emily as a bargaining chip," he said. "She's the primary focus of both the angels and demons. If we can leverage that, we might be able to negotiate a more favorable outcome."

Caught off guard, Caleb took a step back. "What?!" he exclaimed, his muscles stiffening, and fists clenched, ready to fight if necessary. "No, that's out of the question. How could you even think about doing her like that?"

"Look at her," the scientist implored, gesturing towards Emily. "She wants to do this."

"No, she's willing to fight the devil to save the world because she believes she doesn't have a say in the matter."

"Oh please, she wants revenge."

"Can you blame her?" Caleb inquired, closing the distance between them.

"On the contrary. After all she's been through, I think it's natural. But have you considered that the angels might be manipulating the situation in their favor?"

Like a kaleidoscope of emotions, the weight of their discussion filled the room as a voice emitted from the obscure recesses. Its presence carried an air of mystery. "The angel made his stance," it countered.

The duo searched for the source of the voice, but there was nothing out of the ordinary.

"Who said that?" Caleb asked.

However, the voice faded while smoke slithered from a crack in the far corner. In the blink of an eye, a phantom stood in front of them. Dark fog from its body entangled with the ceiling fan, causing it to spin at a rapid speed.

"Oh, I'm prepared for you," Caleb declared, his hand reaching into his back pocket to retrieve the gun loaded with holy water bullets.

After taking aim, his heart pounded in his chest. A cold sweat trailed down his face. His arm hair stood on end, holding the power to strike or falter under pressure of the unknown.

David noticed a twitch in the author's hand, causing doubt to creep into his mind about his conviction. In a decisive move, he used his power to force him to squeeze the trigger. The air crackled as the bullet flew through the fog and lodged itself in the plaster. This unexpected outcome left their eyes wide with disbelief.

"I am not a demon," the phantom assured.

Caleb redirected his attention to Dave. "What did you do that for?!"

"You weren't going to take the shot!"

Then, a realization dawned upon them, triggered by the haunting words that escaped the phantom's lips following the gunshot. Their gaze fell back towards the figure, standing resolute in their presence.

"If you're not a demon, then what are you?" David asked.

The phantom responded with an air of authority. "A being striving to safeguard the future of your realm. Now, I implore you to step away from the mortal, lest you perish where you stand."

Rather than succumb to his fear, Caleb positioned himself in front of Emily. His eyes locked onto the phantom; a defiant glare reflected his refusal to yield.

"I am not moving."

Although he didn't agree with his friend's stance, David stepped in front and forcefully swung his arm in an attempt to send the phantom flying. To his dismay, the dark figure remained in place.

"I don't understand," he said, staring at his hands. He tried again in angst, avail.

"You hold no power over me, human."

Determined, Caleb cocked the gun once more. In response, the phantom shot a piercing glare.

"I refuse to enable this behavior. Either stand down or I will lay you to waste."

Unable to fathom another way out, David collapsed to his knees. "We're out of moves."

"Like hell we are!"

Caleb pivoted and scooped Emily up in his strong arms. Fearing his chances are slipping away, he dashed out of the room, determined to keep her safe. During this time, the phantom divided itself into two separate entities, reforming the other one in front of the exit.

"Relinquish the mortal, or die with her."

Frozen in place, Caleb's fingers constricted around Emily's hands. He fixed his glare upon the phantom, believing any momentary lapse in focus would invite disaster. The thumping of his heart echoed in his ears, a steady rhythm that mirrored the serene cadence of Emily's unconscious state.

Caught in a whirlwind of emotions, his mind struggled to make sense of the situation. Confusion mingled with terror, creating a tangled web of thoughts that threatened to consume him. And then, a flicker of hope took shape behind him, capturing the phantom's attention. Intrigued, Caleb shifted his gaze, turning his body to meet the unwavering stare of Michael.

"I thought you were done with this foolish game, the archangel retorted."

"I'm not going to fight you this time, angel. You're about to have your hands full without my interference."

The phantom's eyes flashed white, while staring at Michael. This broke the enchantment woven by Haines to veil the tumultuous conflict raging outside began to falter, its once steadfast potency slowly eroding. The magical spell that had cloaked the skirmish under a deceptive calm now unraveled, revealing the looming specter of the battle creeping into view with each passing moment. As the arcane barrier weakened, the deceptive facade of peace dissolved. Michael's perception detected the unmistakable presence of diabolical energies.

"Sulfur."

He teleported onto the front lawn, where the pandemonium of the warzone took place. A fleeing Entitle took the opportunity to strike the Archangel. But, with his guard heightened, Michael turned around, ducked, and delivered a resounding blow to its chest.

As soon as it crashed into a bush under the windowsill, Victor twirled on his heel, pausing his assault on another Entitle.

But how can he see us? He pondered, taking a step backward.

"This is where you meet your fate," Michael declared.

Despite the terror pouring upon him, the demon's gaze shifted. His eyes glued to the phantom's reflection in the window. A realization sparked in his eyes, and a mischievous grin tugged at the corners of his mouth.

"You might want to get back inside," Victor advised, his tone laced with amusement.

"No more tricks. This is where you end!" Michael's eyes gleamed with a fiery blue intensity as he prepared to strike. But before he could, a swarm of Entitles leapt onto his back.

With his adversary distracted, Victor regained his footing, his focus still fixated on the shadows lurking in the house.

"I'm not foolish enough to tangle with you."

The phantom's ethereal form stood resolute at arms length from Caleb. The scientist sought to redirect his attention by tugging on his arm.

"Come on, we can get out from the back," he said.

Fueled by optimism, the pair dashed into the neighboring room, convinced they could reach the exit. Smiles cracked on their stern faces as Caleb's hand touched the knob. That's when two shadowy, razor-sharp rods materialized and plunged into his ankle.

The overwhelming pain brought him to his knees while David rooted himself in place. He couldn't help but watch his friend continue to cradle Emily in his arms.

"Caleb, you have to get up!"

The phantom took shape beside David, its presence sending a chill down his spine. Still processing its movements, a hand launched out at him, seizing him by the neck.

"You brought this on yourself," the phantom said.

The phantom tightened its grip, leaving the scientist gasping for air. To end his misery, the shadowy figure propelled him backward, forcing a violent collision that sent shockwaves throughout his body.

Meanwhile, at the abandoned warehouse, dilapidated walls loomed over Victor. As he broached the room, he overheard Haines whispering to himself.

"Why do we continue to play these games?" the Roamer muttered, filled with frustration. "I should be focusing on finding the last three crypts, so that you can…" he paused for a moment, listening to Oswald's voice before conceding. "Fine, if that's what you want."

A confused Victor approached his ally. "Who are you talking to?"

With a flicker of surprise crossing his face, Haines glanced at him. "Never mind that," he said. "I assume there's a reason why you're here."

"It's the phantom," he began. "I saw it at the house."

"Really?" Haines retorted. "Persistent little buggos, aren't they? So, I guess the plan worked after all."

Confusion continued to cloud Victor's mind as he struggled to comprehend. "I don't follow."

"There's only one reason why a phantom would ever leave its post and more so, threaten the life of a mortal being. She must pose some kind of threat to the natural order, at least her powers do." Haines paused, taking a moment to gather his thoughts. "Unfortunately, this means I have to save the day once again."

No matter how hard Michael tried, the energy he unleashed only served to strengthen the Entitles. This time, there were multiple adversaries, causing his power to be evenly divided among them, leaving him on his knees, weakened and struggling.

On the front lawn, Haines materialized, his attention fixed upon Michael. "That's the issue with your kind," he remarked, a hint of disdain in his voice. "Always craving to showcase your power. It's precisely why you lost the previous battle."

However, Haines' words went unnoticed by the Archangel, who was fully engrossed in the ongoing conflict, his attention diverted and unresponsive to the Roamer's remarks.

Gliding forward, the phantom passed through the iron rods as they merged back into its shadowy body. Caleb, desperate and with no other options, crawled across the cold, hard floor, his limbs trembling with exhaustion. Finally, he reached the wooden table, his fingers grasping at the edge, seeking support to pull himself up. But his hopes were dashed as the hand of the phantom descended upon him, its grip tightening around his arm like a vice.

Suspended in the air, held captive by the ominous figure, Caleb's gaze locked with the darkness where the phantom's eyes should have been.

"It didn't have to come to this," it declared. "But you left me no choice."

In an instant, the phantom released its hold on them, hurtling the duo back into the dining room with a force that sent them crashing into a China cabinet filled with delicate trinkets. Caleb, instinctively shielding Emily with his body, collided with the furniture first, absorbing the impact as best he could.

Meanwhile, Haines made his entrance into the house, his presence commanding yet cautious. He stood in the doorway as he uttered a protective incantation - "mortale praesidium."

Glass shattered on the floor, scattering tiny shards in all directions. Caleb's body bore the brunt of the piercing fragments, causing searing pain to shoot through him. Soon, the weight of the falling China cabinet added to the onslaught, burying them beneath its weight. Amidst the trinkets that littered the floor was a small figurine of a speak-no-evil monkey sat upright, facing the phantom.

Believing Emily to no longer be a threat, the phantom vanished. Outside, Haines walked up to the pile of Entitles feasting on Michael's energy and ordered them to flee.

"You'll leave the Archangel alone unless you want Oswald to know of your recent activity."

With those words, the dark entities released the warrior and bolted out of the area. Despite standing right next to him, Haines remained invisible. Michael couldn't understand what had happened or why the energy eaters had retreated. None of that mattered though, when he heard Emily's scream. After all, she's the one who's supposed to be protected at all costs.

A sense of urgency gripped him as he sought to assess the situation. Yet, as he entered the room, the magnitude of the devastation exceeded what he expected. Smack in the middle of all the destruction was Emily, trying her hardest to wake Caleb up.

While scanning the area, the angel's eyes were drawn to a different monkey figurine, this one embodying the principle of see-no-evil, lying behind Emily, facing the ceiling. His focus returned to the enigma that confronted him.

How did she escape unscathed, devoid of any wounds? This singular question echoed within his mind, demanding an answer.

As his gaze swept across the room, Michael's attention was drawn to the shards of glass that adorned the exposed areas of Caleb's lifeless form. The wooden floor, once pristine, now bore a crimson hue beneath the shattered fragments. In a moment of profound anguish, Emily reached out and lifted a piece of wood that rested upon her partner's body, only to be met with the haunting sight of his eyes, still open and unseeing.

A gasp escaped her lips, a visceral expression of shock and sorrow, as tears streamed down her face, intermingling with the weight of her grief. With shaking hands, she gently closed his eyes, bidding a final farewell to the life that had been tragically extinguished.

"You must have shielded yourself from their attack, which would explain why you are unharmed."

"You think I would do something like that?" she began, wiping the tears from her eyes. "I would never put myself above anyone else." Emily stood up, glaring toward Michael. "If anything, this is all your fault. You kept me from waking up until I finished the stupid trial. Had I been awake, I could have done something."

"The only thing you would have accomplished would have been dying."

"Well, I'm done with all of this," she stated, kneeling back down beside Caleb. "I've lost everything."

Michael watched as Emily crumbled under the weight of her grief, her tears flowing freely. Deep within him, a desire to offer guidance stirred, yet he understood the importance of allowing her to navigate her own path of realization. Though the darkness of despair loomed, the angel knew the window of opportunity had not closed entirely; there remained a sliver of time, a chance for Emily to find her way.

28

Δ LIFE REVIVED

Leaning against the weathered exterior of a modest eatery just beyond the outskirts of town, Boris sought solace in the coolness of the building's surface. The frigid air seeped into his bones, mirroring the icy grip of despair that clenched his heart. In his hand, he clutched a stale piece of bread, its texture rough and unforgiving, a meager sustenance to stave off the gnawing hunger that plagued him.

His mind, a tempest of anger, echoed with the resolute words he had whispered to himself. "I am going to find you and when I do, I swear it'll be lights out."

He devoured the last morsel of bread, its bitter taste a reminder of his dire circumstances. His thoughts, however, were consumed by a memory he had painstakingly preserved on his phone. It was a video, a precious relic capturing the essence of his beloved wife, recorded mere hours before the cruel hands of fate snatched her away.

His fingers trembled with sorrow, fumbling to unlock his phone. A bittersweet ache tore at his heart when he pressed play. The screen came alive, illuminating the radiant visage of his wife. Her smile, a beacon of joy and love, filled the frame, casting a warm glow upon his desolate existence. The sound of her laughter echoed in his ears, a haunting melody that both comforted and tormented him. In that moment, as he watched the video in solemn silence, the weight of his grief mingled with the tears that cascaded down his cheeks.

Pausing the recording, Boris lowered himself to the ground, finding solace for his weary knees on the gritty pavement. The scattered array of empty bottles, remnants of past sorrows, were kicked aside to clear space for his anguished presence. His hands, once strong and steady, now quivered as he navigated through the labyrinthine maze of video files on his phone. Each swipe and tap was a delicate dance, a desperate attempt to find solace in the last glimpse of his beloved wife.

The street faded into a blur, narrowing his focus to the screen in his hands. Memories intertwined with the present reality, thinning the line between what was and what is. The video files on his phone became a lifeline, a fragile connection to the past that he clung to with desperate hope.

And there it was, nestled amidst the digital archives, the final testament of their shared happiness. In the captured moment, Boris found himself seated in his car with Rylee by his side, their laughter intertwining with the warm sun. Her delicate hands reached out of the frame, as if yearning to escape the confines of the video.

A smile graced Boris's lips, his laughter mingling with the gentle breeze that danced through the open windows. "I think you should come inside with me," he playfully suggested.

She chuckled, her voice a sweet symphony. "You're just getting milk, babe. Besides, my feet are still sore."

"Okay, but let me capture your radiance before I go," Boris insisted, the camera lens now fixated on her enchanting smile.

Rylee lowered her hands, surrendering to the camera's gaze, her countenance a portrait of joy. "Now go, so we can get home before nightfall," she playfully urged.

The video stopped when a tear embarked on its descent down his cheek, mirroring the cascade of emotions within his soul. Frustration surged through his veins, compelling him to unleash his anguish upon the unyielding brick wall against which he leaned. His knuckles scraped against the rough surface, a testament to the pain that coursed through his being. As he shivered from the cold wind, he noticed the sleeve of an old jacket hanging from the rim of a nearby dumpster.

Tattered fabric fluttered in the breeze, its faded blue reminiscent of the damage done to Caleb's left arm in his North Carolina University sweatshirt. Blood stained the edges of the sleeve as he lay motionless over the glass-ridden floor.

Emily knelt beside him and proceeded to do chest compressions. She hummed, "Stayin Alive" in an attempt to keep rhythm, only stopping when she looked at his closed eyes and said, "Come on, Caleb, stay with me."

Even after her breath labored, she stayed on beat, refusing to give up. This sound dangled in David's ears as he rose up at a leisure pace, grasping his head. He winced upon laying eyes on the heart-wrenching sight of Emily huddled over Caleb, pouring every ounce of her being into reviving him. His heart ached for her and took a step forward to offer solace, only to be intercepted by the archangel Michael.

His words spilled like a clarion call, demanding her attention and focus. "You may feel the emotion, but do not let it cloud your thoughts," he urged.

Emily pressed on, ignoring all outside noises.

"Stop what you are doing. Take a deep breath. And listen to the surrounding air."

Her tear-streaked face locked with Michael's gaze. She paused, her hands still hovering above Caleb's chest. "If I stop, he dies."

Michael stood resolute, his presence a steady anchor amidst the storm. "Hear my voice," he implored. "This man's soul is on the precipice of departure. If you do not act now, the window of opportunity will close."

She looked down at Caleb's battered body and rested a hand on his chest. Reluctantly, she followed his guidance, closing her eyes and focusing on her breath. Soon, the chaotic whirlwind of emotions settled, giving way to a newfound clarity from the depths of her despair.

"This better work."

Michael took a step forward, dismissing her doubts with a reassuring gesture. "I assure you, this is not a ploy, Emily. His life is in your hands and yours alone."

However, the more she tried to push everything aside, flashes of Kota's body flickered in an open field. The weight of her past failures bore down on her, questioning her ability to save those she loved. But amidst the distress, Michael's comforting touch on her shoulder broke through the darkness, like a beacon of solace cutting through the storm.

A gentle, enveloping white light replaced the haunting image, washing over Emily with a surge of tranquility. The room seemed to transform as Emily delved deeper into her being, allowing her mind to settle. She mustered all her inner strength, determined to harness the power within her.

Maybe I can do this. I've witnessed too much suffering lately to not give it a try, she thought.

Yet, a nagging thought crept up, planting seeds of doubt. What if this angel wants to distract me while he launches another attack? Emily's gaze shifted towards Michael, studying his every move, searching for any sign of deception.

Sensing her worry, Michael took a decisive step forward, his eyes filled with sincerity. "This isn't a ploy, Emily. Your doubts are understandable, but I assure you, this mortal's life is truly in your hands."

Emily closed her eyes once more, shutting out the world around her. With each breath, she fought against the chaos of her mind, striving to anchor herself in the present moment. The weight of her past failures and the uncertainty of this moment threatened to overwhelm her, but she refused to let it consume her.

In the depths of her being, a flicker of belief ignited. She had completed the final trial, unlocking a power she had never known before. With unwavering determination, she tightened her grip on Caleb's shoulder, her palms emanating a mesmerizing display of light-purple energy.

The room transformed into a spectacle of ethereal radiance as her energy enveloped his lifeless body. Unaware of the damage, Emily remained calm, her breathing steady and composed. Then, a miraculous change took place. Caleb began to stir, and a series of coughs escaped his lips. The wounds that marred his body started to heal, a testament to the incredible power Emily possessed.

Caleb's eyes fluttered open, and a rush of sensations overwhelmed him. His body tingled, every nerve ending seemingly on fire. The room's brightness assaulted his vision, and sounds pierced his ears with startling clarity. Even the air felt foreign in his lungs, each breath a conscious effort.

"It worked!" she yelled, wrapping her arms around his shoulders.

Disorientation hit him in waves. Fragments of memory - searing pain, encroaching darkness, a sense of falling - clashed with his current reality. He blinked rapidly, trying to reconcile his last conscious moments with his inexplicable present.

"Em?" he croaked, his voice hoarse. "What happened?" He reached out, his hand finding Emily's. The contact anchored him, providing a lifeline to this bewildering new reality. His eyes locked with hers, searching for answers. "Did...did I die?"

Emily, barely able to keep her composure, but her lip. Caleb surveyed the room, noting the shattered glass and splintered furniture. The magnitude of what transpired hit him with the force of a freight train. He was alive, breathing, feeling - all because of his partner's extraordinary gift.

"Now, let's go get Kota," she said, springing back to her feet.

"Yeah, okay. Thank you for saving my life."

Michael took a decisive step forward, carrying the weight of a difficult reality. "I must apologize, but the resurrection of your sister is not possible."

"Why?"

"Excuse me," Caleb interjected, "but I am living proof of what she can do."

"You misunderstand, once a soul departs from its physical vessel, there is no going back," the Archangel explained.

Emily's voice quivered with frustration. "That's not fair. Where were you when we needed you?"

Before Michael could respond, a sudden and blinding surge of electricity descended from above, engulfing him in a whirlwind of light. With a forceful impact, he was propelled back to the realm of Heaven, leaving the trio stunned in its wake.

Reacting on instinct, she shielded Caleb's eyes from the blinding brilliance that poured forth from the lightning. This ensured his vision remained protected, while David blocked his sight with his forearm until the luminosity diminished. As a result, the room was left shrouded in an all-encompassing darkness.

"Thank you for that," he said, lowering her hand from his sight. "Any idea as to what that was?"

"Nope."

"I'm pretty sure heaven just called him home," David informed.

Within the confines of the forgotten maintenance facility, Haines stood by the grimy window, his arms poised behind his back in an authoritative stance. His mind connected with Oswald through telepathic means, their thoughts intertwining in a sinister conversation.

"The phantoms believe the mortal is deceased, so they should no longer pose a threat."

"Excellent. Our plan is proceeding as anticipated," Oswald retorted, his tone dripping with satisfaction.

Haines paused, his expression betraying a hint of concern.

"Well, there is one minor complication. You see, the mortal ventured into the labyrinthine tunnels of Hilltown, likely investigating those murders. As she departed, my men stationed there were incapacitated when the structure collapsed," he disclosed.

"What! It is already troublesome enough that you have yet to locate the remaining five crypts. Losing access to the ones you have already discovered is simply unacceptable," Oswald said, seething with anger.

Haines, aware of the gravity of the situation, clenched his fists as he responded with a hint of defensiveness.

"I understand your frustration, but I haven't had the opportunity to recruit new servants yet, especially with the phantoms causing disturbances," the Roamer explained.

Oswald's voice grew colder, his threat palpable. "No excuses. Rectify the situation immediately, or I will erase every trace of your existence from your own mind."

29

RETURN TO THE SCENE

The car hummed along the winding road, a cocoon of normalcy in their abnormal lives. Emily laid back in the shotgun seat with her eyes closed while David occupied the backseat. As Caleb eased off the accelerator to make a turn, a low rumble emanated from his stomach.

"Man, it feels like an eternity since I've had a satisfying meal," he confessed.

"Well, it looks like we're almost at Burger House," David said. "But I think we should take this time to discuss strategy."

"Michael will be back and throw Emily into all this craziness and, until then, I want us to just enjoy a moment."

Emily opened her eyes and faced Caleb. "What if those shadow things come back?"

A note of reassurance entered David's voice as he responded, "Oh, I think we've seen the last of them. They believe they've achieved their desired outcome, so there's no reason for them to haunt us any longer."

"On that note, let's focus on enjoying a well-deserved meal," Caleb declared, steering the car into the parking lot of Burger House.

Later, the trio savored the aroma of freshly cooked burgers and crispy fries. With each bite, the worries and tensions of their recent encounters faded into the wind. However, the tranquility in the scientist's mind shook when Haines' haunting words resurfaced.

Bring her to me, now!

A sharp pang shot through his head, causing him to wince in pain, his hand reaching for his temple.

"Are you alright?" Caleb asked.

David, his face contorted in discomfort, managed to reply, "Yeah, thanks for lunch, but I need to go."

"Come on, man, we're nowhere near your house."

The scientist stood up, clutching the remnants of his meal in his hands. "Then I'll get a cab," he informed, disposing of his trash and heading towards the exit.

As the door closed, the companions stared at a middle-aged couple who chatted animatedly while standing in line. The man held out his phone so his wife could see the screen.

"Hey, honey, would you look at that," he began. "Mexico's underwater cave, Cenote Angelita, has some weird river flowing through it."

His wife leaned in, squinting at the screen. "Underwater river? How's that possible?"

The man scrolled down to read the full page. "Says here it's not actually a river, but it looks like one. It's some kind of layer of hydrogen sulfide that separates the fresh water at the top from the salt water below. Creates this misty effect that looks just like a river flowing under the water."

News of this recent discovery prompted Emily to rummage through his purse for Caleb's book. "You mentioned the massacre and how not everyone believed that the teens committed the crime, but then..." She paused, setting it on the table and glossing over several pages. "You cut to the legend surrounding the cave we visited. But you never brought up the tunnels under the homes."

"Because I didn't know about them."

"Exactly. There's gotta be something we're missing, something important. We need to figure out what it is." She opened the book to the bookmarked location. "I just feel like we're not seeing the whole picture."

"What are you thinking?" he asked, leaning in to get a look at the page.

"I'm not sure," she admitted. "How did you hear about the Hilltown massacre?"

Caleb's voice dropped, as if the very walls might be listening. "It started with my cousin Jay," he began. "A figure cloaked in darkness wormed into his mind, puppet-mastering him into petty crimes. But you know the source of it all? The contents inside a spell book that uncovered secrets not meant to be heard. I dismissed it as delusion then, but now? Now, I'm not so sure of anything."

Curiosity piqued; Emily leaned forward. "A spell book? Yeah, sure, I guess at this point, why should anything be off the table?"

"This book was filled with ancient incantations and rituals," he explained. "Initially, I dismissed Jay's claims as mere delusions, but given what we've experienced, I can't help but question my initial skepticism."

She stared back down at the page in question. "How does all of this tie into the Hilltown massacre?"

Caleb took a deep breath, his gaze fixed on a distant point. "According to Jay, there's a belief that the truth behind the massacre must be uncovered in order to free the spirits of the accused," he revealed, his words carrying a weight of solemnity.

Emily nodded. "So, you decided to write a book about it?"

"Not initially," he clarified. "The more I delved into my research, the more I stumbled upon unrelated events that held peculiar connections. Some of the missing individuals you said you encountered in the tunnels, for instance, were last seen near Burney Falls, while others had ties to Hilltown."

"One of them was a childhood friend. She disappeared when we were kids. I always thought she'd just moved away, but now..."

"You couldn't have known," he reassured, resting a hand over hers. "You were just a child, unaware of the darkness that lurked beneath the surface."

"I understand that, but what I can't comprehend is why angels, supposed guardians, couldn't prevent any of this from happening."

A spark ignited within her, awakening a desire for knowledge. Emily retrieved her phone, tapping away at the screen. The digital sea parted, revealing an island of intrigue: 'Fear of the Unknown: Even When It Stares You in the Face.' The article spoke of a man whose gaze was a portal to primal terror, his eyes the key to unlocking paralytic fear in others.

Her eyes scanned the page's contents, searching for a plausible narrative. And there it was, nestled amidst the digital tapestry of stories - an article that seemed to radiate an aura of ominous fascination. It chronicled the tale of a man endowed with an uncanny ability to instill paralyzing fear within others through the mere act of locking eyes with them. The article painted a vivid portrait of this enigmatic figure, describing his unyielding gaze that pierced through the souls of his victims, unblinking and unwavering. It detailed how his unwavering stare, devoid of any trace of mercy, unleashed a torrent of dread and panic within those unfortunate enough to be ensnared by his gaze.

Her excitement brimmed as she shared her discovery with Caleb, her voice tinged with awe. She extended her phone towards him, allowing him to delve into the article's chilling contents with a growing sense of concern.

"It sounds like this guy is a demon," he remarked.

"I know. It's still weird to say out loud. But what could they be digging for?"

"As far as I'm concerned, there's only one way to find out."

"You really want to go back there?" Emily's eyes widened with apprehension flickering within them.

"I think it's something we have to do."

The sound of sizzling meat and chatter devoured the room while they finished their drinks. Upon taking in the last drops, a golden glow poured over Long Point State Park, filtering around the trees where David locked himself in a battle. It wasn't of flesh and blood, but of mind and will.

Get out of my head, you fiend. He thought to himself, not anticipating a response. However, to his surprise, Haines' voice echoed back.

You fool, the voice resonated, sending shivers down his spine. If you don't concede, I'll make sure you'll wish you had.

The voice departed David's mind as his nose began to bleed, a physical manifestation of the mental turmoil he was experiencing. The bloody droplets trickled down his face, staining his pale skin.

While he struggled to overcome his invader, the sun had begun to set over the chilling town of Hill. In the fading light, the duo walked in unison, their steps synchronized as they approached the house she narrowly escaped. As he surveyed the surroundings, he felt ominous intentions from every direction.

"This place is giving me the creeps," he stated.

His focus shifted back to his partner in crime, who stood frozen in shock upon witnessing the wreckage. Overwhelmed by terror, her entire being succumbed to the fear that engulfed her after tumbling into the tunnel. Locking eyes with her, Caleb grabbed Emily's hand, applying just enough pressure to capture her focus.

"Don't worry, it'll be okay."

Emily turned around, enveloping him in a comforting hug. He reciprocated, and they both savored the intimate moment.

"I'll go and investigate while you stay here," he suggested, gazing into her eyes.

"Absolutely not. We're not separating. If you're going down there, I'm going with you."

Moments later, they stood at the threshold of the tunnel, its gaping maw a black void that seemed to swallow light itself. Emily and Caleb exchanged a glance, their eyes reflecting a hint of apprehension. They took a simultaneous deep breath and step forward, crossing the boundary between the known world and the mysteries that lay ahead.

Feeble beams of their phone flashlights carved thin paths within the oppressive darkness. A claustrophobic corridor breathed malevolent life before them. The light moved across the surface, exposing slick walls that encompassed an otherworldly sheen. Shadows morphed and shifted in their peripheral vision.

Emily's hand found Caleb's in the darkness, seeking comfort in each other's presence as they ventured deeper into the unknown.

"This is where you saw all those people who were reported missing?" Caleb inquired, looking around the area.

"I mean, they didn't look like themselves anymore, but yes."

As they pressed onward, Caleb's foot teetered on the edge of a treacherous abyss, threatening to plunge him into its unfathomable emptiness. With fast reflexes, Emily lunged forward, snatching him from the clutches of the gaping chasm. Now, frozen in place, he directed his flashlight's beam into the bottomless void, revealing something so profound that seemed to devour all light. Emily's gaze, however, remained fixed on the convergence of multiple tunnels ahead, a labyrinthine network that beckoned with an air of intrigue.

"Are you seeing this?" she asked. "It looks like this single location is what they were searching for."

"Every tunnel seems to lead to this," Caleb informed, walking beside her.

Above them, etched into the stone like an ancient whisper, loomed a protection sigil. A perfect circle, split by a vertical line, cradled a horizontal cross at its apex - strength and unity intertwined. Below, an all-seeing eye peered into their souls, its gaze softened by a whimsical mustache-like mark. The symbol was a paradox of power and playfulness, carved into the very bones of the earth.

They traced the sigil downwards, uncovering a mark resembling a mustache, evoking a sense of whimsy amidst the profound symbolism. Eager to preserve this discovery, he pointed out the sigil to Emily, who opened the photo icon on her phone to capture an image that would forever encapsulate the essence of this ancient symbol.

"Perhaps Michael can provide some insight into this."

"We have to explore what's down there," Caleb asserted, fixating his gaze upon the expansive hole in the ground.

"Really? What if we come across more creepy people?"

"I'm with you, Emily. I get it, but don't you think we have to know?"

He lowered himself to a kneeling position, his hands tracing the weathered fibers of the rope that had been secured around a sturdy rock. With a firm grip, he gave it a series of deliberate tugs, testing its strength and resilience. Despite its age, the prickly cord held steadfast, assuring him that it would bear the weight of his body.

"Awesome, it looks like it'll hold," he said, approaching the hole in the ground. "Stay up here and maybe keep an eye on this thing just in case this ends up being a bad idea."

"Oh, I can tell you right now that it is. If anyone should go down there, it's me. I'm the one with these powers."

"Please," Caleb began, looking at Emily. "Let me do something useful."

As he descended, a mesmerizing sight sprinkled across the ground, he spotted a myriad of luminous purple dots. Continuing downward, he became aware of a multitude of double crosses etched into various surfaces, their presence scattered throughout the surroundings.

How far down does this thing go? He pondered, feeling a bit uneasy.

After reaching the lowest point, he realized that the identical symbol seen above was also etched beneath his feet. Due to the absence of any other discernible features, he experienced a sense of claustrophobia, so he decided to ascend the rope to the surface.

Upon assisting him in getting vertical, Emily gazed at him. "So, what's down there?" she inquired.

"Actually, nothing," he replied, looking up at the rock above them. "I think we need to figure out what that symbol means.

"Well, then let's go outside so we can look it up."

In the wake of exiting the cave, Caleb engaged in an image search for the symbol. However, the results yielded only comparable visuals.

"None of these are exact," he informed, holding his phone out in front of Emily.

"Good thing we know an angel."

After settling into the car, Caleb started the engine as Emily leaned back in her seat. Her thoughts galloped through her mind. The symbol, the tunnels, the missing people - she knew they all had to be connected somehow.

30

CHOICES

Over several days, Caleb and Emily immersed themselves in the Bible, searching for insights about the entity that instilled fear in others. Their quest led them to the bookstore, where they acquired various editions of the sacred text. Despite their efforts, they reached a singular conclusion: this phenomenon was attributed to the devil's malevolent influence. Among the vast collection, only a handful of Bibles dared acknowledge an elusive force capable of driving a person to madness. The mention of the entity's various names sent a chill down Caleb's spine, leaving an indelible mark within him. Determined to preserve their discoveries, they left the books open across the dining room table, pages splayed like the wings of inquisitive birds eager to take flight.

One morning, Caleb roused from slumber and stretched. He leaned over, planting a gentle kiss on Emily's forehead. "I'm heading out. Back in a bit."

Emily's eyes fluttered open as she sat up. "Want company?"

Caleb shook his head, fingers fishing for his keys. "No need. Won't be long."

After his departure, she moved to the living room couch. Sinking into the cushions, she delved into her subconscious.

If I truly possess this power, I should be able to summon it.

A mesmerizing purple aura enveloped her, its ethereal glow pulsating with otherworldly energy. Suddenly, a medium-sized orb manifested in her palm, its sudden appearance startling her. The shock sent her tumbling from the couch, yet as she hit the floor, a sense of wonder and intrigue washed over her, eclipsing any discomfort from the fall.

Meanwhile, Caleb stepped into the hushed interior of St. Paul's Chapel. The sight of holy water near the entrance captivated him, its shimmering surface a mirror to the solemn atmosphere. He paused, bowing his head in a silent prayer for guidance.

As he ventured deeper, awe overcame him. Sunlight filtered through stained glass, painting the polished pews and intricate altarpiece with vibrant hues. Ornate chandeliers hung from high ceilings, their golden glow illuminating the sacred space below. Every corner boasted exquisite religious artwork, scenes from biblical tales and saints of old adorning the walls.

At last, a priest approached, his robes rustling softly. "Hello, my son. How can I be of help?"

Caleb hesitated, weighing his words carefully. "Are you familiar with ancient symbols predating Christianity?" He held out his phone, revealing the discoveries from the cave.

The priest leaned in, his brow furrowing as he examined the screen. "It appears to be a protective sigil," he mused. "But these additional markings suggest a different meaning entirely."

"It's unique," Caleb explained, a hint of excitement creeping into his voice. "I couldn't find any mention of it online."

A visible shiver ran down the priest's spine. He turned to Caleb, his eyes wide with concern. "Where did you find this?"

"It's engraved on the floor and ceiling of an underground cave."

The minister's facial expression darkened, shadows deepening the lines on his face. "Perhaps its secrets are meant to remain there. Consider this: if the devil you've heard about was behind these events, do you believe anyone would have survived to tell their stories?"

Before Caleb could respond, the shrill ring of his phone cut through the air. The priest retreated hastily to his chambers, the heavy doors closing with a resounding thud. Left alone in the vast, echoing space, he realized his quest for answers had hit another dead end.

Back at the house, Emily persevered in her efforts to awaken her abilities. Her eyes squeezed shut in concentration as tiny luminous spheres flickered in and out of existence around her, their soft light dancing in the air. The sudden click of the front door broke her focus, and she opened her eyes to see Caleb entering, the enticing aroma of Chinese takeout wafting in with him.

Emily's face bloomed with a radiant grin. "You remembered."

"Of course," he said, crossing the room to hand her a container of fragrant specialty chicken. The spices tickled her nose as she accepted it.

Setting her food aside, Emily leaned forward. "Did you visit the church?"

Caleb's shoulders sagged slightly as he nodded. "I did, but the priest knew nothing. Actually, he seemed nervous about the whole thing."

"That doesn't sound good at all."

"No, it doesn't," he agreed. "But I think we've exhausted all our leads. We'll have to wait for Michael's return. He should be able to clarify things."

"True," she conceded, her tone resigned.

Caleb set his food down and strode to the closet at the hallway's entrance.

Curious, Emily called after him, "Where are you going?"

Several moments later, Caleb returned, brandishing a worn box of Uno cards. "How about we play a fun game in the meantime?"

A spark of excitement danced over Emily's features. "Wow, it's been ages since I've played Uno!"

As the couple settled in for a pleasant evening, the night deepened around them.

Elsewhere, in Oakwood Park, the clock on the community center struck 10 PM. The sound echoed through the playground, where two young boys were engaged in a spirited game of basketball under the harsh glow of flickering streetlights. Their laughter carried on the cool night breeze, a carefree counterpoint to the tension building in the shadows.

Nearby, a young girl on a rusted swing set watched the boys play, her legs swinging idly. The creak of chains punctuated the rhythm of a bouncing basketball and shouts of triumph. With a crackling buzz, the street light above the court sputtered and died, plunging the area into an eerie half-light. The boys' laughter cut short, and the girl's fingers tightened on the swing's chains.

When the creature, hidden in the void realm, prepared to act, the Roamer appeared, restoring the wind and stabilizing the lights. "Haines, I thought we'd parted ways. Have you come to free me from this Gargoyle encasement?"

Haines grinned, a hint of malice in his voice. "Since you've been such an obedient puppet, I thought you should know: Lucifer's aware of your allegiance to me."

"What?!"

In an instant, he vanished, leaving the creature to grapple with this revelation. Paralyzed by fear, a surge of electricity obliterated the bulbs in every street lamp in a spectacular display.

Across the street, Boris trudged along, the grimy jacket from the dumpster masking his identity. He stopped and plucked the weathered key from his pocket. His thumb grazed the engraved letters—T.A.S—probing each groove as if it might unveil something useful.

Upon stepping into the crosswalk, hushed voices from a narrow alley caught his attention. He edged closer, peering into the dark passage. An anxious man with a trimmed beard, clad in a rumpled button-down shirt betraying a grueling day at the office, murmured to a woman.

"I can't believe I lost it," he muttered, raking a hand through his salt-and-pepper hair. "That key is irreplaceable."

The woman clutched his arm. "We'll backtrack and find it," she reassured. "But first, you gotta see something."

Boris lingered at the entrance, watching as the pair flagged down a cab, melting into the night. He glanced at the key in his palm, doubt creasing his face. He pocketed it and resumed his trek when the flickering lights on the adjacent block commanded his attention.

"Showtime at last," he said, aiming to cross the street.

Screams pierced the night air, followed by billowing smoke. He sprinted toward the chaos, finding two boys and a girl trapped within a fiery ring encircling the basketball court.

Assessing the dire situation, he shrugged off his jacket and flung it onto the flames to create a path to safety. The boys dashed to freedom, while the young girl paused, her eyes meeting Boris's.

"Thank you, sir," she whispered before joining her companions.

While fire raged on, another scent mingled with the acrid smoke—a faint whiff of sulfur that kept Boris alert.

"I knew you were behind this," he murmured, scanning the area. "It's not like you to leave your handiwork unfinished."

Puzzled over the sword swaying on its own, he pulled it from his jacket.

With a shimmer of dark energy, the haunting silhouette of the creature took shape at the edge of the basketball court. A pungent odor permeated the area, a nauseating blend of decay and struck matches left to smolder. The intensity of the smell was unmistakable, clinging to everything it touched. "I'd have thought you'd curled up and died by now," it sneered.

"I'll wipe that grin off your face!" Boris shouted, accustomed to the foul stench.

The sword flickered in and out of visibility, while multiple gashes formed on the demon's body. Feeling lighter than a feather, the scientist wielded the weapon. A low, resonant hum vibrated throughout his arm after every swing, cutting the air with the weight of mountains, creating a rainbow of golden sparks in its wake.

"What the—how did you—"

Boris admired the ancient weapon. "Looks like this thing packs quite a punch."

Emboldened, he extended the sword and advanced. He charged at the demon, aiming for its face. In response, it raised its arms in an X, shielding itself from the blow. Upon impact, the blade shattered under Boris's weight.

"No... you've got to be kidding me!" He stared at the weapon in disbelief.

The malevolent being's lips twisted into a smirk. "I hope you enjoyed that. Now it's my turn."

It plucked a fragment of the shattered weapon from its arm. "I'm a demon of my word. Once I'm done with you, I'll eradicate your other offspring from this realm."

Terror seized Boris. He crumpled to his knees, overwhelmed by his quest for vengeance he'd forgotten about the threats.

"Time to pay the piper," it declared, looming over Boris.

The air fractured with the resonant tolling of bells tearing across the thunderstorm's crackles. The creature, sensing an opportunity, attempted to wisp away in a gust of smoke when a diabolical whisper slithered through its ear. "What's the matter? No juice?"

In a blaze of fiery brilliance, Lucifer showed up facing the demon, his ruby-red eyes commanding attention. Reality warped around him. First, the swing set groaned and bent inward at its corners. Then, the tips of the grass ignited into small flames licking upwards before being snuffed out by blue fire that spread in a circle around his feet.

He beheld the creature as crimson veins burned through its being, a visual manifestation of the power he held over his underling. Yet, as quickly as they appeared, the veins faded, leaving its body unmarked.

Smoke wisped from the creature's body, testament to the intense heat and pressure. He turned to face Lucifer, his expression a mixture of anguish and desperation. "I... I freed you from perdition."

"By aligning yourself with him!" Lucifer spat, his face inches from the demon's.

"I've been trying to devise a plan to strike him down, but his guard is always up. Moreover, he's been communicating with someone."

The devil's mind paused. Locked away and they can still communicate?

"Tell me where he is, and you might live to see another nightfall."

"I... I don't know, but I do know he's been digging tunnels—"

"Where?"

"He never told me. It's what I overheard."

Lucifer's snarl reverberated through the air. "What?! You fool!" he spat, his words laced with venomous contempt. "He trapped you inside the Gargoyle statue and banished you to hell before the battle was won. You couldn't have known, but that doesn't excuse your actions."

The devil's gaze ripped into the creature's soulless depths. "I believe I can make you see the error of your ways without annihilating you... yet."

A fiery sphere formed beneath the creature's feet. Flames flew upward, their intensity towering over its presence. The inferno's scorching hold hurled the creature back to the underworld.

Boris retreated, sprinting as fast as he could down the road. His eyes fixated on his phone, where an ominous message blinked: "666."

Before long, he collided with a couple on the sidewalk. He looked up, an apology on his lips, but recognition flooded their features. Fear coursed through the woman, her scream piercing the night air and drawing the attention of two nearby police officers.

They rushed toward the commotion, hands poised for their holstered weapons. It didn't take long for their own realization to take hold.

"Freeze!" one officer bellowed.

"Drop the phone and get on the ground, hands up!" the other ordered.

With no apparent alternative, Boris complied. He released his grip on the device, lowering himself to the ground. A solitary tear escaped, tracing a path down his cheek as his phone clattered against the unforgiving pavement.

"I have Boris Linderman in custody," one officer dispatched, a hint of triumph in his voice. His partner moved to secure the scientist with handcuffs.

The officers moved in unison, escorting Boris to their patrol car. En route, the partner reached into his blazer's inner pocket, producing a clear evidence bag. He bent down and scooped up the fallen phone, securing it inside the bag.

Once he sat in the backseat of the squad car, the reality of his situation sank in. As they drove off, the faint sound of sirens grew louder, a harbinger of the challenges that were yet to come.

31

MICHAEL'S RETURN

I solated in the woods, David staggered along a dirt path he had stumbled across several hours ago. A rainstorm had since passed, leaving the air thick with the sweet, earthy scent of wet leaves and soil. He took a deep breath, savoring the refreshing aroma that filled his lungs. Upon coming across a medium-sized Red Maple tree with a smooth, gray bark, he crossed his legs and sat down. The tree's leaves glistened with raindrops, the wet foliage almost overpowering.

He closed his eyes, blocking out any and all types of distractions that might occur. The calm wind blew by, rustling through the leaves of the nearby trees with a gentle whisper. The sound of the rustling leaves created a soothing background noise that helped to calm David's mind. In the distance, a Swainson bird's fluting melody filled the air, its sweet, melodic song carrying on the wind. The sound was both beautiful and haunting, adding to the sense of peace and tranquility in the woods.

Then, Boris's voice returned. Bring the girl to me. He demanded.

David's eyes snapped open, his anger boiling over. He slammed his fist into the wet dirt, feeling the cool, damp earth squish beneath his knuckles. The sensation was both satisfying and jarring, the wet dirt clinging to his skin as he pulled his hand back. He glared at the ground, his resolve hardening. He refused to give up the fight.

"I thought you were done with this, Boris!" He stared up into the sky, where the sunlight filtered through the trees overhead, casting dappled shadows on the ground. The warm rays of light created a sense of hope and optimism, even as he struggled to resist the virus's influence.

That's when it hit him. The eerie voice wasn't actually communicating with him anymore; it was the virus replaying his voice.

"I figured you out, did you hear me?!" he yelled out into the clear sky. "You won't drive me mad like you did everyone else."

As he spoke, a few marble-sized rocks with jagged edges glinted in the sunlight, levitating above the ground. They hovered in the air for a moment before bursting into pieces, a testament to the growing strength of his telekinetic powers.

Back at the house, the duo sat in silence, listening to the sound of their racing heartbeats. Caleb and Emily immersed themselves in a tender moment. They found themselves perched on the edge of the bed, their shirts discarded haphazardly on the floor. The room exuded an air of quiet passion, as if holding its breath.

Caleb's gaze, filled with vulnerability, locked onto Emily's eyes. In this intimate exchange, he mustered the courage to reveal a truth that has weighed heavily upon him. "It's been a really long time for me," he confessed.

Emily, her lips curved into a coy smile, playfully teasing him. "Well, ya gotta get back on the horse sometime."

Leaning in, she exerted a gentle pressure, forcing Caleb to yield, his body sinking back onto the soft mattress.

As their bodies met the plush surface, a symphony of sensations enveloped them. The mattress cradled them with its embrace, offering a sanctuary of comfort and support. The fabric beneath them caressed their skin, its softness a tactile reminder of the intimacy they shared.

A radiant azure light bathed the room with a mystical brilliance. Unaware of the spectacle unfolding around them, they leaned in, their lips poised to meet in a fervent and passionate kiss. Just as abruptly as it had appeared, the blue light dissipated, leaving behind a lingering sense of awe and wonder.

Michael took shape in the living room, his face draped in worry. "Emily, are you here?"

The silence that greeted him was deafening, amplifying his mounting concern. Then, a jarring and intense thud reverberated from down the hall. As the Archangel approached the bedroom, a question echoed in his mind.

"Are they constructing some sort of weapon?" He stood in place for a moment before vocalizing his concern. "Is everything okay in there?"

A resounding snap rippled through the room, causing the bed to collapse onto the ground. Emily, taken aback by the sudden turn of events, remarked with sarcasm, "Oh, I can't believe you broke the bed."

Caleb's laughter could also be heard from outside the door as he replied, "I think we can both agree that wasn't me, young lady."

However, their momentary amusement was interrupted by an unwelcome entrance. Michael, appearing in the doorway, was met with the sight of their hastily covered bodies and the wreckage of the bed.

"This is how you choose to spend your time when you are aware that the fate of the world hangs in the balance?"

Feeling defensive, he protested, "Seriously, man, can you just give us a moment and we'll be right out?"

Michael's departure marked a silent condemnation of Caleb and Emily's carelessness. The weight of his disapproving presence lingered just outside the door.

"You think it's possible he doesn't know what coitus is?" Emily murmured.

"I don't know."

Meanwhile, Michael stood in the hallway, his gaze fixed on the ticking clock adorning the wall. Impatience coursed through him as he waited for the duo to emerge from the room. Frustration tightened his fists, the tension evident in his clenched hands.

At last, the door opened, its faint creaks serving as a signal to the Archangel of their arrival. Instantly, they were enveloped by the resplendent luminosity that bathed the house. While Emily perceived a gentle haze, as if veiled by ethereal mist, Caleb blinked and squinted, his eyes adjusting to the brilliance that surrounded them.

"Why is it so bright in here?"

"I have brought you into the Celestial realm."

"Celestial—"

"Why, exactly?" Emily inserted.

"You are here to learn how to use your powers without being detected."

"You think those guys from before are going to come after her?"

"My brethren are still hunting the Entitles, and I am certain they will come for you in retaliation like they have once already. This realm provides the opportunity for Emily to develop her skills without being detected," Michael replied.

Caleb's frustration bubbled up inside him, a seething annoyance that he could no longer contain. He opened his mouth to speak. "So, our lives are in danger," he began with a hint of bitterness. "Yet, you couldn't even give us five—"

"There are serious matters, you understand. You can procreate once we have won, and the world is free from Lucifer's grip."

"It's not like we've been sitting idly by, ya know," Emily asserted. "You've been MIA for almost two weeks. You want proof? It's spread out all over the table in the living room."

As they made their way down the hallway, Caleb led the way with Michael and Emily following his lead. Upon reaching their destination - the living room, the Archangel glanced over the scattered remnants of their labor laying on the table.

"Familiarizing yourselves with the Bible. Not a bad choice."

"No," Caleb said, walking over and picking up one of the books to point out a highlighted verse. "Most of these insisted that the devil could instill fear in mortals just by being present, but others suggested that it was something darker, more sinister."

Emily approached them, inserting herself into the conversation as Michael lowered his sights onto them. "More sinister than Lucifer himself? Doubtful. What is all of this about?" he questioned?

"We found several documents where people claimed to have been under so much fear that they did what was asked of them," Emily explained. "These people were otherwise like your average Joe until one day they just snapped. At least, that's how the police saw it."

Caleb nodded. "The teens accused of the Hilltown massacre all stated that they felt an unbelievable amount of fear after laying eyes on an unknown being hiding in the shadows. We're asking if maybe it's possible something else, something worse than the devil could be out there."

Michael shook his head. "You humans have it in your minds that there is always a bigger threat lurking in every dark corner, but the greatest evil to this world is Lucifer."

Caleb took out his phone and opened the photo gallery. He showed a picture to Michael. "Can you shed some light as to what kind of symbol this is?"

He examined the symbol on the phone. "I am familiar with a protection sigil similar to this, but there seem to be a few more markings here. My assessment is that it means nothing."

"I don't know," Emily insisted. "There are two of these symbols, one directly below the other, in the tunnels under the vacant homes in Hilltown."

"I assure you there is no cause for alarm."

"Yeah, no offense, but I'm not convinced."

"There is no time for this debate," Michael retorted. "It is imperative that you learn how to use your abilities, and fast."

Emily, taken aback by his sudden change in tone, closed her eyes and surrendered herself to the immersive embrace of a vibrant purple light. The energy emanating from her being enveloped her in a luminous aura, casting a radiant glow upon her surroundings. With her left hand outstretched, a small sphere of the same enchanting hue materialized in her palm, pulsating with ethereal power. As she opened her eyes, her irises were adorned with a mesmerizing ring of captivating violet.

"See, we haven't just been sitting around while you were away."

"No, I suppose not. Let us see how well you are in combat."

Emily raised her fists as her aura intensified. A tingling sensation spread throughout her body, her heart racing with a mix of excitement and nervousness.

In a sudden blur, the angel teleported behind her, but Emily's eyes seemed to capture every detail in slow motion. She hesitantly closed them, unsure of how to adjust her vision.

Sensing her confusion, he reassured her, "There's nothing wrong with your vision, Emily. I noticed you were able to track my movements as I teleported here. Your mortal mind might struggle to comprehend it, but my advice is to embrace these powers."

She felt excitement over her newfound abilities. The lavender aura intensified as his words sank in. Closing her eyes, she felt her aura expand, enveloping her entire body. She released the tension in her muscles, unclenching her fists and letting them fall loosely by her sides. A calming energy coursed through her. In the darkness behind her eyelids, she visualized herself standing in a different location, as if she were phasing in and out of reality. With focus and precision, she envisioned herself emerging from the other side.

After granting herself sight, she found that she had been transported beside Caleb. He greeted her with an excited grin and an eager hand raised for a celebratory high-five. She offered a faint smile before shifting her gaze to the archangel, her training partner. His eyes were watchful, expectant.

His voice broke through her thoughts, his tone evaluative yet firm. "Not bad, but it needs to become like second nature or you will lose the fight against Lucifer before it even starts."

"Then let's dispense with the feeble talk and get on with it," she said.

With each passing second, the weight of loss and the memory of Kota's death flooded her thoughts, propelling her forward. She took a deep breath and lunged across the room, her limbs moving with fluid grace as she aimed to take down Michael.

However, the angel moved with impossible precision, effortlessly blocking every strike. Emily caught a whiff of the faint scent of ozone that seemed to emanate from him, lacing the ambiance with the purity of his divinity.

"If you were human, you would have been kneeling on the floor," she remarked, a hint of amusement coloring her tone.

Without warning, Michael swung his fist towards Emily's face. The force of the blow left her feeling defenseless against his overwhelming power and brutality. Her body hurtled through the air, crashing into the unforgiving wall with a bone-jarring impact. Agonizing pain radiated through her, and every breath became a struggle.

Despite the ringing in her ears, she heard Caleb's worried cries as he rushed to her side. Through the haze of pain, the Archangel's words tore through, firm and unyielding. "Do not lose focus."

32

HARDSHIP

D avid rushed back into Creation Labs, his heart pounding with urgency as he darted towards the cabinet. The room was dimly lit, with the only source of light coming from the computer monitors that flickered with data. His eyes were fixed on the cabinet underneath the computer, knowing that the cure he desperately needed was hidden inside. He could feel his palms getting clammy with anticipation as he punched in the code, 4-0-3-1, to the safe box inside.

Maybe he's right and I'll still be able to help in the coming fight, but I need to get Boris' voice out of my head, he ponders, while reaching further into the safe in order to reach a syringe.

His eyes widened after hearing the safe click open. He reached inside and pulled out the last vial of the cure—its liquid substance glimmered in the fluorescent light. This was his last hope to fight against the impending battle that loomed ahead.

With a determined look on his face, he rolled up his sleeve and made a fist with his left hand. He grabbed the syringe and jabbed it into his shoulder, drawing out a small sample of his blood. The needle pierced through his skin, sending a sharp sting down his arm.

Once he had enough blood for testing, he pulled out the syringe and reached for a microscope on the other side of the cabinet. The microscope had been a familiar sight to him, with its metallic body and intricate lenses that allowed him to see the smallest of details. He carefully placed the blood sample on a test slide and adjusted the lenses until the sample came into focus.

As he peered through the ocular lens, he could see his red blood cells contorted and twisted with a yellow glow. This filled him with concern until the distorted color faded away. However, his relief was short-lived as he noticed several red blood cells shrinking in the process.

A whirlwind of dread and doubt twisted through David's mind like a turbulent storm. But he knew he couldn't afford to let these thoughts consume him, not with so much at stake.

Muscle memory. I hope you're right. He dwelled on Micheal's words.

With a deep breath, he acquired the last of the cure from the safe and injected himself. The cold liquid rushed through his veins as he leaned back against the wall, waiting for the effects to take hold.

Just a stone's throw beyond the county, while he fought his personal battle, the city grappled with its own shock. Television screens flickered in homes within the metroplex, broadcasting the latest crisis. Witnesses recounted a nightmare scenario: sudden deafening noise, unexplained fires, and even claims of a demonic presence. While most called for Boris's punishment, believing him responsible, one young woman's tearful testimony stood out:

"I must express my gratitude to Boris," she choked, her eyes brimming with tears. "He saved my life."

The anchors fell silent, grappling with this unexpected twist. As they prepared for an intermission, Jason sat alone in a quiet kitchen, staring at a framed picture of him and Tori smiling at each other. He traced the outline of the photograph, his chest tightening as he stared at their frozen smiles. The weight of absence pressed down on him, heavier than ever.

With all the recent crime scenes he's been at and now the news of Boris's capture, he takes out his phone with a heavy heart. He only has to press a single number as the person is on speed dial. With each unanswered ring, he grows even more anxious than before.

"Hey, it's me," he said, leaving a message on the voicemail. "I'm sorry that I haven't been there, but I'm better now."

Putting down the phone, he walked over to the window and looked out at the city, feeling its hustle and bustle around him.

Meanwhile, at the police station, Boris adorned an orange jumpsuit with chains around his ankles and wrists, walking down cell block six. The other inmates jeered and leered at him as the guards pushed him along.

The former scientist, a man accustomed to being hated, faced false accusations of murder that led to his current situation. Though he remained steadfast to see justice prevail.

As the cell doors locked him in, he slumped down onto a worn-out bench. The sound of his cellmate's heavy footsteps reverberated throughout the dark corridors, startling him as the man loomed over and whispered in his ears.

Boris winced at the harsh words. These accusations, like poison, seeped into his veins, filling him with a sense of hopelessness. He tried to speak, to defend himself, but his voice faltered and died in his throat. The disdain and repulsion in his cellmate's eyes were suffocating, suffusing the air with a palpable tension. It became clear that his side of the story would fall on deaf ears.

"No," Boris managed to protest. "I'm innocent."

Anger and aggression radiated from every pore in the cellmate's body as he clenched his fist and delivered a brutal blow to his face. The force of the punch sent him sprawling onto the stained tile floor, disoriented and dazed. Panic flooded his senses, his vision swimming with spots of darkness as he struggled to regain his footing.

His cellmate sneered, towering over him like a predator reveling in his prey's vulnerability. "You think you can just deny everything and get away with it?" he hissed, venom dripping from each word. "You killed your daughter too. You're sick, man."

Gazing up from his prone position, Boris's gaze inadvertently fell upon the neglected floor, noticing the scars etched upon it over time - the stains, scuffs, footprints, and cracks. It became a chilling reflection of his own crumbling sense of justice, a symbol of his entrapment amidst a sea of doubt and isolation.

Undeterred, his cellmate unleashed another barrage of kicks, each one hitting with a greater ferocity, striking him where the pain lingered the deepest. With each blow, Boris's breath became more labored, tears of agony stinging his eyes. Just when he felt like he couldn't bear another strike, his cellmate withdrew, crouching down to meet his bloodied gaze, a smug grin playing across his face.

"This is your place, understand?" the man jeered, his voice dripping with malice, callously exiting the cell.

Lying there, bloodied and broken, Boris fought to regain control of his body and his shattered spirit, gasping for air as he attempted to rise. As the footsteps once again approached his cell, he glimpsed a guard nonchalantly strolling by, his indifference a chilling reminder of the cruel reality of life within these walls.

He felt a mixture of anger, fear, and sadness while dragging himself to his feet. Each movement became a battle against pain and despair. His legs shook as he stumbled to his bunk, collapsing against the wall. His jaw clenched, fighting back tears of rage and fear, as the cold concrete pressed against his bruised back.

Still maintaining composure, he recounted another moment with his late wife, Rylee. This time, it was when he spoke to her about wanting to take the lead on the next experiment at the lab. She had told him he needed to stand up for himself and not let others walk all over him.

Her voice ran through his mind, already feeling like the verdict had already been decided. Boris jammed his elbow into the wall until he ruptured the outer layer. As He held his arm as a man slothfully entered the cell with his head down.

"I heard they finally brought you in. I just had to see it for myself," the man uttered, his words veiled in a whisper that drifted into a hushed cadence.

"Do I know you?" Boris asked, looking toward the stranger.

"No, you don't. Yet, I'm here because of you."

Boris strained to discern the familiar features of the stranger. Yet, his thoughts yielded no recognition.

"Yeah, that vacant look in your eyes only confirms my suspicions. Maybe this'll jog your memory," the man declared, producing a creased newspaper clipping from his pocket and depositing it in Boris' lap. The headline emblazoned across the page read, "Driver Escapes Unharmed After Crashing Into Split Tree on 4th Street."

"The incident at the coffee shop," Boris muttered, his glance lifting to meet the stranger's probing stare. "I didn't have a choice."

"Bull! There's always a choice," the man began, getting right in Boris' face. "You didn't have to inject me with whatever that stuff was that took away my free will."

"At least you survived, 'cause many didn't," Boris attempted to justify, his tone tinged with regret.

"I would have been amongst the casualties, but given I was speeding and nearly ran someone over, the cops were already nearby. So, when I slammed into the tree, paramedics were called right away and I lived to see another day. But, in prison, thanks to you."

"Reckless driving. That's really what you're in for, right? You'll be out soon and be able to put all this behind you."

"I lost my girlfriend because of you. The only reason I don't beat you to a bloody pole, is because that would just result in me staying locked up longer. And you've already taken enough time out of my life."

The man turned around and left the cell, leaving Boris to dwell on his actions.

Back in the confined space of Jason's kitchen, his heart raced as he made another attempt to reach the woman in the photograph. But once again, an automated voice answered his call, sending shivers down his spine.

Why was she ignoring him? His fiancée, and more importantly, the mother of their daughter, would never cut off communication like this, especially when their child was with her.

Growing more worried by the second, Jason grabbed his phone and opened the "find my friends" app, hoping to ease his anxiety by checking her location. However, his hopes were dashed as the screen remained blank, devoid of the familiar red dot that would pinpoint her whereabouts. It was as if she had vanished into thin air, leaving no trace behind.

He collapsed in the chair and prayed for a sign, desperate to hear from his loved ones. Just as despair settled in, the phone buzzed, jerking him out of his thoughts. A glimmer of excitement sparked within him as he reached over to answer the call.

"Hello!"

But the voice on the other end wasn't who he expected. It was a recorded message, one that sent a chill creeping up his spine. His body tensed as he listened, disbelief etched on his face. The name of the inmate, Boris, echoed in his ears, triggering a surge of anger that coursed through his veins. In a fit of frustration, he clenched his fist and slammed it down on the table.

"Yeah, okay, I accept," he grumbled, recalling the events that led him here.

"Jason, thank you for accepting my call."

"You've got a lot of nerve calling me. I always had my doubts about whether you were capable of killing your wife, but what you did to that innocent child..." Jason's voice cracked with anger.

"You don't understand. We live in a world that's far from black and white. There are horrors out there that you can't even fathom," Boris pleaded, his voice tinged with desperation.

"I should have stopped you when I first saw you on that block. But I was too caught up in the case, too consumed with wanting my fiancée and daughter to escape this madness," Jason admitted, frustration evident in his tone.

"I did not kill my wife. I did not kill my daughter. And I tried to keep them from finding out about that girl's sister."

"What are you talking about?" Jason demanded, his emotions spiraling out of control.

"You wouldn't believe me even if I told you. I can hear it in your voice, the doubt creeping in. I guess I'm no longer Karry's godfather in your eyes."

Jason's grip on the phone tightened, knuckles turning white as anger burned within him. "You got that right. And don't worry, Boris, have you been watching the news lately? You might just get acquitted for all your atrocious crimes," he spat out. With a swift motion, he ended the call, discarding the phone as if it were a poisonous snake.

33

UNCERTAINTY

S ilver moonbeams cascaded upon the grueling battle, imbuing it with an otherworldly allure. Engaged in a perilous struggle against the elusive Entitles, Gabriel and Raphael readied themselves to unleash their divine fury upon the thriving farmland. As their eyes and palms ignited in a vibrant display of emerald and ivory radiance, they sensed an unsettling mirth dancing upon the faces of their adversaries.

"They show no fear," Raphael discerned, his voice tinged with uncertainty.

"It is as if they long for our onslaught," Gabriel observed, his glare piercing through the darkness towards the dilapidated barn. In haunting unison, four other Entitles stood before the weathered doors, their malice grins stretching from ear to ear as they clasped hands.

"I sense no presence inside, but there is deception at play," Gabriel whispered.

"Can you breach their defenses?" Raphael inquired; his tone edged with determination.

"If you fulfill your role, then, yes."

As the ethereal glow dissipated, leaving only the lunar radiance to guide their path, the two celestial warriors prepared to resume the clash. With the battlefield bathed in the moon's tender light, the dark entities regained their focus.

Raphael vanished from sight, reappearing behind one of the three adversaries. With a flicker of celestial speed, he contorted the entity's arm into an unnatural position, the sickening crack echoing through the air. During this act of divine retribution, Gabriel appeared next to his brother, seizing the Entitle's wrists in a vice-like grip.

Raphael readied himself to strike another fiend, disappearing and reappearing behind his target. Yet, in a macabre twist, the creature's head spun around, fixating its chilling gaze upon the angel's eyes as tendrils of inky smoke emerged from every crevice.

"What abomination is this? You wretched creature," Raphael growled, his voice heavy with disbelief and disdain.

Gabriel watched on, muscles straining as he struggled against the relentless onslaught of the first Entitle. "What in the blazes is happening over there?"

The billowing black smoke fractured into three ominous tunnels, ripping through the air with a menacing force, homing in on the outskirts of the tranquil farmland. In an eruption of chaos, a massive chasm materialized at the heart of the land, unfurling a monstrous, vaporous fist that loomed overhead, poised to obliterate Raphael like a mere speck. As the imminent catastrophe hurtled towards him, Gabriel duplicated himself, materializing the clone in front of the incoming attack. The dense misty fist collided with the copy's tangible form, hurtling it towards the ground, while the smoke vanished into the abyss.

Seeing his brother stunned before the Entitle as the smoke dissipated, Gabriel conjured two new replicas of himself, their identical forms materializing beside the healer. His clones seized hold of the Entitle's arms, their grip firm and resolute.

"I have him! Now, go after the last one!" a clone shouted.

Raphael rubbed his eyes vigorously, banishing the remnants of the oppressive fog that had obscured his vision. Gradually, his sight returned as the dark veil lifted, revealing the barn where the remaining Entitles stood defiantly.

"These guys are unlike the other groups we fought," he observed, his gaze darting towards the barn where their formidable opponents gathered.

"If we get a hold of the last one, perhaps we will uncover the reason," Gabriel suggested.

With his steely sight fixed on the weathered barn, Raphael vanished in an instant, his form dissolving into thin air as he teleported towards the lone opponent that stubbornly stood in their path. The Entitle's sinister eyes locked onto the determined angel, a malevolent grin stretching across its face like a sinister promise. And then, in a stunning display of unholy power, the creature conjured two flawless carbon copies of itself, sending a shiver of disbelief down Raphael's spine.

"What in the world?!" he exclaimed, his astonishment echoing through the tense air. "Entitles are not supposed to wield this kind of power."

The three formidable Entitles lunged forward with an ominous purpose, relentlessly driving the archangel further away from the shelter of the barn with each fierce punch. Though the thought of obliterating them crossed Raphael's mind, he couldn't tear his eyes away from the barn, reminding himself of their true mission. And so, with unwavering determination, he seized both of the dark entity's clenched fists, guiding their violent trajectory downward, causing the creature to slam its own knuckles into its malevolent abdomen. This momentary distraction allowed Raphael to swiftly teleport behind the clones, delivering a devastating kick that sent them crashing to the ground alongside their progenitor.

"It is over," the messenger's voice rang out as he stumbled back.

Raphael rushed to aid his brethren, only to find that, in a flash of speed, the dark entity had spun around, its arm a blur as it prepared to unleash a devastating blow that would have surely spelled the end for the real Gabriel. And yet, just as the creature's sinister knuckles were poised to collide with his brother's vulnerable chest, Gabriel's form vanished from sight, evading the deadly strike with a flicker of grace.

A surge of unease coursed through Raphael's veins, a gnawing realization that the situation was spiraling out of control. His gaze flickered towards the other two duplicate Entitles, who were still desperately struggling to subdue their captive. Doubt began to gnaw at his resolve, threatening to unravel the threads of their carefully devised plan.

"Perhaps Michael was right," he pondered aloud, fearing they may have made a grave mistake in underestimating their adversaries.

But then, in a sudden crescendo of clamor, the barn door swung open, jolting the unassuming guards stationed outside, toppling them face first into the unforgiving earth. The world held its breath as the dust settled, revealing the figure of the original Gabriel emerging from the once sealed entrance, cradling an unconscious mother and her daughter in his strong, protective arms. A triumphant smile graced his face, a silent proclamation that their audacious plan had, against all odds, unfolded flawlessly before their eyes.

"What makes you think that?" Gabriel retorted, holding an unconscious mother and child in his arms. "Our gambit was successful."

Raphael turned abruptly, taking in the sight before him. His fellow angels had successfully apprehended the mortal beings, and a mix of shock and satisfaction played across his ethereal features.

The Entitles, however, seemed untouched by the significance of their capture. Their grotesque faces twisted into wicked grins as they slowly advanced on the angels, relishing in their impending victory.

In a sudden burst of light, the heavens parted to reveal a blinding brightness as Michael materialized on the battlefield alongside Gabriel. Seeing his brethren appear, Raphael teleported before him, questioning Michael's unexpected presence.

"Why are you here?" he demanded.

"The mortal has completed her arduous training and is ready to confront the devil himself. Since you two are determined to engage with these loathsome creatures, I propose a plan. Let us distract them, preventing them from discovering her location, while I take on the task of tracking and confronting Lucifer," he explained.

Raphael's icy gaze narrowed. "After all this time, what makes you so certain you will succeed where I have failed?"

"I have a few theories."

With a begrudging acceptance, Gabriel chimed in, his voice tinged with sarcasm. "Well, it's refreshing to know that you actually need us for something."

To carry out their plan, Gabriel relinquished the captive mortals into Michael's capable hands. It was a weighty decision, as they understood the ramifications of their ongoing battles and the destruction they left in their wake.

"No," Raphael interjected. "If we continue obliterating every battlefield in our path, there will be nothing left on this Earth when our work is done."

Michael conceded. "Fine. Do it your way. But these mortals need to be delivered safely to their medical center."

"Agreed," Gabriel said.

Without another word, Michael vanished from the scene, while his brothers steeled themselves for the inevitable clash that awaited them. In the midst of uncertainty, they were resolute in their purpose: to protect what remained and face their adversaries head-on.

The warrior angel reappeared and clutched the mother and child, transporting them to the tranquil confines of a hushed hallway inside of a hospital. He set them down on an unoccupied stretcher, their presence temporarily punctuating the silence. A faint, ethereal glow enveloped the corridor, casting a marble glow as if a portal had briefly opened. As the celestial energy dissipated, a nurse emerged from the doors of the bustling emergency room. Assured of their safety, the archangel left, resolute in his purpose to carry out his mission.

Elsewhere, deep within the depths of the Anzob Tunnel, an eerie silence hung heavy in the air, broken only by the hurried panting of a woman gasping for breath. Her heart racing, she fumbled through her pockets in search of her phone, a lifeline to the outside world. However, her hopes were dashed as she stared at the screen, realizing there was no cell signal.

A chilling sensation crawled up her spine as an unseen presence stirred in the darkness. Fear coursed through her veins, which caused her to lose her grip on the phone. Panic threatened to consume her as she frantically scanned her surroundings, searching for an escape route.

But fate had other plans. In her frantic attempt to flee, her own feet betrayed her, causing her to stumble and tumble to the cold, unforgiving floor. Dust and dirt mingled with her anxious breaths, further complicating her desperate situation. The limited air within the confining tunnel seemed to close in on her, making each breath more difficult than the last.

As she lay sprawled on the ground, her head spinning and heart pounding, a sudden burst of light pierced the suffocating darkness. The alarming blare of her vehicle's sound system shattered the eerie silence, casting a surreal glow with its incessant flashing orange lights. Shadows danced wildly upon the tunnel walls, casting ominous silhouettes that seemed to mock her predicament.

But it was amidst this chaotic illumination that she caught sight of a figure emerging from the shadows, slowly advancing towards her. This creature, thin and agile, exuded an air of primal hunger that was etched in its gaze. Its movements were astonishingly swift, as if propelled by some sinister and otherworldly force. Fear clutched at her, freezing her limbs in a momentary state of paralysis, while her heartbeat thundered in her ears like a relentless drum-roll of impending doom.

Meanwhile, a sense of confusion gripped Michael as he stood above her, unsure of the unfolding scene before him. His head tilted, a puzzled expression crossing his features as he scanned the immediate surroundings for any signs of life, only to be met with emptiness and stillness. The absence of any tangible presence puzzled him deeply, adding to the enigmatic aura that hung in the air.

Burdened with unanswered questions, he couldn't help but wonder aloud, the words couched in a mix of frustration and curiosity, "If he was truly here, why is it that I cannot feel even the faintest trace of his presence?"

Beyond the horizon's grasp, in the sprawling expanse of a damp field in Utah, miles upon miles of tall grass stretched out, enclosing a small group of people in a desperate race for survival. Amongst them, a young woman with a torn sleeve, a scratched shoulder, and a bruised knee sprinted alongside another girl, her short blonde hair similarly disheveled, her shirt torn in the middle with a bloody belly button and a scratched cheek. The man accompanying them bore the marks of countless scratches that etched his body, his feet barely supporting his weight. The two girls clung to him, their grip unwavering as they pushed themselves to run as fast as their legs would allow.

Quick like lightning, a glint of steel flashed through the field as an ax hurtled towards them. With a sickening impact, it cleaved through the man's left arm, burying itself partially into one of the girl's shoulders. She crumpled forward, the weight of the severed limb adding to her pain, while he stumbled backward, agony contorting his features, pushing the bruised girl aside as her screams pierced the air.

"Help! Get this wretched thing out of my back!" the blonde girl pleaded, her voice filled with desperation.

A sudden gust of wind brushed over like a silent plea when Michael's commanding presence took shape before them. "Who brings you harm?"

"Where did you come from?!" questioned the bruised girl, her voice laced with disbelief.

"I do not have time for questions and it appears unsafe for you to remain out in the open. Now, tell me."

"Some deranged man in a mask," the blonde girl retorted, her pain-laden tone trembling.

"He claims to be the devil," the bruised girl added.

Understanding the gravity of the situation before him, Michael carefully removed the ax from the girl's shoulder, his touch accompanied by a wave of healing energy that mended their wounds.

With the three of them miraculously restored to their prime condition, they gazed upon the archangel in awe, a mixture of astonishment and gratitude etched across their faces.

"Who are you?" the man asked.

"Better yet, how did you just fix our wounds?" the blonde girl inquired.

With no desire to linger and explain the situation, the Archangel chose to dissolve into the ether, vanishing from their very sight. Fully cognizant of the repercussions, he manipulated their minds and left no trace of the encounter.

Amidst the eerie silence of their surroundings, permeated by the faint rustling of leaves, a perplexed man broke the stillness with a bewildered query that echoed in the vast expanse.

"Why on God's green earth are we standing out in the middle of nowhere?"

"Good question," the blonde woman retorted, her eyes drawn to the gleaming object before them. "Why is there a random weapon lying on the ground?"

As the weight of unease settled upon their hearts, a haunting symphony of footsteps reverberated through the desolate landscape, growing louder with each passing moment. Sense and instinct melded seamlessly, urging the twins to take flight from the impending danger that loomed ominously ahead.

"We should run," declared the twin.

Back in the bustling streets of New York, Caleb and Emily remained immersed in the familiar confines of their dwelling. While seeking a refreshment, Emily opened the fridge, her eyes shifting through its contents, only to be plunged into darkness as the lights abruptly extinguished. The room was cloaked in eerie shadows while the sun's rays streamed gently through the window, casting patterns upon the walls. Sensing a shift in the atmosphere, she closed the door, scanning her surroundings for any signs of familiarity.

"Caleb?"

Receiving no response, a tinge of worry began to gnaw at the edges of her consciousness. With caution, Emily made her way towards the light switch located on the opposite side of the room. Each step taken in the dimness intensified her apprehension. She inched closer, her fingers trembling as they brushed against the switch, ready to unveil the room from its shrouded state.

Just before flicking the switch, a low, shuffling sound reverberated from the top of the kitchen counter. Startled, Emily instinctively took a step back, her fists tensing nervously.

In that disconcerting moment, a figure lunged down from the furniture, as if primed to attack, before surprising Emily by being captured securely within the refuge of her grasp. A sigh of relief danced upon her lips as her arms encircled the unexpected intruder.

"What are you doing?"

"I wanted to help keep you on your toes," he replied with a playful tone in his voice, his arms enveloping Emily in a warm embrace. The mischievousness of the moment lingered as a smile tugged at the corners of his lips. "I assume you knew it was me even before I landed in your arms."

"I had an inkling," she confessed, her hug tightening in a gesture of reassurance.

After settling Caleb back on his feet, she turned towards the refrigerator, its cool metallic surface glistened in the dim light. With a purposeful motion, she opened the door, revealing the cool oasis within. The chilled air escaped in a gentle breath, causing condensation to form on the sleek bottles of iced tea nestled inside. Droplets of moisture clung to the surface, promising a refreshing respite from the weight of the world. Delicately, she reached for two bottles, their coolness a comforting sensation against her fingertips.

Sensing the need for solace and comfort, Emily extended one to her partner, offering a tangible reminder of her care.

"Thank you," he said. "Considering we don't know when he'll be back, I think we should seize every moment and make them count. So, without hesitation, tell me, what is one thing that you would like to do?"

Caught off guard by this sudden inquiry, Emily's voice escaped her lips, unfiltered and raw with desire. "I want to go see the Wicked play," she blurted, her eyes lighting up at the mere thought.

"Seriously?"

"Oh, it's not what you think," she quickly clarified, "It's a Broadway play with a twist on 'The Wizard of Oz.'"

A flicker of determination ignited within Caleb's eyes, his resolve growing stronger with every passing second. "Alright, then let us embark on this whimsical journey."

He immediately began to take purposeful steps towards the door, beckoning Emily to follow. However, confusion set in as she trailed behind. With anticipation bubbling within her chest as they approached the threshold that led to the wonderful unknown, doubt danced at the corner of her consciousness, questioning the feasibility of the proposition.

"You can't be serious?" she spoke up, interweaving her words with a hint of disbelief.

A soft smile played upon his lips, his eyes registering a profound sincerity. "Of course, I am," he began, his words full of unspoken fears and revelations. "Michael could return at any second and then drag you to the battlefield with the devil. I think we should just live life as much as possible right now."

Touched by his unwavering commitment and the reflections of her own uncertainty mirrored in his gaze, Emily felt a newfound sense of liberation wash over her. In that moment, she decided to surrender to the current of spontaneity and follow Caleb's lead.

Crammed inside the plush, jam-packed Broadway theater, the duo found themselves swept away into a mesmerizing world of theatrical enchantment. The air crackled with anticipation as the cast took their positions and launched into the melodious strains of 'Defying Gravity.' The harmonious voices soared through the theater, reverberating within the ornate walls and resonating deep within Emily's soul.

As the ethereal melody echoed through the air, Emily's eyes lit up like a brilliant constellation, sparkling with an otherworldly radiance. Her gaze was transfixed on the stage, her senses enveloped in an ethereal embrace of music and lyrics. Caleb, perceiving the enchantment shining within her, chose not to disrupt the magic in the air. Instead, he delicately placed his hand atop hers on the smooth, cool armrest.

This diverted her attention to meet a gentle smile etched upon Caleb's face. The sight of his contentment mirrored her own, creating a profound sense of warmth and unity within her. With an affectionate embrace, she nestled her head upon his sturdy shoulder.

"Thank you for sticking with me and not running the other way," she said.

"I would never do that."

Later, the duo embarked on a leisurely stroll through the heart of Times Square, which led them to the enchanting Bryant Park. Rich in its allure, this urban oasis sprawled out before them, a vibrant burst of color adorned the meticulously manicured gardens, where a ballet of delicate flowers danced gracefully in the gentle breeze. Petals unfurled, their hues ranging from fiery scarlets to soothing lavenders, creating a resplendent mosaic that appeared to shimmer and sway with a celestial rhythm.

Caleb's voice broke the silence, filled with awe as he observed his surroundings. "Wow, this is truly amazing. It's no wonder you wanted to come here."

"You've lived around here for how long, and you didn't know about this place?" Amusement colored her tone as she questioned him. "I got here about a year ago and this was one of the first places I visited."

"In my defense, it's only been around six months since I moved here, and during most of that time, we've been preoccupied with running from things I think neither of us thought existed."

"Ever think that if we hadn't met, your life would still be normal?"

"Not at all. Meeting you has been the best thing to ever happen to me. Without you, I'd probably be sitting at home right now, working on my next book," his firm response carried a note of conviction.

"You're not really an outdoorsman, are you?" she inquired.

"Don't get me wrong, I don't mind traveling, just when there's someone to spend time with."

Emily couldn't help but smile back, her own longing for companionship mirroring his.

Their journey soon led them to the magnificent library nestled in the park. As they drew closer to the towering structure, Emily's breath caught in her throat. "Wow, this thing is like a castle."

She craned her neck to take in the grandeur of the lion statue guarding its entrance. Its fierce posture and majestic gaze hinted at the secrets and knowledge contained within.

"You know what, since we're here, there's something I want to look up."

Stepping closer to the library's grand entrance, Caleb couldn't help but appreciate the intricate details that adorned its façade. The arched door, adorned with ornate carvings, seemed to welcome them into a realm of knowledge and discovery. With a courteous gesture, he extended his arm, holding the heavy wooden doors ajar for Emily, allowing her to enter into this sanctuary of wisdom.

"What's on your mind?"

"Did you notice that only a few volumes of those Bibles we read actually provided a name for the entity we believe is the devil? But each version gave a different one," he said, his words layered with intellectual curiosity. "The only thing they all had in common was the overwhelming fear that consumed everyone in its presence."

As they ventured further into the depths of knowledge, the atmosphere within the library transformed, enveloping them in a realm of stillness. The hushed whispers of students engrossed in their studies and the soft rustling of pages turned created a symphony of intellectual pursuit. The scent of old paper mingled with the subtle aroma of freshly brewed coffee served as a testament to the cozy corner café nestled within the walls.

"So, what exactly do you hope to find?" Emily inquired, looking around in amazement.

Enchanted by their opulent surroundings, their every step was muffled by the velvet-like silence that cloaked the gleaming marble floors. The buildings masterful fusion of modernized aesthetics and imitations of a storied past beckoned them with its allure. A harmonious contrast unfolded before their eyes, as sleek computers, beacons of contemporary knowledge, stood in stark companionship with ancient bookshelves, bearing the weight of centuries-old wisdom.

Immersed in their conversation, the duo found themselves enveloped by the very essence of the library. Wasting no time, Caleb lowered himself onto the chair before the computer screen, immediately pulling up the search engine and typing in a singular name - Nyx.

Emily moved closer to get a better look. "Who is Nyx?" she asked.

"It was one of the names given," he said, his fingers navigating the keyboard with swift precision. "But I have a feeling this search will bring up something completely different."

As the digital realm came to life before them, an article popped up on the screen, unveiling Nyx, the Greek Goddess. Cloaked in an aura of mystique, Nyx was renowned for her penchant for the shadows, forever suspended in a dance with darkness.

Pointing at the screen, Caleb began to explain, "You see, she is believed to have been misunderstood because there is scarce information about her. I mean, what's on this page is basically all there is."

Emily leaned in, her eyes fixed on the words before her and questioned, "And?"

"And I just don't believe that a Greek Goddess could have instilled such overwhelming fear in all those people. Beyond that one verse, nowhere is it written that Nyx invaded anyone's mind."

Determined to explore further, he then typed a new name into the search bar - EREBOS.

Curiosity danced in her eyes as she peered at the screen, entranced by the unfolding discoveries. "So, who is this?"

"Erebos," he stated. "Is the God of darkness itself, the son of Chaos and the devoted husband of Nyx."

Emily shifted from the screen to Caleb's gaze, searching his eyes for answers. Doubt hung in the air as she questioned, "So, you think just because angels are real, it means all this mythical lore is too?"

Caleb shook his head, his expression thoughtful. "No, that's not what I'm saying at all. These are merely two names that this entity provided as identification. I believe they are simply aliases. It's also the reason why I don't think the devil is behind all this either."

Emily absorbed the weight of his words.

"If that were true, he would have reveled in taking credit for his own deeds. Plus, I think we both know that had the devil been walking among us all this time, the world as we know it would not exist."

Leaning in, Caleb's voice dropped to a near whisper, his eyes intense with concentration. "What I'm thinking is that there's an entity out there—not the devil, not a Greek god, but something else—that's using these names as aliases. This being seems to have the power to instill overwhelming fear in people, something beyond what even the devil is said to do in religious texts. It's hiding its true identity behind these mythological names, perhaps to confuse us or throw us off its trail."

Emily nodded, processing the information. "And you think this entity is behind the incidents we've been investigating? The ones everyone's been blaming on the devil?"

"Exactly," Caleb confirmed. "It explains why the accounts vary so much, why different names keep popping up, and why the level of fear described goes beyond anything we'd expect from traditional religious or mythological figures."

Renewed hope coursed through Emily as she leaned in, wrapping her arms around him in a warm embrace. The air crackled with the electricity of their shared longing as she whispered, "I hope you're right."

A gentle smile warmed Caleb's face as he held Emily, his heart echoing her sentiment. "Me too."

34

HUNT FOR THE DEVIL

Within the illuminated expanse of Creation Labs, the empty vial laid on the desk beside the microscope, while David lay sprawled on the cold, tiled floor, his body reclined in the overturned computer chair. Unconsciousness held him firmly in its grasp, a silent surrender to the ceaseless current of the cure coursing through his veins.

Anchored on the wobbly desk, his cell phone vibrated, each consecutive ring reverberating an unwavering reminder of existence beyond the contained space. The luminous screen emitted a mystic glow, casting an ethereal hue upon the disarrayed surroundings, simultaneously an unwelcome intrusion and a beckoning lifeline to an awakening consciousness.

As Caleb and Emily departed the library, the persistent ring of the phone continued unabated. The sharp harmony of it clashed with the mellifluous symphony of the bustling streets. After stepping onto the sidewalk, he took out his phone and held it to his ear. It rang several times before going to voicemail.

"Listen, man," he expressed. "Emily and I may have found evidence of something far worse at play, so I think it would be prudent for us to convene at my place."

Having concluded the call, Caleb's sight was captivated by Emily's sudden, prompt movement. With an unparalleled resolve, she dashed towards the nearby fountain, her determined footsteps reflecting the fervor that accompanied their intellectual pursuits.

"Come on, this view is absolutely incredible," she declared.

Determined not to lag behind, he quickened his pace, his determination propelling him forward until he finally caught up with Emily. She stood before the majestic fountain, its cascading waters sparkling in the sunlight.

"See," she continued. "I wasn't lying, was I?"

"I didn't think you were," he retorted, smiling upon Emily.

Emily's eyes twinkled mischievously as she spoke, her voice brimming with excitement. "But you know what would make this moment even more unforgettable?"

Without warning, she playfully shoved Caleb into the sparkling water, his startled gasp drowned out by her contagious laughter. The droplets splashed and danced in the sunlight, creating a symphony of tiny ripples that harmonized with their joyful energy.

Caleb laid there, immersed in the cool embrace of the water, while a gentle current of warmth washed over him. He stared intently at Emily, his heart swelling as he witnessed the sheer happiness radiating from her being. A soft smile played at the corners of his lips, a testament to the joy that enveloped him in their shared moment.

Emily, standing before him, became an enigmatic sight to behold. The water droplets trickled down her face, leaving a trail of glistening trails in their wake. The brilliant rays of the sun, hitting her at the perfect angle, revealed a brief glimpse of exquisite detail—a scattering of precious purple dots that adorned her iris for the briefest of instants.

With his legs drenched from their aquatic adventure, Caleb pulled himself out of the fountain's embrace, his damp footsteps marking his return to dry land. The warmth of the sun's golden touch whispered promises of quick evaporation, reassuring him that he would soon rid himself of the dampness that clung to his clothes.

"Given how hot it is," he remarked casually, "I'll surely be dry in no time."

Little did he know his words had laid a tantalizing temptation before Emily's calculating thoughts. Overwhelmed by the challenge, she succumbed to the irresistible urge bubbling within. Pushing him back into the sparkling water, her laughter echoed through the air, resounding with such intensity that her ruddy cheeks bloomed into a vibrant shade of crimson.

However, Caleb was quick to emerge once more from the water, droplets clinging to his every limb. With determination etched upon his face, he lunged towards Emily, effortlessly sweeping her up into his arms. Their intertwined bodies moved in synchronous harmony as he turned them both towards the fountain's edge. Emily, suspended above the water's surface, looked up, locking her gaze with Caleb's, while nestled in his arms. She curled up slightly, with exhilaration shimmering in her eyes.

The corners of his lips curled into a playful grin as he observed her expression. "Awe, you look scared."

Emily continued to glare up at him, her eyes a mirror reflecting her unspoken thoughts and desires.

"Alright, I won't do it."

He placed her feet back onto the cool ground, her body swaying towards him, drawn to his comforting presence. In an instant, she pulled him into a tight embrace, her warmth enveloping him.

"You truly are the sweetest," she whispered, her voice filled with tenderness.

His lips pressed softly against her forehead, his love evident in the gentle gesture. The connection between them was palpable.

Their moment was interrupted as a small puddle formed beneath them, causing their shoes to squeak as they reluctantly broke apart from their embrace. The joy that had enveloped them suddenly dissipated.

"I think we should swing by Dave's place and see if he's there," he suggested, an air of disappointment lingering in his tone.

Emily nodded, a sense of longing evident in her eyes. The brief respite of happiness had been cut short, leaving them wanting more.

As they retraced their steps to the car, miles away at the community hospital, Jason approached the receptionist desk, his face etched with concern. The worry in his eyes was unmistakable.

"Excuse me," he began, capturing the receptionist's attention as she hung up the phone. "I received a call earlier about my wife and daughter. I'm Jason Silverton."

The receptionist stood up and moved around the desk, her face showing a glimmer of sympathy. She guided Jason towards the room where his family was receiving treatment. His heart raced, fearing the worst.

"We admitted them a little while ago," she explained, her voice tinged with both professional detachment and sympathy. "Ally received a glucagon injection for hypoglycemia, and Tori started on quetiapine for her hallucinations."

"Hallucinations?" Jason asked, his worry deepening with every step. "No, my wife doesn't suffer from anything like that. There must be some mistake."

The receptionist paused, her eyes conveying a hint of understanding. "Given the ordeal they've been through, it's possible that it's only temporary. They've gone through a great deal, and sometimes the mind can play tricks."

The receptionist halted at the threshold, her hand gracing the doorknob.

"The usual protocol dictates that they be kept apart, for the sake of privacy and efficiency," she explained. "But despite their unconscious state, every attempt to relocate her triggered an instinctive squeeze from Ally's delicate hand as if she was afraid to be alone."

"Sometimes she does that," Jason remarked, ushering himself inside the room.

The moment his presence filled the room, Ally's eyes brightened with a mixture of elation and fragility. Her frail body strained to sit upright, defying the weakness that engulfed her.

"Daddy!" A jolt of uncontainable joy erupted from the depths of her being.

"Hello, sweetheart. How are you feeling?"

"I'm... good. They've been pumping me full of some sugary stuff, making me feel all... tingly."

He nodded, a mixture of relief and concern clouding his eyes. "They had to give you a shot once your sugar levels dropped."

With a sharp twist of her head and a flicker of curiosity in her eyes, Ally noticed Tori, her mother, sitting up in the other adjacent bed. The corners of Tori's mouth were tightly pressed together, a clear indication that something had transpired.

"What happened?"

"These... these men, they ambushed us while we were idling at a stoplight on our way out of town. I could sense the malevolence emanating from their very core."

Jason inhaled deeply, attempting to reconcile the horrifying scenario unfolding in front of him, dismissing any inkling that his wife's words were mere figments of her imagination.

"What did these men look like?" He moved closer, a palpable intensity driving his every step.

"They appeared rather ordinary, almost like your everyday individual. Hard to describe, really. One had flowing hair while another was completely bald. They were all diverse."

"And how did they manage to force you out of the car?" Jason's voice quivered slightly, betraying his fear as he drew nearer to her bedside.

"One of them lunged forward, his head colliding violently with the windshield. Stunned, I watched as he retreated, as if to admire his gruesome handiwork. Meanwhile, his accomplices seized us."

His mind reeling, the pieces of the traumatic puzzle gradually assembling in his thoughts, Jason sought to piece together the fragmented remnants of their ordeal.

"Do you recall anything about the location where they held you captive?"

Tori paused, her expression shifting momentarily before settling into a distant reflection. "I believe...I believe it was a farm. It reeked of manure, so there's no mistaking that odor."

"But the nearest farm is roughly twenty-five miles away," he mused aloud, momentarily lost in thought.

"True," Tori retorted, her voice resolute, "but when the overwhelming stench of horse manure invades your senses, it's hard to be mistaken."

Jason nodded and pivoted on his heel, retracing his steps toward the door. A newfound determination etched across his face, he turned to address Tori, whose eyes followed his every move.

"I'll be back soon. I need to find the ones responsible for all this."

Wonder ignited within Tori as she watched him, her voice full of worry. "Where are you headed, Jason?"

"To find those perpetrators," he said, pausing for a beat after flinging the door open, his gaze fixed on the unknown. "Do you remember the street where the attack occurred?"

Recognition flickered across her face as she recalled the precise details. "Yes... I do. Between Lybrith Avenue and Kanter Street."

On that note, he bade them farewell, striding with unwavering determination towards the truth that awaited him.

Meanwhile, Michael ventured through the dense woods, fueled by the chilling tales of the devil whispered amongst the teenagers. The moon cast eerie shadows that danced among the gnarled trees, leading him deeper into the mysterious realm. The air was thick with a sense of impending doom, as if the very forest itself held its breath.

His breath hitched as he stumbled upon a grim tableau of horror. Lifeless bodies, their souls stolen away with brutal precision, lay before him like macabre artwork. His gaze traveled across the gruesome scene, taking in the twisted fate that had befallen them. One wretched soul bore the cruel imprint of nature's wrath, a jagged tree branch driven mercilessly through their neck. Another victim, their life abruptly snuffed out, bore the mark of human-made suffering - two knives, their metal glinting coldly, plunged deep into their heart.

Michael was eager to uncover the truth behind this gruesome display. But his doubt lingered like a lingering fog, refusing to be dispersed. The fallen angel he sought, his once comrade, was known for employing powers beyond the realm of mortals. The crude brutality of these killings did not seem to align with his modus operandi.

"What is wrong with mortals that some would mask as the devil?" he pondered aloud.

A haunting cry echoed in the distance, slicing through the stillness of the air. The sound carried a mix of relief and gratitude, as if the agonizing grip of captivity had finally been shattered. But before the tears could dry, a thunderous BANG shattered the serenity.

Michael's eyes snapped towards the source of the noise, teleporting to the scene of the crime. Once there, his eyes instantly fell upon the ghastly sight before him. The man, now motionless, lay sprawled on the worn, wooden steps of the dilapidated cabin. His gaze fixated on the gaping hole that marred the back of the man's head, the remnants of a life violently snuffed out.

"This is the work of a deranged mortal, nothing more," Michael proclaimed, his voice laced with a mix of sadness and frustration.

His focus shifted, drawn to the markings on the trunk of a towering oak tree. The words, 'I am your enemy, prowling around like a roaring lion looking for someone to devour,' stood out in stark contrast against the aged bark.

"Foolish human."

As he prepared to abandon his search, a distant news broadcast cut through the air. In a small, worn-out living room located eight miles away from the vast expanse of the Great Salt Lake Forest, an elderly man sat comfortably in his recliner, fixated on the flickering images on an ancient television.

Despite the interference of static, the news reporter's voice cut through the crackling noise, its urgency subtly seeping into the room.

"Whether you're a believer or not, there's an undeniable darkness spreading in the heart of the forest. We can't dismiss it without concrete evidence. Who's to say the devil hasn't spawned an unholy progeny? As humans, we're not equipped to comprehend such malevolence."

Unseen by mortal eyes, a shadowy figure lurked in the darkest corner of the room, a sinister grin beginning to form. Lucifer clenched his fists, their evident tension causing the television screen to flicker ominously before being engulfed by an ethereal white glow, forming the shape of a cross.

"I shall put an end to this tormented soul," Lucifer vowed. "I feel Michael is nearby, driven by the same purpose. I suppose it is time to come to terms with the inevitable."

His brooding eyes glowed with a sinister shade of ruby, a flicker of smoke escaping from his intense gaze. His very presence exuded an aura of power, as he tapped into the depths of his dark abilities.

On the farm where Gabriel and Raphael found themselves entangled in a fierce battle with the Entitles, a subtle shiver crawled up their spines, heightening their senses. The air crackled with electric energy, as if the very fabric of reality was unraveling before their eyes.

The healer, struggling to fend off two relentless Entitles, leaned in closer to his brethren.

"Raphael, do you feel it? That undeniable surge of power radiating from the devil?"

"Yes, I sense it. But the timing couldn't be worse. Michael will have to handle it on his own for now," the weight of the situation laced Raphael's voice as he responded.

Raphael tore his attention away from the vicious creatures and focused on the source of the disturbance. The uncertainty in their hearts grew heavy as they contemplated the unimaginable might possessed by their formidable adversaries. Gabriel, his voice filled with a mix of disbelief and apprehension, voiced their shared concern.

"Is it truly possible for these creatures to wield limitless power?"

"Let us find out." Without further hesitation, Raphael's human form faded away, replaced by an iridescent emerald aura that shone through his eyes and palms. Gabriel followed suit, his own body engulfed in a brilliant ivory radiance.

As their energies intensified, the Entitles watched with a twisted anticipation, drooling with excitement at the prospect of the forthcoming onslaught. Grinning wickedly, they locked their gazes onto Gabriel and Raphael, eagerly awaiting their attack.

"Are you ready?" Raphael's voice rang out.

"On your lead!"

Brilliant tendrils of emerald and ivory lightning burst from the angels' bodies, piercing the heavens above. The electrifying bolts, radiant and fierce, descended with a purpose, their path set towards the callous Entities standing unabated.

Anticipating the imminent clash, swirling vortexes formed within the Entitle's very beings, poised to consume the surging energy. However, the angels had their own countermeasures. Gabriel materialized before the Entities, locking his unwavering gaze upon their menacing forms.

"How unfortunate that you are all bound, unable to consume the impending blast," his voice carried conviction, mingling with a touch of taunt.

Drawing upon his mastery of tricks, Gabriel compelled the Entities to divert their attention downwards, where an entanglement of electrical wires ensnared their bodies. Panic took hold as they futilely struggled against their restraints. In the final moments before the lightning's wrath descended, Gabriel teleported beside his fellow angel, Raphael.

A faint smirk graced Raphael's lips as he remarked, "Seems we should have explored this avenue from the outset."

Gabriel, his steady voice a reflection of wisdom, replied, "Indeed, delving into the recesses of their minds demands an immense wellspring of power."

The air crackled with anticipation as the lightning, seething with raw energy, surged into the Entities' writhing forms. Agonized screams erupted from their lips, melding with the tumultuous symphony of destruction. The earth quaked beneath the wrathful assault, leaving behind a ravaged landscape where once a vibrant farm thrived. From their vantage point, the victorious angels beheld the aftermath, confident in their triumph over the Entities.

"Unfortunately, our power is depleted," Raphael lamented, a vibrant green illumination emanating from his weary body.

"We must make our way back to Heaven and lend our aid to Michael on the battlefield," Gabriel insisted, his form enveloped in a radiant aura of white energy.

Meanwhile, in a quiet parking lot in Utah, Michael seethed with anger, his search for the elusive Lucifer yielding no results thus far.

"I know you are here, Lucifer Reveal yourself!"

A blazing blue light surged in his eyes, his energy bursting forth with such force that it threatened to obliterate everything in the parking lot. Cars were left dented and windows shattered, while a nearby street light toppled, crashing to the ground at the angel's feet.

Inside a nearby store, a disheveled man emerged, his shirt in tatters, adorned with scattered bloodstains. Crammed haphazardly into his back pocket, a rubber mask lay crumpled and misshapen. With a wary stride, he made his way to the bathroom, seeking solace amidst its musty air.

In a nearby store, a disheveled man pushed through the entrance, his torn shirt adorned with smears of blood and a rubber mask haphazardly stuffed into his back pocket. Light glinted off his wild eyes as he made his way to the restroom. Once there, he turned on the faucet. Steam billowed and swirled, allowing scalding water to cascade over his hands. He scrubbed his hands with vigor, erasing any trace of the bloodstains that had defiled the fabric of his torn shirt.

Droplets splashed onto his face while raising his gaze to meet his own reflection in the cracked mirror. The man's bloodshot eyes pierced through the glass, a haunting image that mirrored the torment within his own mind.

A faint smirk tugged at the corners of his mouth as he gazed into the mirror, his eyes glassy and unfocused. His lips moved silently, forming words only he could hear. For a moment, his reflection seemed to waver, revealing something darker beneath. He blinked, and the image stabilized, leaving him with a sense of anticipation that made his fingers twitch involuntarily.

The overhead lights flickered, plunging the restroom into darkness. Rather than concern himself, the man embraced the sudden power outage like a twisted gift bestowed upon him.

In that limited space, the fragile bulbs burst into fragments of shattered glass, each explosion resembling the wrathful fury of Lucifer himself. And there, emerging from the darkness behind the man, the figure materialized - the embodiment of darkness and temptation.

"You really shouldn't masquerade as something you're clearly not, especially to carry out such unforgivable acts," Lucifer's voice resonated, thick with contempt and an air of authority.

The man spun, his mouth agape, as he struggled to speak, his words suffocated by fear.

"That's right, you pitiful sinner, words are unnecessary in the face of your despicable actions."

In mere moments, the man's life slipped away, his physical body crumpling onto the grimy bathroom floor, a silent testament to the consequences of his malevolence.

A jarring hum pierced the devil's thoughts, jolting his attention towards Michael's unwavering gaze.

"Well, well, well, it seems you've finally found me," he said, a smirk dancing on his lips. "I don't suppose you are willing to lend an ear?"

"What do you think?!"

"Well, Let the record show I attempted to resolve this peacefully." Lucifer's eyes lit up like fiery rubies as he evaded Michael's punch by ducking down.

In a swift motion, he rebounded, launching himself back into the fray, intent to strike the Archangel square in the gut. Yet, in an astonishing display of reflexes, Michael seized his fist, preventing the blow from landing.

"I know about your mortal," Lucifer divulged, his tone laced with a telepathic resonance that seemed to reverberate through the space between the combatants. "Bring her to me, so we can have our battle."

As the devil pulled away from Michael's grasp, the duo instantaneously teleported to a vastly different location, the barren wilderness of Utah's Red Barn Land Grant stretching before them, that exuded an untamed beauty. As far as the eye could see, the earth seemed to drink in the warm hues of rusted orange, sun-kissed red, and burnt sienna.

"Why have you brought us here?" Michael inquired, his eyes exploring the unfamiliar landscape with a mix of curiosity and vigilance.

"Come now, surely you did not believe that bathroom stall was an appropriate stage for our battle?" Lucifer retorted, an undertone of mockery shimmering in his words. "This is as desolate as it gets. Now, go and bring the mortal here."

35

THE END BEGINS

Amid the sun-soaked day, Caleb and Emily stood outside David's loft, a sense of unease pricking at their skin despite the warmth that enveloped them. The air held a slight chill, as if an invisible hand brushed against their cheeks, inviting shivers down their spines. Caleb's outstretched arm hovered before the door, his knuckles poised to tap upon the wooden surface. Aware of the weight of their purpose, he rapped gently, the sound resonating through the stillness of the residence.

Emily fidgeted with the hem of her shirt. "Maybe try calling him again?"

Taking a moment to heed her suggestion, Caleb retrieved his phone from the depths of his pocket, his fingers deftly dialing David's number once more. The seconds ticked by, each one amplifying the absence of David's presence. But instead of the familiar ringtone, an impersonal automated message met him, signaling that the phone had lost its connection to the world. Disappointment etched itself across Caleb's face as he abruptly ended the call, his hopes for reaching David dashed.

Caleb ran a hand through his hair, his shoulders slumping. "His phone must be dead."

Caught in the grip of the unknown, Emily searched for a glimmer of direction. "Where else do you think he might have gone?" she queried, her voice carrying a yearning for answers.

Caleb's brows furrowed in thought, uncertainty clouding his features. "He could be at More Mellows, or perhaps at the lab. It's hard to say."

A determined glint in her eyes, Emily turned on her heel, facing the busy sidewalk that sprawled out before them. With every step, a resolve settled within her. "Then let's go find out."

As they slipped into the sleek car parked by the dimly lit curb, Emily fastened her seatbelt, while Caleb's hand turned the ignition key. As soon as the headlights burst to life, however, piercing through the obscurity of the evening sky, Michael materialized before them.

The celestial being hovered above the rhythmic hum of the engine nestled under the hood. Emily felt a surge of trepidation coursing through her veins, her heart pounding like a drumbeat in her chest. Caleb, overcome by a momentary wave of weariness, rested his head wearily on the steering wheel, grappling with the gravity of their impending quest.

Summoning her resolve, Emily mustered the courage to step out of the safety of the car, the metallic click of the door echoing in the stillness of the night.

"You found him, didn't you?" she inquired, her voice laced with a mixture of concern and determination.

Michael, his gaze burning with purpose, nodded solemnly, confirming her suspicions.

Drawing closer, Caleb hurriedly joined Emily's side, his breaths coming in quick bursts as he voiced his urgent plea.

Caleb stepped forward, his fists clenched at his sides. "Wait." He took a deep breath. "Before we go, can you lead us to Dave? His telekinesis could be invaluable in the battle ahead."

Pausing for a moment, Michael's gaze flickered with a hint of reluctance, yet his unwavering commitment to his sacred duty compelled him to respond.

"Indeed, the girl is destined to vanquish the devil on her own," he stated, his voice resonating with undeniable authority. "However, I hear your impassioned plea and shall oblige. Something felt amiss when I encountered him. He possessed a knowledge of Emily and cunningly handpicked the battlefield."

The author's eyes widened, his jaw clenching. "Hold up. This is the actual devil we're talking about. The root of all evil, and you let him choose the battlefield?"

Michael, his ethereal presence undeterred by Caleb's outburst, met his gaze with unwavering resolve. "The chosen battleground lies nestled in a desolate corner of Utah, seemingly devoid of any strategic significance," he explained.

"Thus, I did not see a reason to contest his choice. However, I promise you this: before we set foot on that cursed terrain, I shall meticulously scan the area for any concealed traps or treacherous snares. Only then shall I gather your friend to join us in the fight."

Emily turned towards Caleb, a flicker of trepidation escaping her eyes as she placed a quivering arm on his side.

"Thank you for everything," she murmured, unsure if they would live to see another day.

With conviction burning in his gaze, Caleb locked eyes with her.

"I promise you; this is merely the beginning of our story. There is no way we meet our end like this," he declared.

Feeling the weight of impending danger, Emily clung to him, her embrace becoming a bittersweet farewell. Sensing the gravity of the moment, Caleb returned the embrace, enfolding her in his arms with an intensity that surpassed any that had come before.

Their moment of solace was abruptly shattered as Michael approached. Time was truly of the essence, and his urgent command sliced through the tense atmosphere like a razor-sharp blade.

"Come," he began, his voice laced with the urgency of a ticking clock. "We must go now."

Delicate as a wisp of wind, the Archangel's hand pressed on Emily's trembling wrist, a gentle reminder of the imminent danger that awaited them. But in a swift motion, Caleb's hand shot out, instinctively landing on the angel's shoulder, a silent declaration of his unwavering loyalty.

Their eyes locked, an unspoken conversation passing between them in that fleeting moment. Caleb's gaze held a fire that burned with determination, a declaration that he would not be separated from Emily, come what may.

But Michael's stare dug into the depths of his soul. "That weapon is useless against the devil, boy."

Yet Caleb's determination burned brighter than ever as he tightened his grip on the Archangel's shoulder.

"I don't care," he proclaimed, his voice carrying the weight of unwavering loyalty. "I'm not leaving her."

Michael, a master of reading the tides of time, knew that there was no room for debate. The urgency of their situation demanded swift action.

"Luckily for you, there is no time for debate."

In an instant, the trio vanished from sight, leaving naught but a vacuum of bewilderment in their wake. As they reemerged from the abyss, Caleb and Emily found themselves thrust in the very epicenter of destiny, utterly disoriented, their senses overwhelmed by a whirlwind of emotions that seemed to consume their very being.

The sun, in its final descent, painted the sprawling landscape with a fiery palette that transcended imagination. As the celestial sphere neared the distant horizon, hues of crimson and amber cascaded across the heavens, casting an ethereal glow that bathed the land in an otherworldly radiance. The air, however, was heavy with the scent of earth, devoid of any stirring breeze that might offer a sliver of solace.

As the duo gathered their wits, the vault of the heavens crackled with red lightning, illuminating the vast expanse with an eerie flicker, casting haunting shadows upon the rugged terrain beneath.

Watching intently, his arms tightly folded against his formidable chest, Lucifer's presence oozed with an unsettling aura. His piercing gaze, radiating with skepticism, bore into the souls of his adversaries, sending shivers down their spines.

"Is this really the mortal with inhuman capabilities?" he questioned.

As their eyes fell upon Lucifer, a sense of dread washed over their faces, the weight of their trepidation palpable in the stifling silence that enveloped them. Then, like a beacon of hope in the darkness, Michael materialized behind them, his celestial form glowing with ethereal light. His entrance broke the deafening stillness, and relief washed over the mortals as they turned to face the angelic being that stood before them.

"It is clean," Michael said, his voice a soft melody amid the hushed landscape. "There are no traps or snares of any kind in the area."

Glimmers of hope danced in their eyes, but Caleb couldn't help but voice his lingering concerns.

"Are you sure? I mean it's Satan himself we're facing. Surely he does not plan on fighting fairly."

Michael's expression carried a blend of empathy and uncertainty as he responded, his words tinged with the weight of the unknown.

"I do not know what else to say," he stated with a hint of resignation. "Now, I shall fulfill your request and bring Dave here."

With those words, Michael vanished into thin air, leaving Caleb and Emily suspended on the edge of a daunting new reality. Reacting swiftly, Caleb's fingers tightly closed around the handle of the gun, concealed skillfully within the back waistband of his pants. A glint of apprehension danced within Emily's eyes as her gaze fell upon the weapon in his grip.

"Where did you get a gun?"

"It was my mother's, a devout Christian," Caleb began, his tone revealing hints of a complicated history. "She gave it to me for protection when I moved away. But I've made some modifications to the bullets."

He aimed the gun at the devil, who feigned a tremor of fear. Beads of perspiration began to form on his forehead as he prepared to unleash a barrage of specially crafted ammunition.

"Now, these bullets can shield us from inhuman beings," he stated, while pulling the trigger.

In an instant, an electric spark crackled at the end of the barrel, as wisps of salt-infused smoke curled upwards. Two bullets hurtled towards Lucifer. Yet, with a mere flick of his hand, the devil halted their trajectory.

A wicked smirk danced upon Lucifer's lips as he reveled in the failed attempt. However, unbeknownst to the devil, the second bullet continued to spin, gaining momentum with each rotation. Its relentless speed propelled it beyond Lucifer's grasp, eventually burying itself into his shoulder.

An agonizing howl escaped from Lucifer's contorted lips, the piercing sound causing blood to trickle from his earlobes, dismayingly staining his pristine white suit.

Realizing the true power of the weapon now, Lucifer, with a burst of supernatural agility, pounced upon Caleb with lightning speed. In an instant, the gun was torn from Caleb's grip, sent spiraling through the air, and ultimately crashing onto the unforgiving ground. A brutal blow landed with unforgiving force upon Caleb's abdomen and face, sending him sprawling onto the cold, unforgiving earth.

Emily's heart hammered against her ribcage, its desperate beats reverberating throughout her entire being. Fear consumed her, eclipsing any semblance of calm or rational thought.

With trembling hands, she reached out and yelled, "Get up!" Her screams tore from her throat, desperate to break free from the nightmare surrounding her.

Lucifer, in a display of speed too swift for the human eye to perceive, seized her by the jaw, his grip iron-clad and unyielding. Their eyes locked in a chilling gaze as he spoke, the weight of his words carried on the edge of his demand.

"If you truly possess any vestige of power, now is the time to reveal it," he demanded, his grip tightening, a physical manifestation of his menacing presence.

Emily's eyes glistened with tears, her voice a primal war cry as she summoned all her strength. In a surge of determination and sheer willpower, she aimed a forceful kick against the devil's shin, her leg propelled with all the might she could muster. The impact sent her sprawling backward, her body falling in an elegant cascade, akin to a regal tapestry.

"There it is," Lucifer sneered, his tone laced with bitter triumph as he loomed over the fallen Emily. "Revealing itself in all its majestic glory."

While Emily grappled with her fears, drawing upon her wellspring of strength, Michael materialized in the lab. The scientist struggled to retain consciousness while making a garbled attempt to reach the sink along the back wall.

"I cannot heal your physical form," the Archangel informed. "I can, however, rid your body of the contaminant that plagues it."

An incandescent light, reminiscent of polished marble, emanated from the angel's hand, casting a brilliant glow that suffused David's very essence. The sheer intensity of the energy unleashed sent seismic shockwaves pulsating through the lab, wreaking havoc upon the delicate scientific instruments and causing the monitors to spark and fizzle, their screens succumbing to a haze of static.

In the wake of the Archangel's radiant intervention, remnants of his transcendent power were etched upon the walls, leaving ethereal marks that stood as a testament to divine intervention. His essence lingered in the air, casting the room in a serene hue of shimmering blue that whispered of divine grace.

As the light gradually ebbed away, David's wounds were miraculously knit together, his body restored to a state of pristine wholeness. He sprung up from the cold laboratory floor, his head spinning, his breath rapid as he struggled to regain his composure.

"The battle has begun," Michael's voice broke through the disorienting fog. "I shall bring you there on the off chance that your presence is required."

David's mind reeled, his thoughts tangled in confusion. A sudden realization struck him, piercing through the fog of turmoil.

"Wait, do I still possess the gift of telekinesis?"

A knowing look crossed Michael's face. "I would imagine so."

Filled with determination, David's eyes met the wreckage before him, his gaze unwavering. The crumpled mess, a somber reflection of collateral damage, elicited a sharp glare from his piercing eyes. Yet, simultaneously, his focus shifted, cautiously extending his senses to embrace the remnants of his untapped power. Within him, an energy pulse hummed like a coiled spring yearning to be released.

As he stood amidst the mess, his gaze fixated on a single shard of glass, partially obscured by the debris-strewn floor. Inhaling deeply, he infused his lungs with resolve, bracing himself for the task at hand. Then, exhaling with intent, a surge of unwavering determination surged forth, intertwining with the throbbing ache in his temples—a visceral reminder that his powers were stirring from their slumber.

He commanded the object to heed his bidding. Against the laws of gravity, it defied its earthly confines and rose effortlessly from its shattered prison. Floating through the air as if guided by invisible strings, the shard moved with purpose.

With measured precision, it found its place within the wall, blending into the tapestry of destruction. As if solving an elaborate puzzle, its jagged edges transformed into a purveyor of order—a testament to the fusion of power and control that resided within his being.

Witnessing the irrefutable evidence of David's telekinetic powers, Michael stepped beside him with concern etched on his face. He fixed his gaze on the shard embedded in the wall, a testament to David's abilities.

"I hope this display suffices, for we must leave now," Michael retorted.

In a sudden burst of movement, David and Michael departed the lab, leaving behind an empty space. As their presence faded, the room seemed to shudder, as the ceiling light overhead plummeted to the ground with a resounding crash. The fragments of glass scattered across the floor, catching the faint glimmers of light that managed to pierce through the gloom, making the scene all the more poignant.

Meanwhile, on the battlefield, the forces of good and evil clashed in a battle of cosmic magnitude. Against a backdrop of crimson skies, which crackled with searing energy, bolts of red lightning lashed out. These jagged streaks of fire sliced through the atmosphere, illuminating the forest in a hellish glow, casting eerie shadows throughout the land.

Amidst the darkness, however, a radiant glow manifested as pulsating purple dots, shimmering with an ethereal luminescence. These motes of light floated with graceful movement, contrasting with the fierce intensity of the lightning. The purple hues danced around like celestial fireflies hovering around the two opposing forces.

Lucifer stood firmly on his feet, his arms outstretched towards the newly awakened angel. Symbolizing an invocation of unholy power, his stance exuded an aura of darkness. Emily fought with every ounce of strength she could summon. Her back leg stretched to its limit, serving as an anchor, while her front knee teetered precariously, almost grazing the ground. Her arms extended outward, mirroring the devil's own, as their fingers interlocked in an unyielding struggle for dominance.

As consciousness slowly returned to Caleb, his eyes fluttered open in a daze. It didn't take long for the reality of the situation to crash upon him, amplified by the sound of Emily's struggle. Jumping to his feet, a surge of adrenaline coursed through his veins as he instinctively reached for the handgun within arm's reach. However, his grasp was interrupted by the sudden appearance of Michael, emerging alongside David. The scientist doubled over, coughing violently, his disorientation evident. Michael, on the other hand, surveyed the situation, glaring upon the weapon.

"Leave it be, boy," he spoke with an authority that brooked no argument. "Allow Emily the opportunity to shine through."

Fueled by faith, Caleb fixated his gaze upon the angel, desperately holding onto the flicker of hope that burned within. The gun, forgotten on the ground, remained a latent lifeline, ready to be wielded at a moment's notice should the need arise. Then, with a swift motion, Michael's human form evaporated into a myriad of shimmering particles that disbanded through the forest, filling Caleb with disbelief.

Lucifer's grasp on Emily's delicate fingers tightened, knuckles turning white as the pressure threatened to shatter bones. Seeing the pain on her face filled him with much discontentment. In a venomous voice, the fallen angel uttered his chilling ultimatum.

"If you fail to reveal the depths of your power, your world shall crumble into the abyss," he proclaimed.

In the face of imminent danger, Emily's mind became a battleground of haunting memories, each one unfolding with a vivid clarity that tore at her soul. The heart-wrenching scenes of her mother's tragic demise, the searing pain of losing Kota too soon, and the indelible image of Caleb's sacrifice and subsequent resurrection flooded her consciousness. An incandescent fury surged within her, stoking the fires of her resolve while shattering the shackles of fear that bound her.

With a force that defied the limits of human comprehension, Emily tapped into a wellspring of untapped power. Within the unfathomable depths of her irises, a magnificent vortex of regal amethyst materialized, swirling and pulsating with an arcane energy. It coalesced into a resplendent ring, a manifestation of her unleashed might, radiating with an otherworldly luminescence.

As Lucifer bore witness, his body became enshrouded in an infernal blaze of crimson flames. The vermillion fire danced and licked at his form, echoing the intensity of the battle that lay ahead.

"Remarkable," he retorted, his voice tinged with a mixture of awe and malice. "Now, let us witness the true extent of your capabilities." With those words, he withdrew, momentarily retreating before charging towards her with a ferocity born of darkness.

However, just as his fist arced towards Emily's jaw, an astonishing duplication of herself materialized behind him. In a display of exquisite technique, she defied the laws of physics, locking her the devil's arms with an intricate move, rendering him momentarily immobilized and vulnerable in her grasp.

As the original image of Emily slowly dissipated like mist carried away by the wind, her phantom double stood resolute, a testament to her unwavering strength.

A smug smile tugged at the corners of the adversary's lips, his voice oozing with derision.

"Looks like you've mastered super speed," he taunted. "But let's see if you can counter."

Without warning, two spectral hands materialized from Lucifer's shoulders, descending upon Emily's hands with an uncompromising force. Each tendril showcased an ominous power, pushing relentlessly against her resistance. Try as she might, her efforts to keep him bound were deemed futile as the devil's strength prevailed.

Recognizing the precariousness of her situation, Emily's innate instinct surged within her, compelling her agile form to retreat, distancing herself from the clutches of her liberated foe. With a graceful landing, her nimble body poised for action, her eyes locked defiantly with the devil's menacing glare, steeling herself to confront whatever ominous wrath he had prepared.

And in a breathtaking display of mastery, the extraneous hands that once threatened her retreated back into the devil's body.

As Emily's gaze remained fixed upon her formidable adversary, her eyes, radiant with celestial power, discerned the lingering presence of untamed energy in the air. A tangible mugginess soon settled over the area, emanating from stealthy rocks suspended above the ground. The particles of dirt, untethered from the earth, danced in suspended animation, foretelling an impending storm. Emily, however, instinctively took evasive action. With effortless grace, she leaped backward, her agile movements carrying her a safe distance from the impending danger. Her back found solace against the sturdy embrace of a towering, vibrant tree, its branches reaching out like emerald arms against the darkened sky. And just in the nick of time, a cataclysmic sandy spike erupted from the earth's depths, tearing through solid ground as if it were mere parchment shredded by invisible hands.

Despite her narrow escape, Emily's feat did little to impress Lucifer. Unfazed, he stood perched on a higher branch, a malevolent smirk playing upon his lips, as he mocked her with unwavering certainty. His words dripped with disdain, a challenge thrown with calculated nonchalance.

"Surely, you have mastered more than the art of escape. Show me what you can do before I grow weary," he demanded, his voice laced with a mix of contempt and curiosity.

With his gaze fixated upon Emily below, Lucifer conjured yet another illusion, a replica of himself that swung effortlessly from the surrounding branches. Intent on deceiving her, he turned away just in time to face her fierce, blazing fist. But the illusory form of the young angel wavered, fading away before it could make contact with the devil's corporeal being. Now positioned advantageously among the branches, the real Emily poised herself to strike with unwavering resolve.

Swift as the wind, Lucifer defied gravity, springing back onto his feet the very moment his body made contact with the ground. His rising fury was palpable as he demanded more from Emily, his voice tinged with frustration and impatience.

"Show me something new already!" he thundered, his temper becoming a tempest that raged within him.

"How's this?" Emily inquired, her voice laced with determination as she appeared behind the devil, hands pulsating with a vibrant, otherworldly energy, almost as if she held lightning itself in her grasp. The intensity in her eyes matched that of the crackling orbs swirling around her, merging together and converging towards a single point - Lucifer's face.

"Awesome! Way to go!" Caleb's voice echoed through the clearing as hope coursed through his veins, convinced that the battle was won and the forces of darkness were finally conquered.

But as Emily's power dimmed, the residual energy dissipated, intertwining with the smoke that now rose from her eyes and hands as she knelt on the ground. Weak and weary, she refused to be defeated.

The once calm and serene forest, once ravaged by a storm of epic proportions, now found itself in an eerie state of red-blooded shadows. The sky, once a serene blue, now enshrouded in a menacing crimson hue. Fear began to claw its way into Caleb and Emily's hearts, a gnawing, insidious agony settling deep within their souls.

"This ought to show you how perilous it is to lower your guard in the midst of battle," Lucifer growled, his aura piercing through the lingering smoke, casting an ethereal glow upon his malevolent form.

A glowing crimson fist burst into existence, hurtling forward with furious velocity. It pummeled Emily into the earth like a helpless puppet, her body merging with the dirt in an amalgamation of pain and defeat.

"EMILY!" Caleb's voice ruptured through the chaos.

He lunged for the gun, his trembling hands desperately seeking to steady its aim as he fixed his gaze upon the devil. The weight of the weapon pressed against his palm, its cold metal sending a shiver down his spine. But just as he applied pressure to the trigger, an outstretched arm darted towards him, snatching the gun from his grasp with lightning speed.

Suddenly, Lucifer materialized behind him, his presence suffocating as he leaned into his ear. The air grew heavy with tension, and Caleb's entire body quivered in fear. "YOU!" Lucifer's voice boomed, echoing through the depths of his soul. "Quit interfering as Michael commanded or I shall have no choice but to end your existence."

In a swift motion, Lucifer appeared before Emily, who struggled to regain her footing. His imposing figure cast a shadow over her, his eyes burning with an intensity that sent chills down her spine.

"Are you done playing around?" he sneered, his voice dripping with disdain. "Because I am. I know you have an untapped reservoir you have not even begun to pull from."

Emily's mind raced, her thoughts swirling in a whirlwind of confusion.

More power? She pondered, her brow furrowing in deep concentration. I've been giving it my all, pushing myself to the limits. It's been hard keeping up with my own movements.

36

ANOINTMENT

While Emily grappled with her newfound powers, Heaven's warriors observed from above. They couldn't understand the order not to interfere despite all the time spent preparing Emily for this very battle. This especially troubled Michael.

His jaw tightened and fists clenched. "I know she has the ability to fight. So what is the issue?"

Upon hearing his question, Gabriel approached Michael, unsurprised by his lack of comprehension regarding Emily's situation.

"I have mentioned this before, Michael. You are an exceptional warrior, unbeatable. That is why you were the ideal mentor for the mortal. But, you struggle to grasp human emotions."

"What does—"

"She is afraid. Terrified, even. She is a mortal being facing the devil, but did you notice the sparkle in her eye just now? I think maybe the fight is about to get interesting."

On the battlefield, Emily's eyes shone purple as she closed them, focusing solely on the calm breeze and nature.

You can do this, she thought. He wants a fight, not a bloodbath.

While hyping herself up, Lucifer stood firm, anticipating the next round. Flames engulfed his body, only to recede after opening his hand. The fire reappeared as a ring with Emily at its center. Through it all, she remained focused on her core rather than the rising heat.

Taken aback by the unfolding terror, Caleb searched his pockets and retrieved two small vials filled with holy water. Recognizing the devil's preoccupation, he strolled forward, disregarding his inner desire to remain stationary. David attempted to intervene, but his words went unheard.

"Hey, Michael warned us not to interfere."

Once Caleb reached the desired proximity, he hurled one of the vials, striking the devil's back directly. Steam emanated from the devil's skin, yet it had no further effect.

Lucifer's attention shifted to Caleb, his glare fixated on the vial in his hand, causing it to shatter. Shards embedded in his skin as he recoiled in pain. He examined his bloody palm, attempting to extract the glass fragments.

The devil observed, unimpressed by the fragility of humanity. "Perhaps I shall consider you collateral damage." With ruby-red eyes, his gaze intensified as his telekinetically-charged opponent stepped forward.

"Hold on," David cried out. "We are mere observers of this battle. I give you my word that we will not interfere again."

"Take heed of my warning, or I will reduce you to dust."

Suddenly, the flaming ring that encased Emily surged upward, threatening to engulf her. Soon, the energy emanating from her body proved more potent than the devil's surprise attack.

Countless minuscule fireballs shot through the forest, extinguishing upon contact with the calming aura of Emily's energy.

Fixated on Lucifer, Emily took a small step forward, hurtling closer with a swift elbow to his stomach, followed by a forceful punch to his chest. She momentarily jumped back, only to launch herself at him again, delivering an uppercut that sent him airborne.

Lucifer, his gaze locked on the righteous mortal, wiped his chin clean. Filled with anticipation, he dissipated and reappeared behind her, hoping to catch her off guard. Emily, perceptive of the energy coursing through the air, anticipated the devil's attack. She swiftly turned around, catching his fist in her grasp. In response, Lucifer swung his other hand, but once again, Emily deflected the assault.

With both of his hands restrained, a new fist materialized from Lucifer's right forearm, delivering a sucker-punch to the side of Emily's face. In an instant, her body crumpled onto the soil.

Witnessing his girlfriend's face meet the dirt, Caleb was consumed by rage, his desire to charge after the devil overriding any concern for his own safety. However, David utilized his telekinetic abilities to prevent his friend from making a reckless move.

"Let me go!"

"You must calm down. While I don't know the whereabouts of the angels, I am certain that if Emily were in grave danger, they would swiftly intervene."

"She just got pummeled," he retorted. "I have to protect her."

"I'm not going to risk our lives in the process. You heard what he said. He will kill us if we try anything."

A sudden realization dawned upon him. The adversary, Satan, possessed cunning and deceptive qualities, akin to a prowling lion seeking to devour his prey. The words of Peter 5:8 echoed in his mind. "It doesn't add up," Caleb said.

"What doesn't?"

"He cautioned us against taking action," he began, pivoting to face David. "How does that fit with his deceitful nature?"

"I understand your point, but consider this: what if he intends to eliminate us regardless of our choices? Perhaps he merely desires to toy with Emily for a while."

Caleb redirected his focus to the battlefield. "You may be right, and I have no reason to doubt that. Only I do."

The adversary raised Emily's head from the ground, his gaze fixated on her eyes filled with terror.

"My patience wears thin. Surely, this cannot be the full extent of your power."

As her attention oscillated between the mortal and celestial realms, she became aware of the energy enveloping the surroundings. The sky above shimmered with sparks of crimson and magenta, intertwining in a captivating display of ethereal ambiance.

The disconcerting silence only served to further enrage Lucifer. Convinced that she had lost consciousness, he turned to Caleb and David, believing their pleas would unleash the angelic energy he sought.

Witnessing the deranged look in Lucifer's eyes, the duo instinctively took a few cautious steps backward.

"Do you still maintain that he is not evil?" David asked, extending his arms in a defensive gesture towards the advancing adversary.

Leveraging his telekinetic abilities, the scientist exerted increasing resistance, making it more challenging for Lucifer to advance. Each step he took placed an immense strain on David's body. Despite the imminent threat of their impending doom, Caleb surveyed the surroundings, desperately searching for any potential aid. And there it was - a gun, lying several feet away.

Mindful of the risk of being apprehended before he could discharge a shot, Caleb proposed that he employ his powers to empty the gun's clip. David lowered his arm and positioned himself beside the author, determined to outwit the embodiment of malevolence. As the devil took form at the precipice of their destination, David stared upon the weapon. Once the barrel aligned with Lucifer's head, he discharged the firearm in a relentless assault.

Six bullets found their mark in the core of Lucifer's being, causing smoke to emanate from his form as he emitted a piercing screech that compelled the two mortals to cover their ears.

As they knelt in agony, overwhelmed by the deafening scream of the devil, the sky transformed into a vibrant purple hue as the clouds dispersed. Astonishingly, the bullets that had previously pierced Lucifer's form began to reverse their trajectory, exiting his being one by one.

With the final round hitting the ground, the adversary's body underwent a miraculous healing, erasing all traces of the wounds inflicted upon him. Fixing his gaze upon Caleb and David, he seethed with fury, unable to comprehend why God would place any trust in humanity.

"You are all utterly worthless," he spat. "It appears that my expectations of this being a worthy battle have been reduced to nothingness, carried away by the wind."

In that moment, the sky once again flashed, capturing the devil's attention. He looked upward, attempting to grasp the significance of the unfolding events.

What am I experiencing? he pondered.

All of a sudden, a bolt of magenta lightning, tinged with a crimson glow, struck the earth with an electrifying force.

"Of course!" he proclaimed. "She is harnessing the power of cosmic energy."

Emily, still prone on the ground, exhibited irises that gleamed with a mesmerizing magenta hue. Another bolt of lightning materialized, striking in proximity to her outstretched hand.

Subsequently, shockwaves plummeted at the devil, yet he remained unfazed, not even flinching. "You better possess more power than that for me."

Meanwhile, David, positioned on his knees, directed his gaze to the heavens. "Is this storm really Emily's doing?"

"I believe so," Caleb said.

The intensity of the lightning surged, radiating a brilliance that surpassed its previous luminosity, resulting in a palpable tremor within the surrounding atmosphere. Gazing upon the extraordinary occurrence, Lucifer's corporeal manifestation commenced a fluctuation between visibility and invisibility, while his ethereal energy field remained undisturbed. A powerful discharge of electrical energy erupted, releasing a forceful burst of power that struck inches from Emily's feet. Subsequently, a fiery projectile, resembling a pulsating vein, hurtled at him.

It stopped right before impact and twirled until it dissipated. At this time, Emily's body ascended into the sky, enveloped by her radiant aura. Its brilliance was so intense that Caleb and David shielded their eyes from its blinding light. However, the power within Emily was now primed for utilization. Four electrically charged poles emerged from beneath the ground, positioned directly in front of the devil. Startled, he took a step back, only to witness the same phenomenon occurring behind him.

What are you up to, mortal? he pondered, intrigued by the unexpected turn of events.

The air crackled with static, exerting a powerful force that forcefully propelled him backward. His physical form flickered, intermittently disappearing from sight. Then, the long-awaited moment arrived. Purple bolts of electricity descended from the clouds above and surged upward from the ground, converging upon the devil in a simultaneous strike.

The resulting explosion propelled Caleb and David through the air, their bodies colliding with the force of the impact, causing them to crash through several branches along their trajectory. Meanwhile, Emily's aura guided her descent, as if she were descending an escalator. Her eyes returned to their normal state, and she surveyed the scene before her, taking in the magnitude of her accomplishment.

"Did I just beat the devil?" she murmured.

The cloudy sky morphed into nimbus clouds, releasing a steady downpour that soaked the earth below. The lack of wind gave an eerie stillness to the air, amplifying the sense of foreboding that hung heavy like a thick fog. Emily's attention was abruptly drawn away from the brewing storm when she heard the desperate cry of her friend, Caleb, echoing in the distance.

Driven by adrenaline, Emily raced towards the sound, her heart pounding in her chest. However, her determined strides were halted when a wall of fire erupted suddenly just a foot ahead of her. The flames grew and spread with a measured control, as if guided by some unseen force.

Unsettled, Emily turned her gaze back towards the smoke, her eyes widening in sheer terror as a brilliant crimson aura emanated from its core. Within moments, monstrous arms materialized from the depths of the smoke, stretching out towards her with an undeniable malicious intent. Caught off guard, Emily had no time to react or dodge the impending attack.

As the monstrous arms closed in on her, she felt the blunt force of their impact as they struck her body with terrifying strength. The force sent her hurtling backward, her form crashing to the ground uncontrollably. The sudden impact jarred her senses, leaving her momentarily disoriented.

While trying to catch her breath, her surroundings continued to spiral into chaos. From the ashen ground, two scorched hands emerged, their burnt flesh contrasting sharply against the vibrant backdrop. The hands seized her trembling wrists, their sharp nails digging into her supple skin, drawing droplets of crimson blood.

Emily's scream resonated through the dense forest, its raw intensity shattering the silence that had enveloped the surrounding landscape. The intertwining emotions of pain and fear wove an intricate web within her, fueling the magnitude of her vocal outburst.

Caleb struggled relentlessly to free himself from the clutches of the fallen tree branches. Pinned down at the base of the decaying trunk, his efforts were met with futility as the weight of two thick limbs demanded his submission. With each painstaking attempt to extricate himself from his woody prison, the soil beneath him squelched in protest.

He cast a concerned gaze towards David, who lay beside him, his head burdened by a fraction of a fallen branch, while a larger one constricted his hand, subjecting them both to the oppressive weight of the forest's wrathful grasp.

Frustration marred Caleb's face as he implored David, "Come on, you gotta do your mind thing."

David tilted his head, a grimace of anguish etched upon his features. "I can't. I..." His words trailed off as the searing pain intensified, rendering him unable to fulfill his friend's entreaty.

The visceral agony coursing through Emily's body pierced Caleb's empathetic heart, leaving him feeling utterly powerless. Summoning every ounce of his resolve, he mustered his inner strength, endeavoring to sever the branches that enmeshed them in their woody prison. The branches, still wet from earlier rainfall, resisted his efforts, clinging tenaciously to their captive position. Stoic of his own wounds Caleb cleared a path and rose to his feet.

A grotesque sight had befallen upon him as he approached—Lucifer's monstrous arms, enveloping Emily, rendering her vulnerable and defenseless upon the forest floor. Ignoring the looming threat, Caleb fumbled in his pocket, retrieving another vial of holy water. Time seemed to dilate as he propelled himself forward, sliding through the muddy terrain, and kneeling at Emily's side. With swift determination, he smashed the vial against the devil's menacing knuckle, allowing a mixture of holy water and salt to seep into the wound. The adversary recoiled at the searing pain, enough to loosen his grip on Emily's fragile form.

Supporting her in his arms, Caleb tenderly brushed away the tears that ravaged her delicate visage. "You're safe now."

"But I don't know how to fight that thing," Emily confessed, her wounded spirit preventing her from envisioning a path forward.

The celestial soldiers of Heaven remained watchful, their eyes keenly fixated upon the tumultuous battle that teetered in favor of Lucifer. Ready to intervene at a moment's notice, the divine warriors bided their time, poised for action.

Gabriel interjected, voicing his thoughts to the assembly of celestial beings. "Perhaps this conflict requires our direct involvement after all."

Michael, steadfast and resolute, responded with conviction. "The mortal engages the adversary himself. This has always been our battle."

Raphael, inquisitive by nature, posed a question to his comrades. "Have either of you pondered the reason for our inaction?"

"It is not our place to question," Michael affirmed, his unwavering focus remaining fixed upon the ongoing strife.

In the midst of the chaos, Caleb clasped Emily's hand, providing her with a sense of solace amidst the turmoil. Observing the bruised contours of his shoulders, concern etched across her face as she voiced her worries.

"Are you alright?"

Caleb, meeting her gaze with steadfast reassurance, confidently replied, "Of course, I am."

Touched by his valiant attempt to mask his pain for her sake, Emily tenderly held onto his arm. A surge of luminous light, reminiscent of pulsating veins, encircled his injured limb, healing the bruise.

"Wow, that's incredible!" In awe, he bore witness as the wound vanished into thin air, leaving no trace behind.

Emily, her irises once again adorned with radiant magenta rings, began, her voice imbued with determination, "You have supported and been there for me since the beginning. Now, it's my turn to reciprocate."

Caleb, ever the steadfast pillar of support, assured her, "You don't have to face this alone."

Transfixed by the ethereal radiance of the crimson light, Emily found herself captivated by a dark presence emanating from the piercing yellow gaze of a wolf.

Meanwhile, David scanned the surroundings, searching for any trace of the devil's whereabouts. "Where on earth could he have gone?"

Pointing towards the wolf, Caleb exclaimed, "Right there, staring at us like a wild animal."

Emily, her mind honed in on the situation, analyzed their predicament, and concluded, "He's attempting to deceive us, to strike when we least expect it."

The wolf, agile and silent, darted deeper into the labyrinth of the forest, his movements barely registering a sound. Both Caleb and David became increasingly restless, their unease tangible in the air. In stark contrast, Emily's resolve deepened as she took a deliberate breath, closing her eyes, allowing herself to attune to the subtle shifts in the adversary's movements.

Her comrades spun around, their expressions a mix of shock and alarm as they witnessed the wolf hurtling towards them from behind a nearby tree. In this treacherous game orchestrated by their elusive foe, it felt as though they were hapless prey being relentlessly hunted. Within a blink of an eye, the wolf whirled around them, leaving only its distinct footprints as evidence of its presence before vanishing into thin air.

A chilling dread washed over David as he surveyed the circle of prints imprinted on the ground, realization dawning upon him. Turning to Emily, a sense of urgency etched upon his face, he implored her aid.

"If you have any hidden reserves, now would be the time to tap into them. Otherwise, we are all doomed."

Sensing the weight of responsibility resting upon her, Emily felt it deep within her being, an innate knowledge guiding her obscured vision. She opened her eyes and vanished from sight, reappearing beside her boyfriend just as the wolf's razor-sharp claw grazed his cheek. Stepping back, Caleb instinctively covered the wound with his hand, while Emily, her determination unwavering, tightly clamped onto the adversary's paw.

The wolf growled, its ferocious gaze locking with Emily's unflinching stare as it attempted to strike her with its other paw. The creature's nails pierced her cheek, causing her to wince, yet she persisted, seizing the opportunity to grasp its outstretched limb before it could retract. Without averting her gaze, Emily skillfully delivered a powerful knee strike to the wolf's jaw, eliciting a resounding screech from the beast. In pain and disarray, the wolf hastily retreated back into the depths of the forest.

Overwhelmed with admiration, Caleb expressed his appreciation by clapping and launching his fist into the air. "That was incredible! You really showed him."

Just then, the devil phased in front of Emily, aiming a hand at her suprasternal notch. With agility, she sidestepped the attack by teleporting behind him and delivered a powerful kick to his back. Without hesitation, she reappeared in front of him, landing a forceful blow to his stomach. As she prepared to strike the side of his face, a hand emerged from the dirt below, tightly gripping her wrist. Locked in place, Lucifer extended his hand, causing steam to emanate from his fingertips. With a malevolent grin etched across his face, the devil propelled himself forward, poised to launch an attack. Just as he closed in, three fingers of the ethereal hand he had conjured shattered into fragments, allowing Emily to evade the imminent blow.

Rubbing her wrist, She rubbed her wrists and vibrated into the wind. To the devil's surprise, his assault had been rendered futile as his nails passed through her body. Transfixed on her form fading away, he felt a sharp jab on the back of his neck.

His knee grazed the ground as a newfound respect gleamed in his eyes, comprehending the extent of her powers.

"Astral projection. Impressive."

"Actually," Emily began, her voice laced with a hint of amusement, "I think that was more of a mirage."

In a mesmerizing display, another manifestation of Emily materialized beside the devil, delivering a powerful blow to his side before dissipating into thin air. "That was an astral projection."

Four new replicas of Emily took shape, encircling the devil. But as they attempted to strike the adversary with electrifying force from all angles, he intercepted two of them with his hands, while two more emerged from his back, restraining the remaining copies.

"Allow me to offer some advice," Lucifer began. "Avoid conversing during battle. It grants your adversary an opportunity to strike."

His appendages elongated until a portion of his back separated from his being, forming his own duplicate. With a crushing grip, fire consumed one of Emily's copies, erasing it from existence. He proceeded to do the same to another replica, leaving only the two engaged in combat with his own duplicate.

Observing a fiery yellow blaze in the devil's eyes, Emily extended her arm forward, imbuing her other manifestations with a vital surge of spiritual energy. Their forms radiated with a tremendous aura, enabling them to repel the adversary. Suddenly, a set of four celestial wings materialized on their backs, accompanied by a blinding light that consumed their mortal visage. This resulted in a cataclysmic explosion, shattering the ground, and obliterating the devil's duplicate.

Emily stood in bewilderment, uncertain of how to comprehend the unfolding events right before her.

"What on earth just happened?"

37

DISAVOWAL

The heavens opened, painting the sky with a blend of vibrant pink and purple hues. The celestial canvas seemed to crackle, illuminating the surrounding landscape. The air grew heavy as if nature itself held its breath in awe. Soon, a dense mist shrouded the forest, creating an ethereal veil. It clung to the trees and foliage, transforming the familiar surroundings into an otherworldly realm.

Meanwhile, Haines stood just outside the imposing Bayshore Roundhouse, his senses acutely attuned to the unfolding clash between opposing forces. Still reeling from the sheer potency of Emily's recent assault, he gazed up at the ethereal pinkish clouds that adorned the sky above.

"I hope you possess a firm grasp on the consequences, Oswald, for a force of such magnitude does not yield easily," Haines remarked, his voice laced with a mixture of concern and admiration.

"It all hinges on the challenger," Oswald's words reverberated within the Roamer's mind.

Haines leaned forward with narrowed eyes. "Do you genuinely believe you can vanquish Lucifer if he harnesses that kind of power?"

"Do you harbor doubts about my capabilities?"

"No, not at all. I am just contemplating the strategic implications. You deemed it necessary to assemble a mightier force, but with the existence of this extraordinary power, perhaps such measures may prove moot. It is conceivable that this planet need not suffer the same fate as ours."

Having made his perspective known, Haines was met with a profound silence, leaving him to ponder the weight of his words and the implications they held.

Within the celestial realm, Michael's mind raced as he attempted to piece together the puzzle of the devil's intentions. Something felt amiss, but what could it be? Lucifer, renowned as the dark ruler and master manipulator, had always been associated with pure malevolence. If he truly embodied such evil, why did Emily still draw breath? These thoughts swirled within Michael's consciousness, yet no satisfactory answer presented itself.

"Could it be possible that he is actually instructing her in the art of combat?" Michael pondered aloud.

"What?" Gabriel exclaimed incredulously. "Are we witnessing the same battle?"

"It is evident that the adversary seeks to spill blood," Raphael interjected.

"If that is indeed the case, why does Emily remain alive? I taught her how to fight, but it appears that Lucifer possesses greater skill than I recall," Michael mused.

"Seriously?" Gabriel retorted. "Have you forgotten that he taught me the art of multiplication?"

"I believe Michael concerns himself more with the exceptional level of skill Lucifer displays," Raphael clarified, shedding light on the underlying source of the warrior's unease.

"I have questioned his motives in the past, but you were not prepared to entertain such thoughts," Gabriel began. "When he rose up and caught me off guard, he had the opportunity to strike me down. Yet, he chose to weaken me."

"We never did ascertain how he managed to break free from the confines of the tomb in the first place," Raphael reminded Michael.

"Such inquiries are irrelevant. We are well aware that Lucifer has forsaken us, corrupting this world in the process. Our utmost priority is to halt him at any cost."

On the battlefield, Emily remained transfixed, bewildered by the fate of her replicated selves. Overwhelmed by uncertainty, she sank to her knees, grappling with the weight of her own destiny. Caleb and David rushed to her side in haste. The scientist positioned himself in front of her, confronting the devil, while her boyfriend knelt beside her, tenderly clasping her hand.

"I cannot comprehend what just transpired. What was that?" Emily inquired.

"I do not know," Caleb replied, resting his head against her's. "I fervently wish that Michael were present to bring an end to this ordeal."

"Hey, guys, hate to interrupt your reunion, but what's the play here?" David asked, his gaze fixed upon the adversary's sinister grin.

"You need only allow events to unfold as they are meant to."

David attempted to restrain the devil's advance, employing his telekinetic abilities to impede his progress. However, his efforts were futile, as the force rebounded upon him, forcefully propelling him backwards. The more David struggled to hold his ground, the more resistance he encountered.

Once Lucifer halted his approach, he summoned the surrounding roots, which entwined around his ankles and wrists, propelling him towards a sturdy tree trunk, effectively immobilizing him.

"You must have had some inkling of the consequences that would arise upon fully embracing these powers," Lucifer continued, stepping closer to the dynamic duo.

"What are you implying?" Caleb inquired.

"The very events that you all have just witnessed," Lucifer replied cryptically.

"So, what? Either you kill me, or I perish, regardless?" Emily questioned; his tone laced with defiance.

"Foolish sinner. You fail to grasp the grander scheme of things."

"Stop messing with our minds," Caleb demanded.

"Reveal to me the power I sensed, so that we may bring an end to this petty skirmish."

"This is precisely what you want. You're planning on doing something to Emily."

In the blink of an eye, he lifted her into his arms, cradling her protectively, and veered in the opposite direction. Fear and concern etched across his face, he clung to her tightly, propelling himself forward with even greater speed. However, as he attempted to disappear from view, a torrent of searing flames erupted from the ground, obstructing his path. With fast thinking, he managed to evade the fiery onslaught by a mere fraction, maneuvering past two colossal boulders nestled beside a towering tree.

Amidst the lush and vibrant expanse of the verdant landscape, a concealed grove unveiled itself. Its lush foliage formed a natural canopy that provided a shield from prying eyes. Just as he caught sight of this secluded haven, multiple streams of scorching fire emerged from the ground, creating two parallel rings of blazing inferno. Halting in his tracks, Caleb stumbled over his own feet, causing both himself and Emily to tumble to the ground.

"He will not get what he wants; I promise," he declared, locking eyes with Emily.

She smiled in response to his words, though deep down, she knew they were embroiled in a situation far beyond their control. Placing her hand gently atop his, she offered a brief moment of solace before rising to her feet.

"We can't escape this, Caleb," she stated, her gaze fixed upon the distant horizon. "You and Dave must get out of here."

"I'm not leaving without you," Caleb insisted, his voice filled with unwavering determination.

Suddenly, the devil's hand materialized behind him, exerting immense pressure upon his shoulder, rendering him unable to rise. Gradually, the hand contorted, assuming a vine-like form that ensnared his body. As he lay incapacitated, Lucifer's complete form materialized on the opposite side of Emily.

"No more running," he retorted, his voice dripping with malevolence.

Wisps of smoke billowed forth from Emily's eyes while a purple ring once again encircled her irises. She darted towards the adversary with an astonishing burst of speed. She materialized behind him, her agility catching even herself off guard. After regaining her composure, she unleashed a devastating blow, driving her elbow into the devil's lower back.

Without pause, she leapt gracefully into the air, her lithe form ascending to a remarkable height, before descending with precision to deliver a resounding knee strike to his head. The impact reverberated through the air, leaving the devil momentarily stunned. Seizing the opportunity, Emily unleashed a flurry of calculated strikes, each blow landing with a resounding impact. As she finally distanced herself from Lucifer, a palpable aura of power emanated from her outstretched hands, where tiny orbs of luminous light sat in her palms.

Lucifer, his face gripped with intrigue, observed the ethereal orbs hovering before him. Standing resolute just behind the orbs, Emily maintained an unwavering gaze fixed upon him. Perceiving it as a challenge, Lucifer emitted a low growl as he propelled himself forward. However, the instant he crossed the threshold between the two orbs, a powerful shockwave coursed through his being, compelling him to retreat.

Perplexed, Lucifer questioned, "What is this?"

With a hint of uncertainty, Emily replied, "I cannot say for sure, but it appears to be effective, don't you think?"

As the devil recoiled from the shockwave, his expression contorted with a mix of anger and curiosity. Emily maintained her focus. and intensified the energy emanating from the orbs. The luminous light surrounding her intensified, casting an otherworldly glow over the battlefield.

With a snarl, Lucifer lunged forward once more, determined to overcome whatever force stood in his way. However, as his hand extended towards the orbs, a bolt of energy shot forth, striking him square in the chest. The impact sent him hurtling backward, crashing into the ground with a resounding thud.

Emily, propelled by her newfound confidence, stood her ground, but remained cautious. She realized that her abilities had a profound effect on the adversary, but she was unsure of their limits. As she surveyed the battlefield, she noticed Caleb and Dave, who had managed to free themselves from the devil's grasp, watching with both awe and concern.

"Stay back," she called out to them, her voice carrying a blend of determination and protectiveness. "I'll handle this. Find a way to escape while you can."

Reluctantly, Caleb and Dave nodded, realizing that Emily was their best chance at survival. They began to back away slowly, ready to seize any opportunity to slip past Lucifer's weakened form.

Meanwhile, Lucifer glared at Emily, his malevolence boiling over. Slowly, he rose to his feet, a twisted smile forming on his lips.

"Your powers are finally taking light, but I hope you have more in the tank than this, otherwise your fate is already sealed," he hissed. "You have no idea what you're truly up against."

Emily squared her shoulders, refusing to be intimidated. "Perhaps not, but I won't back down. I will protect everyone I care about."

Lucifer's lips curled into a wicked grin. "Oh, my dear, you have no idea what lies ahead. But I must admit, your spirit impresses me. Let us see just how far it can take you."

With a calculated leap, he soared high into the air, confident in his ability to bypass the glowing orbs. However, Emily's powers surged to new heights, causing the orbs to multiply rapidly. They transformed into a swirling vortex of shimmering spheres, numbering in the thousands.

In a breathtaking display, she unleashed the torrent of orbs, propelling them towards the devil with incredible speed and precision. The sky became a mesmerizing spectacle as the orbs streaked through the air, converging on their target.

Caught off guard by the sheer magnitude of the attack, the devil found himself engulfed in a tempest of radiant energy. The orbs collided with him, unleashing shockwaves that rippled through his human form. He writhed in agony, his defenses overwhelmed by the relentless assault.

Emily continued to channel her energy, fueling the onslaught. She refused to relent, recognizing this as her moment to seize control of the battle. The devil, weakened and disoriented, struggled to regain his footing, his malevolent presence diminishing under the relentless barrage.

As the last of the orbs dissipated, a profound silence fell over the battlefield. She stood, her chest heaving with exertion, her gaze fixed upon the devil. Despite the toll it had taken on her, Emily felt a surge of triumph coursing through her veins. She had pushed herself beyond her limits and emerged victorious, if only for the moment.

Lucifer, though wounded, retained an indomitable spirit. He glared at Emily, his eyes smoldering with a mixture of fury and begrudging admiration.

"You have proven yourself to be a formidable opponent," he rasped, his voice tinged with grudging respect. "But I can see our fight is over. Your feeble body is exhausted."

Observing the unfolding events from their ethereal realm, the spectral beings meticulously strategized every potential move that could lead to the devil's triumph. Recognizing Lucifer's inexhaustible arsenal, they concluded that he held the upper hand in the impending battle.

"We must intervene. Leave nothing to chance," one phantom asserted.

"Absurd," the other countered. "The mortal's strength is waning."

"Perhaps, but can you not sense the formidable power emanating from Lucifer?"

After a moment of contemplation, a look of realization crossed the phantom's countenance. "I understand," he began. "If indeed this is the Morning Star himself, then we must intervene, but only once the mortal is no longer shielded by opposing forces."

Back on Earth, Emily's heart raced, her breaths coming in rapid succession. Despite her exhaustion, she refused to yield, her determination fueling her resolve as she witnessed Lucifer's wounds miraculously mended before her eyes. Understanding that she must surpass her own limitations, she braced herself for a final, decisive assault.

With unwavering resolve, she charged towards the devil, her fists clenched and ready to strike. Each step fueled by adrenaline, she unleashed a flurry of punches, aiming to break through Lucifer's defenses. Her movements were swift and precise, guided by a newfound strength that seemed to emanate from deep within her. However, after gaining an understanding of her movements, he caught her fists in mid-air with an unyielding grip.

Despite this, she refused to be deterred. With a burst of strength, she managed to break free, delivering a series of powerful punches that landed squarely on Lucifer's torso. The impact reverberated through the air, momentarily staggering him.

However, before Emily could capitalize on her advantage, Lucifer vanished in a blur of motion. In an instant, he reappeared behind her, his movements almost too fast for the eye to follow. A surge of panic shot through Emily as she realized she had been outmaneuvered.

Luckily, her instincts kicked in at the last moment as she spun around, narrowly avoiding his strike. The air crackled with tension as her mind raced to formulate a new plan of attack.

Lucifer looked down upon Emily with disdain in his eyes.

You were God's trump card? he pondered.

Back in the Celestial realm, Michael grew antsy. Doubts crept into his mind, questioning the righteousness of their actions. If they continued to stand by and watch as the devil prepared to slay Emily, what was the point of granting her powers in the first place?

As these doubts consumed the archangel, a sudden shift in the atmosphere seized his attention. The sky darkened, clouds swirling with an ominous energy. Thunder rumbled, shaking the very foundation of the earth.

Meanwhile, Emily clenched her fists, her aura dissipating in her eyes. Just as doubt threatened to creep into her own mind, a single blue feather gently floated down from above, landing at her feet. Emboldened by a new sense of hope, she propelled herself forward, however, her pursuit was met with a merciless blow to the stomach by the adversary. She fell to the ground in excruciating pain.

"I told you our fight was over," he said.

Suddenly, a crimson glow overtook the palm of his hand. Fire erupted around his arm as his weapon of choice- a trishul, emerged from the light. As he took hold of the handle, the two outer spikes fell back, while the center grew.

Concealed amidst the natural splendor of the forest, the two bystanders observed the unfolding spectacle while hiding behind a log. Caleb, weary of inaction, abandoned his position and sprinted towards Emily, determined to intervene. David hastily pursued, desperate to prevent him from getting in the way.

As the malevolent force behind the devil's action loomed over Emily, her instincts kicked in with split-second precision. The moment the tip of the trishul grazed her skin, her hands instinctively intercepted it, halting its deadly progress. In a display of unexplained power, her palms ignited in a dazzling purple blaze, while radiant angelic wings materialized in the middle, right where her palms met. Gracefully flapping, the wings revealed a mystical connection, conjuring a sword poised between them.

Emily's mind raced as she stared at the ethereal purple sword that materialized before her eyes. Its shimmering glow held immense power, and she couldn't help but feel a mix of perplex and awe. With a firm grip, she embraced the weight of the sword, ready to wield its strength against Lucifer and his devil's trishul.

The clash of their weapons echoed; each strike met with absolute precision. Emily swung the sword, its blade slicing through the air with a graceful swiftness, but Lucifer countered her every move with agility.

Sparks flew as their weapons collided, creating a dazzling display of light and energy. Her eyes narrowed with focus, her mind honed on the task at hand. She channeled her newfound power into each swing of the sword, unleashing a torrent of energy that pushed back the adversary's relentless assault.

Lucifer, a sly grin on his face, acknowledged Emily's prowess. "So, you can conjure a weapon as well. Not bad. You are much further along than you let on," he taunted, his voice dripping with a mix of admiration and challenge. "But this is your last chance to fight with everything you have."

Emily's determination burned brighter as she met Lucifer's gaze.

The angels observed the ongoing battle with a glimmer of hope, their faith in Emily's potential victory growing. Michael couldn't help but crack a slight smile, a rare display of optimism. However, Gabriel interjected to remind his fellow angels of the true nature of their adversary.

"Let us not become overconfident," he cautioned, his voice filled with wisdom. "Remember, he is not the king of darkness solely due to his combat skills, but through his mastery of manipulation. If you need a reminder, just look at the state of the world he has influenced."

"Do not let him in, Emily."

38

THE TRUE PROPHECY

Caleb and David were filled with a profound sense of satisfaction as they bore witness to the mesmerizing spectacle of Emily's unparalleled prowess.

The adversary unleashed his trishul with a tremendous display of force, aiming to strike Emily. However, Emily displayed her remarkable skill by deftly parrying each attack with her Heavenly weapon. With every swift maneuver of her sword, the wings attached to its hilt fluttered vigorously, generating a powerful gust of wind that pushed the devil back. Even as Lucifer regained his balance, Emily was already there, gracefully swinging her sword and piercing through his deceptive human facade. In response, his wounds became shrouded in an eerie, crimson aura that emanated through the surrounding veil of dark fog.

"How does it feel? To have your desires within reach, only to be vanquished by a newcomer," Emily taunted, hovering above the devil.

"Do not count me out just yet."

In a sudden display of cunning, Lucifer swung his foot, catching Emily off guard and causing her to stumble momentarily. However, she refused to remain vulnerable, swiftly regaining her composure. With unwavering determination, she fully extended her arms and lunged forward, aiming to deliver a forceful strike directly to the devil's heart. A vibrant aura shimmered along the blade of her sword, emanating an ethereal energy that coursed from the base of the handle to the very tip of the blade. This ethereal glow served as a testament to her indomitable spirit and the immense power she wielded.

Yet, Lucifer proved to be a formidable adversary, skillfully maneuvering his trishul to block Emily's attack. Undeterred, she persisted, channeling every ounce of her strength into her strikes. As she relentlessly pressed on, a disconcerting transformation gradually overtook Lucifer's countenance. An eerie grin slowly spread across his features, while his eyes gleamed with a malevolent light, revealing the depths of his sinister nature.

"This has been fun," he began. "But this next attack will leave our little skirmish at an end. Whether you are left standing or parish is something we shall see for ourselves."

Lucifer exuded an intense, vibrant red glow that seemed to emanate from the depths of his very being. This fiery essence, shrouded in a dense mist, enshrouded his entire form, casting an ominous aura around him.

Unfazed by his proclamation, Emily tightened her grip on her weapon, preparing herself for yet another fierce assault. As she raised her sword, flames erupted from the devil's body, engulfing him in a blazing inferno. She swung her blade, slicing through the ground with a resounding force.

This time, she hoisted the sword upward, propelling herself backward with a graceful leap. The instant her feet touched the ground, a spectral image of herself materialized behind Lucifer, its ethereal form delivering a devastating strike to his shoulder, unleashing a surge of power that reverberated through the very core of his being.

Caleb's eyes widened, excited over the blow that had been felt to the devil. "Yeah, that's it, Emily!"

The adversary emitted an intimidating growl, unleashing a torrent of searing flames aimed directly at Caleb's face. However, David intervened, exerting his strength to push his friend out of harm's way. Unperturbed by whether his attack found its mark, Lucifer endeavored to strike Emily's spectral clone with a powerful elbow blow. Yet, to his astonishment, she dissipated into thin air, only to reappear in a poised kneeling position, her sword slicing through his stomach with a swift and decisive motion.

Lucifer belched out one aggressive attack after another, determined to strike her down. Luckily, David harnessed his telekinetic abilities and exerted his power to pull Emily out of harm's reach. With a controlled landing, she found herself safely positioned beside her partner and David, their collective presence forming a protective barrier.

"Hey!" Caleb exclaimed, his voice filled with awe and admiration, as he gently placed his hand on the side of Emily's face. "Hey, look at me. You were absolutely incredible."

Emily's gaze shifted, meeting Caleb's with exhaustion. "You did an amazing job, but it's time for us to leave."

However, before Emily could respond, Lucifer interjected with a bone-chilling assertion, "There is no escape, boy."

The sudden eruption of flames enveloped them, trapping them within a ring of fire and scattering embers like fallen stars. Feeling the searing heat closing in, David instinctively extended his hand, wielding his latent powers to carve a narrow path amidst the inferno, beckoning the others to follow as urgency laced his voice.

"Let's go!" His command cut through the crackling inferno, a fervent plea for swift action echoing in the fiery onslaught.

Within the chaos, Caleb's attempted guidance was met with Emily's staunch refusal to flee blindly, her steadfast resolve matching the intensity of the flames that hemmed them in.

"We can't just run. If we do, he might set the entire forest ablaze and still pursue us."

Caleb's gaze flickered back to the blinding figure of the devil, a silent understanding passing between him and Emily before he squared his shoulders, determination etched on his features as he addressed her once more. "I refuse to be a mere spectator any longer," he proclaimed firmly, turning back to Emily with a burning resolve. "How can I help?"

"Your belief in me is all I need." A flicker of gratitude softened her gaze as a dim smile graced her lips.

As an ominous crimson glow pulsed within the devil's chest and tendrils of smoke swirled around his form, a palpable sense of foreboding hung heavy in the air, prompting David to voice his growing apprehension.

"I have a bad feeling about this," David acknowledged, his tone laden with unease as the dire situation unfolded before them.

In the celestial realm, Michael's countenance darkened with worry, the weight of his concern mirrored by the troubled expressions of the other angels as they grappled with the escalating crisis.

"He is consolidating his energy, drawing upon all his power, even the essence that manifests his human guise, to unleash a devastating assault."

"Like a final strike," Raphael said, underlining the gravity of the impending clash with a sense of finality.

Disagreeing with the angel's interpretation, Gabriel interposed, "I doubt his intentions involve bringing an end to this encounter through fatal means."

"Well, it appears as though we are about to find out," Raphael concluded, the looming confrontation on the brink of revelation.

A sinister grin etched across Lucifer's countenance as his form pulsated with an incandescent glow, his predatory gaze fixed on Emily with chilling intent before he vanished into a blaze of crimson light, leaving behind an aura of fiery malevolence that surged in intensity with each passing breath. "Given your purpose, I hope you can withstand this attack, mortal," he declared before disappearing into a crimson light.

Lucifer's human form vanished into the vibrant hues of fiery red energy, its intensity emanating from him growing with each passing moment.

Out of nowhere, a deafening thunderclap rumbled through the sky, its sheer force demanding the undivided attention of all who witnessed this spectacle. The piercing sound sent shivers down their spines, causing everyone's hearts to race. The very atmosphere seemed to vibrate in response, creating a tangible sensation that could be felt even beneath their feet.

Despite his apprehension, Caleb gazed at Emily, still enveloped in her vibrant purple aura, and maintained faith in her ability to succeed.

The intensity of the crimson radiance increased as it rapidly approached Emily. Holding the Celestial sword firmly, she positioned her arms in a protective stance to defend against the impending attack. The wings on the sword's handle emitted strong gusts of wind, piercing through the oncoming energy. A deafening screech reverberated across the land, causing Caleb and David to cover their ears as they knelt on the ground.

As the energy swirled around Emily, it made a sudden lunge towards her grip on the sword. However, she instinctively sensed the imminent danger and swiftly swung the weapon through the air while turning around. However, this was all part of Lucifer's plan to catch her off guard. Seizing the opportunity, the devil dug his claws into her knuckles.

Emily's piercing scream shocked through the earth and sky, causing the clouds above to disperse. In response, she released her grip on the sword, causing it to transform back into pure energy.

The crimson glow continued to intensify, but before it could advance any further, a blinding flash of marble blue light collided with it. Wasting no time, Caleb ran up to Emily and checked her hand.

Caleb bit his lower lip with a muscle in his cheek twitching as he turned her hand to assess the damage.

"Are you okay?"

"I'll be fine."

Caleb ripped his torn sleeve off his shirt to use like a bandage. The moment he went to wrap it around her hand, she healed, leaving no trace behind.

Emily smiled. "I can rapidly heal, remember?"

"That really comes in handy."

Suddenly, a crater burst through the ground, causing everyone to fall from the tremors below. At the bottom was Michael's light fading in and out of sight. Then, Lucifer's aura resurfaced at the edge of the crater, taking human form once more.

"Looks like your time on this rock has weakened you, Michael. At the moment, I suppose that could be a good thing since maybe now you will listen," Lucifer began, staring down at the warrior angel. "Do you truly believe that God would create something as powerful as a mortal being who possesses angelic abilities just to stop me when he had already given you light? No, this mortal is destined to take down the biggest threat to all existence."

Michael's light vanished, reforming in front of Emily as she and the others stood back up.

"The only threat to the world is you," Michael declared.

"No, and in time, you will come to see that," the devil retorted, teleporting behind Emily. "Since you cannot tap into your full potential, I shall take what I need to ensure Haines' defeat."

With an outstretched hand engulfed in flames, the devil ruthlessly squeezed Emily's shoulder, siphoning her power into his own dark essence. Unfazed by the heinous act, Caleb lunged towards Lucifer in a valiant effort to intervene. However, a single glance from the devil was all it took to send him hurtling backwards, crashing into the unforgiving embrace of several towering trees.

Emily's once vibrant magenta aura now danced in flickering flames within the devil, a chilling symbol of her stolen strength. Casually lowering her fragile form to the ground, the adversary locked eyes with Michael. "I hope when you find me again, you will know what is truly at stake."

With a cryptic farewell, the devil vanished into the shadows, leaving a haunting echo of his ominous words in his wake. In the distance, David's urgent cries drew Michael's attention, prompting a call for healing to tend to the wounds inflicted upon Caleb.

"Sorry, bud, he cannot do that," Raphael's voice pierced through the air, suffused with an otherworldly glow as he materialized before the scientist. The archangel's arrival seemed to command the very essence of the sun, compelling its light to bow in reverence and cloak the mortal in a serene emerald brilliance. "But I can."

The celestial being's presence captivated David, wrapping him in a cocoon of warmth as the air carried a rich scent of rosemary infused with cineol, heightening the gravity of the unfolding spiritual confrontation. "Who are you?" he asked.

"I am Raphael," came a serene response.

With much grace, the healer knelt beside the scientist, his appearance enhancing the natural world around them. Meanwhile, archangel Michael approached, a weary Emily cradled in his arms, her fragile form barely conscious and teetering on the edge of exhaustion. Gently placing her beside Caleb, Michael's solemn gesture spoke volumes of unspoken concern and care, Emily's outstretched arm seeking solace in Caleb's reassuring touch.

David turned his attention towards Michael, a curious gleam in his eyes as he sought the warrior angel's insight into the unfolding enigma before them.

"So, what do you make of the devil's words?" David's inquiry cut through the weighty silence, prompting a response from Michael.

"He is manipulative. That is all."

Pondering the depth of Lucifer's cunning, David contemplated the possibility that Caleb and Emily might possess evidence to corroborate the devil's cryptic claims, a glimmer of doubt flickering in his mind.

"How about the symbol you couldn't identify?" Caleb interjected, his words resonating with newfound clarity as he rose from his prone position, his countenance transformed by the healing touch of Raphael's presence.

The mention of the mysterious symbol piqued Raphael's interest, prompting a question as he sought to unravel the intricacies of Caleb's revelation.

"Symbol?" Raphael sought clarification, his gaze shifting between the mortals gathered before him in rapt attention.

"It is a false lead," Michael interjected, his tone resolute in dismissing any semblance of uncertainty. Disappearing in a swift teleportation, Michael's departure left a lingering sense of tension in his wake.

"It seems your line of interrogation may be unsettling his grasp on reality," Raphael remarked, his voice a soothing cadence that carried the weight of profound understanding. Casting a watchful gaze upon Emily's unconscious form, he reassured Caleb and his companions, his commitment unwavering as he pledged to delve into the implications of their revelation, promising a path towards uncovering the truth amid the shadows of doubt and deception.

And then, he was gone, dissipating into a brilliant burst of emerald radiance. Caleb kneeled beside her, nudging her shoulder. "Come on, please wake up."

David surveyed their surroundings, his eyes bearing witness to the devastating aftermath that had befallen the once-vibrant forest. The weight of the destruction hung heavy, casting a somber pall over the landscape.

The towering trees, once standing tall and proud, now lay scattered like fallen giants, their broken branches reaching out like desperate pleas for help. The air was heavy with the pungent scent of damp earth and decaying foliage, a somber reminder of the devastation that had befallen this once-thriving ecosystem.

While taking in the scene, a chorus of distressed cries pierced the eerie stillness. The anguished wails of wounded wildlife echoed, their haunting melodies forming a heart-wrenching symphony of pain and desperation. It was as if the very essence of the forest itself wept for the destruction that had been mercilessly wrought upon it.

David broke the silence with a resolute tone. "I think I can fix this."

Caleb kept his attention glued to Emily as her eyelids fluttered, gradually revealing her awakened gaze. "Oh, it's so good to see those eyes," he expressed, enveloping her in a warm embrace.

"It's great to see you too," she said, her tone full of exhaustion.

As he helped her up, however, she barely had a balance to stay vertical, collapsing in his arms. Concern etched across his face, he quickly adjusted his hold, ensuring her safety as he gently lowered her back down. "Easy now, take your time," he reassured her.

Emily leaned heavily against him, her body trembling with fatigue. "I'm sorry," she murmured, her voice barely above a whisper. "I guess I'm still a little weak."

Caleb's concern deepened as he supported her weight, his protective instincts kicking into high gear. "There's no need to apologize. Let's take it slow and steady, okay?"

They soon overheard the sound of a Quaking Aspen tree, a species that thrived within the Great Salt Lake Forest being placed back into the ground. Caleb looked over in astonishment. "You're really restoring this place back to its prime."

"That's the plan."

Caleb redirected his attention towards Emily, eager to share the moment with her, but their gazes did not meet since she had passed out.

"Em, are you alright?"

David interjected, still fixed on the ongoing task, "She just fought off the devil, utilizing powers that her body is not accustomed to. I'm sure she just needs some rest."

With a surge of mental strength, he directed his powers towards a fallen Quaking Aspen, its once vibrant leaves now wilted and lifeless. As if responding to the call of his abilities, its broken limbs moved with newfound life. Almost imperceptibly, the tree rose, defying the laws of gravity. Inch by inch, it lifted from the ground, creating a small window of opportunity for a trapped fawn to escape.

A burst of energy seized the baby deer, propelling him forward in a desperate bid for freedom. While darting away, the tree settled back into its rightful place.

Meanwhile, watching from inside the crater, Haines observed as they mended the damaged terrain. Yet, attention was directed solely on Emily and her need to revive the once flourishing land. As another tree floated over to its rightful place in the soil, Haines resumed his communication with Oswald.

"Lucifer has taken the bait," he said.

"Marvelous. With the celestial being's perception of the verities, they shall devote every passing instant in pursuit of him, thereby affording you the ample duration required to conclude your expedition, liberating me from my prison."

The following day, David embarked on the meticulous restoration of Creation Labs, determined to rectify the extensive ruins inflicted upon the ceramic surface. In the subdued illuminated room, the absence of electric lights was compensated for by the warm glow of flickering candles that adorned the desk. Their gentle flames cast dancing shadows across the space, providing a soft illumination that guided his hands as he worked. Not far from his reach, two spotlight flashlights were wedged in the cracks of the wall, their beams providing additional assistance.

Beads of sweat glistened on his forehead as he wielded a sturdy pry bar. With each calculated motion, he wedged the tool beneath the damaged tiles, lifting them from their positions. Behind him, a neat stack of new tiles awaited their turn to be laid in place, ready to breathe new life into the once marred floor.

A broken vial on the floor caught his eye, and a pang of realization struck him. I need to figure out how to combat the virus. He pondered, utilizing his telekinetic abilities to restore the ceiling.

First, he removed the wires from the original light sockets. Then stopped after noticing a dark silhouette drawing nearer, revealing itself to be none other than Celsey. Her keen eyes took in the dilapidated surroundings, remarking, "Wow, this place really has seen better days," as she scanned the area.

"I started wondering if you were gonna show," David stated, breaking the silence between them.

"You mentioned that Kyle's true killer is still out there. Although I know they caught Boris, I figured I'd come see what you were thinking that you couldn't say over the phone," she explained.

With a contemplative expression, David inquired, "You're a churchgoer, right?" as he rose to his weary feet.

"I am," she retorted, crossing her arms in a gesture of assurance.

"So, you have no trouble believing in an almighty being watching the universe or in the devil? You believe, good or bad, that everything happens for a reason," David probed, leading the conversation down a philosophical path.

Perplexed by this line of inquiry, Celsey took a step back in an attempt to read him. "Where are you going with this?"

Setting aside the pry bar, the scientist retrieved a folded sheet of paper from his pocket, revealing a copy of the perplexing passage at hand. He passed it to Celsey, his stance expectant as he awaited her analysis.

"What are your thoughts on this?" he probed; the air thick with anticipation.

Engrossed in the ancient text before her, Celsey began to read aloud, "In the annals of time, there arose a specter of unknown origin whose name was whispered fearfully in hushed tones–" her voice trailed off, a frown creasing her brow.

"Is everything all right?"

"This passage is false. It paints the Greek God Nycterus as a malevolent force, yet in truth, she bore no malice."

Handing her another section of text, David pointed out, "This one follows the same false narrative."

As Celsey's gaze fell upon the unsettling reference to the deity Eris, a harbinger of chaos and discord, she questioned, "What significance does this hold?"

Pondering the implications, David settled himself at the worn desk's corner, the room's atmosphere heavy with possibilities. "Perhaps these deities pose a threat to us, or perhaps there's only one force masquerading under these false identities."

"How does any of this tie back to Kyle?"

Leaning in with a sense of urgency, David revealed, "While it's true that Kyle succumbed to a fatal virus, his final moments were tainted by unspeakable acts. What if this cryptic entity was the unseen orchestrator behind it all?"

Despite her skepticism, Celsey made a move to depart the lab, acknowledging David's penchant for delving into the unknown.

"You're gonna look into it," he asserted, standing back up. "I know you, Celsey. You won't be able to let it go until you do."

Beyond the scope of the lab, Caleb's mailbox, its once verdant green paint now faded and chipped from years of exposure to the elements, held a stack of mail nestled within its metal confines. A jumble of envelopes and parcels awaited their recipients. At the top of the pile, a solitary letter beckoned for attention, its official seal and bold lettering declaring its importance: Jury Duty addressed to Emily. In a surreal moment, it shimmered out of sight, never to be seen by the intended party.

While inside the house, he prepared a breakfast fit for a weary Emily. Carrying a tray adorned with a steaming bowl of scrambled eggs and toasted bread, he glided into the cozy living room. There, he found her nestled on the couch, her tired form seeking solace in its soft embrace.

As he approached, the low volume of the radio caught his attention. Spiritual music played softly in the background, creating a serene atmosphere that complemented the moment. Emily looked up at him with a feeble smirk, her senses captivated by the enticing caramelized aroma.

"You really didn't have to go through all the trouble," she said, her voice filled with gratitude as she leaned up on the plush cushion.

"No trouble at all." With gentle care, he placed the plate of warm food on her lap, ensuring she was comfortable.

As the music reached its crescendo, it abruptly stopped, interrupted by a news broadcast about Boris's trial. Emily's eyes turned cold at the mere mention of his name. In a burst of frustration, she grabbed her shoe and launched it toward the radio, knocking it off the shelf. The room fell into silence as Caleb rested a comforting hand on her shoulder.

"I'm sorry."

"No need," he said. "I get it."

Suddenly, the ticking clock on the wall halted, its hands frozen in time. A hush fell over the room as a dark void materialized at the center of the room. Ethereal flashes of violet, blue, and lime green danced and flickered from within.

Caleb rose to his feet, positioning himself in front of Emily as his eyes widened in astonishment. As the unnatural occurrence unfolded, a pale purple hue flickered within Emily's irises. After a moment of awe-struck silence, Emily's voice broke through the tension. "What... what is happening?"

"I don't know, Em," he replied, turning to face her. "But I think we're about to find out."

As the void expanded, the shimmering colors grew brighter, casting a vibrant glow that illuminated every corner of the room, transforming it into a mesmerizing kaleidoscope of light and shadow. The pulsating hues danced and flickered, creating an ethereal spectacle that demanded attention, leaving the duo in awe of the mystical phenomenon unfolding before them.

39

COURT CASE

As the morning sun illuminated the sky with delicate shades of pink and gold, the area around the courthouse bustled with activity. Reporters gathered, holding their pens and cameras at the ready, forming a lively huddle. Their voices intertwined, creating a symphony of intrigue. The air carried the enticing aroma of freshly brewed coffee from the tightly gripped cups many held in their hands.

Amongst the swarming crowd, Jason stood, his eyes gleaming with disbelief as he shared his thoughts on the accused. "It's always the ones you least expect," he reflected, his words carrying a weight of betrayal.

Several reporters focused their attention on a young girl who bravely stepped forward. Her innocent face held a story untold as she began to recount an extraordinary tale of Boris's heroism. She spoke of a fire that threatened her and her brother's lives and how Boris had swooped in like a guardian angel, saving them from the flames. But before she could finish, an older man, his voice tinged with skepticism, interjected, dismissing her words as mere childish imagination.

In the midst of this clash of narratives, a spokeswoman, her tone laced with conviction and her hand pressed against her neck, demanded Boris be condemned to the ultimate punishment: the death penalty. However, her declaration was interrupted by a young mother whose eyes were filled with gratitude. Holding her son's hand tightly, she spoke of Boris's selfless act, proclaiming him a hero for saving her child from harm.

Inside the majestic confines of the judicial chamber, the trial unfolded. The opulent setting enveloped the spectators, their eyes fixed upon the elevated platform where the judge presided. Whispers permeated the space, creating an undercurrent of fervent expectation.

The prosecution, a formidable figure with an unwavering gaze, stood before the jury, poised to deliver their opening statement. With steadfast confidence, they began to weave a narrative of betrayal and tragedy, casting Boris as the villain responsible for the untimely demise of his beloved wife. "If he was innocent as he claims, why run? Why abandon his own children?" he inquired, each word carrying a weight of conviction, leaving an indelible impression on the minds of all those present.

Across the chamber, the defense attorney rose to counter the prosecution's claims. Their presence commanded attention as they meticulously dismantled the narrative, presenting an alternative perspective that challenged the assumptions of guilt. "Mr. Linderman stated that he ran to protect his loved ones. He may have given a wildly obscure story about a malevolent force taking Rylee Linderman's life, but I think it's likely he came home and witnessed the crime as the real assailant fled. The scene was so horrific that as a defense mechanism, his brain couldn't fathom that another human being could do something so evil; it's called confabulation." The counsel's words wove together a compelling counter-narrative, casting doubt upon the prosecution's assertions.

The trial commenced, and the prosecutor called his first witness, Mr. Bremington, to the stand. "For the record," the attorney began. "You lived across the street from the defendant, is that right?"

"Oh, yes," Mr. Bremington replied, "and his children were always up well past their bedtime, let me tell you."

In a calculated reaction, the defense attorney rose from his seat, objecting to the witness's statement. He addressed the judge, stating, "objection, Your Honor. The witness's comment about the defendant's children is irrelevant to the case and does not bear any relevance to the charges against my client."

The judge quickly ruled, "Sustained. Please refrain from introducing unnecessary information, counsel."

Next, the prosecutor called a therapist to the stand, who was also a close friend of Rylee's. He began by aiming to shed light on the victim's overall character.

"Dr. Bianchi," she began. "You knew the victim well, is that correct?"

"Yes," she stated, clearing her throat.

"And how would you characterize her overall demeanor?" he probed, seeking insight into Rylee's personality.

An innate response brought a warm smile to the doctor's face as she recalled her dear friend, envisioning her as a vibrant and effervescent soul with an infectious energy that could light up any room she entered. With each word, Dr. Bianchi painted a vivid picture of Rylee's vibrant and caring nature, leaving a lasting impression on the courtroom. However, the prosecutor wanted to dig deeper into any clear changes she might have noticed.

"And did her attitude change at all prior to her death?" he pressed, leaning in as the witness answered the question.

"About a week or so, she was scared. She used to talk about always seeing a bright future ahead. But, suddenly, it was gone."

"Gone?" the prosecutor began. "In other words, she knew her life was in imminent danger."

"I told her she'd be fine. She was just being paranoid. That she shouldn't let these thoughts keep her from enjoying herself."

"It sounds like she took your advice, but in doing so, Boris was able to catch her by surprise."

"Objection, Your Honor," the defense interjected, rising to his feet. "Prosecutor's statement is speculative."

"Sustained," the judge declared. "Either rephrase the question or move on."

"That's all, your honor. I have no further questions."

As the prosecutor took his seat, the defense attorney rose from his own, striding towards the witness stand. With much confidence, he began to address the court. "Thank you, Your Honor," he said. "I would like to draw attention to the fact that the witness, Dr. Bianchi, testified that the victim was worried about her impending doom seven days prior to it actually happening. The jury, however, may not have noticed that one crucial bit of information was never given." A moment of silence devoured the room, allowing time for wonder to permeate everyone's thoughts. "Did the victim ever say what she was scared of?"

"No," Dr. Bianchi began, shaking her head. "It was just that she felt her time was almost up."

Upon hearing this revelation, a single tear escaped Boris's eye, betraying his otherwise composed demeanor. A mix of emotions stirred within him, and he couldn't help but wonder, *Why didn't she tell me?*

Elsewhere, the brilliance of the vacant abyss intensified, compelling Caleb to shield his eyes. Gradually, a profound and resonating voice emanated from every corner of the room. "Fear not," it declared as a figure of unparalleled luminosity gracefully stepped through the void. Each step resonated with cosmic vibrations as if the very fabric of reality acknowledged their presence.

Cloaked in garments that shimmered with celestial hues, the figure exuded an aura of divine grace and power. Their feet, adorned with jeweled anklets, left behind swirling tendrils of stardust, a celestial ballet in their wake. With a thousand arms swaying in elegant harmony, one hand held a weapon of immense potency - the Sudarshana Chakra, charged with the very essence of divine energy.

As Emily mustered the courage to speak, her voice quivered with trepidation. "Who the heck are you?" she asked, her words laced with uncertainty. Yet, as her gaze met the deep pools of wisdom in the figure's eyes, a profound sense of connection washed over her.

"I am Lord Vishnu," the figure replied, their voice resonating with a soothing timbre that seemed to carry the weight of countless ages. The sound of their words reverberated through the room, filling the space with a divine presence.

Caleb, unable to contain his astonishment, interjected, "Hold up, for real?" His word carried a weight of disbelief.

Emily turned her attention back to him, curiosity etched on her face. "What is it?"

"Lord Vishnu is the God of the cosmos," Caleb explained. "Like an overseer, watching over the vast expanse of creation."

Emily's gaze shifted back to Lord Vishnu, her expression a blend of determination and caution. "We've dealt with a big fish already," she began, her words steady as she addressed the deity. "Are you friend or foe?" Her fists clenched, ready to defend herself, if necessary, as she awaited a response.

"I am the preserver of all things," the deity began. The words held a weight that transcended the physical realm, resonating within the souls of those who heard them. "Trust me, it is in the best interest of creation that you remain in the fight."

Emily's eyes widened, her initial concern giving way to a glimmer of understanding. She realized that Lord Vishnu's presence was not a mere coincidence but a call to action. "Lucifer. The devil. He stole my powers," she informed, frustration evident in her tone. She felt a surge of anger at the memory of the serpent beating her in battle, a fire that burned inside.

The deity's gaze remained steady, his eyes filled with compassion. "Only what you have unlocked, which, trust me, isn't even a fraction of what you are capable of," the deity replied, carrying a soothing reassurance.

With the entity's words lingering in the air, the defense attorney's glare, sharp as a surgeon's scalpel, fixated on the next witness, a neuropsychologist, who sat perched in the witness stand as the trial commenced. She exuded intellectual superiority as the lawyer prepared to delve into the intricacies of a cognitive phenomenon. "Dr. Kelt, can you please explain to the court what confabulation is?"

Adjusting his spectacles, the doctor cleared his throat, ready to bestow upon the courtroom with scholarly confidence. "Confabulation, is a tapestry of distorted information, intricately woven in the intricate folds of the human mind, yet devoid of any intention to deceive. This enigmatic occurrence often manifests itself in individuals afflicted with neurological conditions or those burdened by underlying cognitive deficits."

Satisfied with the given information, the attorney pressed on, the thrill of discovery becoming evident. "And, Dr. Kelt, as part of your examination, you had the opportunity to look at my client's medical charts, did you not?"

"Yes, that's correct." the doctor retorted with absolute certainty.

"And did you find any signs of these cognitive deficits?" the defense inquired.

"No, I didn't, but emotional trauma, the kind I am convinced Mr. Linderman has endured, may also serve as a catalyst for these episodes."

"Objection!" The prosecutor declared, his echoes slicing through the charged atmosphere. "Your Honor, speculation."

"I'll allow it, but only because of the years of experience you have under your belt. From now on, though, stick to the facts," the judge demanded, striking the gavel before him.

"Just one more question," the defense said. "Did you find any evidence of a violent nature?"

"On the contrary, his medical history suggests that Mr. Linderman has never been involved in a violent altercation."

With the legal counsel's questioning concluded, the prosecutor took the opportunity to cross-examine the witness with a smug look on his face. "I only have a single question for you, doctor," he stated. "You have testified that confabulation can occur for many reasons. Including the trauma the accused must have suffered after watching someone else take his wife from him. Even though there's no evidence to suggest that anyone else was present. So, I ask, Dr. Kelt, isn't it possible; no, isn't it more likely that the defendant killed his wife himself?"

"I'm sorry, but without further information, it would be speculative for me to draw definitive conclusions."

The proceedings continued as the prosecutor faced a new deponent. "Now, you requested to testify here today, proclaiming that you possess relevant information, is that right?"

The observer nodded in affirmation. "That is correct."

With his curiosity piqued, the attorney pressed on. "Well, then, I invite you to enlighten everyone with your insights."

The witness's hands trembled slightly as she took a deep breath, her eyes darting around the courtroom. With a shaky voice, she began to share her account, her fear evident in her every word.

"I... I was walking my dog. He had gone to the bathroom, so I stopped to clean it up," she stammered, her voice barely above a whisper. "When I stood back up, I saw all the streetlights were dim... flashing uncontrollably as if they struggled to get their color back. Everything felt... wrong."

Her voice quivered as she continued, her eyes wide with apprehension. "I... I could tell something truly evil was approaching... I felt strong shivers down my back."

The prosecutor, seeking to challenge her testimony, attempted to cast doubt. "Well, you are testifying to walking your dog after ten in the evening," he interjected.

Her nervousness turned into a momentary flash of frustration as she shot a cold stare at the attorney. "I got home late," she proclaimed, her voice steadying. "And it was May, dumbass."

The presiding officer, observing the exchange, intervened with a stern tone. "I remind Ms. Darkwood to refrain from using derogatory language in my courtroom," the judge admonished.

As tensions grew more intense within the courtroom's four walls, the witness's outburst reverberated to every corner. The arbiter's stern reprimand lingered in the air, a reminder of the decorum expected in the halls of justice.

Back inside, what would otherwise be your everyday home, Caleb stood by Emily's side, firmly grasping her hand, his sights undeviating from Lord Vishnu. The deity primed his weapon, the subtle, high-pitched hum of its activation echoing as he aimed it toward the recently roused archangel. "Wait," Caleb blurted. "Doesn't Emily have a say in the matter?"

"I understand your desire to return to your ordinary lives," the deity explained. "However, I promise that without her intervention, the future of creation is in jeopardy."

"Wait, so Lucifer was telling the truth?" Emily inquired, her brow furrowed in confusion, searching for answers in Lord Vishnu's enigmatic gaze.

"I cannot answer that," he replied cryptically, his expression inscrutable.

"You kind of just did," Caleb interjected, his words lacing with skepticism as he challenged the deity's response.

"I have come solely to ensure you don't give up. Now, please step aside."

"If there's a way to actually beat the devil and whatever else might be out there, count me in," Emily declared with unwavering conviction.

Caleb turned to meet her gaze in a silent exchange. She briefly squeezed his hand, offering reassurance with a subtle smile. Sensing her trust in the divine, he released her hand and stepped aside. Suddenly, a mesmerizing, ethereal glow enveloped Emily's body, emanating colors that transcended the visible spectrum. Caleb shielded his eyes, instinctively raising his arms to protect his face as the potent rejuvenating energy of the Sudarshana Chakra consumed every fiber of the newly awakened archangel's being.

The dazzling array of colors was soon eclipsed by the brilliance of a celestial violet essence. Within the radiant energy field surrounding her, Emily opened her eyes, revealing their shimmering indigo hue. Stepping forward as the intense light faded, she exclaimed, "I've never felt quite like this before!" Her excitement was palpable as her eyes returned to their normal state.

"Remember, dear one, the energy I have bestowed upon you will lock on to your dormant powers, but you still must learn to tap into your full potential," Lord Vishnu reminded her.

"Oh, I will. For sure," she informed, full of life as she felt the power coursing through her veins.

"Very well," the deity began as the empty void from before opened up behind him. "I shall take my leave knowing there's still a fighting chance."

Meanwhile, in the courtroom, the prosecutor prepared to continue his line of questioning as the earlier disruption was set aside. The judge, a symbol of order and impartiality, kept a close eye on the witness. "Did you have anything more to add?" the prosecutor inquired.

"Yes," Ms. Darkwood retorted. "I felt a chill, not from any cold weather, but from...what I saw."

"Okay, and what was that?" the prosecutor probed.

In the courtroom, the prosecutor prepared to resume his line of questioning after the earlier disruption was addressed. The judge, a symbol of order and impartiality, closely monitored the witness. "Do you have anything further to add?" the prosecutor inquired.

"Yes," Ms. Darkwood retorted. "I experienced a chill, not from the cold, but from... what I witnessed."

"Alright, and what was that?" the prosecutor probed.

The witness hesitated for a moment, appearing to deliberate on her response. Growing impatient, the judge focused on the observer, insisting that she provide an answer. "The witness must respond to the question," he asserted.

"All the lights... they were flickering," she began. "I - I know anyone's first thought might be faulty wiring, but that wasn't it. You see, I - I saw something inhuman staring back at me from the window of Mr. Linderman's home."

"Oh, no, don't tell me it was a demon," the prosecutor chuckled. "Considering the late hour, it's likely your eyes were playing tricks on you. Ms. Darkwood, how can you be certain that the individual you saw wasn't the defendant?"

"Well, for starters, the figure had these dark, veiny eyes and vanished in a dark mist," she explained, maintaining eye contact with the unamused attorney. "Oh, and this occurred just before Mr. Linderman approached from down the block and rushed into his home."

The testimony caused a stir among the jury, prompting whispers that spread like wildfire throughout the courtroom. The judge sternly called for order, his authoritative voice demanding immediate attention. The witness's unexpected revelations clearly unsettled the jurors, leading to palpable tension in the air as they struggled to process its implications.

After a brief pause to allow everyone to settle down, the prosecutor announced that he had no further questions.

"Very well," the judge responded. "Counsel, you may cross-examine the witness."

"Thank you, Your Honor," the defense attorney said, approaching the stand. "Ms. Darkwood, you are testifying about an event that occurred almost twenty-one years ago. Is it possible that your memory of that evening has been distorted over time, leading you to believe my client was involved in a violent outburst?"

Ms. Darkwood shook her head. "No, I remember exactly what I saw. It's why I decided to self-educate myself —" She stopped abruptly, cutting herself off mid-sentence.

The defense lawyer, however, urged her to continue. "In what?"

Taking a deep breath, Ms. Darkwood hesitated before admitting, "I am a self-taught demonologist."

The attorney seized on this revelation. "So, as a demonologist, you believe you can interpret supernatural occurrences, such as the flickering lights at my client's house, as evidence of demonic activity?"

The prosecutor objected, standing up and addressing the judge. "Your honor, this line of questioning is speculative."

Turning to the defense attorney, the judge asked, "Counsel, where are you going with this?"

Arguing his case, the defense attorney stated, "Your Honor, the witness's expertise as a demonologist is pertinent to understanding her interpretation of events. My client has claimed that a demonic force caused his wife's death, and the witness's background sheds light on her perspective."

The judge allowed the defense attorney to continue but cautioned, "Proceed with caution, counsel."

"Thank you, Your Honor," the lawyer said, repositioning himself to address Ms. Darkwood. "So, what was it you saw that night that led you to believe something supernatural was going on?"

"Well," the witness began, her voice crackling with nerves. "As I mentioned before, the sudden cold breeze that came out of nowhere, the flickering lights, which on their own I admit, mean nothing, but accompanied with the dread that overwhelmed me, as well as what I saw with my own eyes in the window, there's no way it wasn't. It's something that's been imprinted on my brain."

"And you stated that this was right before you saw my client arrive back home?" the lawyer inquired, leaning in slightly.

"Yes," she confirmed, her hands fidgeting nervously in her lap. "Mr. Linderman wasn't home when I saw that thing standing in the window."

"Thank you for your testimony, Ms. Darkwood," the lawyer said, a note of finality in his tone. "No further questions."

On the other side of town, Emily demonstrated a series of precise and dynamic karate maneuvers in the comfort of the living room, highlighting what she's learned from Michael. She initiated her sequence with a flying kick, propelling herself into the air with notable velocity and elevation before executing a swift and controlled strike. Transitioning seamlessly, she followed with a spinning kick, showcasing a graceful and fluid rotation of her body as she made contact with the wall. Exhibiting her acrobatic abilities, she then turned to observe Caleb, who was watching her with admiration from across the room.

"Would you like to spar with me?" she inquired.

"I think I'll pass," he responded. "I might just slow you down."

"I doubt that," she retorted, retrieving her phone and playing "Firework" by Katy Perry. "Come on." Assumed a fighting stance, Emily approached him, ready for a friendly sparring session.

Not wanting to disappoint her, Caleb felt the moment, bouncing a bit in place as he put up his dukes. "Alright, I'm ready," he said.

Emily grinned mischievously before launching herself into a series of quick jabs and kicks, testing his reflexes. He barely dodged and blocked her attacks. As the music blared in the background, they danced around each other, exchanging playful blows and taunts.

Just when he thought they were done, Emily flipped backward into a somersault, successfully catching him off guard. Her knuckles tapped the sides of his stomach as she looked up at him with a twinkle in her eyes.

Their gazes locked, and Caleb leaned in to kiss her on the forehead. Without hesitation, Emily responded by planting one on his lips. "You really have to get better at taking hints or just go for it," she retorted.

"No problem," Caleb replied, moving to return the gesture. However, before he could do so, Emily closed her eyes and concentrated on a new location. The surrounding air began to ripple and distort as a blinding flash of violet hues emanated from her being. In an instant, she vanished, leaving him kissing the warm, empty space where his girlfriend had stood just moments ago.

Feeling a mix of sadness and confusion, his expression darkened as he stared ahead. Before he could dwell on it too much, Emily reappeared behind him. "You gotta catch me first," she teased, causing Caleb to swiftly do a 180-degree turn.

"Oh, it's on," he retorted, a playful glint in his eyes.

He threw a weak punch, prompting Emily to block with a hand. Moving quickly, he tickled her on the left side, eliciting hysterical laughter. In the middle of her giggles and exaggerated movements, she accidentally launched four small beams of energy into the wall by the door. They glanced over to find lavender smoke rising from the points of impact.

"Well, at least you didn't completely obliterate the wall," Caleb retorted.

"I need to be more careful," she said, keeping her sights on the scorch marks.

"It's fine," he began, facing her once more. "If anything, it's my fault."

Emily directed her attention back to her boyfriend as he successfully kissed her lips. Reciprocating, they shared a moment where the world around them faded, leaving only their connection. With a mutual sense of affection, they stepped back, their movements guided by an unspoken understanding. Shifting their weight, they sank into the welcoming cushions of the couch, naturally gravitating towards each other.

Back in the judicial courtroom, the final witness took his place in the box, ready to face the prosecutor's interrogation. The observer, visibly distressed, gripped the stand tightly, his hands trembling with anxiety. Traces of a struggle marked his arms, a silent testimony to the events that had transpired. His eyes were glazed over, as if he was in a daze, not fully present in the moment.

The prosecutor's words cut through the silence, demanding answers. "Can you recount, for the benefit of the court, the events of that fateful morning of July 13th, 2002?" he inquired.

"Indeed," the observer replied. "I was jolted awake by a sharp pain in my arm. Upon opening my eyes, I saw the defendant, Boris Linderman, looming over me. A wave of terror washed over me as I feigned sleep, only to hear his ominous whisper, 'I know you're awake.'"

With determination, the district attorney sought to solidify the case with a piece of evidence. "Your honor, I request the admission of this photo as evidence," he declared, approaching the judge with a document in hand.

The judge inspected the photo intently, his expression betraying the gravity of the situation. "Exhibit A is accepted as evidence."

Turning back to the witness, the prosecutor pressed for more details. "Could you describe the contents of this photo to the court?" he demanded, his tone unwavering.

The observer focused on the image before him. "It's my arm," he started, his eyes locked on the haunting sight. "The wound bled profusely as I struggled against it."

Throughout his account, the witness subconsciously scratched his arm, a sign of inner turmoil and unease.

"Are you aware of other victims who succumbed shortly after a similar injection?" the prosecutor probed.

"I am. I awoke in the hospital to the sound of a flatline. The sight of the victim bleeding out shook me to the core. Drawing closer, I noticed the same fatal puncture on their neck."

With no further questions from the prosecution, the defense attorney seized the opportunity to challenge the witness's narrative. "You claim similarity in the wounds inflicted, yet one on the arm and the other on the neck. Is that correct?" he challenged.

"Indeed," the witness affirmed, steadfast in his account.

"But how can you be so certain? I mean, the points of injection were in different locations, and, to point out the obvious, you're still alive."

"Everyone's body can react differently to the same drug," the witness informed, shifting his gaze toward Boris. "All I know is that shortly afterward, I heard a voice in my head demanding that I pick up a knife and stab that man at the grocery store. As much as it wanted me to commit murder, I fought back, started bleeding profusely, and passed out, but at least I can still say I've never hurt anyone."

"The defense rests, Your Honor."

As the defense attorney settled back at the desk, the prosecutor rose to his feet, requesting permission to address the court directly. "Your Honor, may I approach?"

The judge, acknowledging the request, nodded in approval, allowing the prosecutor to speak.

Approaching the bench, the attorney leaned in and spoke to the presiding officer, "Your Honor, there is one final witness who has proven elusive to locate, yet she was a crucial eyewitness to her sister's murder."

"Is this your attempt at a continuance?" the judge inquired.

"On the contrary, Your Honor," the attorney responded. "I have a handwritten statement that I wish to present to the court."

"Has it been properly authenticated?" the judge inquired.

"It has," the prosecutor confirmed. "It has been verified against the witness's known handwriting."

"In that case, let's proceed. Councilman, you may read the statement to the court."

The attorney turned to face the jury as he unfolded the written testimony. His gaze shifted between the paper and the attentive faces in the courtroom. Clearing his throat, he began to read the witness's words aloud, each syllable resonating through the hushed space.

"I hereby state that the accused, Boris Linderman, slaughtered my sister, Kota Reels, right in front of me. He wasn't alone; however, he was accompanied by her boyfriend at the time, Simon Grieves and Kyle Heem."

The prosecutor's voice remained steady as he continued to read the witness's harrowing account, each sentence painting a vivid picture of the events that transpired on that fateful day. The courtroom was silent, and the impact of the testimony reverberated through the space, leaving a profound sense of unease in its wake.

Meanwhile, in a remote location in the expansive Pacific Ocean, amidst the serene azure waters of Hawaii, the enchanting Island of Niihau emerged as a natural marvel. The landscape showcased rolling emerald hills that gracefully descended to meet soft sand beaches caressed by pristine, crystal-clear waters. The atmosphere carried a fragrant blend of plumeria and hibiscus scents, mingling harmoniously with the briny air, creating a symphony of sensory delights that cocooned the island in a tranquil aura.

However, the once-tranquil beauty of Niihau faced upheaval upon the arrival of Haines, whose foreboding presence instilled fear in the once-idyllic paradise. By directing the inhabitants to excavate along the slopes of the dormant volcano and issuing menacing threats against their loved ones for non-compliance, Haines disrupted the island's peace. As the residents disturbed the ground at his behest, a darkening shadow loomed overhead, signaling an impending shift in the island's fate.

The Roamer gazed up at the darkening sky with an unsettling grin, his voice cutting through the gathering tension. "There is no need for anger. It was your energies that beckoned me here. And soon, Oswald shall be liberated from his confinement."

ABOUT THE AUTHOR

Patrick Menzel is a passionate storyteller who discovered his love for writing at a young age. Born with an insatiable curiosity and a vivid imagination, he has always been drawn to the power of words and their ability to create entire worlds within the minds of readers.

From crafting short stories in middle school to penning novel-length works in high school, Patrick's journey as a writer has been one of constant growth and exploration. His early works, while amateur, showed promise and a unique voice that would only strengthen with time and practice.

Patrick finds inspiration in the world around him, from the bustling streets to movies on television. His writing is influenced by a diverse range of authors and genres, reflecting his belief that great stories can emerge from any setting.

Known for his vivid sensory details and cinematic quality, Patrick's work allows readers to fully immerse themselves in both the mundane and fantastical aspects of the story. His stories are characterized by elements of urban fantasy and mythology that keep readers engaged from the first page to the last.

Patrick's work often explores themes of faith and destiny, inviting readers to ponder life's bigger questions while being entertained by gripping narratives. By blending urban fantasy with mythology, he creates unique worlds that are both familiar and extraordinary, offering readers an escape into realms where the impossible becomes possible.